THICKER THAN WATER

Other books by Geoffrey Carter:

The PS Wars: Last Stand at Custer High

THICKER THAN WATER

(A NOVEL)

GEOFFREY CARTER

Three
Towers
Press

MILWAUKEE, WISCONSIN

Copyright © 2020 by Geoffrey Carter
All rights reserved.

Published by
Three Towers Press
An imprint of HenschelHAUS Publishing, Inc.
www.henschelHAUSbooks.com

ISBN: 978159598-761-7
E-ISBN: 978159598-762-4
LCCN: 2020938060

Cover design by Michael DiMilo

For Kris

The blood of the covenant is thicker
than the water of the womb…
—Proverb

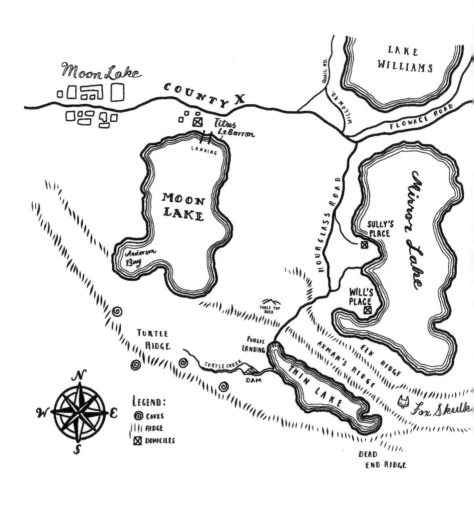

CHAPTER 1

EDDY CAREFULLY STEERED HIS PICKUP down the boat ramp and onto the lake's surface. He wasn't worried about breaking through the ice. The temperature had dropped below zero for five straight nights, so the surface had to be at least two feet thick—plenty strong enough to support the old Ford. Eddy accelerated, spinning the tires and fishtailing a little on the slick surface until the truck gained traction and started crawling ahead toward Anderson Bay. It wouldn't take long to get there. The lake was just a couple miles across. No need to rush.

All he had was time, as business was slow this time of year. He glanced at his watch. It was only after two, and there was still plenty of light left. It had been overcast but was beginning to clear up; the clouds were coming apart, tearing away like pieces of cotton candy. Patches of sunlight glided across the snow-covered surface like great silent birds.

Eddy glanced at the worn Nikon lying next to his sleeping dog in the passenger seat. This wasn't the best time of year for a realtor to take pictures of a property, but he wasn't looking for pretty today—just accurate. The appraisers needed an idea of the lay of the land, and this was the best time of the year to do that. When the trees were bare, the land was revealed—all the dells, rises, boulders, and beds. The forest couldn't hide anything in January.

"A vision," Jay had said. "We need a vision of what we have on Moon Lake." *Well,* thought Eddy, scanning the shoreline as the truck drew closer to the bay, *if you want a vision of the land, Jay, drag your fat ass down here to see it yourself. Walk through it. Smell it.*

Listen to it. There's no other way to know it. Jay had only been down to the lake once, when they first hired him three months ago—and even then he hadn't gotten out of the car.

Eddy's dad had asked him to show Jay around when he'd first arrived, and ever since then, Jay seemed to think of Eddy as his errand boy. "Can you get me some pictures of this lot?" "Can you set up this appointment with the DNR people?" He knew his dad had brought Jay in to consult on "a very important project" and had asked his son to help him however he could, but Eddy was sick of being his gopher. Still, it was for his father.

His dad always did things for a reason, and Eddy trusted him. After all, his father had built up Lakeland Realty from nothing and made it into a good solid business—a business that would be his someday. *And once I get the chance, I'll turn Lakeland into something big. Something special. Someday soon—sooner than anybody would like.* His father had been sick a long time, and they now knew he wasn't going to get better. The old man had waited too long to get into the doctor's office. The cancer was everywhere.

Eddy steered away from the east end of the bay, where one of the springs that fed the lake welled up unceasing, unchanging, no matter the season. It was never-ending, like the lake's heartbeat. The ice was always thinner over the spring, worn away by the current, and while he wasn't too worried about breaking through this time of year, it didn't pay to take chances.

He pulled up by the big boulder next to the beach, the one he and Will used to play on when they were kids. King of the Hill. They found it on one of their canoe expeditions, exploring different locations on the wild shore, discovering secret new places. This had been one of them. They'd come here a lot. The water was deep off the high end of the rock, almost six feet.

Whoever could push the other one off won. *Me, mostly.* Even though he was younger, he'd always been bigger and stronger than his brother, and that had pissed off Will something fierce. Eddy smiled to himself as he glanced up at the treetops.

The light was good, with sunlight streaming in pretty consistently now behind the naked trees lining the shore, exposing the land hiding underneath the sleeping branches. He picked up the camera. Jimbo, his dog, disturbed by the movement, lifted his head and looked up, blinking in the bright sunlight. He was half-blind and a little bit more than half-deaf. His muzzle, once jet black, was now dappled with gray, and his eyes were covered with a milky film. Jimbo looked around and shivered. He'd slept the entire way. *Well, he is sixteen…*

"Hey, Jimbo," said Eddy. "Want to take a walk?" The tail, predictably, started thumping on the seat as the old dog struggled to get up. He stood and stretched as Eddy checked the camera and pulled on his gloves. He opened the car door, stepped out, and gasped a little as the bitter air hit him. His throat tightened as he took a breath. It was always colder out here on the lake; there was nothing to stop the wind.

Jimbo walked across the seat, hesitated as he eyed up the ground, and then jumped down, skittering a little on the ice. Eddy shut the door and walked up to the big rock, the snow squeaking underfoot. It was funny. He hadn't been this close to the boulder for nearly twenty years, yet all its little crevices, rifts, and cracks were as familiar to him as if he'd been there yesterday, wrestling with his brother, trying to push him into the lake. Funny how you remember things.

He walked a few steps to his left, flipped the mitten half off his glove, and lined up the shot. He'd thought that if they could use this land, the first lot would ideally begin right at that white pine and then stretch north about a hundred and fifty feet. That would include the whole beach. If they took it two hundred feet deep, there'd be more than enough room to build. He clicked off one shot of the—his—ideal south lot line. He walked over—sliding, really—on the slick surface, and got a shot of the north line. Jimbo shambled behind him, trying to keep his footing. Eddy wished he had one of those new cameras with the panoramic feature, but his dad said they couldn't afford it. Eddy knew it wasn't the money, though. His dad just wanted to keep things the way they were. That was all. A burst of wind caused Eddy to step sideways.

"Shit," he said aloud. "It's cold." He looked at the shoreline again. Yeah, he had all the photos they needed. If Jay wasn't happy with them, he could drag his own sorry ass out here and do it himself. He looked around. Jimbo was sitting on the ice, one paw raised. He was freezing.

"C'mon, Jimbo. Come on, boy." The dog took a step and then stopped, shivering. Eddy sighed and went over. He petted him, then grasped his collar and pulled. Jimbo pulled back, took a step, and then broke into a gimpy sort of walk. *Poor guy. These trips are hard on him. Especially in the wintertime.* Eddy opened the door, helped Jimbo into the truck, and then climbed in behind him. It was already cold inside the cab. The sunlight had kept it a little warm, but not as much as usual. Eddy started it up and swung the wheel around, letting the back end fishtail a little bit. *Just like when I was a kid, going out on Moon Lake and doing dough-nuts with the boys. Hell, Why not?* He jerked the wheel over, stamped on the accelerator, and laughed out loud as the old truck spun around in circles, sliding sideways across the lake. The shore spun crazily in front of him, the sound of his own laughter almost muffled by Jimbo's frantic barking. *Yeah*, he thought, straightening out the wheel. *Yeah. Those were the days.*

"Hush, Jimbo," he said, patting the still frantically barking dog. *Poor guy. It's got to be tough being deaf and half-blind and not being able to move around much. Well, at least he doesn't know he's dying. That's one small consolation.* Eddy continued absent-mindedly petting the dog as he started heading toward the landing, toward home.

* * *

EDDY PARKED BEHIND THE OFFICE and put the leash on Jimbo. He grabbed the camera and walked in through the back door. His dad's office was empty, although the door was open. Funny—his father hadn't come into the office for over a month. Eddy peered in. Jay was standing next to the filing cabinet. The drawer was open, and he was taking out a file. Eddy watched as he added it to a pile on the desk.

"Hello, Jay," he said. He'd been hoping to startle him, but the guy didn't take his eyes from his work. He merely frowned a little.

"Hello, Eddy," he said. Jay looked up suddenly, his brown eyes magnified through the thick lenses of his glasses. He wore the wire-rimmed kind—big gold rectangular ones. Jay's round face had a quizzical expression on it today, his mouth slightly open and his brow furrowed as he peered at Eddy before continuing to riffle through the files. Most of the time he merely looked disapproving. He was short, a little pudgy and mostly bald; any hair left up there was brown. All in all, a pretty unremarkable looking guy—except for his complexion. Eddy had never seen anyone quite as pale as Jay. It was remarkable how the man never got any color. Not from sun or wind or excitement. He was always the same ghostly white color, like a fish belly or a larva found under a log.

"Did you get my pictures?" The tone of Jay's voice was even enough, but it always had a naggy quality clinging to it, like a fussy mother expecting to be disappointed.

Eddy stood in the doorway a moment, looking at him. Jay was dressed in khakis and one of those pullover sweaters that zipped halfway up the front. It was black with gray stripes on the side and looked like it was maybe two sizes too small. Jay's belly was starting to sneak out underneath it. Eddy smiled to himself. This guy didn't belong up here; he belonged in the suburbs, in a big fancy house with a two-acre lawn.

"I did," said Eddy, walking into the room. Jimbo followed slowly and lay down next to his father's desk. Jay glanced at the dog as his face crossed into the usual disapproving look. He didn't like animals.

"Good," said Jay. "I'd like to have five copies by tonight. Can you do that?"

"I suppose so," said Eddy, walking over to his father's desk and sitting on a corner of it. He looked at the other man a moment.

"So, Jay," he asked, "what exactly are you doing in my dad's file cabinets?"

It was a simple enough question, but Jay suddenly looked a little nervous. If he could, Eddy supposed, he might have blushed.

"Well," he said, "we're getting to a critical point in the project, so Mr. LeBarron wanted me to come in and get some files so we could take a look at them tonight. So I'm getting them."

"Okay," said Eddy. *The mysterious project. The one you and my father are working on. Not me and my dad, but you and my dad. The*

*one that's too important for me to know about. The one my father—
obviously—doesn't trust me with.*

Eddy wasn't sure what this little prick was up to, but it was-
n't right. Eddy knew he'd never quite lived up to his father's ex-
pectations—that in some ways he was a disappointment to the
old man—but he was still his associate, his partner, the future
proprietor of Lakeland Realty. He understood how his father did
things, how he thought things out. *No, I don't trust this guy.*

"There," said Jay, putting another file on the pile. "That
should do it."

"I'll tell you what, Jay," said Eddy, reaching for the files.
"I'm going out to see my dad tonight, anyway, so I'll take these."

"Well," said Jay, putting his hand on the pile, "your father
said he wanted me to bring them out. He said that specifically."

Eddy stood up, stepped forward, grabbed Jay's wrist, and
pulled his hand away from the files. Jay gasped and froze at the
contact. Eddy took the papers and put them under his own arm.
He looked at the other man, his gaze boring into those magnified, watery eyes— tadpole eyes—and as pleasantly as he could,
said, "No, Jay, it's okay. I can do it. I'd be happy to do it."

"You don't understand," said Jay, his voice not even-toned
now. It had a little squeak in it, like a chipmunk sensing a hawk
overhead.

"No," said Eddy, "*you* don't understand. I'm going out to
see my dad tonight. My father. My business partner. He and I are
going to be talking shop anyway, so we'll just take care of this,
too."

"But," said Jay, "there are some things in here that are for
our eyes only. Your dad's and mine."

"Why is it," asked Eddy, "that you and my dad are working
on something that I'm not allowed to see? You know, Jay," he

said, sitting down in one of the office chairs, "I just don't get that. My father and I have been working together ever since I was old enough to hold a job. There were never any mysterious projects or 'for your eyes only' kind of crap here. We never had any secrets." He glanced down at the files in his lap. "Until," he continued, "you showed up. Then, all of a sudden, here's this project you're working on, a project I'd never heard about, a project that apparently involves you sneaking into my dad's office to steal his files."

"I didn't steal anything," said Jay, a petulant tone now in his voice. "I'm following your father's orders."

"Uh-huh," said Eddy, standing up. He turned to leave. "C'mon, Jimbo," he called. The dog didn't move. Eddy went over and scratched Jimbo's neck. He lifted his head, staring about, and then raised himself slowly to his feet. Eddy glanced over at Jay. The man still stood at the filing cabinet, arms crossed, a look between contempt and fear crossing his face.

"I'll see you, Jay," said Eddy, heading over to his own office. Jimbo followed, walking slowly.

Eddy went to his office, took off his coat, and settled into his desk chair. Jimbo had already collapsed onto his bed. He checked his machine for calls. Nothing. Well, no surprise there. It was that time of year. The snowmobilers and the cross-country skiers would be up for the occasional weekend, but not many people were interested in looking at lakefront property this time of year. Nope. So it was time to plan for the spring season, to follow up on prospective sellers, or to plan presentations for some of the outstanding properties.

A faint murmuring came wafting in from the back of the office. Jay. He and Eddy—and Jimbo—were the only ones there. Eddy smiled to himself. *He's probably calling my father. Not proba-*

bly. Is. The guy was a born snitch if he'd ever seen one. Any minute now he'd come walking in, all huffy and self-righteous, saying your father told me to tell you to give me those files right now.

Eddy lifted the top folder off the pile. Unmarked. He opened it. It was a survey report of some land—a lot of land—between Moon Lake, Thin Lake, and Mirror Lake. This was all land his mother's family had endowed to the state years ago. Why would they be surveying it now? They couldn't divide it up. It was state land. He scanned the maps. All the lakefront acreage on Mirror Lake that went back at least a mile, sometimes as far back as ten miles, stretching over Turtle Ridge and up to Moon Lake, had been sectioned off. The lakeshore land was prime—mostly elevated ridges easing gently down to sandy beaches. Even the land behind was nice—not prime—but good. And, holy shit, there was a lot of it. He couldn't even start trying to figure acreage, let alone worth, without a calculator.

He heard something and looked up. Jay was standing in the doorway, a doughy frown stretched over his pasty face, holding a cellphone in one hand and covering the mouthpiece with his other.

"Your father wants to talk to you," he whispered, walking over and handing him the phone. "He's not feeling well today."

No shit, Einstein. He has cancer. He took the phone. Jay gazed down at the open folder and exhaled loudly.

"Hey, Dad," he said.

"Hello, Eddy." The voice sounded distant, whispery, a sound without wind or force; it sounded scratchy today, too, creaky—like an old tree ready to fall. It was difficult to know this voice as his father's, to recognize the booming force that always accompanied the old man's pronouncements.

"What's up, Dad?"

"Well, I hear you're giving Jay a hard time." A sound came over the line like wax paper tearing. It might have been a sigh; it might have been a chuckle.

"I guess that's one way to put it," said Eddy, glancing up at Jay. "I was just asking him why he was going through your personal files. He told me it was for the project. You know, that special project I don't know anything about."

"Eddy, I told you before. There's a good reason why we're doing this the way we are. It has nothing to do with you. You can't take it personally."

"I don't see why I have to be treated like a child," said Eddy. "I am your partner."

His father sighed. Eddy said nothing. A pause. He could almost hear the old man thinking.

"Okay, Eddy," he said, finally, "we will need to bring you in on this anyway. I guess tonight would be as good a time as any."

"What is this thing, Dad?" asked Eddy. "Why all the secrecy?"

He glanced up at Jay, who was gazing down at him, a little smile playing around his prim little mouth. *Little prick. You're all ready to see me get my ass kicked, aren't you?*

"It's complicated, Eddy. I'll explain it all to you tonight." He sounded tired.

"Dad," he whispered into the phone, turning away from Jay. "This is going to be our thing, right?"

As sick as he was, the old man got it immediately; Eddy knew he would. This was code between them—father and son time, but not your typical quality bonding time or that touchy-feely shit. This was how they worked. They debated everything—home improvement projects, selling approaches, hunting strategies, everything. They talked through every detail, every board to be fitted, every nail to be pounded, and every shingle to be set. They pushed each other. Eddy almost never prevailed in these arguments, but that didn't really matter to him. Not anymore. He loved spending time with his dad, the great Titus LeBarron. Eddy was just glad the old man still was up to it.

He smiled to himself. The whole process used to drive Will and his mother nuts. During family home-improvement projects, whether it was painting or remodeling or launching the boat or whatever, both of them would stand off to the side as he and his father debated, wrangled, contested, questioned, and—finally—agreed, or agreed to disagree.

"Of course," his father said, a little bit of the old vigor shadowing his tone. "We'll talk it through. Just you and me." He coughed then, a slight disturbance, little more than a sharp exhalation.

"Why don't you put Jay back on the phone, Ed."

"Okay, Dad," he said. "I'll see you tonight."

"About six."

Eddy handed the phone back to Jay. He grabbed it and turned his back to Eddy as he spoke to his father.

"But, Mr. LeBarron, don't you think I should be there to…"

His voice trailed off as the little man listened to Eddy's father, the words coming over the phone as distant and harsh as radio static. Jay started nodding and shot a furtive look at Eddy. *Our little Jay's not very happy,* thought Eddy, leaning back in his chair, putting his feet on the desk and locking his hands behind his head. *It's not very pleasant being on the outside, is it?*

"Yes, sir." Jay hung up the phone and looked at Eddy. He sighed.

"Okay," he said. "Your dad said that it's time for all of us to pull together. He'll get you up to speed on the big picture tonight, and then, starting tomorrow, you and I are going to have a lot—" He stopped and looked at Eddy a moment, cocking his head a bit, and continued, "—and I mean a *lot* of detail work to do."

Eddy nodded. Sure. No problem. If it involved real estate around here, he was sure he and his dad would be able to handle it. They'd been doing it all their lives. He didn't need a little pasty-faced city boy to tell him about the land, not this land. He knew most of the woods around here better than he knew himself.

Jay stopped and stared at him, frowning a little. *Yep. You're right. I'm not taking you seriously.*

"And," Jay continued, "eventually, we're going to have to talk to Will. He's going to have to be in on it, too."

Eddy felt a frown cross his face. *Why the hell would they want Will involved? He wasn't a land man. He was a goddamned game warden.* Jay looked at him and nodded.

"I know all this must seem odd to you, but it will all become much clearer after you speak to your father."

"All right," said Eddy, sliding his feet off the desk and standing up. "I guess we'll talk tomorrow then."

Jay had acted very decently—not what Eddy had been expecting. He felt a little guilty harboring such animosity toward the guy. After all, Jay had only been following orders.

"Yes," said Jay, turning to leave, but then, apparently changing his mind, he turned back to Eddy and stuck out his hand.

"Congratulations," he said, smiling. Eddy shook his hand absently, wondering what the hell that was supposed to mean. Jay turned and left, leaving a trailing of dust motes floating through the bright sunlight.

Eddy sat down again and gazed at Jimbo, sprawled out in a patch of sunlight next to the desk, oblivious to the world.

Dad hadn't sounded too good today. The cancer was advanced, stage four, and had been for some time—but his father had seemed to be withstanding it through sheer willpower. It had slowed him down, sure, but it certainly hadn't stopped him.

During this last Christmas, he'd been immobilized in the Lazy Boy and tethered to his oxygen tank, but had been laughing and joking with all of them—the kids, the in-laws, everybody. He even snuck himself a little bourbon on New Year's Eve. *But today, his father sounded remote, removed—just a little more removed—from this world.* Eddy knew, on a visceral, biological level, what was going to happen, but he hadn't allowed himself to think about the rest of it.

Eddy stood up, turned to the window, and gazed out at the highway. The street was empty. He glanced at the thermometer—four above, with a healthy breeze. The wind was kicking up a little loose snow. The block of two-story buildings, downtown Moon Lake, faced him. He could see John Benson through the window of the little storefront post office sitting behind the counter—probably dozing. John was a native of Moon Lake, a Moonie born and raised. Forty-five years old and looked just this side of sixty. Moved as little as physically possible. Eddy guessed him to weigh three hundred, maybe three hundred and twenty pounds. He'd been down to Madison once, years ago, to take his civil service exam, but Eddy doubted he'd been out of town since. John still wore his hair like he was living in 1958, greased back into a classic ducktail.

Next door to the post office was the Half Moon Café, mostly a breakfast joint, although they did lunches on Saturdays and Friday night fish fries during the tourist season. Mattie Doolittle owned it now; she'd taken it over from her mom when she got too old to work it anymore. Her old lady had problems with her legs—blood clots, probably, but nobody knew for sure. Mattie was too classy to talk about her mom's bad legs. She was one of the few people in Moon Lake who refused to gossip, and that wasn't easy when you owned a restaurant in a small town.

Eddy liked Mattie. He always had, ever since high school where she'd been—arguably—the best-looking girl in their class. She never had that squeaky-clean glossy cheerleader kind of Barbie look. No, she had something else. There was a depth to her, something pleasant and wild coiled up behind those velvety brown eyes—beautiful eyes, the color of a wild cattail. Eddy smiled to himself, recalling their last meeting, the lazy afternoon they'd spent together at her place.

A movement across the street caught his eye. A man in a dark-blue parka was trudging doggedly along the road, head bent down against the breeze. Doc. Eddy glanced to his left; the shadows were lengthening along the street. He looked at his watch. It was almost four. He watched as Doc came up to The Purple Onion, the corner bar, one of three in the tiny town, and sauntered in.

Doc was up there—nearly eighty. He was a retired oncologist, a cancer guy, who'd moved into Moon Lake about five years ago. He and his wife had bought the old Richards place over on the north end of Lake Williams and settled into the community. Doc—his real name was Mark Henderson—kept to himself pretty much, but Elise, his wife, had thrown herself into town life, making herself an indispensable engine of charitable works at the Episcopalian church. Bake sales, canned food drives—Elise had done it all.

And then one night, about a year ago, when she was driving back from a church function, a deer had leapt in front of her car. Elise had swerved and only clipped the deer, but the car went off the road and struck a tree. Elise had died instantly. Doc buried her, thanked everyone, and went home. Some of the women who had worked next to Elise in church tried to visit him and bring food, but he never did anything more than open the door to thank them. He never took anything. It took a while, but they finally got the message. Doc wanted to be left alone.

But then, after a bit, Doc started showing up at The Onion. He'd sit, have three or four beers, and be courteous—but not friendly. *Maybe he was lonely. Or maybe he just needed to be a little more numb than he had been.*

Eddy's dad had bought The Purple Onion for cheap a few years back, after it had been sitting on the market for over two years. The bar had been a Moon Lake institution since the sixties when it was built. His dad had asked Eddy to help him fix it up and run it, and Eddy figured, *why not? It would keep him from getting bored during the off-season and might even be fun.* And it had turned out to be more than fun; it was lucrative, a nice side hustle. He smiled to himself. He'd have to stop in and visit Lewis tonight.

Eddy stretched. The shadows were even longer now, purplish-blue patches of dusk sliding over the white expanse of the sidewalk and unplowed Main Street. The beginnings of darkness had crept behind the window. He could begin to see the outlines of his reflection outlined against the Moon Lake downtown, his square face planted squarely between broad shoulders. The waning light shined off his reddish-blonde hair; he still had a pretty full head of it. A frown flitted across the weathered but amiable face. He was still pretty good-looking, in a mature, chiseled kind of way. Mattie had always said he sort of looked like a chunky Springsteen. He looked more closely; wrinkles were starting to show around his eyes.

He peered at his reflection and smiled. *Not bad for thirty-six years old. The ladies still thought so. Mattie, especially.* He couldn't see his eyes yet, those pale, arctic-blue eyes he shared with his father and brother. They, as his dad was fond of saying, all had the blues.

Eddy touched the hair above his ears. He was just beginning to get gray, just like his dad had. All in all, he was a lot more like his father than Will, who took after their mother. Eddy shrugged his shoulders. He'd inherited his father's size, too. Titus LeBarron had been a big man in his prime; six foot four, two hundred fifty pounds—all of it muscle. Eddy had never been quite as big or quite as imposing, never the man his father was, even though he'd played football in high school. Running back. Titus LeBarron had a force of character that was hard to measure up to. Until now. The cancer had whittled him down to the point where he wasn't much bigger than Will.

And now, thought Eddy, running his hand over his chin, *my father is dying. How long do we really have?* Eddy turned away from the window and sat down heavily in the chair. What was he going to do? He needed his father. The old man always been at Eddy's side, guiding him, teaching him, pushing him, wanting him to be better, making him better—never quite good enough. Lakeland Realty would be his; he would make it into something bigger, something better than his father ever had—a business his dad would be proud of. Hopefully, in his dad's eyes, that would be enough.

Eddy leaned forward, placing his elbows on his desk and his head on his hands. The despair, the tangle of anger and fear and emptiness started welling up in him again, pulling at him and holding him like the thorny branches in the wild part of the forest. He felt something on his leg and looked down. Jimbo was there, his head in Eddy's lap, trying to console him. The dog slowly raised his head and stared at his master through what must have been a haze of milky light and silence. He blinked, seemingly unsure of who or where he was. *Lost,* thought Eddy, stroking him behind the ears. *You're just lost, buddy.* He stared at the dog as the darkness slowly filled the room.

CHAPTER 2

WILL TROTTED SLOWLY ALONG THE TRAIL, looking for spoor and trying not to hurry. It would be too dark to see anything before long, and any tracks would be easy to miss. He glanced at the sky and adjusted the rifle strap on his shoulder. Sunset was still about an hour away, but darkness came more quickly in the woods' interior. The coyote he was tracking might have holed up in its den already; he'd been hoping to verify it had been the one that attacked Mrs. Rutherford's dog this morning. He'd planned to find it, tranquilize it, and track it to verify it had been the culprit. The old lady had stormed into his office, demanding that he shoot each and every coyote between here and the Michigan border.

Preposterous—killing an animal for following its instinct, doing what nature had designed it to do, was ridiculous. Coyotes were canines, hunters—what they were intended to be. Nature had not designed canines to be bred into defenseless little long-haired dust mops, like Mrs. Rutherford's Lhasa Apso. He doubted that the coyote had even known her pet was a dog. He'd probably figured it was some kind of squirrel or rodent—its natural prey. It had pounced on the little dog during a walk, but before it could get away, Mrs. Rutherford had charged, screaming her head off, causing the coyote to drop the dog and take off.

Will smiled to himself; he would have run, too. The little dog had been bitten and needed some stitches, but it would be fine. Maybe now she'd keep it on a leash instead of letting it snuffle around in the woods on its own. The forest wasn't as serene as it looked. A lot of people didn't know that. It wasn't a playground.

He'd been working in the woods, in its depths, long enough to know what it could do.

Will continued trotting along, glancing at the sides and banked edges of the trail. He'd picked up some tracks about a half-mile back, but they'd disappeared from the path, and he hadn't been able to find them since. Coyotes liked to lurk in cover, taking their prey in surprise attacks. Will had been hoping to find traces of it on the trail edge, but he was starting to think it had gone deeper into the woods or returned to its den. It was cold and getting colder. Will decided to go ahead another quarter-mile or so, and then start again tomorrow. The light had faded into a rich lavender haze that was settling slowly over the snowy woodland. He glanced into the forest; visibility was maybe one-tenth of a mile. There was a full moon tonight, so it wouldn't be black dark in the woods—but still, he'd better start back.

He stopped, took a moment to catch his breath, and glanced around him. When his breathing slowed, he listened. Absolute dead silence. He smiled underneath his ski mask. The woods were generally a very quiet place. You could hear the wind in the branches or the birds in the summer; it was active, alive, but still quiet. Winter, however, was different. Life remained here, hunkered down, conserving heat and energy, waiting, so it was silent—dead silent. You could almost hear your blood flow and your eyes water. He loved it; some people—most—didn't. It spooked them, the absolute absence of sound; they equated it with danger, as if the forest was something that lay coiled up like a cat, waiting for them—the fat tourists—and ready to pounce. Not to Will. The land itself was benign, beautiful. He loved the silence, its purity—no clutter, no confusion, no turmoil. Not like back in "civilization." God, how he hated that word—that world.

Will shuffled around on his snowshoes and started on his way back. He was just about a hundred yards from the northern edge of Thin Lake, about two miles from his work cabin. Technically, his office was in town, but he went there as seldom as possible. Dealing with people irritated him. Always. It wasn't just the jerks or the know-it-alls or the bullies. It was everyone. They all bothered him and always had. Dithering, chattering, selfish, greedy creatures—there was nothing nearly as annoying as them in the natural world. Not rats or cockroaches or even mosquitoes. At least there was a purpose to a mosquito's irritating behavior— it was only trying to eat. People's motives were a tangle to him. An indecipherable puzzle.

Well, I can make it back in forty-five minutes if I keep a steady pace. Once he got back he could start planning out tomorrow's strategies. He had to build tagging time into his schedule before he was supposed to meet with Chief Dodge, the district warden, at eleven, at the DNR office in town. The chief had contacted him yesterday, saying it was imperative that they meet. Mrs. Rutherford had probably already complained to him about the attack. And then, in the afternoon, he wanted to check on the fox family. *The skulk. What a perfect name for a group of foxes. That was genius.* He knew the origins of those collective nouns went back to the Middle Ages; the names themselves reflected aspects of the animals. A prickle of porcupines. Or otters. A group of them was known as a romp. A romp of otters. How perfect was that?

Will stopped suddenly as he spied a shape off the trail to his right—a more concentrated darkness in the distance, maybe sixty or seventy yards away. Big. Not a bear. Taller than that. Bears were down and out this time of year, anyway. You might see one out on a warmer day in the winter, but it would have to be crazy to be out of its den in this kind of cold. He peered into the dusk, the bluish glow now smothering the light. The shadow moved slowly, away from him. It might be a deer, but it seemed awfully big for a white-tail, even a buck. A moose? Unusual, but not impossible. He'd have to come back tomorrow and track it. *Whatever it is*, he thought, continuing to move, *it won't be that hard to find.* He would seek it out. That was his job, and this was his land, his woods, his domain. If someone had wandered in, he would find him, watch him, and then welcome him into his sanctuary—his home.

* * *

Will trotted up to the tiny cabin as the sun was just dipping beneath the western horizon. It was a beautiful sunset, the pink and vermillion clouds hanging over the purpling dusk and beginning to blanket Mirror Lake. His lake. He took a long look around the shoreline, cataloging the familiar landmarks—the old white pine on the far point, the nearly uprooted hemlock leaning precariously over the ice on the far cove. Good. Everything was good.

Will unbuckled his snowshoes and went inside, peeling off his gloves, the ski mask, his gator and outer jacket before tackling his boots. It had been a good jaunt; he was actually sweating. He turned on the lights and then padded over to the refrigerator and took out a bottle of water. He kept his water in recyclable glass bottles, simply filling them with rainwater or melted snow when they were empty. His brother Eddy—and he wasn't the only one—thought he was crazy, sure that he would end up poisoning himself. *But what's worse*, thought Will, *drinking water contaminated by plastics, chemicals, and synthetics, or drinking water that fell straight from the sky? Every living creature here—flora and fauna—drank it, lived off it, or lived in it. They were all healthy. If they can do it, I certainly can.* He took out a coffee mug, threw a teabag into it, and turned on the hotplate.

Will padded over to the wood stove and peered inside. A few embers were still warm. He grabbed a handful of kindling and spread the twigs carefully over the glowing coals. After a few moments, they began smoking; soon, flames were creeping up the sides of the small branches. Will gave them another moment and then threw a smaller log onto the fire. He watched it a moment, and, satisfied it was burning well, he went over to his desk and flipped on the lamp. He sat down and gazed up at the floor-to-ceiling map that covered nearly the entire eastern wall of his one-room cabin. He had never measured it but knew it was at least twelve by ten feet. At least.

Will had drawn the map by hand, using dozens of separate topographic maps put out by the state as his initial references. He had considered simply taping the separate page-sized maps together and filling in the blank spots with his own renderings, but had decided against it. It wouldn't have been big—or accurate—enough. So he had painstakingly copied each separate map onto a seamless roll of paper—editing or adding details when necessary, and enlarging it by twenty percent—and carefully measuring the unmapped distances between the reference maps, he filled in the missing details himself—some from memory and some from his informal surveys of the land. It was all there—the ridges, rises, dells, marshes and bogs, trees, sloughs, and all the landforms. His map was more accurate than anything the state had done. Nothing else contained nearly the same amount of detail.

Sully was amazed by it, still, even after a year. Whenever she stopped in after rounds, she would go up to the map, put her hands on her hips, and study it, trying to determine what he'd been working on. It was a little game they played. They met here twice a month to compare notes. She was the other Fish and Game Warden attached to the endowment, and, through mutual agreement, they'd decided that her primary responsibility should be the lakes and waterways and that his should be the land and animals. He'd been reluctant to work with anyone at first, especially Sully, since she was a woman, but—despite himself—he'd been impressed by her.

During her first year, she had shown him the outline for a winter population study she'd planned out, including samplings, taggings, and both remote and physical observations. He'd helped her do exploratory dives in January to survey winter crappie and walleye populations. Together, using chainsaws, they had cut out a three-foot square entry hole in the ice. She'd changed in the warming tent and then stood there by the water in her dry suit, her eyes smiling at him from behind her facemask. Without a word, she jumped right into about thirty feet of water. She was underwater twenty minutes collecting data while he stood there, helpless, holding her tether. Will had done a winter dive once and although he would never say so, he would never go under the ice again—not in a million years. It felt too claustrophobic, too tight, and too dark. He remembered thinking that a grave must feel like that. It had spooked him. Bad. He'd nearly had one of his anxiety attacks.

But not Sully. The cold didn't faze her, the dark didn't faze her, and the terrifying suffocating anxiety didn't faze her. Poachers didn't faze her, either. In fact, she'd already earned quite a reputation among the locals, who had—only half—jokingly referred to her as Wonder Woman after she'd brought in a group of four down-staters who'd been chasing down deer on their snowmobiles. She'd caught them going after a doe on Thin Lake and chased them onto the aptly named Dead End Ridge. When they came to the end of the trail and one of them drew a rifle on her, Sully blocked the trail with her own sled and hunkered down to wait them out. After the guy took a few potshots at her, Sully stood up and shot his snowmobile. The gas tank took a direct hit. While it didn't ignite, as she told it at the Purple Onion one night, "After I killed his sled, those boys came out of there with their heads down and their hands up."

Will gazed up at the plastic overlay on his map. Lately he'd been studying a skulk of foxes on the southeastern edge of Thin Lake. He always collated his data on the foxes or the otters or the deer by hanging a transparency over the big map and mapping their movements—sometimes over the course of a few weeks, sometimes over a season, and sometimes over the period of a few years. He used a code he'd devised himself—with a little input from Sully. He glanced at the calendar on his desk, which confirmed she'd be in next Monday. And he'd see her in town tomorrow.

Will put his finger on the map and traced the route he had just taken. Mrs. Rutherford's dog had been attacked near the southern end of Lake Williams, right across the highway. He'd found the attack site, picked up the trail, and had gone south along the old path that paralleled the shore of Mirror Lake. He'd lost his quarry a few times, but it always eventually veered back to the trail. It had vanished for good about five miles from the attack site when it had gone into the woods. This either meant the coyote had made a kill—which Will would have heard or seen or smelled—or that its den was in the vicinity. That had to be it. There was an abundance of good habitat there. A lot of stumps and deadfall. Good cover, but close to open ground. He'd find it in there tomorrow.

And as for that shadow he'd seen in the distance, what had that been? Whatever it was had been hanging close to the lake and seemed to be a loner. That definitely fit a moose profile—even though they loved the cold, they tended to slow down during the more frigid months to conserve energy. This one wouldn't have traveled a great distance to these woods—not in January. *But how would he not have known it had come to his forest?* Maybe he'd missed it during the fall months, but it was hard to miss something as big as a moose. He rubbed his chin absently, staring up at the map. *Maybe.*

He looked at the strip of land between Mirror and Thin Lake where the foxes had staked out their territory. If he wanted to observe them tomorrow, he'd probably have to be out there about two or three—during their dinnertime. Depending on which way the wind was blowing, he might have to cross Axman's Ridge after he'd snowshoed over the bay. It'd be easier to come straight from the northwest, but this time of year, that would probably be upwind. He leaned down to make a note in his grizzled binder. He opened it, accidentally knocking over a picture frame on his desk.

Will picked it up and gazed at the photo of his father, his brother Eddy, and himself on a fishing trip to Thin Lake. He'd probably been about twelve; Eddy would have been ten. He half-smiled to himself—*man, that little son-of-a-bitch was lucky when it came to fishing.* Nobody knew why, but Eddy could catch twice as many fish as anybody else—the same way nobody knew why his "little" brother was not little. He was already two inches taller than Will when he'd entered high school. Will had also privately wondered why his brother had always been the popular one and how he got along with people so well. Or why he didn't get anxiety attacks or lose his temper. Why he was the lucky one.

The picture frame was dusty. Will rubbed a little grime off his father's face and sat down a moment, staring at him. He'd been a big guy, too, although he wasn't anymore. When he'd looked into his father's pale blue eyes on Christmas Eve, he'd seen the longing there—the hunger, the need to drink in every detail of his family. The old man knew this was his going to be his last Christmas. He wanted to savor it all, the love and all the tradition. Family. His progeny. His gene pool.

Dad and Eddy had been up to their old tricks that night, having one of their interminable and useless discussions about rebuilding the downstairs bathroom—useless, circular discussions that never reached any point worth getting to. Those two had always been close—the same interests, the same type of personality; hell, they even thought the same—which was pretty frightening in and of itself. His father, Will knew, had never had much use for him. As a boy, he'd been small, spindly, bookish, and anti-social—the antithesis of his father and his father's ideal of masculinity.

His mother, on the other hand, understood him. She shared his love of nature. The constant chattering and verbal arm-wrestling between his dad and Eddy irritated her—possibly even more than it bothered Will. Sometimes she would get fed up, grab Will by the hand, and take him outside. The two of them would wander for hours, walking deep into the woods, stopping and watching or listening to the animals, the birds, the trees, and even the land itself. Once, on one of their walks, they stopped at the shoreline. His mother climbed up and seated herself on a huge boulder and motioned for Will to join her. He clambered up the rock and sat next to her. It was tight on top, and he had to sit close. It was a beautiful summer day. His mother leaned back and turned her face up toward the sun, her eyes shut. Will gazed at her; it wasn't often he was able to study her, to examine her beauty in detail, to analyze it.

Her skin was pale, almost alabaster—but strangely, she never got sunburned. Will, on the other hand, burned easily and often. She used to joke that he would get sunburned looking out the window on a clear day. His mother loved the sun, and the sun loved her right back. She was outdoors every moment possible.

Her hair—dark, thick, and luxurious, like fur—was cut short. She always said she wanted to keep it short and practical, as she didn't have time to fuss with her hair for hours—the same reason she never wore make-up. Her eyes were as silvery gray as the first light of day and as still and serene as a woodland pond. She was beautiful, and, to Will, she seemed to draw her beauty from the land.

Will gazed down at the picture in his hand. It was odd. This was the only photograph of his family that he owned. He had no pictures of his mother or anyone else—nobody. He shrugged. No matter. The boxes of carefully catalogued photos under his desk were the ones that mattered. Data. Artifacts. Proof of his work. Individually, they were shots of animals, plants, packs, kills, and new litters. Together, they comprised his portrait of the land, the everyday transformed into the eternal, the happenstance mutated into the epic. He glanced at the photo again. *Family*. The only photograph he really might have wanted would be a picture of his mother by herself, luminous, a light in the forest.

Will put the picture back on the desk and opened the old binder to his fox chapter and made his notes for the next observation. The DNR always wanted justification for his jaunts into the woods, so he always had to figure out some kind of rationale for his work, which was absurd. *Idiots*, he thought—and not for the first time. *They're supposed to be scientists. They should know that the object of research is knowledge. Now it's all about economics. How does your research benefit the tourist trade? How will changing migration patterns affect the fall deer hunt?*

Will stood up and stretched. He walked into the kitchen and opened the refrigerator. Leftovers from last night's dinner—veggie stir-fry. *That'll work.* He took the plate out and placed it on the stove. It would be warm enough in fifteen minutes or so. Will walked into the bathroom and reached up, feeling for the string to turn on the overhead light. He found it and pulled. The bulb clicked on.

The bathroom was tiny and chillier than the rest of the cabin; it wasn't insulated because he'd never gotten around to installing it last fall. It was colder than hell in the morning. The state had originally set up the cabin as a summer workstation. They'd never intended anyone to stay here in the winter, so he'd had to do a few modifications to make it habitable, including installing indoor plumbing. There was barely enough room to stand here after he and Sully had shoehorned in the toilet and stand-up shower. Will glanced at the thermometer on the bathroom wall and peered at it through the clouds of his breath. Thirty-eight degrees. *I'll have to put the space heater in here tonight. Can't have the pipes freezing up.*

Will opened the medicine cabinet and took out his toothbrush. He squeezed toothpaste onto it carefully, the clouds of his breath steaming up the mirror. He shut the door and started working on his teeth. A pair of arctic-blue eyes stared back at him—the family eyes. "The blues," his dad called them. Well, as far as similarities went, that was about it. He still had a full head of rich curly auburn hair—no gray yet.

He rinsed off his toothbrush and looked into the mirror again. The face looking back at him was long and narrow, accented by high cheekbones flanking a long pointed nose, a thin-lipped mouth and rounded chin. It was a thin face, an austere face. *Scientists, priests, or saints might have faces like this; anyone who might sacrifice himself over to a vision, an ideal, a calling greater than his own existence could have a face like this.* Will stared at the reflection a moment, wreathed in the clouds of his own breath. He reached up and touched the cold glass, his substance hidden behind a cold and lifeless shell. Trapped.

He knew who he was and why he was here. He knew his purpose on this Earth—but no one else, except maybe Sully, had a clue. No one. He smeared away some of the moisture from the mirror and stared at himself; the image was rippled and distorted through the water. It didn't look like him anymore.

Will turned and went back into the main room of the cabin, shutting the bathroom door behind him. He touched the dish of leftovers on the stove. It was barely warm. He moved it aside, opened the oven door, threw a few more logs into the stove, and replaced the plate. He checked the thermometer on the wall— two degrees outside, fifty-five degrees inside. Not too bad. He'd throw a few more logs on after supper, and the old cabin would be as snug as a blanket. The teapot started whistling. Will went over, turned off the hotplate, and filled his cup.

He sat down at his desk again, staring up at his map, the repository and the showplace of his knowledge—his expertise— but it was even more than that. It was his vision of the land. This was art—his masterpiece. He had represented the complex intricacies of the land, its makeup, even its personality, and the dance of life above, inside, and underneath it. He knew the soil, he knew the animals; he knew their psyches and temperaments as well as a mother knew the idiosyncrasies of her own children. This was his life, his mission.

Sully understood this; she understood what he was doing. They hadn't talked about it at length, but he could tell she knew. Will took a sip of tea and gazed down at his desk, at the grimy picture of his family. He needed a picture of Sully. No, two pictures. One to put on his desk next to his brother and father, and another to put in his catalog under the desk—his composite, his mosaic, his map of the webs and interconnected threads of existence in this world. She was part of it, too, just as he was, and her picture should be in both places, as his was, as his mother's should be—as they all were part of the grander vista and the fiber of the land. His world.

He touched the frame again. His father, Titus LeBarron, was not in the catalog. Neither was his brother. While they knew the land, while they were technically part of it, they had absolutely no understanding of it—no sense of wonder, no awe of it. They were blind to its majesty, its intricacies, its subtleties. And it wouldn't matter if they did get it; they'd only haggle about when or where they should hunt or fish or snowmobile or harvest wood. He shook his head. A faint sound caught his attention. He stood and went over to the window. The moon was up. The snow-covered lake glowed blue-silver under the watchful black shadow line of the forest. He heard it again. Wolves. Far off. Their voices were part of this, too—voices that were rarely listened to. *Well,* he thought, gazing out over the bleak landscape. *I hear you, friends. I hear you.*

CHAPTER 3

EDDY PULLED HIS PICKUP INTO THE driveway of his dad's place—an old resort lodge that sat on a little rise on the northern edge of Moon Lake, right on the boundary of the endowment lands. Three other cabins that had been part of the resort stood nearby. They were unoccupied now. Tall pines bordered the path down to the lake. Eddy could barely see the sun setting over the dark crown of trees on the opposite side of the windswept ice. He got out of the truck, grabbing his father's folder from the front seat.

"C'mon, Jimbo," he said, opening the passenger door. The dog stood up on the seat, stretched, and then stepped down to the floorboard, eyeing the distance to the ground. *Come on, buddy,* thought Eddy, jiggling the leash. Jimbo shifted his weight from one foot to the other, unsure, and finally jumped onto the snow-covered drive. His feet splayed sideways when he landed. He tried to scrabble up, struggling to find his footing. Eddy leaned over and pulled up on his collar until he was standing.

"Attaboy," he said quietly, patting Jimbo on his flank. *He's getting bad. But he's tired. He's been with me all day.* He pulled the leash, and Jimbo walked along behind him, then trotted to catch up. Eddy looked down at him and smiled. He was a good dog. He always had been. They reached the back door. Eddy opened it and stepped inside, followed closely by Jimbo. *Well, at least he hasn't forgotten where it's warm.*

The kitchen was cozy, steamy from cooking, and smelled great. Maureen was hunched over the stove working on something. She turned from the steaming pot and glared at him.

"Close the door," she said. "Don't let the heat out."

"Hello, Maureen," he said, closing the door. "It's nice to see you, too." She was working for the family, taking care of his dad now, but they'd known each other since they were kids.

He took off Jimbo's lead. The dog promptly walked over and sat at Maureen's feet. She ignored him. Eddy placed the folder on the table and then took off his gloves, hat, and jacket. He bent over to start working on his boots and glanced up at Maureen. She was leaning over the stove, hand-mashing the potatoes. Her feet were set wide and her were knees bent, like a boxer's. He watched her calf muscles flexing as she leaned into it. *Work it, baby,* he thought, smiling to himself. *She still looked good. She wasn't as thin as she used to be, but who was? We all put on weight after thirty. Everybody except Will, but he's a freak.* He straightened up. Maureen looked supple—trim. She'd always been fine-boned, almost delicate-looking, but that was deceptive. She was strong, almost as strong as a guy.

"What's for supper?" he asked. "When do we eat?"

"Pot roast," said Maureen, without looking around. "Nice of you to invite yourself, Eddy."

She turned and looked at him, her cheeks flushed from the steam rising off the pot. Her auburn hair was, as usual, in disarray, strands escaping from her ponytail and hanging into her eyes. Some things never changed. Maureen usually looked like an unmade bed and was almost always grumbling—mostly at him. Her sharp tongue worked in opposition to her rich, brown eyes, which felt as warm and comfortable as a cup of hot chocolate. In fact, the combination of her rich auburn hair and deep brown eyes seemed inviting, and, in the right light, almost beguiling.

Maureen was a Hansen. Her dad was an OTR driver whose rig had gone out of control and crashed somewhere in West Virginia. He died instantly. Her mom had never really gotten over it and wasn't able to handle the four kids by herself, so she ended up spending most of her time and money at the Purple Onion. The kids had run pretty wild. Maureen was the middle child. She'd tried to take care of her two younger brothers, but it was tough for an eleven-year old.

The Moon Lake women, Eddie's mom included, helped them out as best they could. They'd run food over to the house and tried to help keep the kids in line. Some of the moms would take one or two of the children for a weekend or bigger parts of the summer break. Eddy's mother had always taken Maureen. She'd never said so, but she had a soft spot for the girl. Maureen spent weekends—weeks—during the summer at their place, mostly hanging with Eddy, who was closest to her age and the one kid who didn't mind being scratched by her razor tongue. They'd grown close fishing, swimming, and lying on the pier on summer nights, staring up at the night sky and talking about their families, their friends, and what little of life they knew.

They fought like brother and sister but took care of each other, too. Maureen was a year behind Eddy in high school but had been bumped up to some of his classes. He always stood up for her when the other girls teased her about her mother. Not that Maureen needed help. She could take care of herself.

Most of the time she'd been like a sister to Eddy, but as they grew older, they began experimenting—kissing behind the shed, petting, and more, but they kept it their little secret. They were never boyfriend and girlfriend, but they could never stay away from each other for very long, either. Then Eddy had gone away to college.

Maureen went to college, too, but quit after a year. She said it wasn't for her. She stayed in Moon Lake, working off and on as a waitress or bartender or cook. Eddy came back from college with a wife and no diploma. It didn't take long before he and Maureen started seeing each other again. He'd drop by her place every week or so. It was a good arrangement, stable; they both knew what they wanted. He was pretty sure Naomi, the new Mrs. LeBarron, didn't suspect anything. At least not at first.

Eddy told Maureen she should go back to school—that she was too smart to be working dead-end jobs in a nowhere town. She told him to mind his own business. Eddy shrugged and said sure. He and Naomi had their first baby, and then their second, but nothing else changed. Eddy and Maureen never stopped seeing each other.

Then when his dad got sick and it became obvious he was going to need someone to take care of him, Eddy hired Maureen to cook and look after him. His father had always liked her, and she'd always liked and respected the old man; he was the one guy she never complained to—or complained about. Maybe because she never really had a dad.

Eddy stood up and padded over to the stove, leaning over the pot. Mashed potatoes. That, along with the pot roast, was one of his dad's favorites.

"What have you got going on here?" he asked. "Pot roast, mashed potatoes, and..." he peered into the oven, "peach cobbler." He straightened up and looked at her. "All dad's favorites. What is this, Maureen?" he asked, smiling—"a last meal?"

"That's not funny," she whispered. "What's the matter with you? He's right in the next room."

Eddy shrugged. "It's a joke, Maureen."

Christ. His father was a grown-up. He knew what was happening. He even joked about it himself—not often, but he did.

"How's he doing?" asked Eddy.

Maureen shrugged, her shoulders unclenching themselves a moment.

"He had an okay day," she said. "I gave him his normal prescription today." She raised an eyebrow. Eddy nodded. That was unusual. His dad almost never took his full dose; he said it dulled his mind. *He must really be hurting.* Eddy glanced into the next room. It was dark.

"Is he sleeping?" he asked.

Maureen nodded. She picked up the potato masher and began flogging the contents of the pan, turning her back on Eddy.

"He's been in and out of it all day," she said. She glanced at him, those soft eyes melting him a little bit. He raised his hand to her shoulder and squeezed it, feeling a corded knot of muscle. She sighed and then abruptly shrugged off his hand. She blinked furiously, turned away, and then started working the masher like a piston in a V8 engine.

"I'll think I'll go and say hi," he said, picking up the folder. "He's expecting me."

Maureen nodded. Eddy watched her a moment and then headed into the living room. He paused at the threshold and turned on the light. The old man had winterized the lodge after he'd bought the resort, but he'd left all that vintage Northwoods décor in place. Eddy had never figured out why. His father was not necessarily a sentimental man—he was probably as far away from sentimental as you could get, but being here was definitely like stepping into a past era.

The dining room walls were lined with pine paneling stained that distinctive honey brown he'd seen in a hundred cabins. The vintage patterned linoleum in the kitchen remained untouched, and the faux log façade on the living room walls was still decorated with photos of record-breaking fish, watercolor renditions of loons, and other artifacts of lakeland lore. There was even the obligatory deer head mounted over the fireplace, which was cold. The only thing missing was the smell—that damp, mildewy odor common to so many summer cabins. It was funny how he missed that smell; other people didn't care for it, but it had never bothered him. It always reminded Eddy of summers when they were kids.

His father was tucked into his big recliner, his head lolled to one side. He was wearing the Green Bay Packer hat the grandkids had given him for Christmas. A few stray strands of white hair—the few he still had—peeked out. The skin of his face was yellowish—it had been for a while—but was now tinged with traces of bluish-gray. *That can't be good.* The outline of his shoulders, not rounded and sinewy anymore, but as sharp and pointed as bird wings, poked up through the flannel comforter. He was sleeping; and for once, he looked comfortable. An open magazine lay in his lap. Eddy watched him for a moment, concentrating on the steady rise and fall of his chest. He'd lost weight, sure, but he still had that force around him; you could even see it when he was asleep—that power, that verve.

Eddy felt a draft. He checked the thermostat and then stepped over to the fireplace. *Plenty of tinder, plenty of kindling, and plenty of wood. It was warm in here, sure, but the old man always wanted it warmer.* Eddy wadded up some newspaper into loose balls, placed a few twigs of kindling on it, and fired it up. It took right away. He rechecked the flue, waited a minute or two until the tinder was going pretty well and then put one of the smaller logs on top of it. Eddy stared at the flames as they rose quickly up the side of the log, dancing with the air.

"Hello, Eddy."

He turned around. His dad was awake, smiling at him.

"Hey, Dad," he said. "How's it going?"

The old man placed his hands on the sides of the chair and pushed himself slowly to more of an upright position. He took a deep breath and then reached for his water glass.

"I'm okay," he said, after taking a long sip from his straw. His voice, which had always been powerful, resonant enough to carry across a room of people, was muted, diminished a bit, like a bell stilled by a grasping hand. He levered the chair forward and was able to sit up straight. Eddy noticed folds of skin hanging loose down his cheeks, like they did on an old dog. *He's lost more weight*, he thought, a stab of concern knifing through him.

"So," his father said, smiling, "I heard you've been a little rough on Jay." His eyes were still the same, though. Those blues crackling with light and energy and humor. There he was.

"I don't know if I'd call it rough," answered Eddy sitting on the couch. "I only asked him why he was going through your files."

"Well, he's a little nervous, but he's still a good man," said his father. "He's done a good job for us." He leaned forward, locking eyes with Eddy. "Son, I'm sorry we had to keep you in the dark about this for so long, but this has been, and is going to be, a tricky business. But now it's time for you and me to sit down and figure out how we're going to do this thing. We need to talk it through now."

He paused and took another sip from the straw. Eddy leaned forward.

"You see, son," he said, leaning forward and locking him in with those frosty blue eyes. "You're going to be a rich man. A very rich man." He smiled and started leaning back in his chair but stopped suddenly, as if he'd forgotten something. "Yes, you and your brother, too. We can't forget Will now, can we? You're both going to be very rich men."

The old man sank back into the recliner then, his message delivered. He had just—somehow, with this proclamation—relinquished the family legacy to Eddy. And Will. Whatever that was. As far as Eddy knew, the family only had what they earned. He looked closely at his father. Was the old man getting delusional? Was the cancer getting into his brain?

His father took a breath and then nodded at him, smiling. *No,* thought Eddy, relief flooding through him. *Dad was fine.* Through all the pain, anxiety, and sickness, Eddy recognized that expression—his father was ready to talk, to figure, to plot, to maneuver. To determine the best way to get it done. Eddy nodded. *For his sons. Me and Will.* He caught himself smiling back at his dad. *Yep,* he thought. *Me and Will. In that order.*

CHAPTER 4

NAOMI WAS PISSED. SHE'D GOTTEN off work, picked up the kids, and cleaned up and made dinner—and then Eddy popped in and said he couldn't stay, had to go see his dad tonight because they had to go over some work stuff. *Really? Real estate deals in the middle of winter? Who the fuck did he think he was kidding?*

She stubbed out her cigarette and lit another.

"Mommy," called a voice from the back of the house, "can you come and help me find my *Magic Treehouse* book?"

"Mommy's busy right now, honey." She heard the flutter of little feet running down the hallway. *Shit.* The little girl appeared in the kitchen doorway.

"Don't come in here, Bella," said Naomi. "It's bad for you. This second-hand smoke isn't healthy."

The girl stopped short, a question forming on her face, but then she looked at her mother's expression and stopped. Her mouth closed suddenly, and she abruptly said, "Okay," and trotted back to her room.

"Donny," she yelled. "Don't bug Mommy. She's in a bad mood."

No shit. You are one smart cookie, Bella.

She sighed. *And here we are again. Every goddamned day. What a rut. I work a full shift while my darling husband sits in his office all day or runs around taking pictures, or yaks it up with would-be clients, and I'm the one who ends up picking up the kids and holding the bag here at home while he's over at his dad's place drinking bourbon.*

Except that old man probably can't handle the bourbon anymore. His liver must be pretty near gone—it had to be. She hadn't seen his charts, but she'd seen enough cancers to know when they got to the tipping point, and he was just about there. He hadn't looked good at Christmas. She'd be surprised if he'd be able to make it through the spring.

And then, she thought, leaning forward to ash her cigarette, *Eddy will inherit the family business and maybe they'd finally be able to get ahead, maybe get a new car, and maybe even a new house. Maybe they could move to Eagleton, and take that one step closer to civiliza-*tion. She sighed and bit her lip.

Jesus—what's the matter with me? Titus was her father-in-law, after all, and it was going to be rough when the old man passed. Not only were the kids devoted to their grandpa, but Eddy was still like a little boy around him, doing everything he could to get the old man's approval. And Titus was a decent man. A little rough around the edges, maybe, but he was a good guy. The first time Eddy had brought her up from LaCrosse to meet the family, during her senior year at the nursing college, the old man had sat at the dinner table holding court, bragging about how he was the best realtor the Northwoods had ever seen—about how he could fleece those Chicago lawyers right down to the bone. Right. The old man was a major-league bullshit artist, full of hot air, just like Eddy, but deep down, he was a decent man. He'd done a good job raising his boys after their mother passed. "Raised right," he always said. Especially Will, who was so strange.

That man, thought Naomi, ashing her cigarette again, *is off. He has absolutely no social skills and then he has those freak-outs—those anxiety attacks.* She wouldn't be surprised if her brother-in-law had some underlying mental health issues. He lived by himself way out there in the woods doing his Ranger Rick shit, but he didn't have to stay out there; that other ranger, that girl, Sully, lived in town. She was closer—although not close enough for Naomi—to normal. She was a wild one. Sully drank like one of the boys, laughed like one of the boys, and played around like one of the boys. And she was a big girl, too. Strong. Naomi had seen her loading bushels of hay onto the ranger truck with Will. She smiled to herself. That woman could handle any one of those dipshits that hung out in the Onion. She was smart, too. She'd been to college.

Just like me. College, a nursing degree—my version of the American Dream, and look what it got me. A three-bedroom ranch in the middle of fucking nowhere, so far from nowhere that I have to drive twenty-five minutes to go to work at the nearest clinic.

She looked up. Donny stood in the kitchen doorway, naked except for his undershirt. He held up his underwear. It was soaking wet and dripping on the floor.

"I had an accident, Mommy," he said. "I'm sorry." He looked like he was about to cry. Naomi pursed her lips and put out her cigarette.

"Come here, baby," she said. He walked over to her, staring at the floor. She picked him up with one hand and held the wet underpants away from her with the other.

"What happened?" she asked, balancing him on her hip.

"I don't know," he said, shrugging his bony little shoulders. "I didn't think I had to go."

"Well, don't worry," she said. "This stuff happens." She walked with him to the bathroom, stepped over the laundry basket, and sat him on the toilet. She tossed the wet underpants into the bathtub and reached for a dry pair from the basket. Bella appeared suddenly in the door. When she realized what was going on, she yelled out, "Donny peed his pants. Baby peed his pants."

"Shut up, Bella," screamed Donny, instantly consumed with fury.

"Hey," said Naomi, in the best mother tone she could muster. "Stop it, Donny. You too, Bella. You did the same thing when you were his age. We all have accidents."

"All of us?" asked Bella, stepping slowly into the bathroom. "Even you, Mom?"

Naomi turned and made a mad face at her. Bella giggled and ran out. Naomi smiled and turned back to Donny, catching herself in the mirror. Her brownish-blond hair hung limp and lank around her face, which was as bony and angular as an old man's hand. It always had been. Her skin seemed stretched more tightly around her skull than other people's, and her blue-gray eyes, set deep in their sockets, seemed to shine, luminous, under her straight brows. Her eyes were her best feature. They were nice, big, and a pretty color. Her smile faded as she gazed at the mirror, resetting itself into a line as straight and hard as a rifle barrel. She wasn't pretty. She knew that. But she was smart—smart enough to snare Eddy LeBarron, the best-looking guy on campus—and she was tough, willing to do whatever it took to get herself and her family what they deserved. *And*, she thought, wiping little Donny's rear end, *I deserve a whole lot more than this.*

Eddy, though, Eddy was happy as a clam with their life—his life; he didn't mind cruising along from paycheck to paycheck, and saving a little here and there when he felt an occasional stab of responsibility. He didn't mind living in a starter home for ten years; he didn't mind being an average guy. He loved being the fun parent. Of course he loved it—who wouldn't? If she had known it was going be like this, she never would have married him.

In college, he'd been bright, funny, and popular. It seemed as if he had the world in his pocket. And he did. Naomi decided he was the one. She wanted him, and so she took him. She was relentless, and she was ruthless—those other girls had nothing. She might not have been as pretty or attractive, but Naomi was willing to do anything, anything he asked. Eddy was attracted to her willingness and flattered by her desire. She made sure that he couldn't stay away.

Naomi finished college, they got married and came to Moon Lake, and Eddy starting working for his dad. He played it safe. *He should have done better. He could have grown that business twice as fast as his dad. He's just too lazy, too easygoing.*

She was the one who had to get up at five every morning; the one who had to dress the kids, feed them, potty-train them, and discipline them. *I guess*, she thought, *I should thank my "dear husband" for going out of his way to take his children to school every morning.* And then, after the morning routine, she went to her job—head nurse at the Eagleton Clinic. She did her ten-hour shifts with an additional four days a month of mandatory double shifts. The clinic had been severely understaffed for years. The money was okay, but just barely.

She put Donny on the floor, slid the clean pair of underpants onto him, and patted his behind. He ran into the hallway, looking for his sister. Naomi sat on the toilet, leaned over and looked into the hall, then reached into her pocket for her pack of cigarettes. She lit up another one. *I really shouldn't with the kids in the house, but screw it.* She stared down at her hands. They were narrow with long, tapering fingers. They were getting older now, like the rest of her, but they still looked good. Miss Carson, her piano teacher in high school, had always remarked that they were "the most elegant and graceful hands I've ever seen." *And I was good*, thought Naomi, turning her hand over. *I was really good.* She'd won piano competitions all through high school but then drifted away from playing when she'd gone away to college.

She'd always meant to get a piano after they got married, but they didn't really have the room. Eddy never said so, but she could tell he thought it was a luxury—an extravagance. Even when they'd looked at the more reasonable digital pianos, he would just shrug and mumble something about "maybe when they go on sale." Naomi stood up, lifted up the toilet seat, and threw the cigarette in. She flushed and stretched, looking around the bathroom. Clothes were heaped up around the laundry chute, toys were all over the bathtub, and the sink was a mosaic of spilled mascara and dried-on toothpaste stains. And the rest of the house—except her kitchen—was in the same condition. *No,* she thought, looking at herself in the mirror as she tied her hair into a ponytail. *This is not what I signed up for, this is not what the way it's supposed to be—back-breaking drudgery, chronic exhaustion, and perpetual aggravation. No.* And the kids were still babies. She had twenty more years of this ahead of her.

Naomi sat down on the edge of the bathtub and rubbed her temples with the heels of her palms. She could feel a migraine coming on. *No, she thought. Eddy didn't turn out to be the man she thought he'd be. So either he gets it together with the family business and makes more than simple commissions—a decent living, a real salary—or I will have to explore my options. Whatever,* she thought, gazing up at herself in the mirror, her mouth as straight as the edge of a knife, her eyes as cold and luminous in their orbits as pebbles on a creek bottom—*whatever those might be.*

CHAPTER 5

MAUREEN HELPED MR. LEBARRON GET settled into his recliner, set out a tumbler of bourbon on the table next to him, and stood up. Her back ached. She resisted the urge to stretch. Eddy was wheeling in the map board from the bedroom where his father kept it.

"Okay, Mr. LeBarron," she said. "If you don't need anything else, I'll go in and clear the table now."

"Thank you, Maureen," said the old man, smiling. She smiled back. He'd done a pretty good job with his supper tonight. He'd eaten all his potatoes and a good part of his pot roast. That was good. Dr. Wilson had taken her aside during the last visit and mentioned to her that he needed to take in more calories, so she'd been monitoring him. His appetite was nothing like it used to be, but he was holding his own.

"You need anything?" she asked Eddy. He shook his head. She nodded to him, and he smiled back as he spun the map board around, positioning it for his father, watching his reactions like a hawk. He moved the board carefully, glancing at his father to make sure he had a clear view of it. The face had a detailed map tacked to it showing Moon Lake, Mirror Lake, and Thin Lake, plus all the surrounding land. It was big, covering the entire surface of the corkboard. A lot of the land seemed separated, partitioned into sections, like lots.

Maureen had seen Mr. LeBarron and that other man from downstate, Jay, working on it for a few weeks now, and she had overheard some things. Things like apportionments and levies and abstracts of title and capital improvements. She'd been around the LeBarron family long enough to know that that type of talk meant one thing—land development. That's what they'd been talking about. Somehow, some way, part of the endowed land around Mirror Lake on that map was going to be taken over by private developers. That must have been why Mr. LeBarron had brought in that Jay person, to take care of the legal stuff.

She walked into the kitchen, put Mr. LeBarron's plate on the floor for Jimbo, and started scraping food off the other dishes into the garbage. From what she could figure, Jay seemed to be more of a lawyer than a realtor—realtors were just glorified salesmen anyway—and if they were transferring the land from public to private ownership, they would need a guy like him. So that part of it made sense. But how and why would all that land suddenly come to Mr. LeBarron? Why now? She knew Mrs. LeBarron's family had donated it to the state years ago as a nature preserve of some kind, so, theoretically, they shouldn't be able to touch it—*but here it is*, she thought. *A mystery.*

Maureen turned on the tap and squeezed some detergent into the steaming water. Mirror Lake was surrounded by state land, the endowment land, and it was still completely wild. Will lived back there somewhere, but as far as she knew, he was the only human being who did. She knew that other ranger, that woman—Sully—was back there quite a bit, too, but that was it. There was no hunting allowed on the land, and there was very limited public access, one trail, and all hikers were required to stay on the path. As a result, that part of the forest was teeming with wildlife—martens, mink, badgers, bear—even a cougar had been sighted in there. She'd gone back there a couple times herself; it was a beautiful old-growth forest, silent, foreboding, wise, full of history, and full of ghosts. It would be easy to get lost in there.

Maureen turned off the water and cocked her head. At first, all she could hear was Jimbo slurping away at the plate of leftovers. Then, floating from the living room, like blowing snow, she heard Eddy talking, saying something about the land being donated forever—the exact thing she'd been thinking. She shook her head.

Eddy always made a big thing about how he and his dad were so much alike that they could almost finish each other's sentences. Maureen had seen it and agreed—to a point. But she had to wonder that if they were so good at thinking alike, why the hell did they argue so much? It wasn't an intuitive process. They had to work at it, honing and sharpening their arguments on each other.

In truth, though, she thought—no, she knew—she and Eddy had a much more profound connection. Even when they were kids, she'd known. Lying on the pier on clear summer nights, wisps of vapor rising from the lake around them, the two of them looking up at the stars, talking and wondering, their hands touching slightly, accidentally, neither of them moving away, she'd felt it. She had always known what Eddy would say and why he would say it. And he knew her, too. Not on a conscious level, but someplace deeper. He knew her. Inside out.

Eddy could make her laugh when no one else could. He could defuse or ignore her slashes of acrimony as he chose. It was frustrating that he took her for granted, that he had never really acknowledged their connection, but he knew it was there; she could tell. Eddy just took things as they came without thinking about them too much, like the first time they'd touched each other and made love. It had seemed so natural, so right, that neither one of them questioned it or wondered about it. It had never really stopped, either—even after Eddy married Naomi. It just kept happening.

Ever since she'd spent that first summer with the LeBarrons, with the snappy and wiry little Will, the big, slow, amiable Eddy, and the beautiful angelic Mrs. Lebarron, as ethereal and radiant as light on the water, when she was ten, she'd discovered a connection she'd never known before—or since. Not in college. Not at home. Not in anyone else's bed. *No, it's Eddy. And the LeBarrons. I feel more at home here than anywhere.* She could hear Eddy's voice again, a little louder this time.

"I'm sorry, Dad, but I don't get it. How could we get it back? Didn't Grandfather Wallace give it away forever?" *Exactly. About time, you idiot.*

She heard Mr. LeBarron say something, but it was unintelligible; all she could make out was a sound like crumpling paper, then a low sticky cough. Another throat clearing and then his voice, suddenly full of energy and force, rolled through the living room and into the kitchen.

"Listen, Eddy," it growled, like distant thunder. "Jay and I have examined this in great detail. There's no reason to doubt it."

"But I don't get it," said Eddy, bewilderment crawling into his voice like a frightened child.

"This was the way your grandpa set up the will. Way back in 1984, when you and Will were babies. Your Grandfather Wallace wanted you to have a legacy from your mother's side of the family. The endowment had been set up to be that legacy from day one."

Maureen picked up a dish and pretended to scrub it. The splashing and clanking should make it seem as if she were actually working instead of listening.

"You know your mother's family cut her off when she married me."

"Yeah," said Eddy, slowly.

"Unfortunately," the old man continued, "your mother's grandfather, your great-grandfather, didn't approve of her marrying me. I thought it was me personally, but then I realized that, hell, it wasn't me; he didn't like anybody. Well, he had the controlling interests of all the Wallace family fortunes, and he made sure she would get nothing."

He coughed again. Maureen frowned at the sound. It was sounding more liquid. That might mean he was bleeding again.

"But," continued Mr. LeBarron, "your grandfather wanted to make sure his grandchildren were comfortable. So he built a clause into the endowment that allows you and Will—upon my death—to take possession of the endowment lands."

Silence. Maureen could almost hear Eddy thinking. He would have hundreds, maybe thousands of acres to sell, develop, or keep as they were. *He's thinking that he's going to be a rich man. He's thinking, "holy shit, I don't believe this."*

"Jesus," she heard Eddy say. "Wow." He started laughing. "My God," he said. Maureen could imagine him leaning toward his father, smiling, ready to begin.

"So, Dad," he said, "How are we going to handle this?"

Maureen smiled to herself as she began to dry the dishes. *And so it begins. The great communicators.*

CHAPTER 6

"No, no, no," said the old man, "if you sell to one of the big developers, you'll make less than building on the individual lots. And—"

"But," interrupted Eddy, "what about building costs? If we built and sold units, we'd stand to take in less in the long run."

"No, son," said his father, "you're not thinking this through. We get one of the local builders to put up a model home on Anderson Bay, then sell the lots along with the contract to build. We get the land money along with the subsidy from the builders."

"But," began Eddy, but paused. His father had dropped his eyes and seemed to be working hard to breathe. "Hey, dad," asked Eddy. "Are you tired?"

His father nodded. "A little," he said. "Maybe we should continue with this tomorrow."

"Okay, Dad." Eddy stood and came over to the recliner. Maureen appeared in the kitchen doorway. She locked eyes with him and nodded slightly, the beginnings of a smile starting on the corner of her mouth. Eddy knew that expression; Maureen got that look when she thought she was one up on him. And then it hit him. She'd been sitting out in the kitchen the entire time, listening. She knew.

"It's okay, son," said his father. "I can get up on my own." He pushed himself up slowly—painfully—to a standing position and started toward his bedroom, taking slow, careful steps. He stopped abruptly as if struck by a thought and then turned toward Maureen.

"Maureen," he said. "Would you give me and Eddy a moment, please?"

She nodded, went into the kitchen, and shut the door. Eddy smiled as the old man turned to him.

"I think," he said, "that for the time being we should keep this to ourselves. I know Maureen has some idea of what's going on, so I think we need to be discreet. After all, she's not really family."

Eddy nodded at his dad, but felt a twinge. Technically, no, Maureen wasn't family—but she was pretty damned close. Still, he was probably right.

"In fact," continued his father, "I don't think we should tell anyone else about this yet. Not even Naomi. We need to get everything settled between us first. I want Will to be prepared for this."

Eddy nodded again, but felt another slight twinge. *Naomi should know, he thought. She's my wife.*

"So," said his father, placing his hand on Eddy's shoulder, "we have to figure out how to break this to your brother."

"Yeah," said Eddy. Surprisingly, he hadn't really thought much about Will's place in all this.

"He's not going to be too happy," said Eddy.

His father frowned and nodded. That was an understatement; Will lived and breathed that land, the animals, the lakes; he loved it all. It was all he had. *Well, still, he'll have his share.* It wasn't like they were going to develop the whole forest. Will would be able to keep part of it as his private wilderness preserve with his birds and bees and flowers and trees and all the rest of it.

His dad and Jay had decided to open up only half of the northern shoreline of Mirror and a little less than half of Moon. The old man said that was all they really needed. Will could have the rest. Eddy thought that would be more than fair—as long as

Will agreed to open up all of it for public use. They could do snowmobiling, ATVing, and camping all across the endowment. The tourist industry would finally take off. Moon Lake would grow; the economy would really prosper. Finally. And along Turtle Ridge, man, there would be some fantastic hunting once they got all the regulations lifted. Deer, wolf, fox, maybe even moose.

"Eddy."

He looked up. His father had stepped closer to him and was staring through him with those family blues.

"What is it, Dad?"

"Your brother," he said and paused to catch his breath, "loves that land." He dropped his gaze a moment. "In some ways," he continued, without raising his eyes, "it's more important to him than family."

"Sure, Dad," said Eddy, nervous suddenly. There was a hesitation, a tremulousness in his father's manner; he was tired. Eddy took his father's arm, but the old man shook off his hand. He raised his head and looked at Eddy. The old firmness was back in his eyes.

"Will isn't like us," he continued. "After your mother passed away, he didn't really have anyone else. He was lost."

Eddy shrugged. "He has us," he said.

His father smiled and shook his head. "No, Eddy. All he has is that land. It's more real to him than we are." His dad got a wistful look. "Will got that from your mother. She loved the land, too." He leaned on his cane and cleared his throat. "So, even though he might not need us, he is your brother, Eddy, and, after I'm gone, he won't have anyone else but you."

I know, thought Eddy, suddenly impatient. *I know. You said that. You've said it a million times. Shit. Leave it to Will to turn some-*

thing positive into a giant guilt trip. The old man should be feeling great, on top of the world, but Will and his tree-hugging bullshit was worrying him. Leave it to sensitive little Willie to screw everything up.

"We have to be very careful how we handle this situation," said the old man. "I'm not sure how he might take the news. That's why I want to keep this between us for now." The old man took a step, leaning heavily on his cane, and then glanced back at Eddy.

"I know he's your big brother, Eddy," he said. "But in many ways, you are the more responsible one."

He stood up straight then and clamped Eddy in his arctic-blue gaze.

"I want you to promise me that, Eddy," he said, a little of the old thunder creeping back into his voice. "I want you to promise me to take care of Will. Promise me that."

Eddy nodded and shrugged. "All right," he said. *Ever since they were kids, it was the same old bullshit. Keep an eye on Will. Watch over your big brother. It never fucking ends.*

A movement caught Eddy's eye. He turned his head and caught a shadow sliding underneath the kitchen door. *Maureen. Just like her, sneaking around like some sort of spook. She never could stand to be left out of anything.* His father turned, leaning heavily on his cane, and started toward his bed.

"You need help getting to bed, Dad?" he asked. His father turned and flashed him a smile—like one of the old ones.

"No," he said, "but if you find a nice young thing at the Onion, just send her over." He cackled.

"You dirty old man," said a voice behind him.

Maureen had come into the room quietly, stealthily, just like she always did. Even back when they were kids, he or Will would come out of their bedroom and find her skulking around the hallway outside their door, or walk into the kitchen and catch her hanging up the extension, or see her lurking just out of sight behind their parents while they were deep in conversation. Once when his mother had been putting away towels in the linen closet, she'd looked up and been startled by Maureen, who'd climbed up to the top shelf and was sitting there, hugging her legs to her chest, looking down at her, silently watching. Just watching. Maureen watched, she listened, she knew things. She was good at turning over rocks, finding out stuff nobody else was supposed to know.

"Are you sure you're okay?" asked Maureen to his father. "I laid out your pajamas. Everything is set up in the bathroom, too."

"Thank you, Maureen," he said. He turned to Eddy and said, "Don't forget what I told you, son."

"I won't, Dad," he said. He and Maureen watched as he made his way into the bedroom, turned, and shut the door behind him. Eddy turned to Maureen and gestured with his head toward the kitchen. She raised her eyebrows and shrugged but went. Eddy followed and closed the door carefully behind them.

"So, Maureen," he said, keeping his voice low. "What's new? What have you been hearing around the campfire?"

She shrugged and tried to look nonchalant, but he saw the flash in those cinnamon eyes, and he knew exactly what it meant. She knew something and wanted him to know it. Maureen turned and sauntered to the refrigerator, took out a bottle of Miller Lite, and sat at the kitchen table.

"I don't know much of anything," she said, taking a sip of beer. "I'm just the hired help."

"What do you know about this project my dad's been working on?" he asked again, gesturing toward the living room.

"I've heard this and that," she said, taking a sip from her beer. "Bits and pieces."

"Tell me what you know," he said. "It's important."

"Well, Eddy," she said. "You need to be specific. If you're asking about general knowledge, I know you're an asshole, but everybody in Moon Lake knows that."

He sat down on the opposite side of the table and stared at her. She looked back, a little smile twisting at the corner of her mouth.

"Maureen," he said. "This is no joke. If you've heard anything about what's going on here, you need to let me know. Now."

"I don't know," she said, leaning back in her chair. "What's it worth to you, Eddy?"

He sighed to himself. Maureen. Always playing the same old games.

"C'mon, Maureen. You know what I'm talking about."

"The project?" she asked, motioning with her head toward the living room. "Is that what you mean?" He nodded.

"Yes," she said. "I know a little bit about that." She took a sip of beer.

I'm sure you do. The way you skulk around, you're bound to know something.

"I know," she said, "that you and Will are going to inherit the endowment lands and that your dad wants some of it to go up for sale, but that he also wants to keep a big chunk of it the way it is. I know you're going to be filthy rich once your dad passes away. I know that Will could be rich, too, but he won't care."

Eddy nodded.

"I know you, Eddy," she continued, "and I know exactly what you'll do." Her tone was strangely flat, dead. Her voice usually had that smirk in it when she flaunted what she knew, but not now. "I know," she continued, "that you're going to rip up the woods, build condos and waterparks and McDonald's and all the strip malls this land will hold. You'll build a subdivision of lakefront cottages that those shitheads from downstate will come up here to buy. And they'll cut down all the trees between them and the lake—except one—that one big tree they all have, and then they'll plant a perfect little suburban lawn." She took a long swig of beer and looked up at him, the little twist of a smile gone. "I know that," she said. She stared at him a moment. "Because," she added, "I know you're an asshole."

He exhaled. Yeah, she had a pretty good idea of what was going on. And she was pissed at him to boot. *All right. Fine.*

"And," she added. "I know your dad wants to keep it a secret. And if that's why you're asking me about it, yes, I will respect his wishes."

"All right," he said. "Good. Thank you, Maureen. So why am I an asshole?"

"Because when you do this, Eddy, and I know you will, you're going to change this place forever," she said. "You'll be ripping up your home and your family and this town. Things will never be the same around here. And you don't even care."

She smiled a little and half-shrugged, tilting her head. "But I guess that's who you are, isn't it? Eddy's always all about Eddy. You never even thought about your brother once in all this, did you? Not until your dad brought him up."

A wisp of auburn hair fell across her eyes, but she didn't remove it. She never did.

"Will," said Eddy, "is going to be getting his fair share, the same as me. He'll be fine."

"He won't be fine," she said. "Destroying that land will kill him. You don't have to do this, Eddy. You could do the right thing."

He looked at her carefully. She was peeling the label off her beer bottle; the hair was still hanging across her face. He resisted the urge to reach over and tuck it back behind her ear.

"And what would that be?" he asked, leaning on the table with his crossed arms.

She looked up, her brown eyes narrowed—not cinnamon now, but focused, their light as sharp and hard as knife points. She wasn't flirting now.

"Leave everything the way it is. Don't develop the land. It's not always about the money, Eddy," she said, her voice still flat, emotionless. "You need to take care of your family, too."

"That's what I'll be doing," he said, leaning back in his chair. "I'm doing this for my kids. And for Naomi."

"That's not what I mean," she said slowly.

"What is it then?"

"Come on, Eddy," she said slowly. "You know exactly what I mean. You insult my intelligence. You insult your own intelligence. If..." she continued, taking another sip from the bottle, "that's possible."

He laughed. "I don't know, Maureen. I really don't know what you want."

"I'm talking about Will."

He shrugged. "What about him?"

"You need to start thinking about how this is going to affect him. He's your brother."

Eddy stood up abruptly and went to the refrigerator, opened it, and looked inside. He was sick of hearing about his brother.

"Is that all we have? Miller Lite?"

No answer. He glanced at her. She was glaring at him now. Eddy grabbed a beer and went back to the table. He opened it and took a swig, not hooking eyes with her. Not yet. He knew what she wanted, but he didn't know how to approach it yet.

He stared at the bottle in front of him. Maureen had done it again; somehow she'd turned the tables on him. *No*, he thought, digging in suddenly. *Wait a minute. This isn't any of her business. She's not family. She has no say in this, about me and Will and our father. Not this time.*

He opened his mouth, but she—once again—beat him to the punch. She knew what he was going to say—probably before he knew it himself.

"Fuck you, Eddy," she said. She stood up. He was surprised to see her eyes were moist. "You selfish bastard. If you want to sell the land, to turn it into a strip mall, that's up to you, but to do it without including Will, without even thinking about him, is bullshit."

She put her empty bottle down gently, almost gracefully, on the table, and glanced up, her eyes tearing at him like thorns. "And don't pretend that everything will be okay, in your cool dude Eddy way, because it won't. If you're not careful, you're going to tear this family apart. I think that means more to me than to you."

She nodded, her auburn hair splayed across her eyes— autumn leaves on the forest floor—and smiled, not playing now, but sharp, cruel, toothy, like a hunting cat.

"And," she added. "Don't forget about your precious Naomi. You think she's going to sit still when all this comes down?

Uh-uh. She's going to be all over it and all over you. Once she smells that money, you can forget about Will and your dad and everything your family ever stood for. And you can forget about me, too." Maureen turned and stalked out.

No, Maureen. I have not forgotten Naomi. He glanced down at his left hand resting against the bottle. The plain gold band on his ring finger shone in the light. It wasn't really gold anymore, more of a brassy color, and nicked in a dozen places. The inside of it had been crudely inscribed with their initials—EL and NS, by Peter Martin, her friend from college, the amateur jeweler. Those scratchings, he knew, from seeing them the rare times he took off his ring, were almost worn away by the years.

When they first met at a frat party in college, Eddy barely noticed Naomi. But after seeing her around campus, he began to notice something about her—an elusive attractiveness, some-thing feral and intense coiled up and ingrained into every bit of her sexuality. He was intrigued. It was physical, but it was more than that; there was something dark and animal in her persona, too. Something wicked. The more he became aware of it, the more he wanted her, and when they finally made love, it was violent, delirious stings of pleasure and pain combined in swirls of ecstasy. Eddy had never experienced anything like it. After a year or so, they got married. She was the one who wanted it, but Eddy didn't mind. After all, it wasn't as if she'd be the only woman he'd ever sleep with again.

Naomi was younger than him, not quite thirty-three. She'd been vocally unhappy for at least three years of their marriage, and probably quietly unhappy for longer, although happiness was—at best—a relative thing for her. Satisfaction wasn't a word that was in her vocabulary; neither was forgiveness. Neither was peace. Or quiet.

And, he thought, picking up the beer and emptying it in one solid swallow, *even if she knew what forgiveness was, she wouldn't know what to do with it.* He sighed, got up, and put on his jacket, hat, and gloves. Jimbo stood up from where he'd been lying next to the stove and stretched. He knew it was time to go. Eddy went to the back door and switched off the kitchen light. Darkness, the dark of the deep woods, complete and deep as a well, padded into the kitchen. Then his eyes began to adjust. The deep dark gave way to the moon.

The silver light, reflected off the snow, streamed into the kitchen. It took his eyes a moment to adjust, but when they did, he could see everything outlined in the blue-white glow, every detail—the counter, the print on the wallpaper, the scratches in the linoleum. Everything.

A movement caught his eye. He turned. There, standing in the open doorway to the living room, was Maureen, her hair turned silver, eyes now blue like his, like Will's, like his father's, in the cold, cold light. Lying in wait for him like she always did, like she always had. And she moved then, silent as a doe, stealthy as a wolf, and she moved toward him. She reached up to him, kissing him on the mouth, and then took him by the hand, leading him to her bed.

"Come here," she whispered. "Come here, you bastard.

CHAPTER 7

EDDY WALKED INTO THE PURPLE ONION, Jimbo plodding beside him. The bar was dimly lit and musty-smelling, mostly because nobody cared. The place had been built back in the thirties. A huge circular bar snaked through the main room. A long, vintage mirror—Eddy and his dad had decided it was probably an original item—covered the back wall. There was an assortment of mounted animals and fish hanging on the walls; most of them had come with the place. They had the usual neon ad lights there, too—Bud, Miller, and some of that artisan stuff a guy from Madison had sold them. A vintage pinball machine and some video games were tucked here and there, but it wasn't really that kind of place. People came here to drink, not to socialize. Especially in the winter.

This time of year, only locals hung out here; in the spring, when the tourists came, they'd break out the Pine-Sol and scrub the place down—but for now, it served its purpose. It looked quiet tonight. Bill Cobb, Derrick Friendly, and Danny Long were sitting at the corner booth with some guy Eddy didn't know. He nodded to them. The Wilson brothers were across the bar sharing a pitcher. Eddy acknowledged them and sat down on one of the barstools. Jimbo sat down on the floor next to him and looked up expectantly. *Shit.* Eddy realized he hadn't fed him yet. All the dog had eaten were some of his dad's leftovers. He'd see if there was something in back after he had a beer. He had to wash up anyhow.

Lewis broke off his conversation with Andy Wilson and made his way over to Eddy's side of the bar. He grabbed a bar towel and said something to Doc, who was scrunched up on his barstool next to the wall. Eddy hadn't noticed Doc sitting there; he took a good look at the old man.

"Hey, boss," rumbled a voice. Eddy glanced up.

Lewis was leaning on the bar with his elbows, staring at him.

"Hey, Lewis," he said. "How's it going?"

"Same old, same old," said Lewis. He looked off to his right suddenly. Eddy felt someone coming up on his left. He turned. One of the guys from the booth—the guy he didn't know—was standing there looking at him. Eddy looked back at him. Medium height. Early thirties, overweight, wearing a red down jacket. Round face, brown hair, beard, balding. No expression on his face. He could be pissed off, depressed, or just plain stupid. It was impossible to tell. He looked like a million other guys up here.

"Yeah?" asked Eddy, trying to be the gracious host. "What can I do for you?"

"Are you Eddy LeBarron?" the guy asked, his voice curt, brusque. Eddy nodded.

"That's me," he said. "I own the place."

"Is your brother Will LeBarron, that DNR jerk who lives out by Turtle Ridge?"

Eddy took a deep breath and looked at the guy long and hard. It didn't seem as if he wanted trouble. If it came down to it, Eddy thought he could take him, but he didn't want to fight. He was too tired. He was too old. Lewis was here, anyway.

"Who wants to know?"

"I'm Mark Larson. I'm working for Danny Long."

Eddy shrugged. That meant very little to him; he knew Danny, a contractor, but everybody knew Danny. A lot of guys worked for him. He cocked his ear. Something was different.

What little conversation there'd been in the bar had disappeared. The only sound was some country western song thumping away on the jukebox. They were all listening. Eddy kept his eyes on the new guy; he felt rather than saw Lewis move closer to the bar.

"I'm looking for that bitch he works with," said the stranger. "Her name is Sully. She busted my cousin last year and shot up his snowmobile."

Somebody across the bar snickered. Someone else joined in. Eddy didn't have to look. He knew the Wilsons were laughing into their beers. The new guy looked over at them. His face wasn't expressionless now.

"You want another one, boss?" asked Lewis. The new guy looked over at him. His eyes got big.

Eddy glanced back at Lewis. He was looking at the new guy through narrowed eyes, not sure whether he was trouble or not.

"You know this guy, Lewis?" asked Eddy.

"Nope. Never saw him before in my life."

"Did you hear him talking shit about Sully?"

"I did." Lewis stood up straight and placed his hands on the bar. He was big, a former semi-pro linebacker. The new guy looked from Eddy to Lewis and back again.

"You know she's a friend of ours," added Eddy.

"I don't want trouble," said the stranger, "and I didn't mean to disrespect you. I just want to talk to that woman."

"All right," said Eddy, "but when you find her, I hope you remember she has a lot of friends around here."

"Maybe so, but I need to talk to her about payback for my cousin's sled. She killed it, man."

"You can't get any money from her for that," said Eddy. "She was just doing her job. Your cousin's lucky he didn't get killed."

"And from what I hear," said Lewis, leaning over the bar. "He had it coming. Besides," he added, "she's nobody to mess with. If you two got into it, my money would be on her. Why don't you let bygones be bygones?"

The guy looked Lewis up and down, smirked, and went back to his booth.

"What an asshole," muttered Lewis, glaring after him.

Eddy swiveled around to face the bar and took a sip of his beer. He glanced up at Lewis.

"Yeah, he is," he said, "but we need the money. As long as he pays, he can stay."

Lewis shrugged. He was a smart guy. Knew when to keep his mouth shut. He picked up his bar rag and wiped up some stray moisture on the bar. Besides being big, he had a nasty look, which was one of the reasons Eddy had hired him. He wore his dark hair long, in a ponytail, and his brown eyes seemed to bore through everything they happened to land on. His nose looked like a broken curb, and his mouth was set in a permanent snarl— like one of the stuffed wolverines lurking behind the bar. Lewis's arms were huge, his biceps almost as big around as a normal man's thigh, and he was as strong as he looked. Not too many customers, drunk or not, would mess with him.

Lewis had wandered into The Onion on a Monday night a few years back, and a couple of locals had tried to pick a fight with him. After he'd kicked their asses and thrown them both out the front door, Eddy had offered him work. Lewis had shrugged and said, "Sure, why not?" He had nothing better going on. And, as it turned out, when the opportunity presented itself, Lewis had been pretty enterprising. He'd started the Tuesday night runs into the Twin Cities.

"Those guys running a tab?" asked Eddy, nodding toward the booth in the corner. Lewis nodded. "Put an extra round on it." They would never know, and in his place, being an asshole cost extra. "Make it two," he said. Lewis smiled and nodded.

Eddy glanced over at the cash register. "How we looking this month?"

"Normal for the season," said Lewis. "We're breaking even. And," he said confidentially, leaning closer to Eddy on his folded arms, "that other payment came in last Tuesday. I have it set up for you in back."

Eddy nodded. Good. He could use the money. He was short again this month.

"Hey, Lewis," he said. "Could I bum a smoke?" He, unlike Naomi, mother of the year, only smoked in the bar. She lit up anywhere she could, including the house when the kids were home. Nice.

Lewis reached into his shirt pocket, pulled out his pack of Marlboros, and handed one to Eddy. *State law says no smoking inside, but fuck it—it's my place, and the only customers in it are the Wilsons and the stooges sitting in the corner nursing their beers. And Doc.*

Eddy watched Lewis as he washed out some glasses. From the little he knew, he understood they had a nice operation going, running up to the Twin Cities every other week, picking up packages to be delivered in Madison. Eddy didn't know what was in the mail; he didn't want to know.

All he had to do was let Lewis run some cash through the bar books. Not enough to arouse anybody's suspicions—just the right amount to keep everybody comfortable. *And for me, that's easy money.* Lewis handled his end and did the Onion's books, too. If push came to shove, if things went sour, Eddy would be in the clear. He had no involvement in the operation, and his ten percent of the cut would be virtually untraceable. Of course, after the meeting with his dad tonight, he knew money was not going to be an issue anymore. In fact, he was going to have to figure out what to do with The Purple Onion—keep it to stay busy, or maybe sell it to Lewis.

Eddy stood up, stubbed out his cigarette, and glanced at himself in the vintage mirror behind the bar. *Man, I'm getting fat. I have to start watching it.* He drained his beer, nodded to Lewis, and pulled on Jimbo's lead. The dog got up and stretched, wagging his tail. Eddy leaned over and petted him.

"I'm going in back for a bit," he said to Lewis, who nodded. He walked around the big curve in the bar, Jimbo at his heels, past the old pinball machines and the video gambling games, through the kitchen, and into the office. *Shit. It's cold in here.* He went into the bar kitchen and rummaged through one of the cupboards, looking for dog food. Nothing. He found a can of Sloppy Joe mix and figured that would have to do. He was sure Jimbo wouldn't mind.

"What do you think, buddy?" he asked, looking down at Jimbo, who was gazing up at him, his tail thumping the floor. "That wakes you up, doesn't it?" Eddy opened the can, found a bowl, and poured the stuff in. Jimbo trotted over and started inhaling it. *Well, he still enjoys eating.* His dad used to say, "As long as a dog enjoys eating, shitting, and sleeping, you keep him around." *Well, Jimbo, the way you're going after that Sloppy Joe stuff, I guess you've got a few more years left in you.*

He walked back into the tiny bathroom, locked the door, and turned on the tap. It would take at least two or three minutes for the hot water to start running. He waited until it got a little warmer, washed his hands, then undid his belt, pulled down his pants, and started soaping up the old Johnson. *That goddamned Maureen.* She'd broken things off with him last fall, and they'd gone three months with nothing happening—and then, boom, tonight she comes after him like a goddamned cat in heat. What was he supposed to do?

He carefully soaped up his penis, wincing under the cold washcloth. This was a precautionary move. Naomi had a nose like a bloodhound; she could smell sex on him a mile away. She'd probably know, anyway. *Jesus,* he thought, reaching for the towel. *They're killing me. One way or another, they're killing me. Maureen blindsides me tonight, and what am I supposed to do? Say no? And then Naomi is going to be all over me when I get home, especially if she smells sex on me. 'Till death do we fucking part. Lucky me. Well, maybe things will get better at home now. Maybe she'll cut a rich husband some slack.* He glanced up in the scratched mirror and caught himself smiling. *C'mon, Eddy. Who the fuck are you kidding?*

He finished drying off, zipped up, and went back out into the kitchen. Jimbo was sitting by his dish, his tail thumping the floor. Eddy picked up the bowl and put it in the stainless steel sink, then knelt down and reached underneath. He felt the plastic-wrapped package taped next to the trap and pulled it off. He unwrapped it and riffled through the bills. *Yep. One thousand. The usual.* He stood up, tucked the money into his vest pocket, motioned to Jimbo, and walked back out into the bar.

Nothing had changed. Lewis was talking to Andy Wilson again. Doc was on his stool, still leaning up against the wall, staring into a fresh beer. Eddy walked over and sat on the barstool next to him.

"Hey, Doc," he said. "How're you doing?"

The old man slowly raised his head and took a good look at Eddy, who suddenly felt as if he were standing naked in an examining room. Doc's eyes were bright green and as clear as a winter sky. Eddy had been expecting the misty bloodshot gaze of the daily drunk, but not this time. His hair, almost completely white, was uncombed but not untidy. His face was weathered, dark, and a little wind-burned. *Doc must be spending a fair amount of time outdoors.* He was thin, too—not old skinny or sick skinny, but wiry, lean. *What does he do out there?* Eddy tried to remember how long it had been since he'd talked to Doc. *A long time. A couple of months at least.*

"I'm good, Eddy," he said, his voice so soft Eddy had to lean in a little to hear him. He smiled a little bit.

"How's your dad?" asked Doc, leaning an elbow on the bar. Eddy tried to remember whether he might know his dad was sick. Everybody else knew, but Doc was awfully good at keeping his nose out of other people's business.

"Is he comfortable?" continued Doc, asking the question like a doctor would. He knew. Eddy nodded.

"Yeah," said Eddy. "He's doing okay." He shrugged. "You know him. He wouldn't complain if he was feeling bad. How'd you know?"

Doc smiled. He still had a full set of teeth. "Everybody knows everything in Moon Lake, Eddy. You know that."

Eddy smiled back and looked closely at Doc. He was stooped, wrinkled, about what you'd expect an eighty-year-old to be, but there was still a spark there. It was funny—everybody, himself included—had assumed from the way Doc secluded himself that he was just fading away. *Well, he's definitely still on top of things. I guess we just never bothered to ask.*

"Okay, Doc," said Eddy. "Listen, I've got to go. You take care of yourself."

Doc nodded, patting Eddy on his hand. "Okay," he said, "we'll see you."

"I'm heading home, Lewis," he called out. "You take care."

"You, too, boss," said Lewis, who raised his eyes and gave him a thumbs-up. Eddy nodded to him and started to leave, Jimbo padding behind him.

He happened to lock eyes with the buck over the bar, the thirteen-pointer his dad had bagged over near the flowage. The black marble eye stared at him through the smoky red light. *Watching. Always watching.* Eddy knew everybody in Moon Lake, and everybody knew him. This was a small town. He would know if the county deputies or the feds started sniffing around, and he would know when they were going after somebody and how they would to do it. *That,* he thought, smiling to himself, *is the beauty of a small town.* He glanced at his watch. Time to go. He needed to put in his share of quality family time.

Eddy zipped up his coat and stepped outside into the frigid air. It already felt like it was below zero. He put on his gloves as he glanced up and down the empty main street. Dead as a doornail. No lights, no traffic, nothing. Even Busby's, one of the other taverns in town, was already closed. He looked past the streetlight standing guard over Olsen's Restaurant on the edge of town. Nothing beyond that light but black. Woods. The deep, dark woods. The trees were outlined by the moonlight, but nothing penetrated the inner depths of that forest. *At least,* he thought, smiling to himself, *for now.*

* * *

EDDY OPENED THE BACK DOOR QUIETLY and stepped inside, gently knocking the snow off his boots. He paused to listen and then glanced at the clock on the stove. It was after eleven, way past the kids' bedtime. Naomi might still be up. He listened for the TV. Nothing. Eddy bent over and started pulling off his boots. He had to get up early to get the kids to school tomorrow and then he had to arrange the meeting with Will. That would be a fun one.

He put his boots away, unhooked Jimbo's leash, padded over to the refrigerator, and opened it. The dog was right behind him. Naomi had left a plate for him. Lasagna. He looked at it a minute, decided he wasn't hungry, and grabbed a Schlitz. He twisted it open as he walked into the living room. Naomi was asleep on the couch. The TV was on, but the sound was off. He put his beer down carefully on the coffee table and walked to the back of the house.

Bella's door was partly open and he poked his head in. She lay there asleep with her favorite Winnie the Pooh doll in her arms. She was beautiful in sleep, peaceful and serene, as still and perfect as a china doll. He watched his daughter in the pale glow of her funny bunny nightlight. Her skin seemed even paler than usual, waxy, almost too perfect. She lay still as a statue. He held his breath, listening, then stepped closer and squatted next to her, watching for movement of her tiny chest. Eddy reached out his hand, almost touching her before he saw the quilt moving slightly. He stood up, took a breath, his eyes still locked on her, and then turned. Naomi was standing in the doorway, the line of her mouth fixed and unwavering, as straight and hard as a rifle barrel. Her eyes, as big as steel bearings, glistened in the semi-darkness. She half-turned and motioned him to follow her. He did, semi-shutting Bella's door as he did so. He paused, sticking his head into Donny's room, before following his wife.

The boy was sprawled all over the bed, his limbs as scattered as autumn leaves. The covers were half on the floor.

Eddy walked in, picked up the quilts, covered up his son, kissed him on top of his head, and went into the living room. Naomi was sitting on the couch staring up at him, the angular planes of her face unsoftened by the light coming from the television. She'd been losing weight, and she couldn't afford to; she'd always been rail-skinny, even after the kids came. His wife just had one of those metabolisms that burned everything—that never stopped moving. Ever. He sat down next to her and reached for his beer. Never-ever. She just wouldn't quit. Not at anything—working, mothering, complaining, nagging, or thinking—even at night, when he would wake to the sound of her teeth grinding as she slept.

"Were you at the bar?" she asked, whispering, which almost hid the edge in her voice. It had a metallic quality, like a nail being pulled from a board.

"Yeah," he said. "Lewis and I were tallying sales. How did things go today?"

Naomi looked down at her hands and back up at him. They were shaking slightly. He braced himself. This could be anything from a stinging critique of her co-workers to a detailed description of another harrowing day at the clinic to an upbeat rundown of a nice play date to a bitter evaluation of his own selfish behavior.

"Not bad," she said, shrugging. "The usual. It was pretty quiet at the clinic, except that goddamned Shelly wanted to leave early again to pick up her daughter from figure-skating practice. Like she's the only one there with kids. She wants off early every goddamned day. Selfish bitch." She'd gotten that snippy tone going, her voice cutting off the syllables like a meat cleaver.

Eddy waited; he knew that when he started to ask Naomi questions, she would only get more worked up. He had learned early on it was better to let her vent. He was just glad he wasn't the subject of the rant this time.

"Donny," she continued, "had another accident with the toilet training." She paused. He nodded.

"How's your dad?" she added, almost as an afterthought. Her tone was perfunctory, tired; he could tell she was only asking because it was expected.

"He's doing okay," he said. "We had a good talk tonight."

"Yeah?" asked Naomi, reaching for her cigarettes. "What did you guys talk about?"

Eddy felt the impulse to tell her the good news rising in him, but he stopped himself. He'd promised his dad he'd wait. And he wanted to have a plan for dealing with Naomi after he told her. Maureen was right about that. Once Naomi found out, she'd want to be right in the middle of things. Or right on top of things.

"The usual," he answered. "We talked about an open house at the Fleming place and maybe putting up a website. Just work stuff. I had dinner over there, too."

Naomi lit up her cigarette and sat up straight, looking at him with her eyes narrowed, her irises the color of ice cubes.

"How's Maureen?" she asked with a different, smarmy tone in her voice; she still had it in for Maureen. *And with good reason.*

"She seems good," he said. "We didn't really talk much." Which—at least at the end of the evening—was true.

"Really?" asked Naomi, staring at him. He stared right back. You couldn't back off with Naomi, or she'd be all over you.

"Yeah," he nodded. "Really."

Naomi nodded back but said nothing—still staring; she knew he'd been up to something.

"How were the kids today?" he asked, changing the subject.

"Okay," she said. "They were pretty rambunctious, though. Look at this place."

He glanced around the room. Toys were scattered all over the floor. Unfolded laundry was in a basket on the dining room table, and the floor looked as if it hadn't been vacuumed for a couple of weeks. It was pretty much the same as usual. Except for the kitchen, which she always kept spotless, Naomi wasn't much of a housekeeper.

He nodded, relief starting to flow through him. *So far, so good.* At least his head didn't seem to be on the chopping block tonight. Not yet. He only hoped she wouldn't pick up the sex smell on him.

"Donny said he wants to go to real school with Bella today," Naomi said, smiling a little. The hard edges in her face followed the smile, softening slightly. "He was really cute. I think he wants to be with his big sister."

"That's cool," said Eddy, taking a sip from his beer. "So how are you doing, honey?"

She shrugged and shook her head in that quick way of hers, always reminding him somehow of a shivering Chihuahua.

"Here," he said, handing her the bottle. She smiled a little, took it and drank, then leaned forward and pressed her lips together.

"I'm hoping I can get off the double shift this weekend," she said. "The bitch Shelly needs to take it. It's her turn. I was thinking we could maybe do some shopping for the kids. Bella needs some new clothes."

"Okay," he said. "That shouldn't be a problem. I was thinking, too," he said, taking the beer bottle from her, "that we could maybe stop by Schuelke's and—if you still want to—we could look at a piano."

She turned toward Eddy, mouth open, and stared at him a moment. *Speechless. Finally.*

"Are you serious?" she asked finally. "That would be great. We could get one of those digitals that don't take up much room. We could put it in the dining room right there next to the bookshelf." She stopped a moment, cocked her head and stared at him. "This is awfully sudden, Eddy. Why now? What's going on?"

He shrugged.

"Nothing. Dad and I were going over our prospects and think this is going to be a pretty good year, so I figured, why not—you've been waiting a long time, and you deserve it. The kids are old enough to start taking lessons now too, right?"

She nodded, her eyes on her hands. Thinking. Wondering. Having her suspicions. But he wasn't really worried about that now; he knew her. She was pumped, excited about the piano. She looked up at him again, her eyes bright but not as hard now, more the color of burnished silver.

Naomi smiled and then curled up next to him on the couch, drawing her skinny legs up underneath her. He put his arm around her shoulders. *My God. She's skin and bones. You'd think she was the one with cancer.* He hugged her and glanced down as she buried her face into his sweater. She inhaled deeply, once, twice, and let it out.

Sniffing. The bloodhound in her. He held his breath. Naomi didn't raise her head. She either couldn't tell he'd been with Maureen or she didn't care. She snuggled closer. He cleared his throat.

"I'll be late again tomorrow," he said. "We're going to be having a family meeting at Dad's to talk over some business stuff. Just me and him. And Will."

"Will?" asked Naomi, alert suddenly. *Shit. Her radar was up.* "Why Will?"

Eddy shrugged. "I don't know. Dad didn't really say what it was all about, just that he wanted Will there, too."

Naomi frowned. She was fully awake now.

"Am I invited?" she asked.

Eddy shook his head. "No. Dad said just the three of us. Just immediate family."

"I don't think that's right, Eddy," she said, the edge back in her voice. "I'm family, too."

"It's just going to be about the business," he said.

"With Will there?" she asked. "And suddenly the new piano? C'mon, Eddy. Don't lie to me. What's going on?"

He shrugged again. *Shit.* He was in for it now. She wasn't going to let up until she found out.

"All right, Eddy," she said. "Don't tell me. It doesn't matter because I'm coming to that meeting, too. With you or without you. You know why? Because I don't trust you, and because your business is my business. And I'll find out what's going on. You can count on that."

Naomi got up, her face silvery in the light from the television. She grabbed his half-full beer bottle and took it with her into the kitchen. Eddy watched her as she returned and strode silently past him into the bedroom. He was struck by the similarity between Maureen, bathed in the cold light of the moon, and his wife, covered in the silver glow of the television. He closed his eyes.

Jesus. I'm surrounded.

CHAPTER 8

THE MOON WAS STILL UP, FAT ON THE western horizon, its delicate silver light still lovingly caressing the dark trunks of the old pines. Will turned to the east. Day was coming; the eastern rim of the lake was growing light, and the dawn's faint golden glow almost seemed to breathe warmth into the frosty morning air.

Will watched the sky as the new light seeped slowly over the tree line. In the spring, the songbirds and squirrels would already be stirring. Not now. Not in this cold. Except for the occasional groaning of the ice, it was as quiet and cold as a tomb. He loved the dawn in his woods. Something about this time of day spoke to him of inevitabilities—of the giant tangle of apprehensions and hopes—wound up tight in the sky, looking over them. This was something he could not have articulated, but that didn't matter; some things—most things—couldn't be and didn't need to be explained—only understood. Here, the dawn was his and no one else's; words were unnecessary. These apprehensions belonged to him; they could not be shared. And why try?

His eyes swept slowly over Mirror Lake as the rising sun touched the snow blanketing its sleeping surface, turning the silver-gray crust of snow to gold. It was a big lake, not the biggest around here, but six hundred twenty-four acres, and every inch of its shoreline owned by the state. The endowment lands went deep behind the shoreline, at least one mile in the narrowest places and nine or ten in the deepest—all the way to the far side of Moon Lake. In fact, the endowment covered all of the Thin Lake shoreline, too, and much of the old forest beyond that—all the way past Turtle Ridge. *And,* he thought, nodding, *I know every inch of it—every single tree, every rock, every pebble, and every wormhole.* He knew how everything connected; at least he had a good start to that knowledge, but he knew he had only scratched the surface. But even so—sometimes he could see all of the magnificent web of life distilled in a drop of pond water or reflected in a dying squirrel's eyes, all of it—the joy, the pain, the despair, the patience, and the inevitability.

Will turned and trudged up the hill to his cabin. The path was little more than a deer trail snaking between the old white pines, unshoveled and only wide enough for one. He needed nothing more. He stamped his feet at the door and let himself in. The fire had burned down. He put two more logs on to keep the temperature above freezing while he was gone and then fixed himself a bowl of oatmeal and a cup of hot tea. He sat down, put a few raisins on it, and started eating.

The first thing is going to be tracking that coyote. He'd have to get started soon. Forty-five minutes to get out there, an hour or so of tracking—if he was lucky—and then another forty-five back. That would give him an hour before his meeting with Chief Warden Dodge. Then he needed to go to see that skulk and his little vixen.

Will glanced out, gauging the height of the sun. Just over the treetops. Time to go. He bundled up, took his snowshoes, and walked out into the clearing behind the cabin, into the cold. The sunlight was streaming down now, all brightness and no warmth. He put on his snowshoes and started walking. Will took his time. The cold didn't bother him; it never had.

He trudged down the narrow path to the road. It was only about a half-mile on the old deer trail. The thick pines overhead kept the trail pretty clear of snow, but he still had to keep an eye out for slippery spots. He spotted a couple of deer tracks, the split hooves almost parallel. Just walking, not spooked. They were big, probably bucks. They must have wandered down from the ridge looking for forage. There wouldn't be much here, except for tree bark.

Will walked past his vehicle, the old green Ford Focus his dad had given him. He hadn't wanted it, but his father said to take it just in case he might need to get somewhere quick. Like where? He rarely went anywhere he couldn't walk. The town of Moon Lake was only seven miles by trail; that was nothing. He figured if he got hurt but could still drive, it might come in handy. And he supposed—grudgingly—it was convenient for getting the few supplies he needed. The DNR had given him a mobile phone for emergencies, but cellphones hardly worked out here. You couldn't connect half the time. Not that he wanted to call anybody; it was just for emergencies.

He found the trail off Hourglass Road and followed his own tracks until he came to the spot where'd he left the coyote trail. He followed along, keeping a close eye out, until he spied some fresh tracks. *My friend was up with the sun this morning. And headed north, back toward Lake Williams and the Rutherfords. He must like the taste of Apso.* Will followed the spoor, leading him toward town, until he reached a high point of the ridge looking down on the unbroken white expanse of Mirror Lake. Beautiful. Not one ice-fishing shack or snowmobile track, not one trace of humanity. Beautiful.

Will continued on, following the coyote tracks, until he got to County X, where the animal had crossed. *Yep. He's going to where the people are. Easy pickings. Either scraps from the trash or fat dumb animals.*

He started to cross the road when a movement caught his eye. It was a doe, a yearling. Will could have counted her ribs if he wanted. She was pawing at the snow just in front of the tree line, breaking through the crust to see if there was anything Old Man Winter had left behind. It had been a tough year; the herd was going to be thinned out pretty good by spring. She was probably part of that group that fed down by the south bay of Lake Williams. The big doe had dropped twins last spring—this might be one of them. They wandered down here sometimes in the winter.

Some of the other people who stayed up here year-round would put out food for the deer—feed corn and such. That was wrong. It didn't do the deer any good. They'd keep coming back for the handouts, not trying to seek out forage on their own. They became dependent, spoiled; sometimes they became easy prey for shooters who would lure them in and then lie in wait as they came up for handouts. *Shooters. They're not hunters. That's not hunting.* He felt a flash of anger even thinking about them and their arrogance.

Wolves were the real hunters, and a fair match for the deer, using claws and teeth against the speed and agility of their prey. No long-range scopes, ATVs, or high-powered rifles. That wasn't hunting. Bow hunting was more fair to the deer, but even then the scales were weighted far too much on the side of mankind—lazy, pink, fat, smelly men who couldn't even drag their kill out of the forest.

Will glanced at his watch; he'd like to follow his quarry farther, but he needed to get back and prepare for the meeting. He could've snowshoed into town from here, but he was supposed to give Sully a lift after the meeting over to the shack off Mirror Lake where she kept her snowmobile. He'd have to go back and get the car anyway. He turned around and started plodding back, keeping an eye out for anything new in his forest, including a sign of that big creature he'd seen the day before. *Moose. It can't be anything else.* The morning sunlight was higher now, breaking the tree line and slanting between the black tree trunks and branches—as bare as skeletons, bouncing off the snow, and almost blinding him. Will stopped, dug out his sunglasses, and put them on. The sky was as clear as an icicle now, but those high feathery clouds to the west—cirrus—meant a front was moving in. There might be more snow tonight. Good. It had been a dry fall; they needed the precipitation.

Will finally got to the Ford. He took off his snowshoes, threw them in the back, and climbed in. The sun had been shining through the windshield, and the car almost seemed warm. Will started it up and carefully pulled onto Hourglass Road. He drove slowly, watching for icy patches. They only plowed down here every couple weeks, so parts of the road were glare ice. He continued carefully over the hills and ridges. Will braked at the bottom of the hill where Hourglass Road met County X, then nudged the nose of the car forward far enough so he could see to the curve to his left. The steep turn was close to the intersection and deceptively sharp; people came whipping around it like there was no tomorrow. And for a few of them, there had been no tomorrow. Like the crash three years ago when those two teenagers had gotten killed—the Lancaster boy and his girl.

Will had heard the crash all the way from his cabin and had made his way over to see what had happened. He'd been the first one there. The car had come around the corner too fast and flipped over, probably more than once. It was lying on its side. The boy was dead already, thrown from the vehicle into a tree. He'd been cut pretty much in half; one of his legs was still lying in the road. Will had picked it up and put it next to the rest of his body. The girl was still alive, but not by much. She was still pinned inside the car, the dashboard crumpled around her chest. She was bleeding from everywhere—mouth, ears, and nose. The skin around the top of her head had been sliced away, showing the glossy white surface of her skull. She was still conscious, her eyes skittering everywhere, full of fear and pain, like a trapped animal. She saw him and tried to raise her head and speak through the streams of blood flowing through her mouth.

Will watched her a moment, listening to the gurgle of her voice for any real words. Nothing. She was dying. He stood up, her eyes following, and he shook his head. She closed her eyes then. It was a shame. All that pain. If she were an animal, he could have put her out of her misery, ended her suffering, but because she was a person, he couldn't do that. To put her down would be a crime. Murder. And that wasn't right.

Will looked around and saw some deadfall by the side of the road. He spied an old pine branch, about the size of a baseball bat, and went over and picked it up. The girl's eyes were shut, but she was still breathing. He raised the branch. No, the angle was wrong. The roof was in the way. He had no room to swing it. He wouldn't be able to do it.

He heard the sirens, then, finally, dropped the branch, and faded back into the woods. He lay underneath the pines and watched as the ambulance came and the EMTs picked up the pieces and tried to help the girl. She died about fifteen minutes after they got there, lasting longer than he'd have thought. After she passed, he crawled out of sight and headed back to the cabin.

Will turned west onto X and went around the curve near Flowage Road, taking his foot off the accelerator as he felt the car drifting a little on the ice. He took it easy going down Fletcher Hill—if he missed that curve, he'd end up going straight down Quail Road on Lake Williams and land at Doc's place. He was glad all the lake people were up on Williams; it was easier to keep an eye on them. They didn't come down to Mirror that often because there was no public landing. Tourists only went on Moon to fish. And only to fish—there was a no-wake rule there that Sully enforced to the letter of the law. And nobody lived on Moon Lake except his dad—the one property that survived the land endowment.

After his father had bought it, he kept the big lodge as his house—and the three smaller places, former guest cottages, for family members. *Except nobody wanted to live there.* Will liked his place in the woods—he needed to stay close to his work—and Eddy and Naomi liked to be in town. Nope. Nobody wanted to live there. Maureen was staying with his dad now, which he supposed was good. She was family—almost. He'd always liked Maureen. Maybe it was more admiration. He liked her fearlessness, her ferocity, and her single-mindedness. *She would have made an outstanding mother.*

He slowed down as the Moon Lake, Unincorporated sign came into view. First the sign, then the row of squat, one-story, mostly wood buildings—Olsen's Restaurant, the Martin house, then the U.S. Post Office, Lakeland Realty, the Half-Moon Café, the Purple Onion, Singh's Convenience Store and Pump, Busby's Bar and Grill, then Pinky's Gift and Tackle, Long Contracting, and then, finally, Land of Lakes Hardware. And there was the Episcopal Church behind Busby's. That was pretty much it except for some houses behind the main drag, and the DNR Office—his office—at the very edge of town. They'd put up one of those ugly little pre-fab buildings back in the seventies, just an office and a bathroom, which was fine. He was never there, anyway.

Well, here it is. Two blocks of commerce and civilization; this was Moon Lake. Population four hundred and fifty. Not a bad little town. Not really. They hadn't had a decent grocery store since The Market Basket had burned down seven years ago, but other than that, they had pretty much everything they needed. It was a pain to run up to Eagleton for groceries, but it could be worse. It could always be worse.

He glanced into the front window of Lakeland Realty as he drove by. The lights were on, but he didn't see Eddy's car. Maybe the other guy, that Jay guy, was in there. That, when Will bothered to think about it, had always puzzled him. Why did his dad need an outsider to help with the business? He was sick, sure, but Eddy was there, and while his brother was no rocket scientist, he knew the realty business. He should. That was the only thing he and his father ever talked about.

The Half-Moon Café was open. Will could see a few people at the tables as he cruised by. This was a slow time, but Mattie was probably doing just fine. Bob Singh was stacking firewood outside his convenience store. He had bought the Blue Moon Gas Station nine years ago, and while he'd had to overcome some indigenous suspicion, he was getting along fine now. Bob was a good neighbor. People had learned to trust him.

All of them. All of us. We've been doing the same thing for years. Locked into our small town work and our small town lives. Nothing much changes. Just little things. People get sick. Babies get born. People get married. It's a lot, he realized suddenly, *like the woods, like my forest. Everybody is locked into who they are and how far they can go. Everybody. Eddy and Naomi with the kids. Maureen. Bob Singh. Mattie. All of us. We're stuck. Which suits me just fine.* He was where he belonged—not now, not this moment, but in the woods, back in the brush, back in the heart and soul of a world without voice—without mercy, and without guilt.

Will parked the Ford in front of the office and went in, glancing at his watch. He was about fifteen minutes early, which was good. He got out of the car, unlocked the office door, strode in, and walked directly over to the thermostat, turning it up from fifty-eight to sixty-five. That would be fine. Nobody would be taking their coats off, anyway. He went over to the fridge, took out the coffee, and started making a pot. He knew both Sully and Warden Dodge liked a cup in the morning. He was usually good with his tea.

The office was only one room with a bathroom attached. A small metal desk and filing cabinet, along with the office chair and two chairs opposite, were the only furnishings there. A dead geranium haunted a clay pot next to the window. They had a little sink by the coffee stand, but that was it. The only things on the walls were their degrees and a topographical map of the area. *If*, thought Will, half-smiling to himself, *you want to call that a map.*

Will glanced out the window just as Eddy cruised by in his old red Ford pickup; Will saw the bed was full of wood. His brother had probably been out taking more deadfall from the north side of Moon Lake near their father's place. Technically, they were supposed to let deadfall lie, decompose, and return to the soil, but Will had stopped bringing it up to Eddy and his dad. They ignored him; they didn't give a shit about the soil or the micro ecosystem. It was just free firewood to them. *Well, sometimes you just have to look the other way.* The door rattled in its frame.

He turned as Sully walked in, bringing the winter air with her, stamped her feet on the carpet, and gave him a big smile.

"Hey, hey, Mr. Will," she said, her voice loud enough to make him wince slightly. He wasn't used to that much volume. "How goes it in the deep dark backwoods?"

"Hey, Sully," he said. "Good. Things are going good."

She smiled, showing all her teeth, and took off her glasses as they began to fog up in the warm interior of the office. They were large, black plastic-framed glasses, the old-fashioned kind. He smiled back. He couldn't help it; few people could.

"Jesus," she said, taking off her gloves. "I can almost see my breath in here. Is the heat on?"

"Yeah," he said. "I just turned it up. It's getting warmer."

"I fucking hope so," she said. "We might die of frostbite before the chief even gets here."

She walked over to the coffee machine, leaned over it, and nodded approvingly. Will smiled. Sully was one of the few people he liked—not just got along with, but actually liked. She was loud, big, and blunt, and she—as far as he could tell—was funny. She was tall, taller than him, and carried some bulk on her, although it was not idle bulk. Most of it was muscle. Will had worked beside her, throwing sandbags onto the state truck during the flooding at the Flowage last spring; she was more than able to hold her own, tossing the thirty-pound bags around as if they were beanbags. She had told him—at length—about growing up on a dairy farm and having to pitch hay, herd cows, and build fences alongside her brothers.

Her ruddy, round face was usually creased into a smile, and when she laughed, her blue eyes—bright blue, like cornflowers—smiled right along with her mouth. She took off her jacket, hung it up, and sat down. She kept her knit hat on. Fringes of dirty blond hair peeked out from under it.

"Man," she said. "You missed it, Will. Boy, did we have a blast last night."

"Oh, yeah?" he said, sitting down behind the desk. Sully knew he didn't like to socialize, but that didn't stop her. It was all right. Will knew she was only making small talk.

"Yeah," she said. "We were playing darts over at Busby's with Bob Singh and the Wilson Brothers. Man, is that bastard good." She looked up at him, wiping the moisture off her glasses. "You know Bob, right?"

He nodded. Bob Singh had bought the gas station from old Axel Engel's family after he passed away. After the Market Basket burned down, he'd built onto it, adding the convenience store.

"Well, you know he doesn't drink, and he was just kicking our asses because, you know, we were having a few, and he kept getting better—or at least it looked that way." She shook her head. "Well, Andy started saying it's not fair, that Bob needed to be drinking too, but Bob said, 'No, I don't drink,' but..." she started laughing again, "he says I'll stand back farther to make it fair. And Andy says, 'Cool, okay, that seems like a good idea.' So then..." she said, leaning forward, "Bob looks at the dartboard, looks at Andy, and says to me, 'Sully, you'd better hold the door. I think I'm going to have to stand out on the sidewalk.'"

She laughed, a deep-throated whooping that filled the small office, a laugh that Will couldn't help smiling at. They both turned as they heard the door open and felt a blast of arctic air come in behind it. Chief Dodge stepped in and closed the door behind him. He was wearing the brown uniform jacket with the state logo on it and one of those wool hats with the flaps that came down the sides—*a havelock*, Will suddenly recalled, out of nowhere. *That's what those hats are called.*

Dodge took off his gloves and the hat and smoothed down his hair. He kept it short, above the ears, but not too short. It was actually looking a little shaggy for him. *He's getting gray.* The usual salt and pepper in the hair was definitely taking a turn. Dodge was average height and weight, with brown hair and eyes; he was average in most respects, but not the ones that counted. His face was weathered, the color of an acorn and as lined as the bark of an old pine. His full mustache was frosted up and starting to melt. He unzipped his jacket but decided to keep it on.

"Hey, boss," said Sully, getting up to look at the coffee machine.

"Sully," he said, speaking slowly and nodding at her as he took off his leather gloves. His voice still had traces of a Louisiana drawl even though he'd been trying to get rid of it for years.

"Will," he added, turning to him and nodding. Dodge typically wasn't a man who gave much away; his voice was always very even, very deliberate. He wasn't a friendly man but was always courteous. Whether he was that way with his employees or with everyone, Will couldn't say. He wouldn't know; he was not a good judge of character. Nobody ever called the chief by his first name—Roscoe.

"Chief Dodge," said Will. "What's up?"

"A few things," he said, finally unzipping his jacket, "but let's get at that coffee first."

Sully poured three cups and handed them around. Will got up, offering to surrender the desk chair to Dodge, but the chief waved him off. He sat next to Sully on one of the office chairs. They all took a sip of the hot coffee.

"Man," said Sully, looking at her cup, "this is even shittier than usual."

Dodge chuckled. Will joined in after a beat.

"Yeah," said Will. "Sorry. It's the stuff that was in the fridge. It's pretty old."

"Well," said Sully. "As long as it works."

Sounds of assent floated through the office. Will glanced out the window. It was still a sunny, beautiful morning. He couldn't wait to get out and see his skulk of foxes. Hopefully the snow would hold off until tonight.

"So," said Dodge, "I've got a couple of things on the agenda." He took a brown leather-bound notebook out of his valise and opened it up. Will was grateful that Dodge's meetings were usually informal affairs. He believed in doing whatever got a job done most efficiently and most quickly. And despite the fact he had to answer to the higher-ups with their tourism agenda, Dodge's primary concern was always based on his deep and abiding love of the land.

"First of all," he said, looking at the agenda. "The Eagleton office got a call about a coyote attack yesterday. On a small dog."

"Yes, sir," said Will. "I'm already on that. I ran into the complainant yesterday. A Mrs. Rutherford from over on Lake Williams. I just happened to be in town when she came in. The dog was bitten but survived. Mrs. Rutherford wanted to me to kill the coyote right away. She insisted on it."

Dodge nodded and made a couple notes.

"So I tracked it from the attack site down to the southern edge of Mirror and lost it in the underbrush down there."

"Was that the one?" asked Dodge.

Will shrugged.

"I don't know," he said. "I was going to tranquilize and tag it."

"You know procedure," said Dodge. *Yes, I do.* The procedure was to terminate.

"Yes, sir," said Will quickly, "but what if this animal wasn't the aggressor?"

Dodge raised his eyes and looked at him, a slow and relentless rebuke.

Sully snorted. Will glanced over at her. She didn't like it any better than he did. Will looked Dodge in the eye and nodded. *Procedure.* Well, he didn't care; he wasn't going to kill it. He'd dope and relocate it if necessary, but he would not kill an animal for following its instinct.

"Okay, Will," said Dodge. "I'll expect you to take care of the coyote situation." He leaned an elbow on the desk. "Although it's not the usual procedure, in this case, I would recommend that we look at relocation as an option. I wouldn't think this animal is a repeater. I think we can find him a new home somewhere on the south edge of Thin Lake. There should be enough chipmunks there to keep him happy."

Will nodded at the chief. *Good. That was a good call.* Dodge cleared his throat and looked back at his notepad.

"Now this next item is a little unusual. I got a directive from the Madison office yesterday that we need to prepare for a major reorganization of resources and personnel up here. They're calling it," he consulted his notes, "a management re-adaptation."

Will felt the familiar anxiety rising in him like a flock of startled crows. Reorganization meant change, and change was not good for the forest. This was the threat, he realized suddenly, that he'd been dreading for a long time. Not on a conscious level, but deep—bone deep, like a dog sensing a rising storm.

"Why?" asked Sully, serious now. A crease had appeared between her eyebrows and her mouth was set, not giving. "Why would we need to reorganize personnel? The three of us can handle anything." She glanced over at Will. "Hell, we've already handled everything they've thrown at us."

The chief raised a shoulder and shook his head slightly. *He doesn't know. Or he doesn't want to tell us yet.* Will leaned back in his chair. It could be a lot of things—species epidemic, widespread poaching, criminal activity, or changes in land use or ownership. Disease didn't spread rapidly in the wintertime, at least not that they could see, so that wasn't it. He or Sully would have had some kind of clue about illicit activity, meth labs or drug trafficking, so that wasn't it, either. It had to be land use— but that couldn't be. Everything was part of the endowment—it had been for years. They couldn't touch it; they couldn't sell it. They couldn't hurt it.

"So, boss," Sully was saying, "what is this going to mean? Are we going to be replaced?"

"I don't think so," said Dodge slowly, staring at a point on the corner of the desk. "It's not about us, at least not directly. To be honest, I'm not really sure what it's all about. I've never seen anything quite like it. The county is involved, and I think the state legislature has a hand in it, too. If I had to guess, I'd have to say it looks like they're looking to change the land status."

Will felt the anxiety growing, burgeoning, the crows screaming and cawing in his head.

"But that's just speculation," said Dodge. "We don't know anything for sure yet. It could be something minor, trivial, like a herd census."

"Re-designating the land status," mused Sully. Will could tell she was trying to get her head around what it might mean. Land sales, development, new roads; dozens of animals displaced, hundreds of trees cut down.

"But they couldn't," Will blurted, "they couldn't. This is the purest, most pristine land in the entire Midwest. We have dozens of acres that haven't seen any kind of human presence for years."

"Except yours," said the chief.

"You're assuming he's human," said Sully. The chief glanced over at her and actually smiled. "We all know he's part goat."

"This is not the time to joke around," said Will, hearing his voice rise. "This is serious."

"Hang on, Will," said Dodge, raising a hand, his voice deep, sonorous, reassuring. "Don't waste your energy worrying about what you can't control. Or what you don't even know. This..." he said, tapping his notepad, "could be anything. It could be nothing." He took a sip of his coffee and made a face.

Sully nodded and glanced over at Will with eyebrows raised under her thick glasses. *She does not look convinced of that. She looks as worried as I do.*

"I only wanted to tell you two so that you'll be ready for this event, whatever it's going to be. You might hear something before I do—I don't know. Whatever happens, I'll be in touch immediately. And I would expect you to do the same." He stood up, zipped up his jacket, and started putting on his gloves.

"What do we do?" asked Sully. "Is there any way to prepare for something like this?"

"Just do your usual thing," said the chief, putting on his hat. His havelock. "We don't know what to get ready for yet, do we?" He paused and looked back at Will. "But I'll tell you one thing. I do agree with you about this land, Will; it's one of a kind. It's the last patch of old forest left up here. We don't see habitat like this anywhere else, except maybe in Canada. So," he continued, "if it comes down to it, I'll fight for keeping everything as it is, for keeping the habitat pure. I think there'll be quite a few people on our side, too."

"Oh," said the chief. "One more thing. Let's keep this under our hats for now. The last thing we need is people here getting all excited about nothing."

Will and Sully both nodded. The chief smiled then, waved a little, and left. Will felt the anxiety easing, the crows retreating. Slowly. But his breath was still coming in ragged gasps.

"Well," said Sully. "That ain't good. It looks like somebody's coming to tear up the forest."

Will looked over at her. She was right. He felt it. He knew it. He'd always known. Bone deep. It was coming. He looked over at Sully. She was gazing at him, that crease between her eyebrows appearing again. Will looked down. He could only imagine how he looked.

"Hey, man," said Sully, leaning her elbows on the desk. "Don't worry. The land is still protected. We'll figure it out."

Will smiled and nodded at her, and might have said something to agree, but he knew. He knew. All his life they'd been trying to tear it down, to destroy, to hew, to build; he and Sully and the chief had fought them off. But now it looked as if they'd been backed into the little corner of the world that he'd spent his life protecting. And now they were coming after it—after him. Well, maybe they had him cornered, maybe not. If they did, they'd find out what a cornered beast could do.

CHAPTER 9

EDDY SAW CHIEF DODGE LEAVING AS he walked up to the DNR office. The two nodded to each other; they weren't exactly friendly since the chief had ticketed Lakeland a couple years ago for clearing some hemlocks from a lakefront lot. In turned out the trees were protected, and his dad had to pay a pretty hefty fine. *Over a couple of stupid trees.* The idea of it still pissed Eddy off.

Will was preparing to leave, getting bundled up, when Eddy walked in. Sully was sitting at the desk looking through the mail.

"Hey, guys," he said. They both looked up.

"Eddy. What are you doing here?" demanded Will.

"Hello, Will," said Eddy. "Nice to see you, too."

"Sorry," muttered Will. "You surprised me."

Sully chuckled a little. Will looked at her, grunted, and then went back to lacing up his boot.

"Hello, Eddy," said Sully. "How are you?"

"Good, Sully. I'm good," said Eddy.

Will glanced up at him. *God,* thought Eddy. *He looks at me like I'm part of his insect collection.*

"So," said Sully, leaning back in the desk chair and grinning. "What has the great real estate mogul been up to lately?"

"Selling everything in sight, Sully," said Eddy, smiling back at her. "You know, I sold a truckload of snow yesterday over on Mirror Lake."

She chuckled a little and cocked her head. "Snow, huh? No ice?"

"No, they knew what they wanted. The client talked a tough deal. You know how those Chicago lawyers are."

They both laughed. Will looked from one to the other and even tried to smile a little bit. *He has to make sure it's funny first. He never did have a sense of humor.*

Sully looked at Eddy a moment, and then her smile faded a bit.

"So how's your dad doing?"

Eddy felt Will look up at her but didn't glance at his brother. *Will doesn't like her asking me and not him.* He felt an urge to get cozy with Sully, just to get under Will's skin, but no, not today. He had other fish to fry.

"He's doing okay, Sully," he said, turning his hat over in his hands. "In fact," he said, "that's why I came over."

He glanced at Will, who was getting ready to put on his coat. Will looked up at him.

"Dad wants to have a family meeting tonight at his place, Will."

"What about?" asked Will.

"Family stuff," said Eddy. "You know." Sully stood up.

"Excuse me," she said, heading toward the bathroom. "I got some business to take care of."

"Knock yourself out," said Eddy. She went in and shut the door behind her.

"Is this about Dad's death and the funeral arrangements?" asked Will abruptly.

"Jesus, Will," said Eddy, anger flashing through him. "Why are you talking about his funeral? He's not even dead yet."

Will set his jaw, getting that pinched look in his eyes that came when he was getting ready to be stubborn.

"I just thought Dad might want to get things settled," said Will, waving a hand. "That's all. You know, before..." His voice trailed off.

Eddy paused. *That's fair—a legitimate concern. I shouldn't have snapped at him.*

"All right," he said. "Sorry. I didn't mean to jump down your throat, Will. It's just hard for me talk about. You know. And sometimes you just…you know, you just say shit."

Will nodded. "That's all right," he said. "I know. I'm sorry." He shrugged. "I know it's tough for you, Eddy. You guys are so close," he finished, his tone curiously flat.

He stood awkwardly a moment, looking at Eddy, then glanced outside the window. He sighed, looked back at his brother, and then gestured toward one of the chairs.

"Why don't you have a seat?"

"I thought you'd never ask," said Eddy, unzipping his parka. He plopped himself down and watched as Will settled himself in the other visitor chair.

"How is Dad?" asked Will, his face softening a bit. The sun streamed through the window on him. Weird. When his face wasn't all pinched and tense, and framed as it was by the morning light, Eddy was struck by his brother's resemblance to their mother.

Eddy shrugged. "He's still hanging in there. You know the old man. Tough as a hickory nut." They both smiled; it was one of their father's favorite expressions when they were growing up. "You should come out and see him," added Eddy.

"Well, I'll be out there tonight," said Will, matter-of-factly.

"Yeah, right," said Eddy. "That's right."

"How is everybody else?"

"You know," said Eddy, shrugging. "Good. The kids are doing good, Naomi's still working her ass off over at the clinic. Everything's the same as usual."

"How's Maureen?" asked Will, cocking his head slightly, appraising his brother with those cold blue eyes. Whenever Eddy looked at himself in the mirror, his eyes—the blues—never seemed as distant or as calculating as Will's.

"Maureen is Maureen," said Eddy. "You know her; she's not happy unless she's giving somebody shit."

"Usually you," said Will.

"Usually me." He laughed.

"Why is that, do you think?" asked Will. "I mean, she gives me a hard time, too, but never the way she does you." There was a musing tone in Will's voice, as if he were talking to himself.

Eddy shrugged. Will also had that other tone in his voice—the junior scientist voice, analyzing stuff, figuring patterns, hypothesizing, like he thought this might be worth taking somewhere.

"Maybe she likes you more than me," said Eddy.

"No," said Will, fixing Eddy in his gaze. "No way. No. She was always your friend. Your girlfriend, right?"

Will leaned forward, ready to ask another question, but then stopped himself. He leaned back again, gazing at Eddy and smiling a little bit. Eddy looked right back at his brother. *What the fuck does he want? Scientific proof? A confession? Pictures? Yeah, okay, Will, I slept with Maureen. I slept with her last night. You happy?*

"Yeah, well," said Eddy. "That was when we were kids." He stood and zipped up his parka. "I'm a married man now."

Will nodded and glanced back out the window. Eddy started putting on his gloves. Will was his big brother, but he never acted like it. Most big brothers looked out for their kid brothers. *Except Will didn't know about anything—except the woods, his animals, and science. He was clueless about everything else. He didn't know sports or music or girls. He didn't know how to be a big brother. Hell, I was more of a big brother to him than he ever was to me. And now, years later, I still have to be.*

"If you could be out at Dad's about six or so," said Eddy, "that would be great." Will nodded without taking his eyes off the window. "Maureen will be making dinner. We'll eat, get caught up, and then Dad can let us know what's on his mind."

"Should I bring anything?" asked Will.

Eddy shrugged. *Hell, this was real progress. The mountain man acquiring manners.*

"Yeah, sure," said Eddy. "Grab a six-pack of something." He opened the door. "None of that light shit, though."

Will half-waved as he left. Eddy glanced back at him through the picture window as he trudged past, the cold whispering past his face. Eddy had a weird feeling; he couldn't say how he could tell his brother did it, but Will knew something was going on with the land. *Somehow, the little son-of-a-bitch knows.*

CHAPTER 10

WILL HALF-SLID, HALF-SHUFFLED DOWN the split bank onto the frozen ice. There was a nice little alley for snowshoeing onto the lake that had been formed by the thaw last week. The snow had melted and then refrozen into a perfect slide. It did this, in one way or another, every year. It was better this year than last—smoother. The otters would love it. There was a romp of them two bays over; he had them on his list to check out.

He hitched his pack onto his shoulders and looked around. Barren trees. Drifting snow and black patches of ice lined with cracks—the pocked face of winter. He blinked as the dazzling sun bounced off the lake snow and wished he'd brought sunglasses. It seemed warmer now, although that was probably an illusion, a trick of the senses. He started walking—trotting—straight across the bay. He knew the drift patterns well enough to avoid the long bare spots of ice, places slick enough to cause a real fall. Out here, alone, a bad fall might cause unconsciousness or a concussion. And that could cause a person to freeze to death. Solitude had taught him caution. He went along at a good pace, fast enough to stay warm but not hard enough to sweat.

After Will had dropped off Sully, he realized he'd have to hurry to reach the clearing and chronicle the winter behaviors of that skulk of foxes in the ravine. If he was lucky, he might catch the vixen hunting. Mid-afternoon was a favorite time for her. Their mating time was coming up soon, and she'd be holed up with the kits, so he wasn't sure how many more chances he was going to have to see her before spring.

He'd driven home, packed up his log and his binoculars and his camera, slapped on his snowshoes, and taken off. The clearing was a little more than a mile off, at the tapered bottom of a big ravine just east of Thin Lake. He trotted along the lake ice, quickly but not recklessly, and did a quick calculation. He'd be there in another twenty minutes. It was two-thirty, so it would be dark in a few hours.

Will felt his left shoe sliding, and he nearly lost his balance but quickly caught himself. *Idiot*, he thought. *Keep your mind on the task in front of you.* The last thing he needed was a broken leg out here in the open. He slowed his pace a little and swept the ice in front of him with his eyes, looking for the bald spots. He filled his mind only with the ice, the snow, and his balance between them. After a time, almost completely across, his thoughts—on their own—returned to what Chief Dodge had said.

Will felt a chill run through him. He felt that somehow the endowment would be ending and tried to reassure himself—again—that that would be impossible, that the land grant was for perpetuity. Logically, that was correct, but the nagging feeling—the certainty—that this was the case would not leave him. And that would be a disaster.

Will knew that every robber baron and huckster and carpet-bagger would be standing in line to steal it. He also knew that his brother, Eddy, would be at the head of that line, his left hand doling out deeds, his right hand pulling in cash. That couldn't happen; it wasn't going to happen. Will had been the active steward, the guardian, the defender of these wilds for more than twenty years. His job—his duty—was to protect the land. He'd do that until the day he died.

Will came to the path on the southern shore right under Elk Ridge. He started climbing it, slowly and quietly so as not to scare the foxes. It was a steep climb, and he found himself puffing and sweating as he neared the crown. His father and that damned car—why had he let the old man talk him into taking it? That's why he was so soft and out of shape. He finally reached the brow of the hill and paused to take off his snowshoes. He lay on his belly and crawled up to the top to look down. The hillside dipped gently away from him, merging into a large clearing below. A stream ran through the area but was now covered by snow. He scanned the area quickly, looking for a single orange blur. *Not today. Not yet.*

Will took off his backpack, brought it around in front of him, and carefully took out a small white tarp, then his binoculars, and finally his camera. Step by step, the same every time. *A method to my madness.* He laid the tarp down carefully in front of him, staked it into the snow crust, gently placed the camera on it, and then planted his elbows on the very edge of it. He looked through the binoculars, focused, and scanned the clearing below. *No sign of anything right now.* He settled in to wait. The shadow from the hill started to inch its way down the side of the hill and was just beginning to touch the clearing. He still had a couple of hours before dusk and another one and a half before full dark. And there would be a full moon tonight.

He slowly scanned the clearing and the edge of the woods, moving the binoculars as slowly and as steadily as he could. *Like a shadow nudged by the sun.* He scanned the wood line slowly, trying to spot deer. While they didn't move much during the day, and while he knew many of them stayed in the heavy brush on the south end of the clearing, he thought he might catch one or two coming out to forage. Since it had been so cold the night before, he thought that perhaps they still could be yarding up, lining up shoulder to rump to conserve body heat. There wasn't much to eat out there anymore. They'd probably be going after the bark by now and pretty much be living off body fat until April.

Something moved in the corner of his field of vision. A fox—the vixen. She was just coming into the south edge of the clearing, stepping slowly and carefully on the thinly crusted snow. Will started to take mental notes, notes that he would transcribe later in the cabin. The fox started moving forward stealthily, ears cocked forward, tail twitching behind it. She stopped suddenly and leaned forward, listening. *She hears one,* thought Will, scrabbling under the snow. He watched her slowly squat down on her haunches and hunker there, still listening. *Snow can't be deeper than two feet there. She'd have no problem getting deep enough to get one.* He noted the direction she was facing—north by northeast. That would be about right.

She leapt suddenly—arcing gracefully through the air, landing headfirst, and disappearing up to the middle of her back in the snow, her rear legs pawing the air. The vixen came up quickly with something dark clamped between her jaws. *She got one,* he thought, feeling a sudden and unreasonable surge of pride. He noted the time, pulled up his glove, and wrote it on the exposed skin of his wrist. It was amazing. They were much more successful, almost three or four times so, when they leapt toward the north. It was something he'd first noticed last year. He'd been meaning to mention it to Sully, but it kept slipping his mind. He made a note to do so on his wrist.

He slowly put down the binoculars and picked up the camera. He was well over seventy-five yards away, but he knew this vixen spooked easily, so he was extremely careful in his movements. He zoomed in on her. There wasn't much left of the mouse. Fast eater. He snapped a couple of pictures. She started suddenly, cocking her ears. She picked up what was left of the mess and trotted back the way she had come, carefully stepping in the same footprints she'd made on the way out. She disappeared into the eastern thicket. Will waited.

A moment later, he heard what had spooked the vixen. Something was crunching slowly and ponderously through the snow, from the north, breaking through the crust with every step. It was too clumsy even for a bear, and no sane bear would be out in the dead of winter.

Trespasser. This was a restricted part of the endowment land, the preserve. *My land.* This was five miles inside the closest boundary line. This was no "honest" mistake. Will raised the binoculars up, sighted in the western tree line, and waited. The crunching came closer; in the silent backdrops of snow and woods, it sounded like a tank crashing through the forest. Finally, Will caught a glimpse of color through the trees—a red down vest. Will focused in. He didn't know the guy. Not from Moon Lake. That was good. It was always harder to bust people you knew. The man was middle-aged, fat, and had one of those scraggly little beards.

Will slowly put down the binoculars and carefully lifted up the camera. He found the man in his viewfinder—still crunching like an elephant across the clearing—and snapped off a couple of shots. The intruder stopped a moment, probably to catch his breath, and took a look around. Will continued snapping pictures, especially as the guy turned toward him to look up the ridge. Will was ready to say something or to even go down to confront him, but he wanted to see what the intruder was up to.

The man walked over to the brush on the eastern edge of the clearing and cleared away some snow. He took off his backpack and unzipped it, and then took out two metal objects. Will zoomed in on them and immediately bit back his rising fury.

Traps. Leg traps. Spring traps, whatever you wanted to call them. They didn't kill, they only caused excruciating pain—and when trappers didn't bother to return to inspect them for three or four days, slow death from thirst or starvation. His first impulse was to tear down the hill and attack this predator, this fat pink killer, but he didn't; he closed his eyes and breathed instead, calming himself.

Will opened his eyes. The guy was setting the first trap under low branches of the hemlock tree. *That's stupid. She would never go there.* Will snapped several more pictures of the guy and waited. The man got up, brushed off his hands, and looked around. He trudged back across the clearing, going right over the vixen's tracks, and set the other trap on the clearing directly below Will. Then he stood up, looked around, and started back the way he had come.

Will knelt down and carefully swept off the white tarp, folded the camera within it, and packed it into his bag. He slipped his snowshoes back on and backtracked off the top of the ridge, planning to circle around the clearing and come up on the southern edge, where the vixen had gone. He'd wait until the poacher left, take the traps, and follow him out. That way he'd be able to see and collect any other traps. Then, when the guy got to his car, probably at the Thin Lake Public Landing, he'd nail him.

Will came out on the southern edge of the tree line and saw the flash of red disappearing on the other side of the clearing. He trotted over to the first trap, tripped it, put it on his belt, and then crossed to the second and did the same. The man in red was going faster than he'd been on the way in, but it was still easy—ridiculously easy—to keep up with him. From the way he was going, Will saw he was right—the guy had parked at the Thin Lake Landing and had walked the one and a half miles over Axman's Ridge to get there. He picked up four more traps on the way in. It was child's play to see where they'd been placed.

As they got closer to the landing, Will cut from the trail and circled through the woods down to the ice on Thin Lake and was able to reach the landing before the man in red. He leaned on the lone car there and folded his arms to wait.

Red burst onto the parking lot and looked behind him. *Spooked—he must sense he's being followed.* The man turned and started for the car, then stopped dead in his tracks when he saw Will.

"Who are you?" he asked Will, still somewhat out of breath. "What are you doing here?" The guy looked him up and down and saw the traps—his traps—hanging from Will's belt. It took a second for that fact to register.

"Hey," he said, finally catching his breath. "Are those my traps?"

Will stood there, his arms folded, not moving a muscle, looking at the interloper, his hands, his breath, his boots, and his eyes.

"I asked you a question, asshole," said the man, his voice flying out over the ice before it was swallowed up by the snow.

Will kept taking in the details of the man, painting a picture with the pieces—his hands, the fearful eyes, the cold-reddened face. The fear. The man moved suddenly and started walking toward him; Will never flinched; he didn't even blink. The man stopped about ten yards away, his hand edging toward his waistband.

"I don't know who you are or what you want, but you need to get away from my car," said the man. "And now."

"My name is DNR Agent William LeBarron," said Will, still leaning on the car. "I'm the warden assigned to the protect these endowment lands. Access to these lands is restricted. Hunting and trapping are strictly prohibited and punishable by fines and or prison time."

The guy stopped. His hand went up in a half-gesture and he started to say something, but stopped.

"Where's your ID?" he asked, belligerently.

Will reached inside his jacket for the ID hanging on the lanyard around his neck. His hand brushed his shoulder holster as he hauled it out. Will didn't take his eyes off the man as he raised it up. The poacher took a tentative step forward, peered at the card, and then stood up straight. He looked at Will and raised his shoulders slightly.

"You were trespassing on protected lands," Will said, his voice sounding thin and feathery in the cold, even to his own ears.

"No," said the man. "No way. This is public land."

"These are not public lands," said Will. "You were setting illegal leg traps on protected property," said Will, watching him. He didn't think the guy would run, but he might try something stupid. "This is a nature preserve."

Red swallowed and shifted his feet a little. His hand went to his waistband and then back into his jacket pocket.

"What are you doing with my traps?" he asked.

"I confiscated them. I'm going to sink them in the lake tomorrow."

"You can't do that. Give them back."

"No," said Will, not taking his eyes from the man. "That's out of the question. By the way, do you have your trapping license?" Not that it mattered, but he wanted to nail this guy as hard as he could. Red shrugged and then shook his head. Will reached into his jacket for his ticket pad.

"Let's see your driver's license."

The guy took out his wallet and handed Will his license. The wind started kicking up as he handed it to Will. Red stamped his feet and put his hands in his pockets.

"Trapping in a restricted area is a five hundred dollar fine," said Will, using his best cop voice. He took out a pen and started writing. "Trapping without a license is another one hundred dollar fine."

"Come on, man," said the guy. "I didn't know." The wind blew again, a stronger gust. *Snow's coming.*

"Ignorance is no defense." Will glanced up at the guy, who was glaring at him. He was shivering. *Too bad. Let the bastard freeze.* Will took his time writing out the citation, then ripped the ticket off the pad and handed it to the man along with his license.

"And," he said, "if I ever see you or find your traps here again, it won't be a fine," said Will. "You'll do jail time."

"Hey," said Red, snatching the papers, "fuck you, Ranger Rick. I have a right to come on this land. I pay my taxes."

Will felt the anger rising inside him like a volcano.

"This," he said to the man, gesturing to the lake behind him and to the forest beyond, "is a nature preserve. Everything north and west of here, including all of Mirror Lake and most of Moon Lake, is protected. This," he continued, pointing down at the boat landing, "is public property. The waters are public, too. Everything else is restricted. So get out and stay out." Will leaned toward the man. "And I'll tell you one more thing, sir. If I see you here again setting your illegal traps, I'll kill you myself." Red grimaced, stood up straight, and stalked off toward his car.

Will watched him a moment and smiled to himself. He reached into his jacket, to his shoulder holster, and took out his pistol. It would be the right thing to do, and so easy, too. One pounce, one quick strike and it would be done. The snow would cover up all traces at the scene and there would be plenty of places to put the carcass. He brought his other hand up to the pistol, caressing the barrel. It would be so easy. And so right.

Will sighed, turned, and started walking onto Thin Lake. It was getting late. The shadows of the trees were stretched almost across the ice. He heard the car start up and pull away. *That asshole doesn't know how lucky he was.* Will glanced up at the sky. Clouds were sliding in from the west, riding the cold wind. Snow was in the air. Clean, pure, white snow that would cover the land in a blanket of quiet and solitude.

CHAPTER 11

MAUREEN SAW THE HEADLIGHTS SWEEPING past the shed through the kitchen window. That would be Will. He was always early; Eddy was usually late. The two of them were like clockwork that way. The door was open; Will could let himself in. Maureen kept stirring the soup. She heard the door open, felt a blast of cold air on her back, and said without turning around, "Shut the door, Will."

The door creaked shut.

"Hello, Maureen," he said. She finally turned around. Will was already sitting at the kitchen table, taking off his boots. He looked okay, but thinner than the last time she'd seen him. She wondered if he'd been eating. He was out there all by himself and didn't always remember to eat. She saw he'd brought a six-pack of beer. Rhinelander.

"Hello, Will," she said, wiping off her hands. "How are you?"

"Good," he said.

"What've you been up to?" asked Maureen.

"I apprehended a poacher today. He was over by Thin Lake setting traps for foxes."

"What were you doing way out there?" she asked.

"Research," he said, and went back to working on his boots.

"What happened?"

He shrugged again. "I saw him setting a trap, trailed him, confiscated the traps, and gave him a fine."

"Just a fine?" asked Maureen. That was surprising. Will hardly ever let anyone get away with just a fine.

"Yeah," he said, finally pulling off his boot and taking the sock halfway with it. "I was on snowshoes. We were in the middle of nowhere. There was really no way to bring him in."

Something creaked in the living room. Will lifted his head and cocked it, looking like a skinny bird. *A woodpecker*, thought Maureen, smiling to herself.

"Your dad's up," she said. "You can go in and say hi."

"Okay," he said, and bent over to start working on the second boot. She knew he'd take his time, that he needed to prepare himself. He hadn't seen his father since the holidays and probably didn't know what to expect. Will never had been that close to his dad; he was his mother's son.

"What are you cooking?" asked Will, standing finally.

"Roast chicken, baked potatoes," she said, "along with braised carrots. And," she said, gesturing toward the pot, "my homemade tomato soup."

Will nodded and walked over to the stove, but not too close, and took a look at the pot of soup simmering on the stove.

"It smells good, Maureen," he said, staring at the pot of soup. "Really good."

"Thanks," she said.

Will seemed nervous, even more strained than usual—like he was talking to a stranger. He had never been good with people. Not even his family. Even though they'd known each other for years, Will still kept Maureen at arm's length. It wasn't that he didn't like her. She knew he did. In fact, when they were teenagers, Maureen suspected Will had a crush on her. When she felt wicked, she would tease him—goose him, maybe brush him with one of her boobs—but he would just shrug and ignore her.

She would have dropped dead of surprise if Will had ever tried anything with her; he was just that clueless. Not that she would have minded. She might even have been flattered. Will was a good guy. He was. He had a heart of gold. But anything romantic with him just seemed outside the realm of possibility. Not like her and Eddy. Hell, no. She and Eddy knew exactly what to do with each other.

Will turned and started toward the living room, shoulders hunched. She watched. He looked back at her suddenly. She dropped her eyes and pretended to stir the soup. *He's not looking forward to this. It can't be easy seeing your father this sick.* She heard him go through the door and into the living room. Voices wafted through the door, exchanging hellos, then nestled down into an uneven hum, punctuated by measures of silence. Maureen strained but couldn't quite make out the words.

Frowning, she turned down the soup and opened the cupboard door. She took out two tumblers and a serving tray and went over to the six-pack of Rhinelander on the kitchen table. She pulled two cans from the plastic holder and put it all on the tray. She walked to the door, paused, and listened.

"Well, Dad, you know that ravine just off Thin Lake, near Axman's Point?" Will's voice was loosened, pouring out as he described his land. "Between Thin and Mirror Lake?"

"I think so." Titus's voice was reserved, but Maureen thought she could detect pleasure in it. And a quiet pride.

"Well, there's a skulk of foxes living near there, and I've been researching their hunting and feeding habits." Maureen opened the door and stepped through, balancing the tray on her left hand. Will stopped talking abruptly as soon as he saw her.

"Well, look at this," said Titus. "Refreshments."

"Will brought some beer," she said, placing the tray on the table next to him. Will gazed up at her, his pale blue eyes not searching or looking, but simply resting on her, taking her in. It wasn't his usual penetrating stare. He almost—for a moment—looked relaxed. Then Will dropped his eyes to the beer, grabbed a can, and began pouring.

"You boys have at it," said Maureen, and went back into the kitchen. The hum of voices started in behind her once more. She was a little surprised. Will wasn't usually that talkative. Not at all. *Change*, she thought. *Change is in the air.* She went back to the soup, turned it up, and stirred.

Another set of headlight beams swept past the shed. *Either Eddy or that Jay.* She turned and watched the door this time. A knock. It was Jay.

"Come in," she said. "It's open." The door popped open and Jay walked in, his hat already off. A gentleman.

"Hello, Jay," she said. "How are you?"

"I'm all right," he said, sitting down at the table to take off his boots. He took off his glasses, already fogging up in the warmth of the kitchen. "Lord, is it cold out there. I'm beginning to think it's never going to warm up."

Maureen grunted and went back to stirring the soup. She was used to Jay's running commentary on the weather. After all, he'd been here almost every day for a month.

"My goodness, that smells good," said Jay. "What's on the menu?"

"Well," said Maureen, turning around. "We have baked chicken and carrots, roast potatoes, and homemade tomato soup."

"Wonderful," said Jay, standing up and rubbing his hands together. Maureen noticed that his sweater was already riding up over his belly. That usually didn't happen until after lunch. Jay examined his glasses, which were now clear again. He put them on. Maureen gestured with her chin toward the living room. "They're in there." She glanced at Jay, who was staring at her quizzically through his thick glasses.

"Mr. LeBarron and Will," she said. "Eddy's not here yet."

Jay nodded and padded through the kitchen to the living room. She heard Mr. LeBarron's voice raised in greeting. Nothing from Will. Then the hum of voices.

Just one more. Just Eddy. And then, she thought, raising her eyes to the living room door, *things will never be the same. Not for any of them.*

Laughter rolled in from behind the door. Maureen could make out Mr. LeBarron's creaky guffaws and Jay's high giggle, and—there it was—Will's breathy chuckle, which never seemed to get too far out of his throat. Maureen smiled to herself. It had been a long time since she'd heard Will and his father laughing together. She supposed there really wasn't much opportunity for it. Eddy tended to monopolize the old man's time. It was good to hear Will and his father enjoying each other's company again.

Maureen caught lights sweeping across the shed again. She glanced up at the kitchen clock. Quarter after. That was about right. Eddy couldn't be on time if his life depended on it. Maureen turned back to the soup. The door opened, and she heard boots clomping across the floor.

One set—no, two. Maureen turned and saw Eddy already taking off his hat and gloves and Naomi, standing in the open doorway, still bundled up and staring at her with those eyes, watery and cold as dirty March snow.

Eddy peeled off his coat and gloves, said hello to Maureen, grabbed the remaining beers, and went to join the other boys. Naomi took off her gloves and coat and sat down. She exchanged greetings with Maureen, but nothing more.

Something was wrong. Naomi was not supposed to be here. Why on Earth had Eddy brought her? Maureen felt Naomi's eyes drilling into her back as she finished cooking. Not for the first time, she wondered how much Naomi really knew about her and Eddy. *She has to suspect something. She's not stupid.*

When dinner was ready, Maureen called the boys in and brought in the extra kitchen chair from the pantry. Will, Jay, and Eddy walked in and sat. Jay raised his eyebrows when he saw Naomi. Will's face was like stone. Titus walked into the kitchen a little after them. When he saw Naomi sitting at the table, watching Eddy, who couldn't stop fidgeting, his mouth tightened and his eyes narrowed a bit.

It wasn't that Titus didn't like Naomi, but this meeting was supposed to be immediate family only—LeBarron and Sons. Maureen had been thinking about that and figured Titus wanted the boys to work things out between themselves before anyone else got involved. It was made clear to Maureen that she was not invited. That didn't bother her. She'd find out what was up anyway—she always did.

"Hey, Dad," said Eddy, who'd been quiet. "I hope you don't mind that I decided to bring Naomi. I know this was supposed to be immediate family only, but this is a big deal, and—"

"Well, truth be told," interrupted Naomi, smiling a little, "it was my idea. When Eddy mentioned there was a family meeting here tonight, I assumed I was invited. When he said it was important, I knew I needed to be here."

Eddy grinned sheepishly and raised his eyebrows.

"What do you think, Jay?" asked Titus, his voice thin and whispery, but still sustaining a seriousness, a gravity.

Jay, who seemed oblivious to the tension, looked up from his plate and shrugged.

"She's related by marriage," he said. "So I don't see any problem as long as she understands the need for confidentiality." He glanced around the table. "But that goes for everyone. We'll be going over all that during the presentation."

"Presentation?" asked Naomi. "What on earth is going on? Can't we just talk about whatever it is?"

Titus wiped his mouth with his napkin, a slow and deliberate process. "No, Naomi," he said. "It's not that simple."

"Well," persisted Naomi, "I don't get it. Why would you need a presentation? Why does it have to be so complicated?"

"I imagine we'll all find out soon enough, Naomi," said Will quietly.

Maureen glanced over at Will. His face was expressionless, but his eyes were locked onto Naomi. She looked back at him, her gray eyes cold as pebbles in the bottom of a stream.

"Yeah," said Eddy. "Don't worry about it." Naomi shrugged and slurped a spoonful of soup.

Why doesn't he stand up to her? thought Maureen, glancing at Eddy. Mr. LeBarron had asked him not to bring her. Specifically. She was sure that Naomi had just pushed her way in when she heard something was going on. So what had Eddy told her? And what had he been thinking?

"So, Dad," said Eddy. "I ran into Morris Wenzel this afternoon."

"Really?"

"Yeah. We were up in Eagleton looking at pianos." Eddy glanced over at Naomi, who smiled back at him. "I finally decided it was time to get one for Naomi."

"And the kids," she chimed in. "It's about time they started learning how to play."

Titus nodded and picked up a slice of bread.

"That's nice," he said, his voice quiet, but reserved now. Coiled up. "So what's up with Morris?"

Eddy swallowed and shrugged. "Nothing much. You know Morris. Hustling every minute of the day. He was asking me about Doc's place up on Lake Williams."

Titus frowned. "Is Doc selling?"

"That's what I asked Morris, and he said no, that he was just curious."

Titus smiled. "That old vulture." He turned to Jay. "Morris always keeps an eye on the retired homeowners," he explained. "He wants to get a jump on their properties when they pass." He looked at Eddy again, not the friendliest of looks.

Maureen got up to clear the soup bowls. She put them in the sink and served the rest of the dinner. Conversation petered out as they ate. A few compliments about her cooking drifted back to Maureen, and she answered graciously—she hoped. She knew she could be abrupt sometimes without meaning to.

Dinner finally ended. Maureen got up to clear the dishes while Naomi went out to have a cigarette. Jay and Titus went into the living room, followed by Eddy. Will offered to help, but Maureen declined. Still, it was sweet of him. Will nodded and followed the others. Naomi came in, took her coat off, and brought her plate over to the sink. Maureen gave her a smile, took the plate and placed it with the rest of the dirty dishes.

"Nice dinner, Maureen," said Naomi.

"Thank you," she said, starting to rinse the dishes. Naomi leaned on the counter, crossing her arms.

"You must be tired of entertaining," said Naomi. Maureen turned and looked at her.

"I mean," continued Naomi, "I hear Jay's been out here a lot, almost every day, all day. It must be kind of tiring to cook for him all the time."

Maureen shrugged. "I cook for Mr. LeBarron anyway," she said. "One more plate is no hardship." Naomi nodded and smiled slightly. Maureen waited. Naomi would show her hand soon enough; she had almost no patience. She was like Eddy that way.

"So, Maureen," she said. "How's Titus doing?" Her voice had that smarmy little twang in it that popped up when she was after something.

"You saw him," she said. "He's doing all right, considering."

"Considering," repeated Naomi, nodding.

Maureen started running the water to wash the dishes.

"What are you going to do after he passes?"

The question caught Maureen off guard, partly because she hadn't really thought about it and partly because it was so abrupt, so rude. She felt herself flushing.

"I hadn't really thought about it," she said shortly. That was true enough.

"Oh," said Naomi. She pursed her lips. "It's too bad you don't have family in town anymore."

"Well," said Maureen, smiling sweetly, "I still think of the LeBarrons as family. Me and the boys are still pretty close."

Naomi's mouth widened slightly. Her fingers drummed on the countertop. *Somebody wants a cigarette.*

"It's funny that a family member would get paid for helping out," said Naomi. *Not much of a shot. Pretty weak, actually.*

"Well, you know what they say," said Maureen. "Every family is different. Some are more generous than others."

"Yeah," said Naomi. "Well, I guess some families can afford to be generous. Others can't. Well," she said, standing up. "I better get in there. I don't want to hold things up."

"Yep," said Maureen. "I'm sure they're all waiting on you."

Naomi turned on her heel and left. *Well,* thought Maureen, watching her go, *there are times I don't feel bad about cheating with Eddy. Like every time I talk to his wife.*

CHAPTER 12

JAY WHEELED THE OLD CHALKBOARD INTO the living room. It was, Will saw, just like the ones they used to use in school. A map of about twenty square miles, including all the endowment lands, was thumbtacked onto it. There were blue demarcation lines along some portions of the land, from north of Anderson Bay around the southern edge to the east side of Moon Lake. And parts of Mirror Lake were marked, too. They looked like lot lines.

This is odd, Will thought. There was no reason for boundary lines there, unless it was some kind of a wildlife population survey. He knew that the University of Wisconsin-Stevens Point did some occasional work up here for their conservation program, but they didn't mark off animal populations like that. Will felt a kernel of apprehension forming in his stomach and took a deep breath. Chief Dodge had said something this morning about a redistribution of resources—that something could be going on with the land. He looked up; his father and Eddy were both looking at him. His dad looked sort of sad. Eddy had sort of a half-smile on his face. Naomi was chewing gum.

"Well," said Jay, standing and making his way over to the board. "Now that we're all situated here, I think we can get started. What we've got here is going to become a very complex situation. Mr. LeBarron called me last summer and told me that there was going to be a major transfer of resources in the near future." He paused and took a breath. "By resources I mean land. And by the future, I mean now."

"Land?" asked Naomi. "What land? I thought everything up there belongs to the state."

"Yes, it did," said Jay. "At least until recently."

Will felt pressure—the anxiety—rising up from his neck, pounding into his head. He felt flushed, hot. He could hear the crows cawing in the distance.

"Eddy. Will," said Jay quietly. Will looked up, his vision blurring. "Your mother's family left the endowment lands to the state of Wisconsin as her dowry. It was meant to be a slap in the face to her and your father. Your mother had defied her family's wishes by marrying your father, so they cut her off from any real money. They just gave her stewardship over endowment lands..." Jay looked down to read from a page in his folder. "For the preservation of these lands in perpetuity for the enrichment of all."

Will nodded. *Yes, that was right.* He felt his breath coming a little easier.

"But," continued Jay, "apparently your grandfather, Ariel's father, snuck a clause into the appendix of the endowment that said upon the deaths of his daughter and her husband, possession of the endowment lands would devolve onto the sons."

Eddy sat forward in his chair with his hands clasped, nodding and smiling. He looked over at Naomi, who had put a hand over her mouth and was making a gasping sort of noise. Will looked up at the map of the land—his land. His life work. They were taking it—taking it from him.

"How can this be?" he heard himself saying. "It was given to the state in perpetuity. That was what everybody said. That's what Mom wanted."

Titus cleared his throat. "Your grandfather Malcolm wanted you boys to have something from the Wallace fortune, Will. This was his way of going around his father. The old man, Great-grandfather Artemis, didn't want us to have anything."

"Is it legal?" asked Naomi.

Jay nodded. "We've been over it with Dick LaBlon, who was referred to us as an estate attorney—and yes, it is completely legal. In fact, Dick believes it's airtight. Upon Mr. LeBarron's... passing, the lands will devolve to the sons."

"What does this mean for the land?" asked Will. "What's going to happen to it?"

"It means we're going to be rich, Will," said Eddy. "Filthy rich." He turned to Naomi, held out his hands and said, "Surprise, honey."

"Omigod." Naomi was sitting back with her hand over her mouth. Jay was beaming at the two of them, even giggling a little bit. Will kept looking at the map. He was paralyzed, as if struck by lightning. He couldn't have gotten up if he wanted to. His father leaned toward him.

"Take it easy, son," he whispered. "Wait for the rest of it. It's not all bad."

Will looked at him and nodded. He swallowed and breathed and took a long drink of his beer. The cawing subsided a little.

"Hey, what's the matter, bro?" asked Eddy, looking at Will with a big smile on his face. "Can't you take the good news?" Naomi was looking at him too, her thin lower lip tucked up under her front teeth.

"Eddy," said Titus. "Enough."

Will looked up at them, a red mist—anger—suddenly rising up behind his eyes. *They love the idea. And they hate me. They hate everything I stand for.* Will clenched his fist, stood, looked away from them, and strode over to the map.

He turned and looked at all of them, Eddy and Naomi still exultant over their good fortune, crowing over what would be a clear-cut forest and the bodies of hundreds of dead birds, animals, and trees. All those souls. *Bastards.* Jay standing next to him at the board, smiling like a fool. His father sitting, frowning at Eddy, but then looking up at Will and pursing his lips.

"Will," he said, his voice carrying across the room. "Why don't you have a seat? You'll want to hear this next part."

Will looked at his dad, who nodded to him. He felt his fists unclench and went back to his chair. They were looking at him—Eddy with that familiar expression of impatience, and Naomi with one of contempt. Titus LeBarron stood up slowly, leaning on the bars of his walker.

"Jay and I have been working on this project for a long time," said Titus. "There were a lot of details we needed to work out. One of the thorniest issues was balancing the renewed private status of the land with the original qualifications put on it by the endowment." The old man paused a moment, staring at a point beyond the map. "We all know that Ariel loved the land in its original pristine state, just as Will does. She loved walking in the woods, swimming in the lakes, and just sitting in the forest. She felt it was fate she ended up here rather than in Chicago." Will saw his dad had a look in his eyes that wasn't there very often—he was wistful.

Will glanced at Eddy, who was leaning back in his chair with arms crossed, a wary look lurking on his face.

"We tried to work out a compromise to make everyone happy," Titus continued. "This is what we came up with." He nodded to Jay, who flipped a transparent overlay from behind the board to lie over the map. Most of the endowment lands were labeled green. The waterfront on the west side of Moon Lake from Anderson Bay to the opposite shore was colored red. There was also a smaller section of Mirror also colored red.

"So," said Jay. "We decided the prime lake frontage on Moon Lake, marked red here," as he pointed, "and a smaller section of Mirror Lake here," he pointed again, "will be marked for development. Everything else will stay as it is. Wild."

Will looked at it. So the red was land marked for development. Maybe four total miles of lake frontage. The otter dens were in there; so was the old beaver lodge and countless birds, squirrels, chipmunks, moths, salamanders, and others. He shook his head and looked down at his hands. All gone, and for what? More houses and speedboats and people. Useless people.

"Is that it?" Naomi was saying, gesturing toward the map. "Is that all we're going to get? Out of all that land? Those little red pieces?"

Eddy stood up, his hands in his back pockets, frowning and looking at his father.

"This is over twenty thousand feet of prime lake frontage," said Titus. "That's well over twenty million dollars worth of land. And that's before development. You make the investment, get in there and build before you sell, and you'll make substantially more."

"This isn't exactly what we talked about, Dad," said Eddy, glancing at Naomi. A hard edge had moved into his voice. He was staring at Titus, his mouth set.

"Yes, it is, son," said Titus, returning the stare ounce for ounce. "We talked about you receiving a substantial piece of land, which is what this is. We talked about you inheriting financial stability for your family, which you now have." The old man glanced at Naomi and then turned back to his chair and sat down heavily. "We never talked about developing the entire endowment, and you know it."

So Eddy knew about this. He's known about this for a while. And here I am. Left out again.

Naomi stood and looked at Eddy. "You knew about this?" she said. "And you didn't tell me?"

Eddy smiled and shrugged. Naomi's cheeks flushed with anger; her body seemed to coil up like a spring. Eddy whispered to her, but she retorted angrily.

"Because I should have been here," she said. "That's why. I would've fought for more. I would've gotten our fair share."

Will looked back at his father, who was standing, trying to get a word in. He started coughing. Will cleared his throat, trying to be heard over Eddy and Naomi arguing.

"Hey," said Will, his voice loud and grating even to his own ears. The two of them stopped and looked at him.

"Dad's trying to say something," he said, his voice falling back into its normal range.

"Thank you, Will," said Titus. He sat down. "I'm a little surprised at this display of selfishness." He looked at Eddy and Naomi, who were still standing. "How much land, how much money, does one person need? How much, Eddy? How much would make you and Naomi happy? Would thirty million be enough? Forty?"

Eddy opened his mouth to answer, but Naomi cut him off.

"How much is all this land worth?" she asked, her voice grating like the turning of a rusty pipe, gesturing toward the map. "We deserve to know. How much money are you taking from us for—him," she said, gesturing toward Will, "and his stupid forest preserve?"

Eddy grabbed her by the arm and whispered to her. She jerked it free and glared up at him.

"Stop it," said Titus. "Stop it and sit down."

Naomi hesitated, and then sat with her arms crossed, glaring straight ahead like an angry child. Eddy gazed down at her a second, his mouth working, and then sat himself. Jay had taken a step back; he was almost standing behind the map.

"All right," said Titus. "Let's start over. The green areas on the map will remain endowment lands with all the same rules that are in force now. The red lands are to be passed on to my sons, Eddy and Will. The red portions will be split by them however they see fit."

Naomi made a noise. *She doesn't want to share. She wants it all.*

"So that's it," said Titus. "I was hoping we could sit down as a family and celebrate our good fortune." He glanced at Naomi and Eddy. "I hope that's still possible."

Will got up and looked at the map. If he could keep the stretch of frontage from the wetland to the southern point and block it off, they could keep the waterfowl nesting area pretty safe. The otters they could relocate over to Thin Lake, which wouldn't have any development. Most of the other damage, he calculated, could be minimized. It would be bad—really bad— but it could have been a lot worse. His dad could have taken the entire shores of both lakes, like Naomi wanted. Another thought occurred to him, out of the blue—a thought that took his mind out of the land for a moment.

"Dad," he asked suddenly, turning toward his father.

"Yes, Will?"

"What about Maureen? Will she get anything? I know that technically she's not family, but she is almost one of us."

Naomi laughed, a harsh grating sound. Will turned. She was staring at the floor and shaking her head. Then she looked up suddenly at Eddy and smiled.

"I had thought," said his father, "that I might leave her this house. Or, if you boys object to that, we could leave her one of the cabins instead. I'd winterize it so she could use it year around."

"That sounds fair," said Will. "I think leaving her this house would be nice."

Eddy shrugged; his wife glared first at him, then at Titus. Will almost felt sorry for his brother.

"Okay," said Titus. "Obviously, there are going to have to be a lot of details worked out in the coming weeks. There will probably be some papers to sign. I know not everyone is happy. In fact, I'd say that everyone seems remarkably unhappy, but remember—there are some bright spots here. You will all have financial security. There will be growth, but it will be a controlled growth. Most of the endowment will still be pristine, and your mother's wishes will have been honored. On that note..."

He turned and looked at Jay, who had suddenly produced a bottle of champagne and glasses. "On that note," he continued, "I thought that we could all have a drink to celebrate."

"Will," said Titus, "would you mind fetching Maureen, please? You're right. She should be part of this, too."

Jay started passing out the glasses as Will went into the kitchen. Maureen was sitting at the kitchen table, peeling a label off a bottle of beer.

"Maureen," said Will. She didn't look up. "Maureen," he repeated, "Dad wants you to come in. We have some news for you."

Maureen looked up, and Will was surprised to see her eyes were moist. A strand of hair spilled onto her face as she looked up.

"What does he want?" she said, her voice quiet, unusually subdued.

"He wants to tell you something," said Will. "I think it's good news." He smiled, hoping to get one in return, but Maureen only nodded and pushed the stray hair back behind her ear. She took a long drink of beer and stood up.

"All right, then," she said. "Let's go face the music."

She walked past Will into the living room. He followed her. Jay was filling up Titus' champagne glass. When he saw Maureen and Will, he gestured for them to come over. Jay beamed at them as he filled their glasses. He nodded to Titus, who raised his glass.

"I would like to propose a toast," he said. "To all of us here, the LeBarrons. Although we might not all be family, I feel as if, for tonight's intents and purposes, we are." He raised his glass. "To family." He drank. Will glanced around the room. Eddy drank his in a single gulp. Naomi held her glass, raised it, and took a sip. Maureen sipped hers and smiled a little at Titus.

Naomi was staring at the map, biting her lip. *What*, thought Will, *is she thinking*? What does she want? She and Eddy already had over ten million dollars worth of land, although it was worth much, much more than that in richness of life and beauty—but they didn't see that; they never had. No. She was looking for something else up on that map.

Will saw Naomi reach over and grasp Eddy's hand, gripping it so hard that her knuckles starting showing white. Eddy didn't move. They both stared at the map. Naomi clenched Eddy's hand even tighter; he could see her nails digging into the heel of Eddy's palm. Despite himself, Will winced.

But neither Naomi nor Eddy moved a muscle. As Jay and Titus, and now even Maureen, who had risen out of her little funk, laughed and joked, Eddy and Naomi stared ahead, united in a single vision underlined by pain, inflicted and endured, and desire, inflicted and endured. Will took a drink of his champagne, intending to go and speak to his father, but he couldn't. He couldn't move. He couldn't look away.

CHAPTER 13

"THOSE DIRTY BASTARDS. I CAN'T believe they did this to you. I can't."

Fifteen minutes in the car and Naomi was still ranting. Eddy sighed, keeping his eyes straight ahead on the road in front of him.

"Will must have been in on this from the very beginning," she continued. "We never had a chance."

"C'mon, Naomi. Will didn't have a clue about it."

"How do you know that? You didn't know yourself until yesterday."

Eddy shook his head. It was pointless arguing.

"Well, he can't be in control of all that land. No way. They're not getting away with this, Eddy. Not if I have anything to do with it. We have rights, too. That land should belong to you. All of it."

"Part of it belongs to Will, Naomi."

"Huh," she said. "That crazy bastard doesn't deserve it. He won't do anything with it. He'll just leave it wild. It's a waste to give him all that land."

"He's my brother, Naomi," said Eddy, feeling defensive suddenly—oddly. "He's got as much right to it as I do."

"No," she said, shaking her head. "No, he doesn't. This is all about family, Eddy. You are the one who's worked alongside your father, building up the family name, the family business. You're the one who's kept things afloat since your Dad got sick. Will hasn't done shit for the family. He doesn't care about us. All he cares about is his stupid wildlife and forestry and animals."

She turned suddenly in her seat and punched the car window with her gloved hand, the dull thud of the impact echoing through the car.

"Hey," yelled Eddy. "Take it easy."

"No," she said, her eyes gleaming in the dashboard lights. "I'm not taking it easy. Not any more. This is it, Eddy. This is our chance. Now listen to me. I know what I'm doing. Listen to me."

She leaned toward him, restrained only by the seatbelt. "We can do something great here." She hunched toward him further, the seatbelt straining against her body. "This is the opportunity of a lifetime. We can make ourselves rich and make a lot of other people rich too. We can put Moon Lake on the map."

"What are you talking about?" asked Eddy, sneaking a sidelong glance at her. In the darkness of the car, her eyes glowed, two tiny beads of white light.

"We can develop all the land and make it work for all the people. Your brother doesn't want that. Will wants it for himself so he can rule over his own little animal kingdom. That's not fair to everyone who wants to come up here and enjoy it. This is public land, right?"

Eddy nodded. That was true.

"So the public should enjoy it. They should be able to use it. And think of what this could mean for the town. Construction jobs, real estate jobs, businesses, schools. Moon Lake wouldn't be just a two-block town anymore. We could make it a real community."

Eddy nodded again. That was true, too. He looked at Naomi, her teeth gleaming in the light.

"And they'd love you," she whispered, "because you're the one would give them all that. You'd give them better houses, better jobs, and better lives. Yes, Eddy, you could make this place really special."

An opportunity to grow the business, thought Eddy. *To be somebody. To finally make his father proud.*

"All we have to do," continued Naomi, leaning closer to him across the car seat, "is to figure out how to get Will out of the picture. How to show them he's not fit to inherit this land. How he's not fit to be a LeBarron, to be part of your family."

He shook his head. He couldn't.

"Eddy," she whispered. "This is your chance. You can be the man you always should have been. I knew when I first met you that you were special, that you were going to do great things. That's why I married you. But you've been wasted here. There's been nothing for a man of your talents here. Until now."

It all flashed in front of him—the sales, the building, the boom for Moon Lake, the recognition. He could get a building, maybe a new school, named for his dad. Naomi was right; he could finally be somebody. But Will...

"Jesus, Naomi," he said suddenly, turning toward her. "Are you talking about cutting Will out completely? I couldn't do that—even if we could figure out a way—I couldn't do it. He's my brother."

"He's an obstruction," said Naomi. "He's in the way. He's in everybody's way. And he's never been a brother to you. He's been nothing but a burden." She sat back in the seat and crossed her arms. "If you can't rise up to the occasion, then I will. This is my land, too, you know. I'll do whatever it takes."

She sat silent, staring out the car window.

"I'll tell you what," she said at last. "I know exactly what we're going to do. You go find a good lawyer. Don't tell anybody, but let him know what's going on. I'll work on the rest of it. Pull over."

He looked at her.

"Pull over," she repeated, her eyes glowing in the dashboard lights.

He did. She unhooked her seat belt, leaned further over, then crawled over the console to Eddy. She turned his head with her hands and kissed him full on the lips, hard, her tongue driving into his mouth, full of desire and fury. She pulled back, still holding his head.

"You are my husband," she said, holding his head in her hands. "I chose you and I got you. You are my future. You are my destiny." She bared her teeth, the white glistening in the darkened car like the cleaned bones of a kill. She reached down into his pants and latched onto his penis as if she were an eagle and it was her prey.

"You're mine, Eddy LeBarron. You're mine."

Later, in their bedroom, she mounted him, riding his monstrous erection as if she was driving them both off the edge of the world, into the abyss, into oblivion.

When they were done, she snuggled in next to him and whispered in his ear, "Tell me Maureen can do that for you, Eddy."

He breathed slowly, unable to answer. "Tell me Mattie can do that for you."

He stared straight up at the ceiling.

"Eddy." Her voice was in his ear, worming into his consciousness, into his very soul. "Eddy, this is our chance. Yours and mine. We can leave everything else behind us, everything and everybody. All those sluts. This is the key to everything we've ever wanted."

And he began to see it, there in the dark. He began to see a new city rising out of the wilderness, a new vision, a new life.

Naomi was right. They could really do it. They could start over. They could make something. He could be somebody.

"Do this, Eddy," the voice said. "Do it for yourself. Do it for the kids. Do it for me, for all the times you touched those other sluts. You do this for me. You have to."

He felt her hand stroking his penis again.

"You owe me that much, Eddy. You do."

She grabbed his penis so tight that he winced. He could almost feel her smiling in the darkness. And she rolled away, her back toward him, and was almost instantly asleep.

CHAPTER 14

SULLY RAN OUT TO THE WORK CABIN TO tell Will that the people from the hospice were trying to get hold of him. It was one of the first nice spring days. The sun was showing real warmth, and there was that faint smell of soil in the air.

"I don't know, Will," she said, hanging out the car window. "I think it's bad this time."

Will got in his car and drove out to County X, past Moon Lake to the Oak Grove Hospice in Eagleton, where Titus LeBarron was getting ready to die. They'd moved him out there in late March after he collapsed. Maureen wanted to continue taking care of him at home, but Eddy and Naomi overrode her. The doctors wanted him closer to medical care, too, so they took him to the hospice.

Will hadn't been around for that decision. He and Sully had been out collecting tissue samples to analyze the threat of Chronic Wasting Disease. A couple of deer in neighboring Dreyfus County had shown symptoms, so they'd been tranquilizing, tagging, and taking samples from the local population. This had been after a busy month of working with Chief Dodge and the DNR to come up with a plan to mitigate problems with the new land development. They'd finished that up just the week before. Will had been working on relocation strategies for the romp of otters over on Mirror Lake when Sully had come by.

Will pulled up to the one-story brick building, stopped, and leaned back in his seat. He didn't really want to see Naomi—things had gotten worse between them lately. They'd been seeing each other more often since his dad had been moved, and Naomi had been curt, even rude with him, and with Maureen, too—

especially with Maureen. She seemed constantly irritated, even contemptuous of her. Naomi wanted Maureen out of their dad's house after he'd been placed in the home, but Will had vetoed that. Eddy had been strangely silent about it.

Will finally opened the car door and stepped into the warm March sun. He stretched, looking up into the pale blue sky—clear, but hazy—and then made his way up to the building. He nodded to the woman behind the receptionist desk and went toward his dad's room. They'd been there so often lately that most of the staff knew them. It was a dismal, dark place.

I would never want to die here. Give me a frozen field or a deep lake or the warm earth. Not a place like this. It reminded him of the caves off Turtle Ridge. Dark. Dank. He stopped at Room 199, took a deep breath, and stepped in. Sunlight filled the window behind the bed.

"It's about time," said Naomi. He couldn't see her; she was hidden somewhere in the block of sunlight, but Will would know that grating voice anywhere.

"Hello, Naomi," he said. Will glanced to the side of the bed, where Eddy leaned back in his chair, staring at their father. The old man was thinner than ever. His cheeks had sunken deep into his jaw. The oxygen mask hid his mouth, but Will knew most of his teeth were gone. He glanced around the room. No one else was there.

"How is he?" asked Will, looking over at Eddy, who shrugged. Will knew Eddy was taking this hard. Even after months of knowing the inevitable, he still hadn't been able to come to terms with their father's death. *That*, thought Will, glancing again at his brother, *is absurd. Everything dies. Everything. It was just a matter of when.* He was going to miss the old man, sure, but life would go on. He would go on. Eddy would go on. The forest would go on, even after they cut into it. God knows Naomi would go on.

"He's dying," said Naomi, making it a proclamation, a fact.

She can't wait. Will walked around the bed past Naomi, who never took her eyes from his father, and sat next to Eddy. Will looked at the old man from this new angle, down low next to the bed. Titus looked imposing, almost regal, on the raised bed, almost like a king lying in state. Eddy looked down to his hands and started fidgeting with his Swiss Army knife, opening and closing it.

"Has the doctor been in lately?" asked Will. Naomi said nothing, not altering her vigil. Eddy breathed out, shook his head, and said, "No, not since this morning when they called us." His voice was muted, distant.

"What did they say?"

"Umm..." Eddy finally turned and looked at Will, as if realizing he was there for the first time. He had an unexpectedly hard look in his eyes. Will had gotten used to seeing Eddy get pretty emotional with their dad in this state, but his brother seemed to have a better hold on himself this morning. He seemed more controlled.

"They said," Eddy continued, "that his body is starting to shut down." He stopped as the old man's arm jerked suddenly. Will looked at Eddy, who shrugged.

"He does that sometimes." He glanced up at Naomi, who said in a clipped, professional tone, "It happens in the later stages. It's normal."

"Normal," said Eddy, looking up at her. "You call this normal?"

She looked back at him and shrugged. "For a stage four terminal cancer patient, yeah—I call this normal."

Eddy stood and stretched.

"How long have you been here?" asked Will.

"Since they called. About six."

Sully hadn't come out to get him until about nine-thirty.

"How come you didn't let me know sooner?" he asked Eddy.

"How are we supposed to know where you are?" asked Naomi. He looked up at her. She had him fixed with those stony eyes.

"You could have called," said Will. "I do have a cellphone."

"There's no reception out in those woods," said Naomi curtly, focusing again on the monitor. "Why even try?"

Will felt anger swelling up, the blood rushing to his head.

"Because he's my father," said Will. "I have a right to know whether he's dying or not."

"Then maybe you should stick closer," said Naomi, crossing her arms. Will was about to reply when a young nurse walked in. She was dressed in scrubs with patterns of penguins on it.

"I'm sorry," she said. "I don't mean to disturb you, but I needed to monitor his signs. I'll be in and out before you know it."

Naomi scowled but stepped back to let the woman through. The nurse took out an iPad, examined the numbers on the patient monitor, and started poking at it. She was young, in her twenties, thin, and Will thought she might have an athletic build, but it was hard to tell under her uniform. She finished up, smiled radiantly, and was leaving when she suddenly stopped and turned.

"Oh," the nurse said to Eddy, "I almost forgot. Your lawyer friend called and said he was going to be out of the office, but that you should call him on his cellphone." She swung around and bounced out of the room.

Eddy had turned his head away and was staring at their father again. Will glanced at Naomi, who was smiling slightly. Will felt that familiar panic, the crows rising up into his head, their cawing and beating wings drowning everything else out, a rush of blood coursing through his brain.

"A lawyer?" asked Will. "What's that about?"

"Nothing," said Eddy, looking at him strangely, as if he were a child. "We just had a few questions." He shrugged and smiled. "About the inheritance."

Will looked at Naomi. Her smile was broader now, and she was standing perfectly straight.

"What sorts of questions?" asked Will.

"We don't agree with your father and his lawyer's interpretation of the will, and we're going to have our own man look at it," said Naomi.

"You're questioning the will?" Will asked Eddy. "You can't change anything. Dad said the will is solid."

"When Dad dies," said Eddy, glancing at his father again, "our lawyer will serve a notice to probate court that we want a hearing."

"That we want our fair share," said Naomi.

Will thought a moment. It hit him suddenly. They were going to steal the land. He looked at Eddy.

"I don't believe it. This isn't what Dad wants. It's not what Mom would have wanted, either."

Eddy smiled at him and opened his mouth to say something, but he caught Naomi's eye and stopped.

Will took a breath, fighting the noise in his brain, and tried to think. He should get an attorney, too, but who? He didn't know anybody. Where should he go? Who could help him? And he knew—in a flash—that there was only one person he trusted, who might be on his side. Maureen. She wouldn't want this. She wouldn't be part of anything like this. He stood, looked at Eddy, who said something to him, something he couldn't hear over the roaring in his head, came around the bed, and found himself face -to-face with Naomi.

"Don't even try, Will," she hissed. "Or we'll squash you like one of your precious bugs." She smiled then, baring her teeth, reminding him of a cornered rat guarding her burrow. He backed away from her, from Eddy, from what was left of his father—his family—and fled from that claustrophobic death space to somewhere he could breathe, somewhere he could gather himself. He had to find Maureen.

CHAPTER 15

BOB SINGH STOOD ON THE CURB OUTSIDE his gas station, watching as the burly building inspector finished looking at the foundation of his store. He turned away and lit up a cigarette, hoping to hide his anxiety. This was the big moment. This could be the turning point. If the inspector gave his okay to expand, then he would be able to start building his full-size supermarket right here, right behind his gas station. Doing that would be infinitely less expensive than building anew.

He glanced up the street. There was that land next to the lumberyard, but he would have no room to put in a parking lot. He knew he could expand on the land at the edge of town, but that would mean clearing it and installing all the improvements. Expensive, expensive, expensive. He took a deep puff off his cigarette. This would be the best place. And if he could start immediately, the new store would be open in time for the land sales. At least that was according to Eddy LeBarron's attorney, that friend of Wenzel's from Milwaukee; what was his name? Burr. That was it. Wilson H. Burr.

Burr had come to visit Singh in his store about a couple weeks ago, saying that he was on the team to help with the growth and improvements that were going to happen in Moon Lake once the land inheritance went through.

Bob had known something was up with the land; everybody did, although no one was sure exactly what. Mr. Burr had been happy to enlighten them, visiting all the business owners one by one, telling them about the land privatization inheritance and how glad Eddy and Naomi would be to assist them in growing their businesses. This had been great news, and, if it were all true, it would be a great boon for the town.

Burr had been in town a couple of days. After he left, Bob got a call from Jake LaRoche. He said that he, Mattie Doolittle, Dickie Terwilliger, and Bill Swanson were getting together at the Half Moon Café to talk about Burr and the land deal. Mattie had called the meeting. Jake owned Pinky's, the gift and tackle shop, and Dickie owned the lumberyard. Swanson was one of the town supervisors. *Hardly a brain trust*, thought Singh.

They met in the café after hours, about four. Mattie started off by saying she didn't like all these lawyers sneaking around and going behind people's backs and making plans that would affect the whole town. It wasn't fair. She asked where the mayor and council were in all this. Bill Swanson said he and the mayor had not heard a word about it until tonight. And where, Mattie had asked, was Will LeBarron? This was his land, too. *These were concerns, sure*, thought Singh, *but they pale in comparison with the potential gains. Anyone could see that.*

Everyone at the meeting, besides Mattie, was for expanding the land developments and supporting Burr whole hog. *They, and they includes me, want the money. And there was going to be a lot of money, at least if you could believe this Burr character.* Mattie didn't back down. After a lot of haggling, she had convinced them that they should meet with Eddy to verify the details and call a council meeting to get everyone's input. Mattie said she didn't want to live in a town run by one family.

And so here we are, thought Singh, flipping his cigarette to the street and grinding it out with his toe. *Mattie would be overruled; they all knew that. Even she knew that, but she was still probably right. Everyone deserved a say.* He felt a movement behind him and turned.

"Hello, Mr. Singh," said the inspector. His name was Skink. He was a big man, broad across the shoulders. He had long, reddish-blonde hair, and, like so many American men his age, he sported a wide belly. The man was slightly shorter than Singh, but seemed larger—more imposing. He wore reflective, tinted sunglasses and sported a full, red beard. Singh thought he might have looked like a young Santa Claus.

"I'm afraid I've got some bad news for you," he said. He glanced down at his clipboard, frowning.

"Yes, Mr. Skink?" Singh was hoping he didn't sound impatient but knew he did. He never could control that in himself.

"Yeah, we're going to need to upgrade your wiring, your sewage, and your well to complete the remodel. After costs," he said, flipping up a sheet on his clipboard, "you'd almost be better off starting from scratch."

Singh sighed, audibly this time, and nodded.

"But," said the inspector, putting his board aside, "I think we might be able to come to an arrangement."

"An arrangement?"

"Yeah," said the big man, smiling a little. "An interested party called me at home last night. He said he would be very disappointed if this project got stalled and wanted to do every-thing possible to..." He paused, searching for the word, "Expedite things."

"Who was it?" asked Singh, his antennae up. This sort of thing had happened to his grandfather all the time back in India. Singh felt the disgust rising up in his belly—the corruption, the subterfuge, the payoffs that never ended. This was why his grandfather had left to come to America. *Forgive me for saying so, but I am glad my grandfather is dead; I'm glad he never lived to see that America has become exactly like the home he fled.*

"I'm afraid I'm not at liberty to say who the concerned party is," said Mr. Skink. He paused a moment, took a step back, and then spit onto the asphalt. *He just spit on my property.* Bob felt no anger or rancor—just more disgust, although it was a different type of disgust.

"What would be the terms of his assistance?" asked Singh. He knew what the answer would be, of course. More money. Payoffs and then more money after that for Mr. Skink to keep his mouth shut. He would be like a cockroach, impossible to get rid of. *But one could learn to live with cockroaches. One could learn to live with anything.*

"I'm not exactly sure of that," said Mr. Skink, taking off his sunglasses to polish them. His eyes were small, sunken atop the fleshy mass of his nose. "All I can tell you is that our mutual friend"—*what an odd phrase for a man like this. He probably picked it up from a James Bond movie*—"will be in touch with you soon."

"I see," said Singh. "What might I expect?"

Mr. Skink shrugged. "I'm not sure," he said. "But," he said as he leaned conspiratorially toward Mr. Singh. "I can assure you it will be lucrative."

Mr. Singh smiled and nodded. Mr. Skink, looking a little disappointed at what he perceived was probably Singh's lack of enthusiasm, went back to his vehicle, one of those gigantic six-wheeled pick-up trucks. *Who needs that much vehicle? A farmer perhaps, or a contractor, but certainly not a building inspector. These Americans were so similar. Everything had to be bigger, shinier, faster, and more powerful. And for that you needed money—a lot of money.*

Singh turned to go back into his store. *I am no better than any of them. I am just as greedy, just as lascivious, just as lusty. I want wealth as badly—worse—than any American. I guess my grandfather has succeeded,* he thought, going behind the counter of his business. *He has made us into true, authentic Americans.*

CHAPTER 16

EDDY PULLED INTO THE DRIVEWAY. Naomi was working late—thank God. He needed a break from her. Eddy was behind the plan to get more of the land, but, *my God*, he thought, *I'm not obsessed with it.* Naomi lived and breathed it twenty-four seven. She never thought about anything else.

Eddy opened the car door and stepped out into the March twilight. It wasn't quite spring yet. It could still freeze tonight. He glanced at his watch. Naomi's sister would be bringing the kids by in about a half-hour. That'd give him a little bit of peace. *And,* he thought, trudging up the driveway, *a little time to figure out how to handle Mattie. It looked like she was going to be difficult.* Eddy opened the front door and stepped into the darkened living room; he moved carefully. Through experience, he knew there'd be something lying on the floor—toys, clothes baskets, books, shoes, anything. He once stepped on a saucepan in the dark.

Eddy finally reached the switch and turned on the light. He glanced around the room. Pretty much the same as he'd expected. Toys, clothes, books. *What a mess.* He didn't know if Naomi was physically incapable of cleaning anything besides the kitchen or if it was some kind of stubbornness. As much as he bitched at her about it, she just wouldn't do it. She always blamed it on the kids.

Eddy took a deep breath and paused. Something stunk. Poop. Maybe there was dirty underwear lying around somewhere. That wouldn't be surprising. He walked toward the hallway leading to the bedrooms and saw a coil of dogshit lying on the floor. Jimbo. Another accident. It was getting to be a daily thing. He got some toilet paper and cleaned it up. Eddy glanced around, expecting to see a pool of urine nearby. Nothing else in the hallway. Nothing in the dining room. So far, so good. But where was Jimbo? He typically met Eddy at the door. He knew the old dog's hearing had been going, but this was bad, worse than he'd thought. Eddy whistled and clapped his hands. Something rustled from behind the couch, and he heard Jimbo moving along the wall. The old dog appeared. He looked around the room, disoriented, and then spotted Eddy and moved toward him.

"Hey, buddy," said Eddy, patting the dog on his head. Jimbo wagged his tail feebly. He was panting. "Let's get you something to eat." He walked into the kitchen. Jimbo followed him slowly. Eddy glanced back, taking a good look at the old dog. His coat was losing its shine, and his eyes now had that same milky cast. Eddy knelt down and took the dog's head in his hands. Had this happened that suddenly, or had he just not noticed? He'd been pretty distracted lately, but still. Jimbo had gotten old. Really old. How had it happened so quickly?

"C'mon, buddy," he said, standing up. Eddy went over to the cupboard and took out a pouch of some wet food, Jimbo's favorite. The dog sat, one leg splayed to the side and looked up at him, tongue lolling off to one side. Eddy opened the packet and emptied it into the dog bowl. Jimbo moved over to the bowl, sniffed, and turned away. He padded slowly into the living room and disappeared behind the couch.

Eddy frowned. This wasn't good. The accidents, the loss of appetite, and the loss of interest all spelled out one thing. It might be the old boy's time. *Shit.*

He heard a thump and then the storm door open. The kids were home. He glanced at the couch. A year ago, Jimbo would have been barking up a storm. Now he couldn't even hear them.

The door slammed open, and Bella came racing into the room.

"Daddy," she said. "Daddy. Guess what?"

"What?" he asked, scooping her up in his arms.

"I got three gold unicorns today."

"You did?" he said. "That's great."

"Daddy." Eddy looked down. There was Donny, staring up at him.

"What is it, son?"

The boy raised up his arms. Eddy knelt down, his knees cracking, and scooped up the boy with his free arm. The kids laughed and hugged him as he twirled them around the room. He went to the door and waved to Naomi's sister, who waved back and pulled out of the driveway. He walked back to the kitchen.

"What's for supper?" asked Bella.

Shit. He'd forgotten about supper.

"What would you like?" he asked, putting the two of them down on the floor. Both kids shed their winter outerwear like butterflies escaping their cocoons.

"Pizza!" exclaimed Bella.

"Pizza," said Donny, probably just to repeat it.

"Hang up your coats," he said. Pizza wasn't their usual weeknight fare, but what the hell? Pretty soon, they'd be able to treat themselves all the time.

"Pizza it is," he said. "But first, you need to go into the living room and clean up all your toys."

"Mom never makes us clean up our stuff," said Bella.

"You want pizza or not?"

Bella stuck out her lower lip. Donny imitated her. Eddy cleared his throat to keep from chuckling.

"Okay," said Bella. "C'mon, Donny." They both raced into the living room.

Jimbo had come into the kitchen and lay down. Eddy knelt down and petted him slowly along his flank. The old dog was panting. He raised his head suddenly and looked at Eddy and then tried to rise up. Eddy gently pushed him back down.

"Take it easy, buddy," he said. "It's okay."

Eddy reached up and took one of the pieces of dog food out of the pouch and held it to Jimbo's mouth. He sniffed it, licked it, and finally ate it. Eddy repeated the process a few times, then went and filled Jimbo's bowl. The dog followed him and started eating.

Finally. Poor old guy. They'd had a dog growing up—a big, dumb Labrador named Ralph—who lived to the ripe old age of seventeen. When he started to go, it had looked a lot like this— loss of appetite, no bowel control, and disorientation. Ralph got nippy, too, which was not like him. He'd gotten to a point, just a little worse than Jimbo was now, where his dad took him out for a walk in the woods. His father had come back alone.

No way. I could never do that. Not with Jimbo. No matter how bad it got. Eddy would take him to the vet. No way would he be able to do it himself.

"Daddy."

He looked up. Bella was standing in the doorway, looking like she was up to something.

"What is it, honey?"

"Donny stepped in some dog poop. Now it's all over him." Donny appeared. He had poop all over him—his shoes, pants, hands, and even his face.

Eddy sighed.

"Okay," he said. "Time for a bath, young man." He led Donny into the bathroom, turned on the water, and told him to get undressed. *No need to get dogshit on both of us.* When the boy was done, Eddy plopped him in the water and balled up his clothes. He'd put them in the laundry tub to soak before throwing them in the washer.

"Bella," he said. The girl, who had been watching from the doorway, walked in.

"Watch your brother while I order the pizza, okay?" She nodded. "Don't let him put his head under." She nodded again.

"So, Bella, where was the dog poop? Where did Donny step in it?"

"In the living room over by the Barbie Dream House."

"Thanks, honey." *Another accident. Damn it. God damn it.*

Eddy ordered the pizza and then cleaned up the mess. He stuck his head in the bathroom, saw that Bella had joined Donny in the tub, told them to use the soap, and went back to the kitchen.

Jimbo was lying next to his water dish, sleeping. Eddy opened a beer and sat at the table, watching him. Except for all the tubes and medical monitors, the dog looked a lot like his father lying in his hospital bed. Neither one could control their bowels or had any idea where they were. Neither one was free from pain. The one difference was that Jimbo woke up every now and them.

After his dad had collapsed, the doctors said all they could really do for him was to make him comfortable. He'd been at the hospice since February, just hanging on. And even though he was barely there, not the father he knew, Eddy still liked going there and just sitting next to the old man. He'd talk to his father, chatting or conducting one-sided arguments, sometimes pretending to listen. It seemed to him that sometimes the old man would nod a little. He even thought he saw him wink once.

Eddy knew the end was near—inevitable—but, as he gazed down at Jimbo, also on his last legs, he knew he still couldn't really admit it to himself. He couldn't bring himself to say goodbye. Even though putting it off caused nothing but pain, he still couldn't let go of his father.

"Daddy," called a voice from the back of the house.

Eddy finished off his beer and went to the bathroom. He got the kids in their pajamas. After they had their pizza, eating it in front of the TV, he tucked the children in for the night and went back into the kitchen. Jimbo hadn't moved. Eddy watched him for a moment, making sure he was still breathing, and opened another beer.

Titus LeBarron. A legend. His father. His teacher. Probably the only person he really trusted. When his father was gone, who would he have? Naomi? Will? Maureen? None of them understood the first thing about him. Not like his Dad. He'd be alone in the universe, floating through the void with no light to guide him. Eddy had always had that light, that direction. Without it, he was lost.

Lost. He wasn't even sure who he'd be anymore. He wasn't sure who he was now. Eddy had always tried to be like his dad, but he never measured up—not in his dad's eyes or his own eyes. He wasn't as smart or as tough or as charismatic. His dad never said so, but Eddy always felt his disappointment. He was a better son than Will, but that wasn't saying much.

Who else did he have? He and Will barely talked. Maureen and he had been close at one time, but not so much anymore. Mattie was a strictly casual relationship. They'd both wanted it that way. The townspeople liked him, but only because he was going to make them rich. All Naomi wanted was for him to become some sort of fucking tycoon. "Grow a pair," she'd said. "Take what belongs to you." She was after him all the time now, pushing, pushing, pushing.

Well, he thought, taking a long drink, *I do have a pair*. And he had the expertise. He'd grown up knowing land, how to buy it, sell it, appraise it, and use it. Will didn't know shit about it; Will didn't appreciate what land was, what it meant. He didn't appreciate what their father had done, the legacy he'd created. *Naomi's right. Will doesn't deserve it. So I should take matters into my own hands; I'll do what my father would have done. I will do what needs to be done. That's who I am, and that's who I'm going to be. I have to be the one to step up after my father goes, to be the leader. Maybe I'm not the man my father was, but I'm going to make my mark before I die.* He took another sip of beer. *Naomi's right. This is my shot—this is what I was meant to be. And I'll do whatever I have to do.*

Tomorrow, he thought, opening another beer and looking down at the sleeping dog. *Tomorrow, Jimbo, you and I will be taking a ride.*

CHAPTER 17

EDDY PULLED THE SHOTGUN OUT OF the truck bed and walked into Lakeland Realty, not bothering to put out his cigarette, and put Jimbo's leash and collar on the table. He stuck his head into Jay's office. There were still a few boxes on the table, but he seemed pretty well moved out. *Good.* Naomi had made the point that they didn't really need the little man anymore, so Eddy had fired him. They had their own lawyer now. He walked into his own office and sat down at his desk. He ashed his cigarette on the floor and took a legal pad out of his desk drawer.

Things were going according to plan so far; Burr had made his rounds to all the business owners, and, except for Mattie, they all seemed to be falling into line. What the fuck was her problem? You think she'd want to be a success instead of a washed-up, middle-aged waitress running a breakfast dive. Eddy nodded. Yeah, Naomi had been right about her. She'd predicted that Mattie would be stubborn, that she wouldn't be bright enough to see the big picture.

Well, he thought, putting his cigarette butt into a coffee mug. *We'll see how things go with the meeting this afternoon.* He and all the principal business owners, and that was a laugh—as if there could be a principal business in Moon Lake—would be gathering at the town hall that afternoon. Eddy figured he would let them talk and see where things stood. Mayor Coogan hadn't weighed in on the land transfer yet, but once he got his slice of the pie, Eddy was sure he'd be no problem.

Eddy drew two columns on the legal pad. On the left side, he put Will's name, Sully's, Chief Dodge's, Mattie's, and then, with a question mark, Maureen's. Not that her opinion mattered.

On the right side, he put his own, Bob Singh's, Dickie Terwilliger's, Mayor Coogan's, and Jake LaRoche's. He put Bill Swanson's name in the middle and circled it. The rest of the town council was still a wild card. So was the state, but Burr thought he had a good handle on that.

Eddy glanced at his watch; it was time to get going. He put on his coat and walked over to the town hall building, a vinyl pole shed with central heating. It actually wasn't bad inside. They'd done a decent job designing the office space. He walked over to the conference room and went in.

Mattie sat at the far side of the table, staring straight ahead with her hands clasped in front of her. Jake LaRoche sat next to her, his fingers drumming on the tabletop, and glanced at Eddy, frowning a little. He was a little older than Eddy, fortyish, and trim. He kept himself in good shape. He wore the same Mark Spitz moustache he'd had since high school and still combed his dark hair straight back. He was sharp—a good businessman.

Dickie Terwilliger sat next to Jake, fidgeting. He was thin to the point of cadaverousness, balding, and always moving. He reminded Eddy of one of those wading birds, all legs and throat. On workdays, Dickie was always tearing around the lumber store, barking out orders, running down inventory, and yapping away. That was the other thing. He usually never shut up, although he was quiet now, peering at everyone in turn through those old-fashioned wire-rimmed glasses he had. Granny glasses.

Bob Singh was sitting still, his hands folded on his lap, staring straight ahead at nothing. According to Skink, he had seemed pretty receptive to the modifications to his inspection. But he was still a wild card. Eddy had known these other guys all his life, but Singh was an outsider—even after living in Moon Lake for ten years.

Johnny Redd, who owned Olson's, and Regina Schnell, who owned Busby's, didn't live in town, so they weren't technically part of the inner circle. They hadn't been invited. Danny Long hadn't been able to make it; he was out remodeling the old Jacoby place on Lake Williams. The Wilson boys were working with Danny, but they were minor league and stupid as rocks to boot. They didn't need them here. They'd have their chance to make some money, though. All of them would. Eddy would see to that. But the Wilsons shouldn't be here to make policy.

Mayor Coogan came bustling in, Bill Swanson trailing behind. They exchanged greetings with everyone and sat.

"Hello, everyone," said Mayor Coogan. "I'm glad we all could make it." He had a very deep, smooth voice. *Silk,* thought Eddy.

"First of all," said the mayor. "Our thoughts and prayers are with your dad, Eddy. He always was a great friend to Moon Lake. Give him our best."

A ripple of assent flowed through the room. Eddy nodded.

"Well," continued Mayor Coogan, "since this is more of an informal meeting, we decided that we really don't need to convene the entire city council."

Even though it was a cool March day, barely topping fifty degrees, a glossy sheen of sweat was already appearing on Coogan's forehead. He was a big man—fat—topping three hundred pounds. *It has to be a lot of work hauling all that weight around, but the extra baggage doesn't seem to slow him down much.* Coogan was always on the move, driving up to Eagleton or over to Rhinelander, always trying to bring a little more economic life into Moon Lake. His small brown eyes—pig eyes—flitted around the room, gauging who was there and why. He ran his hand through the sparse hair on top of his head and took a breath.

"We all know why we're here," he said. "There's been a development with the LeBarron land endowment. It is no longer in the public trust, and, as such, can now be bought, sold, and developed like any other land." He turned to Eddy. "Is that right, Eddy?"

Eddy smiled at the mayor and nodded.

"So the question seems to be how exactly we are going to manage this. It's Eddy's property, and it's obviously his to do with as he wishes, but he has graciously decided to include us in the transition process."

He looked at Eddy. "Would you like to tell us about what you're envisioning with this, Mr. LeBarron?"

Eddy stood up, looked around the table, and smiled.

"It's just like the mayor said. This is going to be a pretty big deal, and it's going to affect almost everybody in town, so Naomi and I thought it would be fair to get everybody's input about how to go about bringing this land to the people."

"I thought the people already owned it," said Mattie.

"Sure," said Eddy. "Theoretically it's theirs. But nobody really ever had a chance to go back there and enjoy it. Now we can open it up so everybody can experience it."

"How much are you planning on selling?" asked Jake, leaning back in his chair and smoothing down his moustache with the fingers of his left hand.

Eddy knew Jake wanted to open a resort on Mirror Lake. Burr had gone into negotiations promising him a sweet deal on interest rates if he played ball; not that Jake would need much persuasion. Jake knew what was best for Jake.

"We're not sure yet," Eddy lied. "We might go with my dad's idea and do a relatively small development, or, if we decide to open it up to the people, we might go bigger. We're just not sure yet."

Jake nodded. Eddy started to sit down.

"How many new domiciles would that be?" asked Dickie. His voice always reminded Eddy of a ventriloquist's voice, the fake one they used for the dummies.

"Well," said Eddy, standing again. "Anywhere from one hundred and fifty or so, if we stay with my dad's plan, or up to four hundred, if we open it up completely."

Dickie let out a slow whistle. A silence settled over the room. Eddy glanced around. Dickie had his calculator out, and Singh was doing it in his head—figuring out their profit lines. Jake was staring straight ahead, probably dreaming about his lake property. Mattie, though—Mattie was staring right at him. She looked pissed.

"What does Will say about all this?" she asked suddenly, her voice as crisp as a bell.

"He's got his share of the land," said Eddy. "But he's worried about the development. You know how he is."

"Is he okay?" asked Jake.

Eddy shrugged and made what he hoped was a "Jeez, I'm a little worried" type of look and said, "I don't know, Jake. Ever since he found out that land is going to be opened up, Will's been acting a little bit, I don't know, I guess a little bit off. He's been erratic. To be honest, Naomi and I have been worried about him."

Mattie smiled a little and shook her head, the smile moving slowly into a smirk.

"Naomi," she said. "Worried about Will? Since when?"

Eddy shrugged. Mattie stood up and grabbed her jacket.

"You are so full of shit, Eddy." She turned to the others in the room.

"Mayor," she said, pivoting toward him. "I would like to call for a general town meeting with all interested parties present. All interested parties. I think Will and the rest of the town deserve a chance to be involved with these negotiations, rather than having all this sneaking around behind closed doors."

The mayor opened his mouth and then shut it; he nodded for her to continue.

"We have to ask ourselves," she continued, "why this lawyer Eddy and Naomi hired is so involved with town business, and why the only people at these meetings are the ones who stand to make a profit. Why isn't Chief Dodge here to talk about the environmental impact of all this development? Why," she said, "do I feel like somebody is trying to sell me a timeshare?"

Dickie chuckled, caught himself, and glanced around the room, blushing.

Eddy felt all the eyes in the room fall on him. He looked back at all of them and tried to smile reassuringly. What would his dad do? He shrugged.

"Sure," he said, turning to Mattie. "If you think it's necessary, I'm all for it. I think a town meeting would be a great idea. Air everything out." She nodded and sat back down.

Jake looked around the room, stroking his moustache again. He didn't look too happy. Dickie shrugged and nodded in one twitchy motion, agreeing—the guy was oblivious. Swanson looked at the mayor, who shrugged. *Yeah, Coogan was smart enough not to get in the way of a town hall. Swanson would follow his lead.* Bob Singh was looking down at his hands; he'd been awfully quiet the entire meeting. Eddy had to wonder whether he was truly on board with them. He and Bob might have to have a heart-to-heart.

And Mattie. She was the last one he'd been expecting trouble from. He couldn't count the times she'd complained to him about being stuck working at her mom's business in Moon Lake, being unable to get out from under. *Well, here it is,* he thought, looking at her across the table. *Here's your chance.* She stared back at him with that mulish look she got when she was being stubborn, chin stuck up in the air and eyes half-lidded. He'd seen it a hundred times before—when she was pissed about him taking her for granted, coming over to her place drunk looking for a little action, or lying in bed talking about how claustrophobic Moon Lake was.

"Well, then," said Coogan, "if there are no objections, I'll call for a town hall two weeks from tonight at the Community Center. That'll give us time to give everyone appropriate notice. Are there any objections?"

Eddy looked around the table. Nobody was saying anything. *Well, we aren't going to be able to get around this one. The whole town will have their say. Naomi won't be happy.* She'd wanted merchant support, a solid base to work with, both economically and politically, before things started happening. Once the old man died, they were going to have to move fast to get things into probate court. Coogan would have been helpful with that.

"We're adjourned, then," said the mayor, lumbering to his feet and then trotting out, looking like a milk cow at feeding time. Swanson followed him out the door. Dickie left next, muttering to himself. LaRoche frowned at Mattie as he stood. He glanced at Eddy, raised his eyebrows, and left. Bob Singh rose up slowly out of his seat. He looked a little distracted.

"Hey, Bob," said Eddy. "How did things go with the inspector?"

Bob looked up at him as he stood, blinked, and then shrugged.

"Good," he said. "I think he's going to let me remodel the old place. It is going to be a little more expensive than I thought, though."

Eddy nodded. "You were kind of quiet, today, Bob. I thought you might have been a little more enthusiastic about the redevelopment."

Bob smiled. "I think you said everything that needed to be said, Eddy. Things seem to be well in hand." He smiled in that naïve way of his, but it didn't work with Eddy. He didn't trust Singh; he never really had. Bob tried too hard to fit in. He was a little too agreeable. Eddy smiled at him as he left.

That left him and Mattie. Eddy looked around the room. It was partitioned out of the big pole shed, definitely not sound-proofed and probably not very discreet. He'd have to be careful.

"What's wrong with you, Mattie?" he whispered. "I thought this whole deal would make you happy. I thought you hated being stuck here."

"I do," she said, standing up, "but what you're doing is wrong, Eddy."

"What are you talking about?"

"C'mon, Eddy, do you think I'm stupid? Do you think everybody in town is that stupid? I know why you and Naomi hired that lawyer. You're lining people up so you can push this development thing through as fast as possible and grab all the land you can. I know what Naomi's thinking. If you get enough popular support, Coogan will feel the pressure and bend to you. All you have to do is wave that little carrot in front of the merchants. That'll put all the pressure on Will."

She put her hands on her hips. "What did you promise Jake? A good price for that resort he's always wanted?" He tried to keep his face as expressionless as possible as her eyes bored into him. "This will be great for business. For Bob and Jake," she continued, "and Dickie and everybody else."

"And you," he added.

She grabbed her coat. "You make me sad, Eddy. I don't know what happened to you. You used to be a good guy. You used to care about other things besides money."

"Mattie," he said. "You've got this all wrong. I don't know why you think we're trying to rip off Will. I don't know how that's even possible. The will is written—it's solid."

She put on her jacket.

"C'mon, Mattie," he said, walking around the table toward her. She tracked him as he moved, her eyes never leaving his face. "C'mon," he said, approaching her. "Let's be friends again." He tried to put his arms around her. She shoved him away violently enough to cause him to stumble backwards.

"Don't you ever touch me again, Eddy," she said. "We're through. Stay away from me." She turned and walked quickly out the door.

You little bitch. You're going to pay for this. Eddy looked around the empty room at the bits of paper left behind. *Yeah, we don't need Mattie. She can work in her little shitty diner the rest of her life for all I care. And if she tries to get in our way,* he thought, shrugging into his own jacket, *she'll realize that we are not fucking around. This is happening, with or without the people of Moon Lake.* It was his fate, his destiny to shape the land. If there were problems, he had solutions. He had Lewis.

CHAPTER 18

WILL STEERED THE OLD FORD INTO THE muddy driveway. Maureen's car was sitting next to the shed. *Good.* He stopped the car, leaped out, and sprinted up the back steps. He paused a moment, remembering suddenly that this was Maureen's house now, not his father's. He should knock. He knocked. No answer. He stood a moment with his hands in his pockets and then glanced down the path toward the lake.

He saw someone sitting on the edge of the pier, gazing out over the lake. A flash of reddish brown moved with the steady wind traveling up the hillside, whispering with the trees, until it reached Will. It had to be Maureen down there. She liked sitting by the lake.

He started down the path, careful not to slip on the coating of pine needles. It was a steep path, but a familiar one. This was the same cabin they'd visited as children—the cabin their dad rented for the summer.

Will reached the pier and stopped. There were still some patches of ice and slush on the lake, and most of the trees were only just beginning to come out of dormancy. The shore was brown and black, rather than green, and the lake was a murky gray of slush and snow. It was, to Will, the ugliest time of year on the lake.

Maureen, sensing someone behind her, turned suddenly. She was sitting cross-legged on the end of the dock, and even though it was barely fifty degrees in the sun, she wore only a frayed black t-shirt and jeans. The shirt had a picture of a wolf painted in striking colors on it. *Not realistic at all,* thought Will.

"Will," she said. "What are you doing sneaking up on people?"

"Hello, Maureen," he said. "Pretty day."

"Yeah," she said, looking back out over the lake. "I like it when it's deserted like this, when no one else would want to be out here."

Will said nothing. He wanted to be out here; he always wanted to be out here.

"What is it?" she asked after a few moments. "What do you want?"

"I think there's going to be trouble," he said. "I think there's going to be a problem with the land."

Maureen looked up at him a second, frowned, and then, gathering her legs underneath her, she rose and motioned for Will to follow her. She walked up the path quickly, knowing it as well as him or Eddy. He watched her legs moving efficiently, effortlessly. *She was in good shape*, he thought, gauging the gait and thrust of her thighs. *Like a deer.* Maureen stopped suddenly and turned, fixing him with her deep brown eyes.

"What are you looking at, Will?"

He stuttered out an answer. "I was watching the way you walk, how surefooted you are. It's easy to see you know the path."

"Of course I know it," she said, turning and continuing up the path. "I was practically raised here," she added, over her shoulder.

We've spent a lot of time here. Seven—no, eight—summers. His dad would rent the cabin for three months, June through August, and bring everyone out. His mom had started bringing Maureen after the girl's dad had been killed.

Maureen reached the cabin and went in. Will followed her into the kitchen and stared a moment. The sink was full of dishes, and there was a collection of beer bottles, dirty plates, a bag of pot, and rolling papers on the kitchen table. Maureen was leaning over the opened refrigerator.

"You want a beer?" she asked, her voice muffled by the door.

He shook his head, then cleared his throat and said, "No."

She stood, beer bottle in hand, and came over to the table.

"Pardon the mess," she said. "I haven't felt up to doing much housekeeping lately. It doesn't seem worth it when I'm the only one here." She sat, putting her bottle in an empty spot, and shoved some other stuff aside, clearing a place for Will.

"So what's up?" she asked, twisting the top off.

During his years with the DNR, Will had dealt with enough boaters and snowmobilers to know when someone had been drinking, and Maureen had been drinking. She wasn't to the point where she'd have been in trouble driving, but she was getting close. This last beer might do it. She looked at Will, half-smiling, as she took a long swig. Would it do any good to talk to her now? Well, considering the situation, how desperate things had become, Will didn't really think he had much choice.

"I saw Eddy and Naomi this morning over at the hospice in Eagleton," he began.

"The Oak Grove," said Maureen. "Yeah. How's your dad?"

Will shrugged. "The same. They thought he was dying and called me, but it was a false alarm."

"Thank God," she said. "I need to get out there to visit him."

Will nodded and looked down at his hands. "Eddy was talking and mentioned they hired a lawyer." Detecting motion, Will glanced up. Maureen was sitting up straight now.

"What did he say?" asked Maureen. There wasn't a trace of alcohol in her manner now, Will noticed. She was good.

"That the lawyer is going to ask for a probate hearing."

"It figures," said Maureen. "It just fucking figures with those two. I've been hearing that there's been somebody hanging around town talking about the land deal. Eddy's been trying to line people up on his side."

"What do you think they want?" asked Will.

Maureen laughed, almost a snort. "All Eddy and Naomi want," she said, "is more." She took another drink of beer. "I think they want it all."

"That's not what Dad wants," said Will, looking down at his hands.

"No, it isn't. We all heard him," she said. "We all heard what he said." A dark expression crossed her face, a passing thundercloud. She was angry, angrier than Will would have guessed.

"I was thinking," said Will, "that if they have an attorney ready to argue in probate court, I should probably get one, too." He held up his hands and shrugged. "But I don't know who to call, Maureen. I don't know anybody. I was hoping you might."

Maureen furrowed her eyebrows a moment and leaned forward. Her hair dangled loosely over her face. *Her hair is beautiful. A beautiful color—like a vixen, although not quite as light.* Will fidgeted and looked down at his hands. He curled them into fists, loosened them, and looked up at Maureen again. She was still staring straight ahead, thinking, trying to figure it out, her brown eyes locked on some point straight ahead of her. Focused.

She turned to him suddenly. He dropped his eyes, embarrassed at being caught staring at her.

"I think," she said, "that we could talk to Everett Bradley up in Eagleton. He's mostly a criminal attorney, but I think he handles some probate. If not, he can turn us in the right direction. Who are they using?"

Will wracked his brain. He couldn't remember, but he had to remember. Suddenly, he could feel the familiar anxiety, his old nemesis, starting to coil up inside his gut. His heart started fluttering. And then it came to him.

"I think somebody named Burris? Or Burr?" he said.

She nodded. "Burr," she said. "I've heard about him. He works with Wenzel. He's a real sleazebag." She looked closely at him. "Are you okay, Will?"

"I'm—I don't know—Maureen, I'm worried. I'm worried that they might do this, take it all, take away everything." He found himself standing next to the table, gesturing toward the lake, the woods. "I don't know," he continued, feeling himself starting to stutter, to hesitate.

The familiar panic, the raucous sound of the angry crows started filling his ears, screaming through his head. Will clamped his hands over his ears to shut it out, but it grew, louder, more raucous, unbearable. He heard something cutting through the noise then, something lower, calmer, rhythmic. He opened his eyes. Maureen was standing in front of him, holding him by the shoulders and talking softly, quietly, her voice as soothing as the sound of falling rain. The sound of the crows slowly subsided, and he found himself looking into her eyes—eyes peering deeply into his own.

"Will, it's all right," she was saying. "It's all right. They're not going to get everything. We won't let them. We'll stop them, Will. Will, relax now. Just relax."

Will's breath was still coming in spurts, and he felt the sweat beading on his face and running in rivulets down his sides. He nodded, took a deep breath, and put his hands on Maureen's shoulders and leaned on her. The cacophony in his head, now a faint echo, continued to fade.

"It's okay, Will," said Maureen, stroking the back of his head. He felt enveloped in her softness, her warmth, her presence. He felt safe suddenly, comforted, as if he were being held in his mother's arms. He took another breath and stepped back.

Maureen was looking at him with her cinnamon eyes. Her hands were still on his shoulders. Will could feel their warmth seeping through his shirt. He nodded, trying to smile a little. Maureen smiled back and dropped her hands.

"Are you okay?" she asked. He nodded again, unable to speak, the familiar tongue-tied sensation he always got whenever he became attracted to Maureen rearing up again. *Why is that? Why am I always this way around her? Why can't I be normal?* He'd always been nervous around girls, but it shouldn't be like that with Maureen. She was more like a sister to him. It didn't make sense that he got nervous around her. He didn't with Sully. He could talk to her just fine. Being with Sully was like talking to Eddy or his dad.

Maureen went back to the table and sat. She took a long sip out of her beer and started pulling strips off the paper label. Will watched her a moment, and then decided to make the leap—to say something, to talk, to make small talk. To be normal.

"Why do you do that?" he asked.

She looked up, frowning.

"Do what?"

"Why do you always pull the labels off the bottles?"

"Oh," she said, looking down as if surprised to see it. She smiled and half-shrugged. "I don't know. Just a nervous habit, I guess."

"You always do it," he said. "It's just something I was wondering about."

"I guess I do," she said. "I don't even notice it anymore." She put her head in her hand and gazed at Will a moment.

"What's with you, Will?" she asked, looking intoxicated again. "Why do you always get so nervous around me? Don't you like me?" She giggled. He felt himself blushing.

"Sure," said Will. "Sure, I do."

She giggled again. *It's funny*, thought Will. *As soon as the adrenaline left, the alcohol returned.* Maureen smiled, leaned back in her chair and stretched, her breasts straining against the black fabric of the old t-shirt. She pushed some of her stray hair behind one ear and sat back, staring at Will. He stared back, his eyes straying down the front of her shirt. He couldn't help himself.

"Why don't you sit down?" she asked. He did.

"We've got to think about this," she said. "We've got to figure out some sort of strategy. Did Eddy or Naomi say anything else while you were there?"

Will shook his head. Maureen started picking at the label on the beer bottle again.

"So," she said, "if they do this, they're going to have to figure out a way to cut you out of the will."

Will nodded. That made sense. But how? What were the rules for inheritance? He didn't know, and he couldn't think. His eyes kept returning to the wolf resting on the curves of Maureen's t-shirt.

"I wonder," she said suddenly, looking up at him. "Have you ever had any psychological testing or anything?"

"What?" asked Will, surprise jolting him out of his reverie. "Why?"

"I'm thinking they might want to try to prove that you're incompetent, that you wouldn't be mentally stable enough to handle the inheritance."

"They want to prove I'm crazy?" asked Will.

He stood up, shocked, but—now that Maureen had said it out loud—it made sense. He wasn't crazy. Eddy knew it. Naomi knew it, too. The doctors had diagnosed him with a mild form of autism when he was a kid. That was the source of the anxiety problems and the reason he had a hard time relating to people. He and his family had managed it, but it had been hard—so, so hard.

It wasn't that Will didn't like other people; he just didn't understand them—how they picked out what to talk about, what they laughed at, or what they liked. It was a mystery to him. Some of them knew it and took advantage. He'd been called names all his life—weirdo, brainiac, and worse. It didn't mean he was crazy.

"Will," said someone sharply. Maureen. He turned and looked at her. She was standing now and glaring at him.

"Take it easy," she said, her voice stern. It made him blink. He took another breath and sat down. She sat down opposite him and took a sip from her beer.

"That is one thing you cannot afford to do, Will LeBarron," she said. "If they're looking to prove you're nuts, they're going to be trying to flip you out every chance they get. You've gotta be cool."

He nodded, feeling embarrassed. She was right. He couldn't lose control.

"C'mon," she said, standing suddenly. She walked over to the closet and grabbed a coat.

Will stood. "Where are we going?" he asked.

"Eagleton," she said. She smiled. "It's time to get you counsel, sir. It's time to get us a lawyer."

* * *

EVERETT BRADLEY WAS SKINNY, almost stork-like, although he was slightly bent in the upper back. He had a long face that tapered down from steep cheekbones into a chin as firm as a stone. He wasn't wearing a suit and tie like most lawyers. He had on a corduroy jacket over a plaid button-down shirt.

"Hello," he said abruptly, turning to Maureen. His voice was nasal and sharp. Will breathed a sigh of relief as Bradley's eyes shifted off of him. "You must be Maureen Hansen," he said.

"Guilty as charged," she said.

"That used to be a funny joke," he said, not changing his expression. "Maybe the first nine or ten times I heard it."

Maureen shrugged and looked at Will with raised eyebrows. "Sorry," she said. "I didn't mean to offend you."

"No need to apologize," said the lawyer. He turned to Will. "Young man," he said, extending his hand. "I'm sorry to hear about your father. Titus and I used to hunt together."

"You know my dad?" asked Will, shaking the man's hand.

Bradley nodded. "A long time ago. How is he?"

Will shook his head. "Not good. The doctors say he might die anytime."

"That's a shame," said Bradley. "Please." He motioned for them to sit in the two office chairs opposite his desk. Will lowered himself into a chair. Maureen plopped down. Bradley sat and stared at the two of them a moment and then said, "So what can I do for you?"

Maureen started talking, describing the situation in some detail to Mr. Bradley. Will didn't mind her taking over. In fact, he was relieved he didn't have to talk about it himself. It wasn't just that he didn't like speaking. Will got upset just thinking about what Eddy was doing. He was surprised Maureen knew of the situation in such detail. She was telling Bradley about the original plan outlined by Titus and was citing property values, tax rates, and DNR regulations off the top of her head.

Bradley leaned forward on his elbows, listening to Maureen intently. She continued on with what Will had told her about the conversation that morning and the fact that Burr had been meeting with some of the Moon Lake merchants. It seemed she was about to start in on her theory about Eddy questioning Will's competency, but she stopped suddenly and waited.

"Well," said Bradley, turning his pen back and forth in his hands, "what we have here is perhaps a little suspicious, perhaps a little shady, but I'm not sure if passes for anything illegal."

Maureen nodded. Waiting. She was waiting for more. She could tell there was going to be more.

"If you're right," Bradley continued, "and the brother wants to go to probate..." Bradley put the pen down. "He wouldn't have any legal grounds to your half of the inheritance." He looked at Will a moment, then glanced up at Maureen, who made a sound in her throat and then nodded to him.

"Unless," Bradley continued, "he could question Will's competence."

He peered at Will. "Are you listening?"

Will nodded, squirming in his chair a little. He took a deep breath, let it out, took another deep breath, and let it out.

"Would he have grounds?" asked Bradley.

"Yeah," said Will slowly. "He might have grounds. I was diagnosed with autism when I was a kid."

"Have you ever," asked Bradley, "had occasion to be hospitalized in a mental institution?"

Will looked up at Bradley and shook his head. Bradley made some notes on his legal pad.

"Have you ever been examined by a mental health professional?"

Will cleared his throat.

"Yes. Well, does a school psychologist count?"

"Why did you see him?"

"Problems in school," Will said quickly, the memories rising up as clear and sharp as if they'd happened yesterday. "Bullying mostly, but he did some tests. That's where I found out about the autism."

"All right," said the lawyer. "Are you presently on any medications?"

Will shook his head. "Not now," he said, "but I was on anxiety meds when I was younger."

"Any recreational drug use?"

Will shook his head.

"Were you ever on medication for depression, psychosis, or hallucinations?"

"No," said Will, more strongly than he had intended. He was getting a little irritated.

Bradley smiled a little and said, "Don't worry, son. These are all standard questions."

He scribbled a little more on his pad.

"All right," said Bradley, pushing himself away from the desk. "Right now, we have a lot of ifs. If this is the case, if your suspicions are correct, if your brother might want to contest the will, then we will need to be prepared."

He stood up relatively quickly for a man his age—or so it seemed to Will—and came around to the side of his desk. "I have done probate in the past. I don't think the particulars of this case will present a problem; if they do, I have some extra help I can enlist. The cavalry, as it were." He came around to the front of the desk and leaned against it, facing the two of them.

"So what do we do?" asked Maureen.

"Sit tight," he replied, "and keep your eyes open. Nothing stays secret in a small town for long. All right?"

Maureen nodded and stood up. Will followed suit.

"I will need a copy of the family will," said Bradley. "Can you get me one?"

"I think so," said Will. "I'll talk to Mr. LaBlon. He's the family attorney."

"Good," said Bradley. "Don't tell him what it's for. Just bring it to me. Can you do that?"

"I think so, sir."

"Good," he said, and clapped Will strongly on the back. "Good boy." Despite himself, Will flinched.

"I'll do some digging on my own and see what I can find out," added Bradley. "Miss Hansen," he proclaimed, shaking her hand as he walked her to the door. "Thank you for coming to see me."

"You came well recommended," she said. "I know Liz DuBois. You handled her divorce a couple years ago."

Bradley pursed his mouth and nodded. "I remember," he said. "That was a difficult case."

"Yeah, I know," said Maureen. "I heard all about it."

Bradley stopped at the office door. "I'll be in touch. Let me know if your father's status changes, and get me that document." Will nodded. He and Maureen left as Bradley closed the door. Maureen looked at him and smiled.

"I think we're set," she said. She grabbed his arm and walked him to the car. "Let's eat."

She took him back to the house, and while he straightened the place up, Maureen put some dinner on. Will made a quick call to Sully to let her know that he had been tied up all day with family business. As she picked up and said hello, he could barely hear her over the clamor in the background.

"Where are you, Sully?"

"The Onion, Will. You should come down; we're having a great time."

"Well, maybe not," said Will. He didn't know why Sully always asked him the same thing. She knew he didn't like hanging out in bars. Too loud. Too crowded.

"Hang on a second," said Sully. Will could hear moving around on the other end—a door opening, closing, greetings, and begged pardons. Sully finally came back, and the background was quiet. "There," she said. "I stepped outside so I could hear."

"Okay," said Will. "What's up?"

"Well, the news is that there's going to be a town hall meeting about what your family's land transaction is going to look like. You know Bob, Dickie, Jake—all the business owners love the idea of Eddy opening up more land. Some of the residents and others like us—and Mattie—are against the idea. Everybody gets to weigh in. It's only to be fair to the town. I don't think there's any kind of binding policy you guys have to follow."

Will nodded, then remembered to say okay. "Who wanted to have the meeting? When did they decide?"

"I guess it was Mattie's idea. They met a couple days ago. Your brother agreed but didn't seem too happy about it." She paused a moment. "Didn't they tell you about it?"

Will looked down at the floor and then out the kitchen window, at the gray slush covering the lake.

"No, they didn't."

"Well," said Sully, "They probably weren't able to get back to you."

"Yeah," said Will. "That must be it." They were going behind his back. Again. He should have been consulted; he should have the power to veto such a meeting. It was his right.

"So, anyway," said Sully. "I talked to the chief, and he's planning to speak at the town hall. He's also thinking about bringing in some experts to talk about building codes and home designs that have minimal impact on the environment."

"I can talk about moving the otter romp," said Will.

There was a pause. "Yeah, I'm sure that'll have them on the edges of their seats, Will," said Sully. "I'm going to speak about keeping Mirror Lake wakeless and some other measures that we might have to take. Ha," she continued. "I might even have to buy some make-up for my big debut."

Sully roared at her own joke, the boisterous laughter bouncing off the phone like a boulder rolling down a hill.

"Ha," said Will.

"C'mon, Will. It's funnier than that."

"If you say so," said Will.

"Ouch. Burn. Okay," Sully continued. "Well, we'll see you soon. Dodge wants us to meet and coordinate everything. Should I call you tomorrow? Or stop by the cabin?"

"Either one," said Will, glancing over at the stove where Maureen was putting some cauliflower into a pot. He'd leave to go home right after dinner. And maybe a beer.

"All right, Will. Take care." Sully's tone got serious. "And don't worry. We'll figure this out."

"Okay," said Will. "Bye." He hung up and turned back to Maureen, who stood at the stove watching him, steam rising around her.

"What?" she asked.

Will shrugged and sat. He thought about the news of the meeting, the weight of it growing heavier by the moment. Eddy had left him out. Again. They were trying to submerge him, to push him under, and it was working. He felt as if he'd been swallowed whole.

"Nothing," he said to Maureen. "They called a town meeting to talk about the land." Will looked up and blinked. The kitchen was a little blurry. He could barely see Maureen. He felt his breath hitch, and his breathing became noisy. He recognized from somewhere outside himself that he was crying.

"Hey, hey, hey," he heard Maureen say from somewhere. He heard her coming closer and felt her hands on him, pulling him closer to her, holding him like a piece of glass against her. Will put his arms around her waist and sobbed—the years of frustration, loneliness, and aggravation coursing out of him like river water gushing down a spillway.

Maureen said nothing; she just stroked his hair. He held her and then felt her kneeling down next to him, taking his face into her hands. She raised it, her brown eyes staring into his own, beyond his own, deep into his interior. She wiped the tears from his eyes with her thumbs, smiling a little—a smile that reminded Will of his mother.

He stared back into those dark eyes framed by the unruly fox hair; she pulled him closer and then kissed him. Will felt the softness of her lips, her cheek, and he smelled her—a strong musky smell. Without thinking about it—for once—he felt his arms go around her as she clasped his head closer to hers.

Will's head was spinning; he'd never kissed a woman before, but the sensation was somehow familiar to him. He knew he had felt this before—there was a physical memory of touching a woman etched somewhere deep in his consciousness.

She broke off the kiss suddenly and smiled at him, still holding his head.

"Hello," she said. "What was that, Will LeBarron? What do you think you're doing?"

Will started to stutter a reply. Maureen chuckled, put a finger to her lips, and then stood, pulling him to his feet. She went to the stove, turned off the burner, and pulled Will along, like a child on his first day of school, to her bedroom.

CHAPTER 19

NAOMI SAT ACROSS FROM MR. WILLIS Burr, Esquire, swinging her crossed leg. Eddy fidgeted in the chair next to her. She reached down into her purse for her pack of cigarettes.

"Naomi," said Burr, looking up from his reading. "No smoking in the office. You should know that by now, young lady." He had put a mock stern tone into his reedy voice.

She shrugged and said, "Sorry. Habit."

"I'll be finished with this in a second," he added. "Sorry to keep you waiting."

She nodded. It had been a long day. Eddy had come home with the news that the mayor had scheduled a public town hall meeting. She had called Burr right away to let him know what was happening. He listened and told them to come in right away so they could work out a strategy—"To keep all their ducks in a row," he'd said.

"You can go outside if you want."

She looked up. Burr was looking at her and smiling his crooked little half-smile. It was funny. He had nice teeth, but he almost always smiled with his mouth closed. Burr was a tall man who would ordinarily have been good-looking, but he was what her mother had called cross-eyed—what they called "lazy eye" these days. When he spoke to you, one of his brown eyes fixed on you while the other one looked over your shoulder. Naomi could never remember which of his eyes was the good one, so she never knew where to look first. He also combed his hair over the bald spot on the top of his head, which looked awful. But otherwise, he was attractive. He looked big, even muscular under his suit coat, and had a raw, chiseled look to his face—

kind of a cross between Clint Eastwood and Daniel Craig. Not bad.

"What?" asked Naomi.

"Outside," he repeated. "To smoke. You could step right out the back door and have a puff while I finish reading through this."

"No," said Naomi. "No, thanks." She smiled. "I can wait."

He nodded and went back to his memo or whatever the hell it was. Why she and Eddy had to sit there and watch their lawyer do his homework was beyond her. It was stupid. She took a breath, ready to say something, when Mr. Burr held up his hand.

"There," he said. "I'm done. Thank you for being so patient." He glanced over at Eddy, who was still staring at his hands.

"Mr. LeBarron?" asked Burr.

Eddy looked up at him and then glanced over at Naomi.

"Are you feeling okay, Eddy?" asked Burr, putting his elbows on his desk. "Because if you don't mind me saying so, I would say you seem a little off today."

"I'm fine," said Eddy, sounding a little irritated. "This whole thing with Mattie is pissing me off."

"Okay," said Burr. Naomi thought he was going to say something else, but he held back. Instead, Burr stood up and walked around his desk. Eddy had to scoot back his chair for him to get by. Burr leaned against the front of the desk.

"The reason I ask," he said to Eddy, "is that in order for us to continue winning the good people of Moon Lake over to our cause, we have to keep presenting a sympathetic front. We need the people on our side, Eddy. We've done a pretty good job of that so far, but being surly and disagreeable will not win over many more of them. Or let us keep the ones we have."

"Yeah, I know," said Eddy.

"And you," said Burr, crossing his arms and looking at Eddy, who peered at one eye and then the other, "would not like it when people stop backing you up, when you no longer have political and moral support for your claim."

He stopped, smiled—with all his teeth this time—and waited.

"Moral support?" asked Eddy. "All they care about is what they're going to get out of it. The money."

Burr shrugged and smiled—without teeth this time. "Yeah, so?" he said. "What did you expect? Who says moral support can't be bought?"

"I'd like them to show a little more respect for my father," said Eddy. "He did a lot for this town. Shit, he's not even dead yet and everybody's already counting their money. Fucking Dickie Terwilliger had his calculator out this morning figuring out profits."

"Hey," said Burr, putting up his hands. "I know what you're going through. I've been there myself—divorces, involuntary commitment hearings, probates. People can be animals. Believe me, I've seen the entire gamut of bad behavior. But, Eddy," he continued, "you've got to keep the big picture in mind. This whole enterprise is going to make you and Naomi very, very rich. We just have to stay on track. Get the townspeople wanting the jobs, get the merchants wanting the business, and get the mayor wanting the votes." He threw his hands in the air. "With all that energy and desire behind you, your brother and those other tree-huggers won't stand a chance."

"What does it matter so much if they're behind us or not?" asked Naomi. "They have nothing to do with the probate."

"Not technically," said Burr, "but if all of the townspeople are pushing for more land, what's the mayor going to do? He'll be all for it; he has to be. And Judge Reinholz will be presiding at any probate hearing. He has an election coming up next year, too. He's been a judge for over twenty years. You think he'll risk pissing off the entire electorate over this? Nah. He'll lean toward our side. He won't be able to do anything too overt, but he'll look out for himself. You can bet on that." Burr walked around the desk and sat back in his chair.

"So, Eddy," continued Burr. "Tell me about this town hall meeting."

Eddy raised his head and smiled. Naomi saw that the anger had faded—at least for now. He had that spark in his eyes that she'd begun to see that night in the car, that night when she had told him about her vision—their—destiny, that this land, all of it, belonged to them and only to them.

It was what she had privately termed his "hit man" look. He'd had that look when they sat at the kitchen table and started planning how to get their due, their fair share—when he decided to go after Will. He'd had it when they'd first talked to Burr and when he began his campaign on the Moonie merchants. He had it now, talking up the meeting with Burr, planning on who to work on and when, how to get at the malcontents—Mattie, Maureen, and Singh.

"I don't know what's up with Mattie," Eddy was saying, "and I don't know if we can get her to come around."

"Would a little extra green help?" asked Burr, smiling again.

"I don't know," said Eddy, "This isn't about money for her. She thinks that we're railroading Will."

"All right," said Burr. "We could try to change her mind, but do we really need her?"

Eddy shrugged. "She's stirring people up," he said. "Some of them think she's right. I think Bob Singh isn't sure anymore."

"Let's quit screwing around," said Naomi. "Let's put Lewis on the case."

"Lewis?" asked Eddy.

"You've had him handle tough situations before, right? He took care of those guys who were messing with Danny Long, right?"

"You want to me put him after Mattie?" asked Eddy.

Naomi smiled, reached down, put a cigarette in her mouth, and looking Burr straight in his good eye, lit up.

"You're damned right I do," she said. *Fuck that bitch. She screwed my husband one too many times.* "Let's quit fucking around."

Burr looked at Eddy with raised eyebrows. "Well," he said. "I like a woman with an attitude. You got yourself a winner here, Edward." He leaned in his chair, clapped his hands, and laughed. "A real gem."

Chapter 20

Maureen awoke suddenly. It was still dark. She blinked, trying to get her bearings. Through the dim light, she recognized the Rembrandt print on the wall. She was home, in her bedroom at the LeBarron house. Maureen stretched and glanced at the clock on her nightstand. Three forty-six. She lay back, stretching under the covers, still covered with the fog of sleep. Yesterday began coming back to her in patches — sitting down by the lake. Will.

Will. It all came back to her.

She slept with him last night. *Shit.* Maureen tentatively reached over to his side of the bed, although she already sensed he was gone. Empty. The sheets were cold. He'd left silently, not waking her. And apparently he'd been gone a while.

She lay back and dug the heels of her palms into her eyes. Patches of yesterday started coming back to her. Will had come by; he needed her help. They went to see Mr. Bradley. Then they came back and she started to make dinner and then somebody had called. Sully. Will had freaked out, upset about the town hall. It was a classic all-out Will freak-out — crying, shaking. She'd tried to calm him down. A couple hugs, some nice words; she'd stroked his hair and whispered to him. Innocent. Completely innocent. But then that something inside of her took over, that something wild. And suddenly — inexplicably — she wanted him. And she took him.

What had she been thinking? She hadn't been thinking. It just happened — the lust, the want had reared up inside her, a chasm with a screaming need to be filled. She'd felt this with Eddy; she always had. But why Will?

Maybe it had started during the beginning of the land thing, at the house when Mr. LeBarron had first announced it. Will had looked so lost, so helpless, so frightened when he began to understand what was happening. He'd been surrounded. Maureen had seen that Naomi and Eddy were out for blood right away. Mr. LeBarron and Jay hadn't seen it. Will hadn't—not at first—but Maureen had known from the get-go. Eddy and Naomi wanted it all.

Maureen sat up in bed and opened the nightstand drawer. She knew Eddy had left a pack of cigarettes the last time he'd visited. Maureen rummaged around and finally pulled out the pack of Marlboros. Maureen didn't smoke often, but sometimes it helped her think. She found a pack of matches in the wrapper and lit one up.

What was wrong with her? Why had she seduced—there was no other word for it—Will? She liked him but had never been attracted to him. Not really. There'd been moments in the past where she felt something might be there, but never in a way she thought twice about. Not like with Eddy. She'd never been able to help that; that was chemistry, hormones, whatever. A spark. But she never had that urge with Will.

But, to be fair, she'd never really given him a chance. She'd been so absorbed in Eddy that Will never seemed a real possibility. He was a good guy. Odd, awkward, even weird, but his heart was in the right place. He really cared about his forest, his animals. And he liked her. Maureen had known that since she was eleven, but she dismissed it curtly, cruelly, as only an eleven -year old could. She only had eyes for Eddy. He was the one.

Eddy. He used to be a good guy, a really good guy, but this land thing had turned him into a real asshole. Maureen took a drag off the cigarette and grimaced. Stale. But she supposed it wasn't all Eddy's fault. Naomi was the driving force, whispering in his ear, plotting, manipulating, bullying. Maureen knew that Naomi was the one who'd hired Burr. It was just like her.

Naomi was one of those people who thought life had shortchanged her, so now she was going to take whatever back payments she figured she deserved. In spades. *That woman,* thought Maureen, *is a dangerous combination of frustration and ambition. And she's got it in for me. She's made that clear. Well,* she thought as she took another drag. *So what?*

There were times when Maureen almost felt sorry for Eddy, but, truth be told, he'd dug his own hole. He chose to marry Naomi, to stay in Moon Lake, and to fuck around like a billy goat. He thought he had it made. She turned to look at the nightstand. Her eyes had adjusted to the dark well enough to see the outline of the ashtray. She guided the glowing orange tip of the cigarette to the tray and snubbed it out.

There'd been a time back in high school when she'd thought about her and Eddy getting married. A clear and glorious vision—a very pretty dream. Eddy had been damned near everything; not just to her, but to the whole town. He was handsome, funny, smart—although he rarely had to use his brains—and charismatic. He was the starting running back on the football team. People loved him. And he loved them back. Every time he possibly could. She'd been his first—at fourteen; at least that was what he said, and she didn't have too much reason to doubt it. But since then, he'd been spreading it around like Johnny Appleseed.

But this land battle was doing things to him; Maureen had never seen Eddy be so mean, so cruel. He was always used to getting his own way, but he was assertive in a genial sort of way. But now he was angry in his manner—unnecessarily aggressive, almost brutal. Naomi. That's what it was. Why in God's name had he married her?

A motion caught her eye; she turned her head and peered out the window. There, in the scant moonlight, barely visible on the other side of the window, was the figure of a man. Maureen gasped, her heart leaping, instinctively pulled the sheet up over her bare chest, and lay completely still.

She took a deep breath, two, then turned her head slowly and looked back toward the window. She could just discern the outline of his body in the moonlight. Everything else was black. He stood, not moving. All she could make out was the shape. She couldn't even tell if he was watching her or not. If he decided to come in, there wouldn't be a whole lot she could do. Mr. LeBarron kept a gun in his desk, but she didn't even know if it was loaded or not. If she could make it to the kitchen, she might be able to grab a knife or some other weapon.

"Maureen."

The sound was light, feathery, but she knew she'd heard it. She knew that voice. And then it hit her. It was Will standing out there. She knew it was true the instant the notion hit her. She knew his outline, his stance, she didn't know what else. God damn him.

"Will, what the hell is wrong with you?" she said, whispering for some reason. "Standing there scaring the hell out of me. What's the matter with you?"

"Maureen," he repeated. And she realized that one of the bedroom windows was opened slightly. Will must have done it. That's why she could hear him.

"What?" she asked. She knew she sounded pissed and exasperated, but she didn't care. He didn't have the right to scare her like that.

"I'm sorry, Maureen," he said and she saw the dark outline of his hand going to his face. "I'm so sorry." And then he melted away, off the porch and into the blackness of the forested night.

Maureen got up, put her robe on quickly, and ran out to the porch. The wooden boards were cool on her bare feet. She scanned the dark yard, looking for Will's shape in the gradations of blackness. Nothing. It was as if he'd never been there. Maybe he never had been. Maybe she was dreaming. *No,* she thought. *No. I'm not dreaming. He's out there watching me, checking every move I make.*

"Will," she said, the loudness of her voice almost swallowed up by the expanse of the lake and the woods. "Will," she repeated, "if you're out there, come on in. I'd like to talk to you."

Maureen waited, trying to distinguish movement or coherence in the layers of black. She could make out the tree line, a few of the boulders lining the path down to the lake, but little more. Something rustled in the underbrush.

"Will?" she called. Still nothing.

Shit. What did I do to him? She knew that Will had little—no— experience with women, so she'd taken it slowly with him. They had kissed, touched, and when she had reached down to grab him, he'd spurted right away. And, then—miraculously, as if he were nineteen—he was immediately hard again. And ready for more. She'd taken him in hand and guided him inside her. As he entered, he moaned, a low and sonorous sound, almost like the mooing of a cow.

Will had lasted longer that time, almost three minutes, but those three minutes were a frenzy of flailing and shaking, uncontrolled spasms, as if he had lost complete control of his body. Maybe that was why he was so freaked out now. *Well,* she thought, turning to go back into the cabin, *maybe he just needs time and space, a chance to go off into the woods, to go back to what he knows.* She had frightened him off as if he were a wild animal.

A wave of almost maternal concern swept over her as she walked back into the kitchen. She knew he'd be okay out in the woods—that was his element—but she had no idea what his mental state might be. He could be frightened, disgusted, or ashamed. You never knew with Will. He barely knew. Maureen flipped on the light and scanned the room. What a mess. She started clearing off the table, stacking the dirty dishes on the counter next to the already-full sink, and then turned on the tap. She squirted in some dish soap and started in on the pile in the sink.

Maureen would get hold of Sully and ask her to contact Will. Sully knew all his hangouts in the woods, all his secret places. But only she could know. The last thing they needed was to have Naomi get hold of this; she'd use it to prove Will was mentally unstable. *But maybe,* thought Maureen, scrubbing at some dried-on gravy, *maybe the truth is that he is unstable. Maybe he really is mentally ill.*

Will had never really had a great grasp on reality. He'd always been hidden in Eddy's shadow. When they were kids, everything he did paled in comparison to his brother— everything except his passion, his dedication. That sank him even deeper into himself. *But at least Will can love something. At least he can be faithful. That's his strength. And his weakness.*

At least Mr. LeBarron can't see this. She couldn't have faced him if he knew she'd slept with both his sons. He would have expected more from her. He always had. And he'd always been good to her. She would never be a member of his family—she knew that—but she wanted to be closer to them. She always had.

When she'd first slept with Eddy, she'd felt another type of connection to the family—a strengthening, another twig in the nest. The feeling would last a moment or two afterwards and then fade slowly—until the next time. And now she'd had Will. But this was different. This hadn't just been about getting into the fold. She had felt a connection, a definite connection, but it wasn't only about the LeBarron family or that feeling of belonging. Instead, she felt as if she were linked to something deeper, older, and stronger—a primal type of memory, like the first time Eddy had slept with her and entered her and the feeling of his penis inside her seemed familiar, eternal, as if she'd done this a long time ago.

Maureen finished drying the dishes and glanced out the window. The eastern sky was just beginning to gray. Her eyes scanned the tree line. Still no Will. She glanced at the clock. Eight after six. She put on a pot of coffee and sat down at the kitchen table. She knew what she had to do. The hospice didn't open until seven-thirty, and she was going to be there when the doors opened. She'd go and tell Mr. LeBarron what had happened, what she had done, and apologize.

"I'm sorry," she imagined herself saying. "I know there's no excuse for what I did, but something snapped in me when I saw Will shaking and crying like a child. I wanted to hold him, console him, and ease his pain. And I did. I wanted to help you by helping him. But I hurt him worse, Mr. LeBarron, in a different way. I scared him, I made him ashamed. I didn't mean to. It just happened. I'm sorry, sir. I'm so sorry."

Maureen stood up, took a deep breath, nodded, and went to get dressed. It was time to face the music.

Chapter 21

WILL KEPT WALKING; HE WAS ON Turtle Ridge proper now, about four miles past Axman's Point and seven hundred feet above sea level. He was getting into the old growth, the part of the forest no one came to. He could just see the sun through the leafless trees. It was well over the hills behind Mirror Lake now. It was right around seven. Maureen was probably just waking up. He felt a spasm pass through him—a shiver. It still felt like a dream. He and Maureen weren't just friendly anymore. They were partners. Mates.

He felt himself smiling. *All that time,* he thought, *all those years of hoping and looking and waiting and finally, bam, without warning, it hit.* It had been fast, too fast. He needed time to absorb the events, what it meant. There were too many possibilities to work through; would Maureen want to stay with him? Would she think the whole thing had been a mistake? Would she tell Eddy?

Will stopped abruptly. Would she tell Eddy? A wave of emotion passed through him; he couldn't tell what it was exactly. Not at first. Fear maybe. Anxiety. Maybe jealousy. He'd never been jealous of a girl before, but he'd been jealous enough of Eddy. Then he recognized it. He was angry—deeply angry with his brother. Eddy didn't care about Maureen; he treated her like shit. He used her. He used her for sex and for pumping himself up. *Well, he'll never do it again. Not when I'm in the picture. I'll take care of Maureen.* Will started walking again, staring at the deer path in front of him, seeing but not looking.

All he saw was Maureen, her naked body straining against his, her eyes locked onto his and her breasts swaying with the rhythm of their common movement. Sex. He'd observed animals doing it hundreds of times—squirrels, otters, rabbits, foxes, and others. Fish. Will smiled to himself. He'd never imagined. He never knew what he'd been missing. Those lucky otters. *Now I know. Now I know.*

Will reached the mouth of the outermost cave a little later. It was a narrow one, barely two feet across in some places. The opening was sheltered by an outcropping of rock that hid it from plain sight and also kept the rain out. It was a decent shelter. He'd used it more than once when summer storms popped up suddenly, as they had a tendency to do around here. He kept going. Further on beyond the crest of the ridge lay three more cave entrances. *Mouths. They're called mouths, as if the earth is hungry and wants to swallow us up. It should. There'd be fewer people that way.*

The first two mouths were actually connected to the same cave, a long tunnel that opened up into a large cavern, approximately seventy by fifty feet. On the other side of the chamber, a third tunnel opened up on the hillside over Turtle Creek. The cavern's ceiling was high enough for a man to stand in, but as far as Will knew, no one ever came there but him. He continued on. The mouth to the third cave was hidden under a large granite boulder, perched on the hillside like a silent guardian. The entrance was barely large enough for a man to crawl through. Will got down on his hands and knees and squeezed himself into the narrow space. He grabbed onto the old oak root overhead and pulled himself into the main chamber like he had a hundred times before.

The cavern was huge, maybe two hundred feet long and half that wide. Will took out his pocket flashlight and went over to the lantern. He lit it and surveyed the room. His gear lay undisturbed on the floor. He only kept a bedroll, a medical kit, and a change of clothes here. There was plenty of water in the stream that ran through the back part of the cavern, and he only brought food when he knew he'd be staying over. Otherwise, the place would be infested with raccoons, chipmunks, or worse. The last thing he'd want to find in here would be a hungry wolverine.

Will went and sat next to his bedroll on the narrow ledge. It was comfortable enough. He liked to come here when he needed to be alone, either to think or to relieve his ever-present anxiety or to just simply enjoy some solitude. He liked being alone. A lot of people didn't like isolation and didn't understand why others did. Will just liked the absences—no people, no noise, no distractions. Just him and the rock walls. And the faint sound of the constant dripping or the stream running through the back part of the cave; it would be pretty full now. Come summer, it would barely be a trickle.

Will leaned back and closed his eyes. Maureen, the wild Maureen of last night, kept popping up in his mind's eye. He tried to push her away but couldn't. She kept coming back, her face contorted with ecstasy. Will opened his eyes. Would it be like that from now on? Would it be weird, strange? Just being attached to anyone was terrifying to him, but being attached to Maureen would be all that plus—strange. It would make everything different. All these thoughts had gone through his head last night, circling the inside of his skull like water going down the drain. He had gotten up and opened the window, hoping fresh air would clear his head, but the clutter, the noise, the sound of the crows grew unbearable.

Will had to leave. He opened the kitchen door silently and stepped out on the porch, but then he turned back and saw Maureen like a vision, lying bare-chested on the bed. He stood on the porch, looking at her, unable to look away, unable to even blink. There was no way of knowing how long he'd been standing there. She stirred finally, woke, and reached for him. She seemed upset to find he wasn't there. That was good. She lay there, muttering under her breath, and then had lit up a cigarette.

Will was overcome as he watched her, not as he would observe one of his subjects but as something overwhelmingly beautiful. She turned her head toward him and covered herself up. He realized he had said something out loud but had no idea what.

"Will?" he heard her say. "Is that you?"

He opened his mouth to say something but couldn't. The old paralysis had taken hold of him. What was he supposed to say to her? Embarrassment washed over him, and then shame. Will turned and walked away into the woods, onto the path he knew so well that would take him to his places of sanctuary. His places of freedom.

CHAPTER 22

MAUREEN STOOD AT THE DOOR OF THE hospice room staring at the name that had been hand lettered onto an index card and slid into the aluminum frame on the door. Titus LeBarron. She reached up and touched it, sliding her fingers along the letters. It was so powerful, that name. To Maureen, as a young girl, it had seemed like a fairy tale when the beautiful woman had showed up at her door and told her she'd be spending the summer at their cabin.

Mrs. LeBarron had looked like an angel or a sprite, some sort of otherworldly creature. She was slim, elegant, beautiful; everything Maureen wasn't, and—even though she was only eleven—knew she never would be. The woman reminded her of Audrey Hepburn—the same grace, bearing, and goodness. And then the boys—big, buff Eddy, wiry, wound Will, and the father, who'd treated her like one of his own. They'd been her family. After her own father had been killed, Maureen's family had slowly and painfully disintegrated, melting away like a salt block. And then Mrs. LeBarron had picked her up and taken her—home.

Maureen walked quietly into the darkened room, peering closely at the figure on the bed. She could barely make out his face in the dim light. The boxes and little monitors surrounding the bed beeped and flashed. *He's still alive*, thought Maureen. *I made it in time.* She walked slowly to the side of the bed, took off her beret, and held it in her hands. His chest rose and fell slowly, rhythmically, almost painfully, it seemed to Maureen. She cleared her throat.

"Hello, Mr. LeBarron," she said. "It's me. Maureen. I know you can't hear me, but I have something to tell you. Something important." And then the thought suddenly struck her. *What if he can hear me? What if he wakes up and sees me? He'll know. No,* she thought, staring at the skeletal face with the tubes running from his mouth. *No. He's oblivious. He's close to the end. But I still have to tell him.*

"What I need to tell you, Mr. LeBarron, is that I haven't been behaving very well. I know you consider a person's private life to be their private life, but this has to do with me and the boys."

Maureen pulled one of the chairs up next to the bed and sat. She grasped one of the old man's hands, the skin clear and as delicate as tissue paper.

"I've taken advantage of your kindness, sir. You took me in when my father died and my mother was having troubles. You let me stay with your family all summer. And it was great. It was perfect, sir. I felt like I belonged there. I really did. Mrs. LeBarron was so sweet and so nice, and the boys accepted me, too." She felt herself smile, remembering. Eddy had given her a fair amount of shit, but she'd given it right back. "At least after a little while."

"And then you took me into your own home. You gave me a job helping and taking care of you. You trusted me. You treated me like family. You took care of me."

She took a deep breath and watched as his breath condensed and then faded on the inside of his oxygen mask.

"What I did, Mr. LeBarron, that was wrong, was to take advantage of Will. I took him to bed last night. I shouldn't have." She sighed. "He's not equipped to handle that." She looked up at the old man's face. "I mean emotionally equipped. Everything else works fine. What happened was that he was upset about something—"no need to tell him what, that the boys were fighting—"and he started crying, and I held him, and one thing led to another." She looked at her hands wrapped around the old man's fingers.

"It was because I wanted to, Mr. LeBarron, not because he wanted it. I wanted to help him. I wanted to make him feel better. Like a..." *Like a wife*, she thought, but didn't say it. *Like a good woman, a faithful woman.* Which was something she had never been. Except to the LeBarrons. She'd been faithful to them. She'd always loved them. She would do anything for any one of them. That was all she'd ever wanted to be part of. It didn't happen with Eddy, even though they kept ending up together, and now Will was part of it, too—part of her sad little dream.

"That's it, sir," she said, standing, but still grasping his hands, the fingers as light and brittle as chicken bones. "I just came to apologize."

The light on the heart monitor kept flashing at the same rate, the machine next to his bed kept beeping, but there was nothing else—no other response. *Of course not. What did I expect? He's in a coma; he's dying.* She sat back in the chair and stared down at her folded hands. *And what do I do? What does stupid Maureen do? I come in and confess to him. I increase his burden.* Even though he was comatose, even though he was out of it, he still had heard.

Eddy had always said when a person hears something, even if they're asleep, they remember. "Psychologically," he had said, "they understand it. They remember it." Of course, they'd been twelve or thirteen at the time, but she'd always felt there was a grain of truth in that. Although whispering, "I love you," to Eddy when he was asleep hadn't done a goddamned bit of good.

A wave of guilt, tinged with shame, flowed over her. Here was the one man in the world whose family had saved her from poverty, maybe jail—her brother had ended up there—but mostly herself, and all she could find it in her heart to do was increase his misery. Maureen stood up, touched Mr. LeBarron's hand again, then leaned over and kissed him on the forehead.

"I'm so sorry, Mr. LeBarron," she said. "I never wanted to disappoint you." She started walking out, then turned back. She knelt by the bed, her vision blurring with the tears starting to fill her eyes.

"All I ever wanted," she said, staring up at the profile of the one man she admired, "was to call you Dad."

Maureen stood, grabbed a tissue, and, dabbing at her eyes, walked out. As she reached the nurses' station, she saw Naomi coming towards her.

"What are you doing here?" Naomi demanded.

Maureen shrugged. "Paying my respects."

Naomi turned to the nurse on duty.

"This woman is not family to my father-in-law. She shouldn't have been allowed to visit him. It's family members only."

The nurse looked at her, glanced at Maureen and then shook her head.

"C'mon, Naomi," the nurse said. "Everybody knows Maureen is practically a LeBarron. Hell, she lived over there the past couple of years."

Naomi glared at the woman.

"Family only," she hissed. "That's the rule." She stalked off to her father-in-law's room.

The nurse shook her head and smiled up at Maureen.

"Thanks, Ruth," she said.

"Well, I call them like I see them," she said. They both chuckled.

"You know," said Maureen, blowing her nose. "I don't know if I'd leave her in there alone with him too long."

Ruth nodded. "You know, I can never help thinking that woman's up to no good."

Maureen nodded, watching as the door to Mr. LeBarron's room slowly shut on its automatic closer.

CHAPTER 23

THE PARKING LOT OUTSIDE THE MOON Lake Community Center was filling up. The town hall wasn't going to start for another fifteen more minutes, but it was already a good turnout. Maureen glanced at her watch. She'd spoken to Sully earlier, who'd said that Will had been doing some work beyond Turtle Ridge. Sully said she'd go out there to remind Will about the meeting, that he needed to be there to speak up for himself and to speak up for the land.

A red pick-up turned the corner of Martin Road. Eddy and Naomi. There was another car behind them, one Maureen didn't recognize. It followed the red pick-up and parked next to it in the lot. A man got out. Maureen knew she had seen him before, but she couldn't place him immediately. It wasn't until he walked over and shook hands with Dickie Terwilliger that she recognized him. He was that lawyer who'd been running around town trying to line people up to get behind the land development. Maureen felt her anger rising; those two had some balls bringing him here. This was supposed to be a fair meeting. People were supposed to be able to make up their own minds, but now this son-of-a-bitch shyster was going to be sitting there reminding them what they'd be missing if they voted to keep the land pure. Who knows what he'd already promised them?

Maureen was pretty sure that Dickie would be happy with a couple of supply contracts from developers. She knew Jake LaRoche had always wanted land on one of the lakes. That's probably all they had to promise him. Mayor Coogan and the others were a different matter; they'd go for everything they could lay their hands on.

Maureen watched as the lawyer went from Terwilliger and shook hands with Bob Singh. Bob. She'd never have guessed. Who'd be next? Mattie?

"Well, well, well," came a voice from behind her.

Maureen turned. Naomi stood there, hand resting on her cocked hip, a narrow smile playing on the sharp angles of her face.

"Hello, Naomi," said Maureen, keeping her voice measured.

"I don't know what you think you were doing at the hospice the other day. You know it's for family only."

Maureen crossed her arms and said nothing. The March night was on them now, and the temperature was already dropping. She was already feeling chilled in her old windbreaker. She noticed Naomi was wearing a new Kate Spade spring jacket. She smiled. Somebody was counting their chickens.

"What's so funny?" asked Naomi, suspicion marching across her face.

"What do you mean?"

"You were laughing."

Maureen shrugged. "No, I wasn't. Get a grip, Naomi."

Naomi frowned. "Fuck you, Maureen," she said. "Stay out of our way." She strode past Maureen, turning her sideways with her shoulder as she did so.

Maureen glanced at her watch. Five minutes. Lights illuminated the blacktop, and then Sully's little jeep zoomed into view. Maureen held her breath. *Come on, Will. Come on. Be there.*

Sully pulled up at the far edge of the lot and clambered down from the Jeep. The passenger door opened and a form slowly climbed out. Even in the spring twilight, Maureen could tell it was Will. The scarecrow-thin frame—even thinner than usual—his awkward stance, the hesitancy. Sully hurried forward, motioning for Will to join her. She trotted up to Maureen.

"I got him," she said, taking off her glasses and wiping them. She ran a hand through her blond hair, trying to smooth it down. She leaned in close to Maureen. "It took some doing," she whispered. "He doesn't want to be here. He said that more than a few times."

"And," she added, watching Will shamble towards them, "we didn't have a chance to stop at home. He's fairly ripe."

Wonderful, thought Maureen.

Will came up behind Sully and stopped, keeping her between him and Maureen.

"Hello, Will," said Maureen. "It's good to see you."

She hadn't, in fact, seen him since their encounter two weeks ago. He'd been hiding out in the woods all that time. He mumbled a hello and smiled. Maureen caught a whiff of him. Campfire smoke, pine, and the smell of sweat—strong, but not overpowering.

"Chief Dodge is here," said Maureen. "He's up front getting his presentation ready. I don't know if you guys want to join him or go off on your own or what."

"Well, the first thing," said Sully, "is for Will to stop in the office and wash up the best he can. Right?"

Will shrugged again. Maureen smiled at him, but he still wouldn't make eye contact.

"Right," said Maureen. "Will, if you want to save that land and keep it the way it is, as much as that's possible, you have to make your case tonight. And you need to look presentable. Sully's right. Why don't you go over to your office and get cleaned up? I'll tell them you're on the way."

Will finally looked at her—finally. His eyes were brimming with fear. His mouth opened and shut and then shut tight. He nodded.

"You're right," he said. "Yeah." He nodded to Sully. "Let's go."

Maureen watched the two of them walk over to their small office and turned to walk into the Moon Lake Community Center.

God help us all.

* * *

MAUREEN ENTERED JUST AS THE people were getting settled into the main room. It was pretty nearly full, containing almost the entire population of Moon Lake. Jake LaRoche and Dickie Terwilliger were sitting together near the front. Dickie's wife, Alva, was sitting two rows behind him. It was funny with those two. They never sat together in public. Not in church, meetings, picnics, school events, not anywhere. Alva was a quiet woman, as still and deliberate in her manner as Dickie was jerky in his. Maureen shifted her gaze to the other side of the room.

Mattie Doolittle was sitting next to Bob Singh, who was leaning over and whispering something in her ear. She nodded and said something back to him. *Where is she in all this?* She knew that Eddy and Mattie had been carrying on for years. Hell, everybody knew. Which meant, Maureen realized, an unexpected wave of shame sweeping over her, that everyone in the room knew about her and Eddy, too.

There was a long table on the stage. Mayor Coogan and Bill Swanson sat in the middle. They were flanked by Eddy and Naomi on one side and Mildred Tennyson, the other town supervisor, and Eric Parmenter, the town clerk, on the other. Mildred was a retired schoolteacher who, at one time or another, had taught nearly everybody in the meeting hall. She'd retired in her seventies, a few years ago now. She was a friendly soul, always chattering, but sharp as a tack. She seemed like a harmless little old lady, but once those gray eyes of hers latched onto you with a question or an assertion, you stood up straight.

Eric was an accountant who worked in Eagleton. He was younger, with a couple of kids. They'd basically twisted his arm to run—unopposed—for clerk. He was a nice enough guy. He kept to himself most of the time. When he did talk, it was in a quiet monotone. Maureen would have to lean in to hear him, always giving her the feeling she was falling into a well. And that she would rather fall into a well. Chief Dodge sat on Eric's left. He was going through a folder.

Maureen caught Chief Dodge's eye, walked up to the stage, and whispered to him that Will had just come in with Sully and would be joining them in a few minutes. He thanked her and continued working. On her way back to her seat, Maureen saw the Wilson brothers were sitting in the back next to Bill Cobb, Derrick Friendly, and Danny Long—the builders' lobby—and, off by himself at the end of a row, sat old Doc Henderson. She made her way over to him.

"Hello, Doc," she said. He looked up, his green eyes flashing with—what? Anticipation? Amusement?

"Hello, Maureen," he said. "How are you?"

"I'm good. Say, Doc, did you want to come and sit by me? I mean you're all alone up here and I thought you might like some company." Halfway through, she realized she was sounding as if she were speaking to a four-year-old or a moron, or a moronic four-year-old, and she stopped. Doc just smiled.

"Don't you worry about me," he said, his voice smooth and reassuring. He still sounded like a doctor. "I like to sit by myself at events like this. It helps me focus."

"Okay, Doc," she said. "We'll see you later."

She continued back toward her seat. Most of the other families were there—Milt Winston and his crew, Maxie Wright, the plumber, who was there with his wife and kid, and Bob Singh's family, his wife Rosa and their four kids. What a brood. Extremely well-behaved, but still full of it. You could tell. That family wasn't sitting together, either.

Johnny Redd, who owned Olson's Restaurant, was here with his wife. They were sitting next to Regina Schell, who owned Busby's. As far as Maureen knew, neither one of them had been in on the early negotiations with that slimy lawyer. John Benson, the fat postmaster, was near the back, looking bored, but he'd made looking bored a profession. Lewis was back there, too, as far back as he could get. A guy in a suit and a lazy eye was sitting next to him—Naomi's lawyer. She turned back toward the front. Musky Jack was sitting on the other side of Mattie. It was funny Maureen hadn't noticed him before.

Jack had been a fishing guide in Moon Lake for the last fifty years. He worked mostly for Jake LaRoche, but sometimes he hired himself out directly to the resorts. His specialty was musky fishing, although he knew how to catch anything. He was a hunting guide, too, and would go after duck, geese, and deer— but, strangely, he refused to hunt wolves. No one knew why. Jack's face was as worn and brown as an old wallet. He wore his straight gray hair tied back in a long ponytail that always dangled behind the same John Deere baseball cap he'd been wearing for years, and his untamed beard—salt and pepper, not gray like his hair—reached down almost to his belt.

Jack was skinny as a rail, and absolutely no one had any idea how old he was. He didn't smoke or drink or hang around town. The only thing you could really see under all that hair were those eyes, and they were almost hidden under the folds of his eyelids, burned the color of stained pine by years of exposure to the sun and wind. They were brown eyes, but that was really all you could get from them. There was speculation around town—gossip—that he was full or part Chippewa, but, as far as Maureen knew, no one had ever asked. And Jack never said. She was a little surprised to see him here; he usually didn't care much about town business.

Maureen glanced over at him; Jack didn't move a muscle. He just continued to stare straight ahead. Maureen craned her head around, taking in the people, nodding and waving at Alva and some others. She caught Mattie's eye and—after a beat—she smiled. Mattie smiled back. Maureen turned away. They used to be close, especially back in high school, but they'd drifted apart over the years. The Eddy factor. *Well*, thought Maureen. *I guess it is possible to have too much in common.*

Mayor Coogan started banging a gavel on the table—softly at first, but then louder, until he had everyone's attention.

"All right," he said. "I'd like to welcome everyone here tonight. I'd say we have a real good turnout. A real good turnout." He paused and cleared his throat. "I'd like to start by each of us saying a silent prayer for Titus LeBarron, who is up at that hospice in Eagleton."

Jesus, thought Maureen. *At least find out the name of the place.* Everyone bowed their heads with the mayor. After a moment, he raised his head and continued.

"We all know why we're here. The endowment lands that were donated to this state by the Wallace family more than fifty years ago are no longer going to be public lands. They are now to be under the private ownership of the LeBarron family."

He turned and gestured to Bill Swanson, who rose and wheeled a corkboard in from the side of the stage. A map of the greater Moon Lake area had been tacked onto the surface. The mayor navigated his bulk off his seat and waddled in front of the map.

"The original endowment lands are marked in blue," continued the mayor. "They go from west of Moon Lake, past Mirror Lake here, over to Thin Lake down here, and as far back as ten miles over Turtle Ridge. As you can see, there is quite a bit of land. We estimate there's a total of nearly ten thousand acres. Much of it is prime lake frontage."

Chief Dodge looked over at Mayor Coogan and frowned a little bit. *He doesn't like the mayor's interpretation,* thought Maureen. The chief was a straight shooter. He wouldn't sit still for that. Not for long.

"Now this is going to be LeBarron land," continued the mayor, "and like any private landowner, Eddy and Will LeBarron will be the ones with the rights to keep or sell or do whatever they want with it. Eddy here," he gestured to the end of the table. Eddy half-rose and waved to some healthy applause, "recognizes that any decisions he and his brother make will have a huge effect on our little town. The economics alone will bring huge changes. Never mind the problems with growth, taxation, et cetera. So we're bound to consider all the possible changes that might come of this. That's why we're here tonight."

The mayor took out a wrinkled handkerchief and coughed into it. He folded it up as he stared around the room.

"I don't see Will LeBarron here," he said.

"Will's on his way," said Chief Dodge, his voice flat and dry. "He was performing a population count on the deer over on Turtle Ridge," continued the chief. "He's been at it all week. He's over at the office cleaning up right now."

The mayor nodded.

"All right," he said. "Why don't we go over the initial proposal while we're waiting. Will knows about that, right?"

Eddy and the chief both nodded.

"Well, I guess Titus LeBarron had a tentative plan for developing some of the land. I think we should let Eddy give us some of the background on that proposal."

Tentative, my ass, thought Maureen. Mr. LeBarron's plan had not been presented as a suggestion. He and Jay had it figured down to the square foot.

Eddy stood. He put his hands in his back pockets and surveyed the room. Maureen watched him carefully. There was something different about Eddy tonight— something hidden, something calculated.

"My father called a family meeting last winter," he began, "to tell us that there was going to be a big change with the endowment lands. The LeBarron lands," he added. "For those of you who don't know the history, my mother's family originally owned that land. After my parents got married, they gave it to the state to be a preserve. Our family was to be the stewards, meaning we have gotten a yearly stipend to watch over it. The DNR and Chief Dodge," he nodded to the chief, who didn't react, "and my brother Will did a great job keeping the land the way God had intended it to be."

"So," he continued, glancing over at Naomi, who smiled sweetly, "then at this meeting, my father surprised the hell out of me when he told us that there was a provision in the will that stated the land will be handed down to the LeBarron heirs, my mom's family, upon his death. So when my dad passes away," Eddy swallowed. "The lands go to me and Will."

People in the audience were nodding and clucking. This much they knew.

"So," Eddy continued. "My dad wanted me and Will to be comfortable with this inheritance, so he and Jay Pilsner, who worked with us earlier this year, came up with a way to develop some of the land that he felt wouldn't be too harmful to the environment."

He nodded to Bill Swanson, who pulled a transparent overlay from behind the corkboard and laid it over the original map. Maureen thought it looked like the overlay Jay had used that night of the family meeting, but it seemed a little different. Had they altered it? A few people in the crowd stood to get a better look. Murmurs and comments filled the big room. Maureen looked at the overlay closely. She couldn't swear to it, but she thought there was more developed land on it than on the original. She glanced up at Eddy, who was nodding to the crowd. Chief Dodge was looking closely at the map, his eyes narrowed.

"That's it?" someone exclaimed. Maureen couldn't make out who it was. "That's the whole development?"

"I know it's not a lot," said Eddy, "but it's what my Dad thought would be fair."

"But it's not even a tenth of what's available."

Maureen looked back. Andy Wilson was the one doing all the talking. That figured.

"We know, Andy," said Eddy, trying to sound patient, "and that's one of the things we'd like to talk about tonight. Naomi and I are still the caretakers of this land, and we want to find a balance between what's best for us, for Moon Lake, and what my dad wanted."

"And Will," said Mattie suddenly. "Don't forget that Will's a caretaker, too."

Eddy looked at her a moment and then nodded.

"Of course," he said.

"Well," said Andy, "the best thing for the town is to get more jobs, right? And the more land we sell, the more jobs we get. Am I right?"

There was a smattering of applause and a few voices chimed in agreement. Maureen turned around, looking for Will.

Another voice cut through the noise, not loud, but sharp.

"There are other factors to consider," it said. Chief Dodge.

It's about time, thought Maureen. The chief stood and surveyed the crowd, his jaw set.

"What we seem to be forgetting is why people come to Moon Lake in the first place. Do they come to live in a subdivision? To be able to choose from the finest restaurants? Although," he added, nodding to John Redd, "we do have some fine restaurants up here. No," he continued. "They come up here to enjoy the beauties of the natural environment—the lakes, the woods, the wildlife, and the solitude. If you take that away, you take away your own bread and butter. People who want to live in a suburb don't come to Moon Lake for a week. No. They come to stay in the woods, to see the deer, to hear the loons, to catch a fish or two."

"What you see on this map," he said, "is probably all the development these lakes can take without drastically altering the ecosystems. As it is," he continued, gesturing to the areas earmarked for development, "we have to be very careful that construction standards are obeyed to the letter."

Some grumbling came from Andy Wilson's corner of the world. Maureen—and the rest of the room—heard Danny Long tell somebody to shut up.

"In short," Chief Dodge said, "if we have to alter these lands, and I would hope we don't, this is it. This would be the maximum load the environment would bear." The chief surveyed the room, then sat back down.

"In your opinion."

It was Naomi.

"Excuse me?" said the chief.

"In your opinion," repeated Naomi. "I mean this is only what you think, right? This isn't necessarily the final word."

"This isn't an opinion, Mrs. LeBarron," the chief replied, his voice flinty. "This is a scientific conclusion based on the carrying capacity of an environment altered by habitat destruction, introduction of contaminants and pesticides, and all the other destructive forces that occur when parts of the forest are destroyed. You won't find too many environmental scientists who would disagree."

"So, Chief," said Danny Long, standing up, "what kind of construction standards would we be talking about?"

"Well, we would prefer not to see lawn cultivation. Those of you up on Lake Williams know what happens when everybody fertilizes their lawn in the springtime. It runs off into the lake and creates algae growth, sometimes blooms. It can kill aquatic life. Fish. Game fish."

"We would also," he continued, "prefer not to alter shorelines and to leave at least a thirty-foot protected shoreline buffer zone between properties to help preserve habitat."

Someone snorted. The chief frowned.

"Also the minimal use of treated lumber and paints and stains that would be detrimental to the water table. Those are the main restrictions. Of course the normal restrictions concerning septic tanks and wells also apply."

"All right," said Danny. "That sounds fair." He turned. "Right, Andy?"

A small laugh circled the room. Andy half-smiled and slouched forward but was still not looking happy.

"Okay," said Mayor Coogan, "that voices some of the environmental concerns we might have about these improvements. I think we might need to hear about what we could gain. First of all, as mayor, I can testify to the fact that if and when this development would take place, the taxpayers of Moon Lake would feel significant relief." Maureen glanced around the room. Most people looked puzzled.

"Let me explain," said the mayor. "Since this land has been state-owned for as long as any of us can remember, there has no property tax attached to it—and so we haven't been able to collect municipal taxes on it, either. The state doesn't pay taxes on its own property. So, in other words, if there is to be private ownership here, these new owners will pay property taxes, part of which is money we use to improve our city streets, traffic signs, all that. We've been carrying that burden by ourselves. With private ownership, we can get a little relief or use the extra tax money for more municipal improvements like finally building a park, expanding the police force, and maybe having a full-time fire department."

There was a smattering of applause. Dickie Terwilliger stood up and cleared his throat. He glanced around nervously, took a deep breath, and started talking in his rushed, rapid-fire manner.

"You all know me. I'm Dickie Terwilliger, and I own the lumberyard. I was doing a little figuring the other day when we were sitting around and talking about this, and, if all these lots up on the map sell and the new owners build, I myself, as a business owner, will have to hire at least three more full-time people. At least."

There was murmuring from the crowd. A couple of people started nodding.

"And," Dickie continued, his voice rising a pitch, "if that's true for me, it's going to be true for everybody. Bob Singh will have to hire, Mattie will have to hire, Danny will need more guys, and Eddy will probably have to take on somebody new, too.

"That makes sense," came a voice from behind Maureen.

"Yeah."

"Wait a minute." Mattie rose from her seat to face Dickie.

"You said you did some figuring, Dickie," she said. "How did you come to these conclusions? What data did you use?"

"Well," he said, glancing quickly up at Eddy on the stage. Eddy didn't move a muscle. Dickie looked back at Mattie. "I looked at the map and then I figured what building a cabin costs. And then I multiplied it."

"When did you see the map?" asked Mattie.

"Eddy called a meeting with all the Moon Lake merchants. You know that, Mattie. You were there."

"Yes, I was," she said. Mattie turned to face the room.

"For those of you who weren't invited to Eddy's little pre-meeting, I can tell you what happened."

"Hold on, Mattie," said Mayor Coogan. "Everybody knows what happened. It was just an informal meeting."

"Really, Mayor?" Mattie turned to face the crowd. "Did everybody know about this? Mr. Redd, did you?"

He shook his head.

"Regina, did you?"

Another negative.

"Jack?"

"No," said Jack, his voice startling in its range and clarity, a voice that would carry across a long meadow or a wooded ridge.

"Will wasn't there, either. So it seems as if a lot of people here were kept in the dark. Could you tell us why, mayor?"

"I can answer that," said Eddy. "We thought that resident merchants, including you, Mattie, would feel the most impact from the project, so we wanted to give you a heads-up. That's all it was. There was no deep dark conspiracy."

"But you managed to line up support for your development, right? Why didn't you invite Chief Dodge to that meeting? Or Musky Jack? Or Will? You didn't even invite your own brother, Eddy, the man who has just as much a stake in this as you do. Why not?"

"We were worried about him," said Naomi suddenly, her rasping voice cutting across the room. Eddy turned and locked eyes with her. Naomi turned her head and looked back at Mattie. "We still are. We thought the pressure might be getting to him and didn't want to give him any more stress."

"What are you talking about?" Maureen heard herself saying. She had wanted to stay on the sidelines, but Naomi's whiny voice had set her off.

"Excuse me?" asked Naomi, smiling sweetly. *Charming as a skeleton*, thought Maureen.

"What do you mean when you say the pressure is getting to him?" asked Maureen. "Will came out to visit me a couple weeks ago and he was fine. I'm not sure what you're talking about, Naomi."

"Chief Dodge," asked Maureen, "has Will been acting odd on the job lately?"

Somebody in the back of the room snickered. Maureen didn't turn around, but she was pretty sure it was Andy Wilson.

The chief looked toward the back of the room, stared at Maureen a moment, then glanced at the others sitting at the table.

"No," he said. "Will is a dedicated worker. He's very focused on his work. He may come across as a little eccentric to some people, but he's fine. He may seem edgy, but it's the way he is; as far as I know, it's the way he's always been."

Naomi nodded, looked toward Eddy with her eyebrows raised, and shrugged. Her meaning was clear, at least to Maureen, that Will had always been that way, that he'd always been off-kilter. Eddy raised his head suddenly and nudged Naomi. She looked up. The mayor and some of the other board members followed suit.

Maureen turned around. Will and Sully stood at the entrance to the room. Will was dressed in a DNR uniform shirt that was too big for him. His hair was uncombed and his pants were streaked with dark splotches and grass stains. He looked like the forest floor. Will glanced about the room, his eyes flitting nervously from person to person. He nodded to Chief Dodge, acknowledged Eddy, and frowned slightly as his eyes crossed Naomi. Will looked toward Maureen's side of the room. He smiled and waved a little when he saw Musky Jack and Mattie.

When he made eye contact with Maureen, he looked away, swallowed, looked back, tried to smile, and then turned to Sully, who pointed out his place on the panel next to Chief Dodge. Will walked stiffly down the center aisle, made his way to the stage, and sat next to the chief, who leaned in and whispered something to him. Will nodded and whispered back. The mayor stood and looked at the two of them for a moment, waiting. The chief looked up at the mayor and held up a finger. Maureen could hear people shifting in their seats. Someone behind her sighed.

Will stood up and looked behind him at the map and shook his head. He leaned next to the chief and said something.

"C'mon, man," somebody behind her muttered. *It wasn't Andy this time*, thought Maureen. *Maybe Lewis?*

Will finally stood up and asked the mayor, "When was my father's map altered?"

"Altered?" asked Mayor Coogan. "What do you mean?"

"Somebody altered it," said Will. He walked over to the map. "Here," he said, pointing at the upper left side of the Mirror Lake development. "This spot, from the old white pine here to the creek mouth here, was originally undisturbed." The piece of land was tiny, barely an inch long on the map. He stood up and faced the crowd. "Someone altered it," he proclaimed, his voice strident with outrage. Somebody snickered.

"Well, Will," said the mayor, looking toward Eddy and Naomi, and then back to Will. "Who would have done such a thing?"

"I'm not sure," said Will, "but it's not what my father had put up there. This wasn't what he wanted."

"That little piece of land is significant," chimed in Chief Dodge. "It may not look like much, but the creek supports habitat for quite a few species, some of them endangered."

"Somebody altered it," Will repeated, looking fixedly at the mayor. Jake LaRoche shifted in his seat. Bill Swanson half-stood up. He didn't have to; Will wasn't threatening anybody.

Maureen wanted to tell Will to breathe, to calm down, to sit.

"Will," said the chief. Will turned, looked at him, nodded, and then went back to his seat.

"So," said the mayor, "we'll look into how this map was altered." Naomi shook her head as he continued. "But until we figure that out, let's see where Will stands on this whole thing."

He turned his bulk in his seat and gestured toward Will. "Would you like to address the audience?"

Will took a loud breath, exhaled, and put his hands on the table in front of him. Maureen saw his hands were balled into fists. His eyes skittered over the audience, taking in everyone—friends, foes, and those he was indifferent about. *But we're mostly foes to him,* thought Maureen. *Even me.* Will's eyes fell on her at that moment, and in the instant before he looked away, she saw something fluttering behind the fear hardening in his eyes—a longing, almost a plea. Then it was gone.

Chief Dodge put his hand on Will's arm. He looked over at the chief and nodded jerkily. A sheen of sweat already covered his forehead. He took a drink from the water bottle in front of him, something he almost never did because of the plastic.

"Most of you in this room know me," said Will, his voice surprisingly clear and firm. "I know most of you. Most of us grew up here. A few of us moved here." He nodded toward Bob Singh and then to Doc.

"You know me," he repeated. "I've lived on that land my whole life. I tend to it now. I know it better than anyone or anything. And I know it's strong. I've seen it recover from disease, fire, and poisoning." He paused and glanced over at Eddy, who was looking at his hands, and Naomi, who was staring at him with those big cold eyes of hers.

"But it can only take so much." Will shrugged his shoulders and coughed. He glanced over at Chief Dodge, who nodded.

"Many of you remember what Lake Williams was like before it was parceled out. There used to be otters on that lake. There used to be a robust bullfrog population. Loons. They're all gone now. The fish population is one-quarter of what it used to be."

Maureen heard a conversation start behind her. She turned. It was Andy Wilson whispering to his brother.

"The reason the lake was irreparably harmed was because of the development on it," Will continued. "Thirty homes caused those changes."

"What do you mean, irreparably harmed?" asked Jake LaRoche. "My mom lives over on Williams now. It's fine. There's nothing wrong with it. I caught a big largemouth on it just the other day."

Will nodded. "There's largemouths there, sure—plenty of them. And smallmouths. But you won't find as many walleye, perch, or bluegills. And no bullfrogs. The ecosystem has been taken over by a few dominant species."

"And a lot fewer water birds," chimed in Sully. "They don't like too many people around."

"That's right," said Musky Jack, his voice startling the room. "I don't take clients up to Lake Williams anymore. Too much pressure from powerboats, jet-skis, and all that other crap."

"So what if there's no loons?" shouted out Andy Wilson. "You can still get smallmouth, right? C'mon, Jack, are you telling me the tourists don't like to catch smallmouth bass?" Jack turned toward him, still expressionless.

"They like deciding what they want to catch," he said. "And the choices are running out on Lake Williams."

"Whatever," Andy continued. "I don't get what the big deal is. So the loons move out of Williams. People can go and see them somewhere else, right? I mean is making sure we have every animal that was on Noah's Ark alive and kicking in Moon Lake more important than protecting our people?"

"It is imperative that the ecosystems stay as undisturbed as possible," said Will, an edge creeping into his voice. "When one species is disturbed or eliminated, it affects everything else in the system. Eventually the changes make their way up to us."

"That's true," said Chief Dodge. "I don't know how many of you remember when the American eagle went on the Endangered Species List. That was because of DDT being used as an insecticide. It made its way up the food chain until it got into the bodies of these eagles, causing their eggs to have skins that were too thin to protect them. They came close to becoming extinct. The government banned DDT, and you can see the result right now. There are eagles everywhere."

"And the tourists love them," said Mattie. "I had a family in the restaurant the other day talking about how exciting it was to see one in the wild."

"Where were they staying?" asked Jake. Mattie hesitated a beat.

"I'm not sure," she said.

"You're not sure?" said Jake. "Really, Mattie? What's the one lake people can stay on up here?"

Mattie didn't answer.

"It's Lake Williams," he said. "Nobody's allowed on Mirror or Thin Lake because they're endowment lands." He paused a second.

Mattie stared at him, her mouth set in a straight line.

"Eagles get high enough to be seen for miles around," said Will. "It's unfair to say their habitat is restricted to one lake. They range miles looking for their prey."

"So you're saying it doesn't matter if there's development on the lakes they fly over?" asked Naomi.

"No," said Will, turning to her. "Development affects everything. Their food source, their habitat, their habits. Too many people might scare them off."

"But Mattie just said the family on Lake Williams saw it up there and were happy with it. They didn't care if it was living on Thin or Mirror or wherever. They just loved seeing it."

"It's not just what you see on the surface," said Will, leaning forward on the table as he looked over at Naomi. She leaned back in her chair and crossed her arms. Maureen could see the color starting to rise in Will's face. She knew what would be coming—the stuttering, the shaking, and then the shouting, the loss of control.

"You just don't get it," said Will. "You don't understand about the complexity, the interdependence, the beauty of it all." He turned to the crowd. "It's all connected. Our environment is sort of like a car engine. If you have a fouled spark plug, it doesn't run that well. If you have a bad belt, it doesn't run as well. If you neglect it enough, it won't run at all."

Maureen nodded to herself. That was good. She could see Bob Singh and Danny Long nodding their heads.

"So you're telling us we should care more about the land and the animals and the fish than we should care about feeding our families?"

Maureen turned in her seat to see who was doing the talking and saw it was Bert Wilson, Andy's brother. She felt herself frowning. Andy was a loudmouth and a jerk, but Bert was mean. And big. He was standing now and staring angrily at Will.

"You need to take care of your families," started Will, stuttering a little. "I know that. But we need to take care of the environment, too."

"You know, you make me sick," continued Bert, taking a step toward Will. "You and your science and your big words and stupid theories. None of that means shit, man. Not when people ain't working."

Will watched Bert closely as he started making his way up the aisle. He stood and slowly stepped his way around the table to the front of the stage.

"You know some people around town say you're not quite right in the head, that you're a little bit crazy," said Bert. Will flushed. Eddy started to stand up, but Naomi grasped him by the wrist and pulled him back down.

"I think they're wrong," said Bert, continuing up the aisle. "I don't think you're a little bit crazy. I think you're really fucking crazy."

Bert stopped at the foot of the stage. Will was still staring down at him, not moving a muscle. Maureen noticed he had crouched down, bending his knees slightly. She glanced over at Mayor Coogan, who was watching the two of them. *He should be putting a stop to this*, thought Maureen.

"I'm not crazy," said Will quietly, tension coiled in his voice like a snake.

"Hey, Bert," said Eddy, his voice stern. "Cut it out." Everybody turned to look at him. Eddy was standing and staring at Bert, who laughed.

"Defending your retard brother again, Eddy? Just like high school, ain't it?"

Bob Singh had gotten up and was moving toward Bert and Will. Dickie had risen but was simply standing there, looking bewildered. He wouldn't be much good in a fight, anyway. Maureen saw Andy coming slowly up the aisle. She started moving over to cut him off. Chief Dodge had gotten up and was trying to pull Will back behind the table. Lewis stood near the back, hands at his sides and watching closely.

Mayor Coogan banged his gavel suddenly, startling the room. He banged it again.

"I want everyone to sit down. Right now," he said. Everybody just looked at him. He banged it again. "Right now." People sat down. Bert grimaced and started back to his seat.

"I do not want to see a demonstration like that again," he said. "Bert Wilson, you threaten or insult anyone here again, I'll have you removed from this meeting."

Chief Dodge had gotten Will back to his chair. Bert, back in his seat by this time, smirked at Coogan. The mayor shifted in his seat.

"Will," he said, "you were talking about the environmental impact this development might have. Could I ask you something? You and Chief Dodge, of course. What if we built it up slowly, like maybe four lots a year? Would that give the lake and everything a chance to get used to it?"

Chief Dodge nodded.

"That's a good question, mayor—," he began.

"I'm not crazy," Will interjected suddenly. "I resent the implication that I am."

He glared at Bert and then looked over at Naomi, his face frozen in an angry mask. *He's on a slow burn,* thought Maureen.

"Wait a minute, everyone. Let's just wait a minute." Eddy was standing and was motioning for everyone to settle down.

"Will," he said, "just take it easy. We'll get this whole thing cleared up. All right?" He turned to the crowded hall.

"I can tell you all right now that my brother Will is not insane. You got that, Bert?"

Maureen glanced behind her. Bert sat glaring, his arms folded on his chest. Lewis had moved up and was sitting next to him. As large as he was, Bert seemed dwarfed by the other man. She turned back toward the stage. Eddy had turned toward Will, who was still flushed and breathing heavily.

"My brother," said Eddy, turning back toward the hall, "has bad anxiety. It comes from a very mild form of autism, a form of childhood schizophrenia." A murmur flowed through the crowd. "Right, Will?"

Will didn't look up.

Eddy, you asshole, thought Maureen.

"Is that why he almost killed my brother in the sixth grade?" called out Bert.

"No," said Eddy. "That was because Andy was picking on him. Will finally gave him what he deserved."

"He busted my arm," said Andy, holding up his left hand. "He was crazy. I thought he was going to kill me."

"C'mon, Andy," said Eddy. "That was twenty years ago."

"That's not to say he's not nuts," retorted Bert. "He's violent, man."

"So will he be fit to handle the inheritance?" someone asked.

Maureen didn't recognize the voice. She turned and saw it was the man who'd been sitting in back, the one with the cocked eye. The lawyer.

"Excuse me," said Mattie suddenly. "Do we know you?"

"Probably not," said the stranger, smiling. "I'm Wilson H. Burr, Attorney at Law, and I'm representing Eddy and Naomi LeBarron in this matter."

"What matter?" asked Mattie. "This is just a town meeting."

Burr laughed. "I know that. I'm just here to guarantee that Will's condition does not affect his judgment about the land in any way. After all," he said, raising his arms and facing the audience, "we're all in this together, right?"

Maureen stood up. Enough. Will was being railroaded.

"I think," Maureen said, "that you had better speak to Will's attorney from now on."

The smile slowly faded from Burr's face.

"Who might that be?" he asked.

"Everett Bradley," she said. "Of Spencer and Bradley. Up in Eagleton. I don't think he'd be very happy that you're talking about this matter in public. Doesn't that violate some sort of confidentiality or something?"

"I'll call him first thing in the morning," said Burr. "Thanks for letting me know that. I appreciate it."

He sat down and crossed his arms. Everyone stared at him a moment. Chief Dodge cleared his throat.

"I think," he said, "we should let Will finish his statement." He looked at Will, who nodded and then stood. Maureen noticed his face wasn't as red and that he looked calmer. Will wiped his palms on his pants and swallowed.

"I'm sorry all this had to come out," he said. "I think that my anxiety problems are my problems. And to be honest, I don't think it has anything to do with the land transfer. The way I am doesn't affect what might happen to these woods, this land. It's virtually unspoiled, almost exactly the same way it was before the settlers and the lumberjacks came and cut it down the first time. It's all back to old growth status. It's beautiful. You all should come and see it more often. When you walk the trail, you can see dozens of bird species you can't see anywhere else, like long-eared owls and bobwhites." Will held up his hands. "There's just not a lot of those around here anymore. But you can see them back there. And they're beautiful."

His hands started moving as if they had a life of their own.

"And the animals, pine martens and lynxes and fishers and other mammals. I've even seen moose spoor back there." Will's voice rose as he described his land, his creatures, his world.

Maureen glanced around her. Some of the audience members, like Doc and one of the Singh kids, were leaning forward in their seats, listening intently. Others were obviously bored, although Andy Wilson leaned forward when Will mentioned the moose.

"What we have in these woods," continued Will, "is an incredibly beautiful, complex, and intricate system of existence." He stopped and stared out at the crowd, hands clasped.

"Don't you see?" he asked. "It's all there. Life, death, survival, birth, love, devotion, sorrow—it's all there."

Somebody in the back of the room belched and a titter flitted through the room. Will didn't flinch; Maureen doubted if he'd even heard it.

"It's all there," Will repeated. "Everything they experience, we experience. Wolves mate for life, just like us."

"Well," said Mayor Coogan, "most of us." There was genuine laughter. Will forged ahead, still oblivious.

"I saw a vixen, a female fox, that stood by its dead mate for days before giving up on it. Just like us." Musky Jack nodded.

"I've seen swallows go after hawks three or four times their size trying to raid their nest. Just like us defending our young."

Will stopped a minute, staring at the floor and clenching and unclenching his hands. He looked up suddenly.

"What you don't see," he said, "is that when you cut down the trees and plow the land, you're destroying animals, food sources, and homes. And you're destroying part of us all."

Will took a deep breath, looked around the room, and sat down. Chief Dodge clapped him on the shoulder. Maureen glanced over at Eddy, who was staring at his brother and nodding slightly.

"So, Will," said Mayor Coogan suddenly, breaking the silence. "What is your position on the proposed development here?"

"I don't like it," said Will, "and if it was up to me, I'd leave everything the way it is."

A few angry murmurs made their way toward the front. Mayor Coogan banged his gavel. "Let him finish," he said.

"But the map my father shared with us," said Will, gesturing toward the board, "not this map—is what he wanted. I don't want to go against his wishes, so I'll go along with that one."

Will stood up and made his way toward the map.

"What I propose," he said, "is that Eddy's lots alternate with the ones that I'll inherit, so it'll be his, mine, his, mine, and so on," said Will, pointing at the map. "That way, there'll be less impact on the habitat."

"Do you mean to say," said Danny Long, rising from his seat, "that only half the land we see up there will be developed?"

"Yes," said Will, nodding. "I'll be leaving all the land I inherit as it is."

Andy and Bert stood up simultaneously; Andy started shouting angrily while Bert kicked a chair over. Milt Winston was yelling something about pulling the rug out from under all of them. Maxie Wright was sitting with his arms folded but was scowling. Maureen scanned the room. Nobody looked happy except Naomi, who was grinning like a fool as she watched Bert yelling at Will and Mayor Coogan banging on the table with his gavel.

Eddy was sitting down now—just watching the free for all. Not smiling, but not looking too distressed, either. Naomi held his hand in both of hers. Danny Long got in front of Bert and started pushing him back toward his seat. Bert pushed back, shoving Danny onto some empty chairs. Bill Cobb came up on the other side and tried to pull him aside, but Bert grabbed him by the coat lapels and threw him down.

"That's enough."

Everyone stopped and looked up. Mildred Tennyson had stood up next to Mayor Coogan, who was still banging on the table.

"Mayor," she said sharply. "Stop that racket."

It all came back to Maureen in an instant. Mrs. Tennyson in the fourth grade classroom telling everyone to sit down and behave. It worked then, and it was working now. Of course they all recognized the voice and the tone. Mrs. Tennyson had taught nearly everyone there at one time or another.

Bert Wilson glared at her a moment, then looked around him. Danny Long was getting to his feet. Bill Cobb was trying to help him up. Danny had a cut on his face.

"Sorry, boss," said Bert. "I got carried away."

Danny got up and walked slowly over to Bert.

"Don't call me boss," he said. "Not anymore."

Bert swallowed.

"Hey, Danny," started Andy, "Bert didn't mean nothing. He got pissed off. You know how he gets."

Danny looked over at Andy, his face flushed with anger. "Shut up, Andy," he said, "before I fire you, too."

Andy looked at his brother and shrugged. Bert started to say something but stopped. Mayor Coogan banged the gavel on the table, more slowly this time.

"Thank you, Mrs. Tennyson," he said, a note of genuine gratitude in his voice. "I think that before we continue, if might be advisable if Bert Wilson would leave the meeting."

"Hey," said Bert, his voice subdued now. "I got a right to be here."

"Not anymore," said Bill Swanson. "You're lucky the sheriff's not here. You'd be down in Eagleton jail right now."

"Go ahead, Bert," said Andy, guiding him toward the back of the room. "I'll let you know what happens."

He led Bert out the door. Mayor Coogan looked at Ms. Tennyson and the rest of the panel before continuing.

"So," he said, "we're looking at probably about eighty developments over two lakes divided by wooded lots." He glanced over at Eddy, who shrugged.

"I guess," he said. "Ask Will." The mayor looked toward Will, who nodded.

"Although," interjected Eddy, "things might change in the future."

"So this is how it stands right now. Do we have anything else to add?"

Mattie stood up.

"Yeah, Mattie. What is it?"

"I just wanted to say that I'm a little ashamed of everyone here tonight," she said. "Will owns this property; it's his by law, but some of you seem to think that he owes it to you to develop it, which is the last thing in the world he'd ever want to do." She held up her hands.

"Do you think he owes you something?" she asked. "Do you think the LeBarrons owe you something? Do you? Dickie, do you think so?"

He shrugged.

"What about you, Jake?" Nothing.

"Danny?"

Danny shook his head. "What's his is his. I know I don't have any say in the matter. I just came here tonight for the doughnuts."

There was a general laugh and a lessening of the tension in the room.

"Anyone else?" asked the mayor.

Musky Jack stood up. A hush fell on the room. He nodded to the panel and then turned to face the crowd.

"Will is right," he said. "You don't appreciate what we have here. I don't think you really understand it. Because of the LeBarrons, this forest has been allowed to go back to the way it was before this land was settled." He smiled. "Almost the way it was. That would probably take another hundred years. This is the last of the old school land. There is no more of it. There will never be more of it." He turned to Jake.

"You say Lake Williams is fine because it still has small-mouth bass, but it's not a healthy lake. People pour poison into it every day. Fertilizer and weed killer. A lot of the animals that used to live there are gone. More birds and animals will die out because people don't understand the land. They don't know how to take care of it. They don't want to."

"Will," he said. Will looked up. "If I were you, I'd fight all the development. Fight to keep the land as it is." He turned back to the crowd. "All of you people want to take the land. You want to build houses and piers and cut down the trees and plow up the shoreline. And for what? So you can have more money to buy your toys—your snowmobiles, speedboats, jet skis, and all the other noisy machines that ruin our country. No. We don't need more of that. We need to keep what we already have."

He turned to look back at the stage. "You fight, Will, and I'll fight alongside you." Musky Jack sat down. Will nodded.

"Thank you, Jack," said the mayor, glancing over at Bill Swanson. "We'll take your comments under advisement. Anything else?"

Chief Warden Dodge stood up.

"I think what Will has in mind is the right thing. Putting a buffer between domiciles will help mitigate the effect on the ecosystem. But I also agree even more strongly with Jack. There is nothing like these woods in the entire United States anymore. They are a treasure. They should be preserved. Thank you."

He sat down.

"Anyone else?"

Silence.

"All right," said Coogan. "I think we have more of an idea of what this might look like. We're adjourned."

Maureen shook her head. Mayor Coogan had a perfect idea of where things stood; he just didn't like it. Eddy stood and shrugged into his coat while Naomi got her Kate Spade off the coat rack. Chief Dodge was speaking to Will, whose eyes were still darting over the crowd.

He's hearing those crows, thought Maureen. *Those awful crows.* Sully was moving toward the front of the room. Maureen fell in behind her.

"Quite the show you put on here, Agent LeBarron," said Sully as she reached the stage. Will opened his mouth but shut it immediately. Chief Dodge frowned and shook his head slightly. Maureen came up behind Sully and grasped her by the elbow.

"I think he's still a little spooked," whispered Maureen.

"Yeah?" asked Sully, her voice laced with sarcasm. "You think?"

"Okay," said the chief. Maureen turned. Will had gotten up and was following the chief off the stage. Sully motioned for Maureen to join them. They followed the chief and Will into a little room behind the stage. Will was bent over with his hands on his knees, taking deep and regular breaths.

"That's right," said Chief Dodge, "just breathe."

"Hey. You okay, there, buddy?" asked Sully. Will looked up.

"Hey, Sully," he said, his voice little more than a whisper.

"Hello, Will," said Maureen. He looked up. "You did a great job in there," she said. "What you said was beautiful."

"Yeah," said Sully. "You did good."

"Thanks," said Will, standing up. "Thanks. I hope they listened."

Maureen smiled, but no one said anything.

"Well, I don't know about you guys, but I could use a beer," said Sully.

"That's not a bad idea," said Dodge. "What do you say, Will?"

Will shrugged and tried to smile. He turned as someone else entered the room. It was Mattie.

"I think maybe we should get Will something to eat," said Maureen. "How long since you've had a decent meal, Will?"

"I had some mushrooms and jerky this morning," he said.

"No twigs and berries?" asked Sully.

Will shook his head, still all serious. Maureen looked at Sully, thinking that maybe she should lay off the teasing. But it wasn't aggravating Will; if anything, it seemed to be calming him down.

"Well, I'll tell you what," said Mattie. "Why don't you all come over to the café and I'll cook up some burgers."

"All right," said Chief Dodge, unexpectedly exuberant. "Let's go."

"Jeez, Chief," said Sully as they filed out of the room. "I don't know why you're so excited. I doubt it's going to be free."

Chapter 24

Eddy followed Naomi into the Purple Onion. There was already quite a crowd gathered. Lewis was there, leaning on the bar, and Bert Wilson was planted on the barstool next to him. Eddy glanced toward the tables on his left. Jake was sitting with Dickie and Bill Swanson. That was good. Doc was on his usual barstool, halfway through a beer. Burr was sitting a couple seats down from him, leaning against the bar and surveying the room.

Eddy nodded. That was almost everyone. Bob Singh wasn't there. Mayor Coogan wasn't there either, but he wouldn't be; he'd sit on the sidelines until he could see how things stood with his electorate—all four hundred and fifty of them. Naomi greeted Lewis and sat at the bar next to Bert Wilson, who had a shot and a beer in front of him.

"Hey, Bert," said Naomi. "How you doing?"

"Not too fucking good," said Bert, turning his head and glaring at her. Most guys would have backed away from that angry stare, but Naomi just smiled at him before greeting Andy, who was pulling beers behind the bar.

"That fucking Danny," continued Bert. "I can't believe he fired me."

Nobody said anything; they all knew Bert. Any attempt to talk him down would only piss him off even more. Lewis was now sitting sideways on his stool, watching him. And, thought Eddy, letting Bert know he was being watched.

Eddy walked behind the bar.

"Hey, Eddy," said Andy. "I didn't think you'd mind if I got everybody started."

"That's fine, Andy," said Eddy. The Wilsons never missed a chance at a free beer. Ordinarily, Eddy would've called Andy out on it, but he was going to need those boys in the near future. It wouldn't hurt to give out some good will tonight.

"I'll take over now." Eddy poured himself a beer and refilled Lewis's mug. He glanced over at Naomi.

"What would you like?" he asked.

"A brandy Old Fashioned," she said. It figured. It could never be anything as simple as a beer with Naomi. He nodded to her and started making the drink.

"Fuck Danny Long," said Bert. "Fuck him. Give me another shot."

Eddy stopped making the Old Fashioned for a minute and poured another rail whiskey for Bert.

"Hey, Bert," said his brother. "You know, I bet if you go talk to Danny tomorrow and apologize, he'd let you have your job back. Danny's a good guy. He doesn't hold a grudge."

"Fuck him," muttered Bert, although Eddy could tell he was thinking about it.

"I'm a little surprised at Danny," said Lewis. "I thought he'd be one to be pushing a little harder to get things moving. I can't believe he asked Dodge about what kinds of modifications the DNR wants. Fuck the DNR. Fuck all those guys. We're talking about good money coming in, and they're pissing and moaning about loons and shit."

Eddy put the Old Fashioned down in front of Naomi and raised his eyebrows. She half-smiled and took a sip.

"Excellent, sir," she said. He nodded.

Bill Swanson cleared his throat. "Well, you know, Andy," he said. "I think Danny's a realist. The DNR's not going away anytime soon. We're just going to have to live with them and their requirements."

Spoken like a true politician, thought Eddy. He glanced over toward Burr, who was watching everybody with that shit-eating grin on his face. *C'mon*, thought Eddy. *Let's go.* As if he heard him, Burr cleared his throat.

"To tell you the truth," he said, "I'm not as concerned about Chief Dodge and the DNR as I am about Will. I mean, did you see him up there? It didn't look to me like he was playing with all fifty-two cards. No offense," he said, turning to Eddy, "I know he's your brother, but, man, he was shaking and stuttering when he started going on about the wonders of nature, just like he was on *Mutual of Omaha's Wild Kingdom*. I don't think he's living on the same planet we are."

"Take it easy," said Eddy. This was how they'd planned it, that he shouldn't look too eager to go after Will, but he almost felt himself meaning what he had said. *Old habits die hard*, he thought.

"Like I said," continued Burr, not missing a beat. "No offense."

"I never knew about the autism," said Dickie. "I guess it would explain a lot."

"What do you mean?" asked Lewis, his voice gruff. He always did enjoy intimidating Dickie.

"Well, you know," said Dickie, shrugging quickly, "the way he is. Jumpy, nervous, not good around people." He turned to Eddy. "That's what autism looks like, right?"

Eddy smiled. "Actually, that kind of sounds like you, Dickie."

Everybody laughed. Dickie flushed and smiled, trying to look like a good sport. *He actually is a lot like Will, except that he's better with people. Maybe just a little better.*

"Maybe we should ask Doc," said Bill. They all turned and looked at Doc, who was gazing into his beer. He looked as if he hadn't been listening.

"So what do you say, Doc?" asked Jake, his voice a little louder than it needed to be.

"I can hear you fine, Jake," said Doc, without looking up. He motioned for Eddy to get him another beer, which he did. Doc thanked him, took a sip, and then surveyed the room.

"My father was a doctor," he said, "and one of the first things he taught me about the profession was the importance of confidentiality. A patient has a right to his or her privacy. We all do. I won't talk about Will or the state of his health, and I think it's shameful that anyone in this room would do so. Especially," he added, looking over at Eddy, "family."

Eddy shrugged. Doc shook his head.

"Will," said Doc, "is leading a healthy and productive life. That's all you need to know."

Someone guffawed. Andy. Eddy started washing glasses.

"That's all fine and good, Doc," said Jake, "but what do we do when Will's judgment affects everybody? I don't know, but I think he's got a perverted sense of what that land out there is for. I mean are we supposed to look at it and say how pretty it is, or is it something we use to better ourselves? I mean, this isn't just about Will. It affects us all."

"Jake's right," said Bill. "With that extra tax money, we could build a school in town or get a library. The mayor was even talking about a new park."

"Or tax breaks," said Dickie. "You know how much we'd save if all that land were taxed? I bet our bills would be cut in half."

"And think how much we'd make in development," said Andy. "Hell, we'd be working all year long."

"Yeah," added Bert, "and maybe we could even get a McDonald's in town."

Eddy looked at Naomi, who was sipping her drink. She wheeled around on her barstool to face the room.

"Will's not going to change his mind," she said. "You know how he is. What I'm wondering is if he realizes exactly what this means to the rest of us. He doesn't have the same problems we do. He doesn't have kids, and he doesn't pay property taxes because he lives in that little shack out in the woods. He doesn't care about a new school or a clinic or a library or any of that stuff. Hell, even his health insurance is paid for by the state."

She stood up, put her hands in her coat pockets, and walked over to the table.

"I really don't know," she continued, "if he gets it. Like Mr. Burr was saying at the meeting, I don't think he can see the situation clearly."

"He can't see the forest for the trees," chimed in Burr.

Swanson and Dickie chuckled, but that was about it.

"Exactly," said Naomi, looking around the room, table by table, man by man, her silver-gray eyes bright, almost glowing. "Exactly. He's too caught up in his own little world to care about the rest of us. He doesn't see the big picture."

"It's like he's in another reality," said Lewis, not sounding—to Eddy—too rehearsed.

"Exactly," said Naomi, returning to her bar stool. "Like he's delusional."

"Does that mean he's all there mentally?" asked Jake. "Is that some kind of a mental illness?"

Doc stood up abruptly, finished his beer, and put on his coat.

"You leaving, Doc?" asked Eddy.

"Yes, I am," he said, leaving a ten on the bar. "I've had quite enough of this conversation." He started putting on his gloves. "I know what you're up to, and I think it's despicable."

Naomi stared at him, her straight mouth set as firm as a knife edge, her eyes not glowing now. He glared right back, his green eyes snapping.

"I don't know what you mean, Doc," she said, her voice steady, measured.

"The hell you don't," said Doc, and strode out, slamming the door behind him. Lewis stood, went to the door, and locked it.

"What's with Doc?" asked Dickie. No one would look at him. Jake started stroking his moustache. Bill Swanson leaned forward on the table, his hand covering the lower part of his face.

The Wilson boys stood at the bar, waiting. They knew something was up but weren't sure what. Naomi leaned on her barstool, smiling slightly and staring off into the distance. No one was saying anything. But they knew. They were all waiting for it. Naomi turned and looked at Eddy. It was time.

"Let's finish up these beers and close up," he said. "It's been a long day."

Jake nodded and took a sip from his beer. Dickie drained his and stood up.

"C'mon," Dickie," said Jake. "I'll give you a ride home."

"Okay," said Dickie.

"I'll go with you, guys," said Bill, glancing back at Eddy and nodding.

They went out; Lewis locked the door behind them. That left Eddy, Naomi, Lewis, the Wilson brothers, and Burr.

"All right," said Burr, standing up and rubbing his hands together. "I thought they'd never leave. Let's get started."

CHAPTER 25

MAUREEN FINALLY FOUND THE PACK of Marlboro Lights in the kitchen drawer, tapped one out, and sat down. She put it in her mouth and started lighting it before looking up at Will.

"Do you mind if I smoke, Will?" She might be living there, but this was still his dad's house.

He smiled, shrugged, and finally shook his head. *Well,* thought Maureen, *if you don't like it, you need to say so.* She lit up, took a pull off her beer, and leaned back in the kitchen chair. He still seemed a little wound-up from the meeting, but better now. She was glad he'd come back home with her.

"Well," said Maureen. "We'll get hold of Mr. Bradley tomorrow and let him know what's been going on." She took a sip from her beer. "I'll give you a ride into Eagleton."

Will nodded.

"Thanks," he said, and took a sip from his own beer. Maureen leaned forward and started pulling at the label on the bottle.

"What do you do now, Maureen?" asked Will suddenly. Maureen looked up. He was staring at her fixedly, his head cocked slightly to one side.

"What do you mean?"

"I mean since my dad's been in hospice, what do you do here all day long?"

Maureen felt a pang of annoyance. The last thing she needed now was a mother.

"I don't know," she said. "I read, keep the place in shape, you know."

Maureen had continued getting paid even after Mr. LeBarron had been moved out. She figured it was probably an oversight and hadn't cashed any of the checks. When the time was right, she'd give them back. Maureen had saved enough of her own money to hold her over, and the house was well provisioned enough to keep her from going hungry.

"Don't you get bored?" asked Will.

Sure. She missed the old man. She missed any company.

"Nah," she said, taking a drag off her cigarette. "Like I said. I read a little, watch TV a little, and, you know, think about things."

"Oh," said Will.

She waited for him to ask about what things, but he stayed quiet, just looking at her from across the table. Waiting. Staring at her. Staring some more.

"You know," she said finally, exasperated. "I think about a lot of things. I like thinking about the summers we spent here when we were kids."

She glanced up at Will, who was smiling slightly.

"I think about your mom and your dad and how much I wanted to be part of your family. I was thinking about when your mom died and when we all went out on the pontoon boat to scatter her ashes."

"Yeah," murmured Will, barely audible. "I remember."

"You were the closest to your mom. Eddy and your dad were as thick as thieves." She chuckled to herself. "I guess that shoe fits now."

"Eddy's not behind this," said Will. "He would never do this on his own. He's not like that. It was Naomi. She put him up to it."

Maureen nodded. She would never say it to Will, but she knew Eddy better in some ways than his own brother did—and yes, she'd have to say Eddy had it in him to do something like this. Having Naomi around didn't help, but she'd seen that streak of selfishness, even cruelty, in Eddy. It wasn't always obvious, but it was there in the way he treated most of the women he knew. *He doesn't really care about any of them—us—* thought Maureen. *All he cares about is getting laid. Will was right, though,* she thought, getting up for another beer, *Eddy hadn't always been that way.*

"You want a beer?" she asked.

Will made a face and then nodded. "Sure," he said. "Why not?"

"That's right," said Maureen. "Why not?"

She opened the bottles and gave one to Will. He took a sip and yawned.

"You must be tired," said Maureen.

"Yeah," said Will. "It's been a long day."

"Well, when you're ready, you can just go and lie down in there," she said, gesturing toward her bedroom. "I'm probably going to stay up for awhile."

Maureen figured it was best to get things out in the open. She hated tiptoeing around sensitive subjects. Will glanced toward her room and swallowed, then nodded.

"Okay," said Will. "If you want. Otherwise, I can sleep on the couch."

Maureen looked at him as she sipped her beer. *Of course I want. You dope.*

"The other night was—" he started and then stopped, tongue-tied again.

Maureen put her bottle on the table and started picking at the label.

"You don't have to worry about it, Will," she said. "I'm fine. I had a good time. Did you?"

He nodded vigorously.

"It's the most natural thing in the world, Will. Birds do it, bees do it, right?" Will smiled tentatively and nodded.

"It doesn't mean you have to stay with me or live here or any of that, Will. We're just two people giving each other companionship. That's all. If it turns into something more, that's fine, too. If not, not."

Maureen glanced up and was surprised to see Will looking pained. He cleared his throat.

"You mean it's nothing special to you?"

"No, no," she said. "That's not what I meant, Will. Of course it's special. I mean I've known you all my life. We've been friends forever."

Will nodded and took a long drink of his beer.

"What about Eddy?" he asked, a strange note entering his voice. Jealousy?

"That's over. It's been over quite a while."

"You've known him forever, too," said Will, smiling a little.

"He's not like you, Will. He changed," she said, realizing as she said it that it was only partly true, that Eddy always had been sort of a prick. He just used to be better at hiding it.

The phone rang suddenly, shrilly, startling the both of them.

"Who could that be?" asked Maureen, getting up to answer it. "Nobody ever calls out here."

She picked up the receiver and said hello.

"Maureen?" It was Eddy.

"What is it, Eddy?" She glanced over toward Will and made a face.

"I thought you should know," he said, his tone clipped. "Dad passed away about an hour ago."

Maureen felt a sudden clutch, a stoppage, in her chest, as if she'd jumped into the cold lake.

"What happened?" she asked.

"He just died," said Eddy. "We got the call a little while ago. Nobody was there. He was all alone." His voice was flat, dead-sounding.

"Well, at least he's not in any more pain," she said, thinking it was a dumb thing to say as soon as the words came out of her mouth. Everybody said that.

"Yeah," said Eddy. "Is Will over there? We saw you guys over at the café."

Maureen glanced toward Will, who was sitting at the kitchen table and sipping his beer, oblivious to the outside world. She wanted to spare him any more pain, but he needed to know.

"Yeah," she said. "Hang on. Will?"

He looked up and she extended the receiver to him. His face fell immediately; he knew. Somehow. He stood and walked toward her. *Of course it's not unexpected.*

Will mumbled something into the phone. Maureen could hear Eddy's voice crackling through the line, but she couldn't make out what he was saying. Will nodded, said all right, and hung up.

"Well, the old man's gone," he said. "He's finally gone."

Will went back to the table, sat down, and finished his beer. He stared straight ahead; his face completely closed off. For once, Maureen had no idea what he was thinking.

"He wanted to be cremated and to have his ashes spread over Mirror Lake," said Will flatly, as if reciting instructions. "We'll do that in a couple days. Eddy's going to take care of the funeral home stuff."

"Will?" she asked.

He looked up suddenly.

"Are you all right?"

He nodded and smiled a bit. She came over and knelt on the floor next to him. He looked down at her as she leaned on him, putting her head on his knee.

"I'm going to miss him," she said. She felt him move slightly.

"Yeah," he said, "me, too. I think Eddy's going to take this pretty hard. I didn't like the way he sounded over the phone."

I don't like the way you sound now. She had never seen him quite so—well—self-contained, so still.

"Will you stay the night?" she asked suddenly, almost surprising herself. "It gets lonely out here, Will."

He nodded, but she knew he wouldn't stay the whole night. If she knew Will—and she did—he'd bolt the first chance he got. He didn't like being cooped up; he never had. She went to her chair and started peeling the label off the bottle again, feeling Will's eyes on her, full of want—wanting her, wanting his freedom, wanting the land.

CHAPTER 26

THE DOORBELL RANG. BELLA RAN TO OPEN IT. Burr stood there, briefcase held in front of him, grinning like a monkey. Eddy forced himself to smile. He couldn't help it; he just didn't like the guy. Eddy told Bella to go play with her brother. He guided Burr through the worst of the clutter on the living room floor and into the kitchen, where Naomi was already sitting at the table, writing down figures on a legal pad. There were two cigarettes burning in the ashtray.

"Hey, Naomi," said Burr, gesturing at the cigarettes. "Working a little overtime, today, huh?"

Naomi glanced up at him, frowning, and then looked at the ashtray.

"Shit," she said, stubbing out one of the cigarettes. "Sorry. I'm just really distracted. Eddy, would you make sure the kids are in their rooms?"

"I just talked to Bella," said Eddy, motioning Burr to sit. "You want a beer?" he asked the lawyer as he got up to get one. Burr shook his head. He turned and looked at Naomi, who held up a finger.

"I think she's almost done," said Eddy.

"What's she doing?" whispered Burr. Eddy shrugged.

"I'm not sure," he said. "I think she's working on profit margins for different development strategies. For the land."

"Okay," said Naomi, sitting up and putting legal pad aside. "Sorry about that. I wanted to get those figures down while they were still in my head."

"Absolutely no problem," said Burr. He turned to Eddy.

"I just wanted to give you my most heartfelt condolences about your dad," he said. "That was a very nice service." Eddy murmured a thank you. *His condolences,* Eddy thought. *Right. The old man's death was probably the best news Burr had all year.*

"So," said Burr, folding his hands on the table. "The time has finally come, and we're ready to proceed with the next phase of our little project." He rubbed his hands together.

"Are you going to file the competency papers?" asked Naomi.

"Well, I did the background on that, and right now it doesn't look as if we have enough to make a competency ruling go our way." He turned to Eddy. "Your brother is definitely one odd duck, but there's no evidentiary trail that would prove he's incompetent. No arrest record, no record of medical treatment for mental problems, and a spotless work record. He takes care of his own finances. In short, Will LeBarron is weird, but he's legal."

"What about the meeting?" asked Naomi. "He looked pretty nutso there."

"Well," said Burr, "he was acting strangely, but not unbalanced. If anybody looked unstable, it was that Wilson character. Him I could work with."

"Shit," said Naomi.

"Yeah," said Burr. "That's exactly what I said. It's not the best news, but it's also not the end of the world. We still have a few alternatives."

Eddy leaned back in his chair. The lawyer was staring at him—or at least Eddy thought he was. One of his eyes was on him but the other one was skewed over Eddy's right shoulder. You could never tell if he was looking at you or not. One less reason to trust him.

"We could," continued Burr, smiling a little, "accelerate matters."

"What do you mean?" asked Naomi.

"Well, Will is notorious for having poor social skills and sometimes having a short fuse. Am I right?"

"Right," said Naomi, looking toward Eddy, who made an effort not to look at her. He kept his eyes fixed on Burr.

"So the chance of him displaying some type of unstable behavior is more likely in a tense social situation. Am I right?"

Eddy saw Naomi nodding out of the corner of his eye.

"Yeah, like at the town hall," said Naomi. "But you said that wasn't good enough for the court."

"Well, he's also a zealous protector of the land, right? He's kind of fanatical about it, right?" Burr paused a beat and continued. "So if he were provoked enough to react inappropriately, we might be able to use that reaction as evidence in a hearing."

"What are we talking about?" asked Eddy. He didn't like where this was going.

Naomi looked at him, her eyes narrowed.

"What if," said Burr, "Will ran across poachers on his land, people trying to shoot game illegally. What would your brother do?"

"He'd freak," said Naomi, her voice rising. "Oh my God, he'd go nuts. He might even hurt somebody."

"I thought so, too," said Burr. "So if that situation would somehow arise, and Will overreacted, and we documented it, that might be enough to swing our case for incompetency. Or even criminality."

"So what exactly are you suggesting?" asked Eddy.

Burr smiled at him, his eye skewed somewhere over Eddy's right shoulder. *Funny, I thought that was his good eye.* Eddy looked at the eye focused on him. *Is that his good one? Or is this asshole fucking with me?*

Naomi turned in her seat and looked Eddy full in the eye. She was staring at him with that expression that turned everything on her face into sharp angles and hard points. It was a look that said "don't you dare fuck with me on this," and despite all his misgivings, his self-loathing about betraying his father's wishes, and his growing anxiety about Will, despite it all, Eddy knew he wouldn't say no to her. He could, but he wouldn't. He owed her that much.

"Well," said Burr. "Maybe if Will happened to run into some trespassers poaching on the land, we might get what we need."

"Yes," said Naomi, nodding in that quick way of hers. "Something could happen out there."

"Something terrible," added Burr.

"A shooting," said Naomi hopefully, as if she were a child asking for a treat.

"Very possibly."

Eddy said nothing. It all seemed abstract, as if they were talking about some movie or television program—some stranger. Not his brother. Or anyone else they knew. This didn't seem to be part of his life anymore. It didn't seem to have anything to do with him. Eddy felt a difference in the room and looked up. They were both staring at him. Naomi spoke first.

"We'll need your help, Eddy. We need someone reliable to help us out with this. Somebody good. Somebody who can keep his mouth shut."

Eddy looked at her. Her eyes were on him, but they seemed as if they were a million miles away, too, like she was already seeing all that money.

Eddy sighed. He knew what they wanted. They would want Lewis to do it. Or maybe friends of his. Outsiders.

"All right," he said, sitting up. "What do you want me to do?"

CHAPTER 27

"SO YOU GUYS KNOW WHAT TO DO NOW?" asked Eddy. "Any questions?"

Bert and Andy both shook their heads. Eddy leaned on the bar and looked at them standing there dressed in their camouflage hunting outfits, looking like a couple of stupid kids, which was basically what they were. Their jackets actually had fake leaves and branches hanging off them. Eddy thought it was the dumbest thing he had every seen, but the boys had walked in proud as punch, thinking that those plastic suits would fool Will. He would spot them in a minute. Or smell them. Hell, Will would probably be able to hear these guys a mile away. But that wouldn't matter. All they needed to do was flush him out. Then they'd be able to finish what they were going out there to do.

He really wished Lewis would have been around to supervise this one, but his Twin City run was his bigger priority. Eddy had been tempted to wait for him, but Naomi had insisted they go ahead immediately. She said it was so simple even these two dumbfucks could handle it. Now, actually seeing them here in the Purple Onion, he wasn't so sure.

Bert picked up his rifle, checked the magazine, and then took out his pistol to check that. Dan took the video camera out of his backpack and turned it over.

"Remember," said Eddy. "Nobody gets hurt."

Bert smiled. "Nothing human, you mean, right?" he said and laughed.

"That's right," said Eddy. "There should be plenty of game out there. Shoot whatever you want to. Shoot as much as you want. Don't worry about fines or tickets." He glanced at his watch. "I'll drop you off down by the Thin Lake landing. You guys are solid about where to go from there, right?"

Andy nodded.

"Yeah," he said. "We go between Thin and Mirror Lake toward Turtle Ridge and shoot whatever we see until Will finds us. And then I videotape whatever he does."

"All right," said Eddy. "You got that, too, Bert?"

Bert grinned, lifted his rifle to his shoulder, pointed it at Eddy, and said, "Bang."

Eddy stood up straight, went around the end of the bar, and walked up to Bert.

"You stupid asshole," he said quietly. "Point a gun at me again and I'll kill you."

Bert frowned and laid the gun on a table.

"If either of you hurt my brother," Eddy continued, looking at the both of them, "I'll kill the both of you. And your mother. Now go out back and wait in the truck. I'll be out there in a second."

The Wilsons turned and went out the back door. Eddy lit up a cigarette and watched the door as it closed behind them. He was getting a bad feeling about this.

Eddy turned as he heard a door open. Naomi walked out of the women's bathroom, her hands in her coat pockets. She looked at him, her eyes shining as brightly as ice cubes. She looked strangely calm, almost serene. Her face, usually clenched like a fist, was relaxed into lines he rarely saw, even when she was sleeping. She smiled suddenly, slow and easy, relaxed. Eddy took a deep breath. Something didn't feel right. He almost liked Naomi better when she was clenched tight. At least then he knew what to expect.

She put her arms around Eddy's waist and gazed up toward him but not at him, eyes locked on a point somewhere over his shoulder, somewhere beyond him, somewhere beyond herself. He held her tight, as if she were a balloon trying to float away, tugging at the lines, moored only with the one anchor—him, and he was hanging on by a thread.

Chapter 28

WILL HAD BEEN UP BEHIND THE RIDGE, away from the lake, when he heard the first shots. He had been mapping salamander habitat, hoping to relocate part of the lakeside population up here when the developments began. Three shots—four—quickly spaced. That was no target shooting. Somebody was hunting. Will put his notebook into his backpack, shrugged into his jacket, and started trotting along the trail toward the lake. It was April. It could be small-game hunters, who were in season, but they were still trespassing.

These are still, he thought, *the protected lands. Hunters have no right to be here.* Will came to the top of the ridge, squatted down, and peered at the few blue patches of Thin Lake he could see through the aspen and white pines. He could not sight the opposite shore from here. More shots. They were definitely between Mirror and Thin Lake, probably in the ravine.

Will reached into his backpack, took out his shoulder holster and strapped it on. He probably wouldn't need it, but you never knew. These could be drunks or kids or squatters or just tourists. From the reckless way they were shooting though, Will wouldn't be surprised if there was alcohol involved. He left his backpack next to a big white pine and trotted along the trail toward the ravine, staying behind the trees for cover. If he went down to the beach, they'd see him in a minute, and then he'd never catch them.

He reached for his phone but remembered he'd left it in at the cabin. Sully was back in town. He was alone out here, but he wasn't about to go back now. Four more shots rang out, rapidly, close by; then he heard a faint whoop, a yell. Will's heart sank.

They'd gotten something—someone. He started up Axman's Ridge. He was pretty sure the intruders would be on the other side of the ridge, down in the ravine.

Will was sweating now, chugging up the narrow deer trail, up to the top of Axman's Ridge. He reached it and dropped to his hands and knees. He paused a moment to catch his breath, and then crawled slowly over the top of the ridge until he could see down into the ravine below. The meadow along the bottom was bathed in warm April sunlight. It was the first really warm day of the year. Will ran his gaze along the ravine and spotted tracks where the young grass had been trodden down. He could see a few muddy prints near the swollen creek.

Will rose up on his haunches, stood, and started slowly inching his way down the hill. As he reached the edge of the meadow, a murmur of voices drifted in beyond the tree line. Will squatted down, his hand resting on his gun, and waited. The voices got louder. They seemed familiar.

Will watched, counting his breaths, keeping them regular. He braced himself. Two figures emerged out of the woods near the edge of the meadow. The taller one held an adult fox by its hind leg. Three others were hanging from his belt.

A red mist rose before Will's eyes; a pounding filled his head; he could hear the crows begin their screeching. *The skulk,* thought Will. *They wiped out my skulk. All four of the adults. God knows what they'd done with the new litter.*

The smaller man was taking a video camera out of a backpack. The taller man started laying the dead foxes in a row. They were going to tape them and probably post the kill all over the Internet.

Will realized he had risen and was walking. The pounding and screeching in his head was so intense he could hardly see.

He realized, on an almost abstract level, as if seeing himself from the outside, that he was moving towards them. Through the pounding and the mist, he saw the killers and realized that he knew them. Bert Wilson. Andy Wilson. Those bastards.

They had spotted him. Bert was watching him closely and holding his rifle in the crook of his arm. Andy took a step backwards when he saw Will coming. He brought the camera up to his hip. As Will came up to them, he realized he still had his hand on his shoulder holster.

"What the hell are you two doing?" he asked, his own voice sounding like a knife on stone to him.

"Just doing a little hunting, Nature Boy," said Bert, smiling. "We thought we'd get rid of a few of these pests."

Will looked at the mangled fox. He was the younger male with the gray highlights in his coat. Half his head had been blown off. Will raised his eyes to Bert's face. Through the red mist, he could see the bigger man taking a step toward him and bringing the rifle barrel upwards, toward Will, though not quite pointing it at him. Not yet.

"Back off, Nature Boy," he said. "You don't have jurisdiction here no more. This is Eddy's land, and he gave us permission to hunt here."

"You're under arrest," said Will. "The both of you. Trespassing. Hunting small game out of season. Poaching." Saying the words felt like spitting.

Bert glanced at Andy, who nodded back at him. The smaller man cradled the video camera in his hand, pointing the lens at Will, but trying to hide it. He didn't have to; Will didn't give a damn.

"How you gonna arrest us, Nature Boy?" asked Bert. "There's two of us and one of you. You're too much of a chickenshit to do anything, anyway. You never did have any balls."

Will drew his revolver and pointed it at Bert. He resisted the urge to do it now, to exact the justice.

"Drop your weapon," said Will.

"What?" laughed Bert. "Are you going to shoot us over a couple of foxes? These guys? This is nothing, LeBarron. You should have seen what we done with the brood of babies back in the den."

Will felt his fury rising even higher. The red mist grew. He looked at the row of foxes—the young male, his mate, the other vixen, and the father. Three kits, too. Gone. Obliterated. Just like that. Stupidly. Because one asshole had the power to do it.

"Hey, LeBarron," yelled Bert. "I said put your gun down. I don't like people pointing guns at me."

Will shifted his gaze from the dead foxes to Bert Wilson. The big man was grinning through his matted beard, his beady eyes focused on Will's pistol. Will could smell the rank odor coming off him, even upwind. The man stank worse than any wild animal. He was worse than any animal. He killed for no reason.

"Hey," said Bert, swinging the rifle barrel around. "I said put your gun down."

Will didn't move. His anger had settled into the space behind his eyes. It had congealed into intent. Will saw the gun barrel pointing in his direction. The thought occurred to him he might be in danger, but he didn't care. Will did know one thing. These boys weren't getting away with this.

Bert took a few steps off to his left, toward the center of the meadow. Will followed his progress with the nose of his pistol. As Bert continued to his left, Will took a step back, trying to keep both brothers in his line of sight.

"Will," said Andy, still holding the camera. "You know why we're here, don't you?"

Will kept his focus on Bert, who kept edging away.

"We're here," Andy continued, "because we were invited."

Will continued tracking Bert but could perceive Andy moving out of the corner of his eye.

"Eddy invited us, Will," said Andy. "He told us to come out and shoot anything that moved."

Andy took a step forward.

"He said not to worry about you, that you weren't a part of this anymore. That you couldn't do a damned thing about it."

Will's silence emboldened Andy. He took another step forward. Bert continued circling around, trying to get behind him. Will stopped backing up and turned toward Bert.

"Stop," he said.

Bert chuckled, a raucous guttural sound, and kept gliding to Will's right.

"I said stop," said Will. His vision cleared suddenly. His path showed clearly in front of him. This was it. Last warning. Any more provocation from Bert would be threatening an officer of the court.

Bert lazily brought the barrel of his rifle up, pointing it at Will. As the barrel came level to his chest, Will dropped to one knee and fired. The bullet caught Bert near the shoulder and spun him around. The rifle dropped to the ground. Will turned and zeroed in on Andy, who stood gaping, his arms at his side. The video camera hung loose in his hand. Will stood up and without taking his eyes from Andy, walked over to Bert and picked up his rifle. He glanced down. Bert lay still on the ground, arms thrown over his head. His breath was coming in short gasps. He was alive but unconscious. Will turned toward Andy. He was gone.

Will took a last glance at Bert and then trotted after Andy, spotting his trail easily. This was going to be child's play. He caught up to Andy huffing and puffing on the trail to the boat landing in about half a mile. He still held the video camera in his left hand.

"Stop," yelled Will, "in the name of the law."

Andy didn't stop. Will increased his pace and closed to within a few steps of Andy. Leaning forward, he swung forward with his open right hand, hitting Andy on the back of his head. He stumbled and fell. Will stood over him holding his pistol. The other man looked up and then raised his hand in defense.

"Give me the camera," said Will.

Andy looked at him and then slowly raised his hand with the camera. Will took it. He reached down and took Andy's pistol from his waistband. He stepped back.

"Go back and get your brother," he said. "You still might be able to save his life."

"Help me," gasped the man on the ground. "Help me save my brother."

Will glared at him a moment and then in a high-pitched mocking voice said, "Help me. Help me."

He raised his pistol, aiming it at Andy's head. It would be easy enough. Take care of Andy, then go back, finish off Bert. Then wait until dark and sink them in the lake. It was nothing less than what they deserved. They'd come into his territory, his home, and ravaged it. They'd killed his children. It was unacceptable. It would happen no more. No more.

Will tightened his finger on the trigger, aimed, and then, with the screeching rising and mounting in his brain, he stopped. Somehow, his guts began to loosen and his vision began to clear. No. Will lowered the pistol. He wasn't that kind of an animal. Andy lay on the ground. Will turned and walked into the forest, into his home.

Chapter 29

By the time Eddy had answered Andy's call, run out to Axman's Ridge, and gotten the Wilsons back to the landing, Bert had lost a lot of blood. They'd called ahead to notify Doc, who was waiting with the EMTs from Eagleton. Doc patched up Bert the best he could and rode along in the ambulance with him to the clinic.

Andy wasted no time getting back to town. He stood outside the door of the Purple Onion, shouting to the crowd that had gathered that they all needed to go out into the woods and get "that son of a bitch who shot my brother." He stomped into the bar. Most of the crowd followed Andy into The Onion.

Eddy made his way around them, stepping into the back kitchen to wash the blood off his hands before going into the bar to serve up some beers. Everybody was talking at once. Eddy could barely hear himself think over the clamor of voices and clomping of boots.

"What happened?" asked Jake, loud enough to carry over the din. He was leaning against the bar next to Dickie Terwilliger and looking concerned. Or trying to.

"Will shot him for no reason," Andy was saying from his perch next to the bar. "No fucking reason."

An angry murmur rose from the crowd.

"Bert and I were just standing there in the ravine talking and Will busts out of the woods and starts blasting. He got Bert right in the shoulder. I was lucky I got out without being hit."

"Where did all this happen, Andy?" asked Mattie. She was standing near the back of the bar.

"What?" asked Andy.

"Where did it happen?" repeated Mattie, making her way to the front. "Where were you?"

"Who cares about where we were?" retorted Andy. "He shot Bert. That's all that matters. What the fuck, Mattie? Are you saying this was our fault?"

"I was asking you where you were," repeated Mattie, finally reaching the bar. "No one's accusing you of anything." She motioned for Eddy to get her a beer. He poured her one without saying anything.

"It is kind of an unusual question," chimed in Jake. "Considering the circumstances, I mean."

"Well, what were the circumstances?" asked Mattie. She turned to Andy. "That's all I'm asking. You make it sound like Will is tearing around shooting anything that moves. If that's the case, I'd like to make sure he's stopped, too. But," she continued, "that doesn't sound like him. So I'm wondering how it all happened." She took a sip from her beer. "The circumstances."

"Fuck the circumstances," said Andy, stepping up to the bar, putting his face close to hers. "And fuck you."

A couple people in the crowd started saying things—nasty things. Mattie didn't flinch. *You have to give her credit*, thought Eddy.

"Hey," said Eddy. "Back off, Andy. Give her some room."

Andy glared at him, looked back at Mattie, and then turned and put his elbows on the bar. Jake smiled a little bit and then glanced over at Eddy conspiratorially.

"Give me a beer," said Andy. Eddy poured him one.

"How is Bert?" asked Dickie. "Do we know anything?"

Andy slugged down his beer without even looking at Dickie.

"Doc said it could have been a lot worse," said Eddy. "It looked like the bullet just missed the lung, but they won't know for sure until they get him to the hospital."

"He's really lucky. By all rights, he should be dead," said Andy. His voice rose. "Will LeBarron tried to kill my brother. We should go out there and get that son of a bitch right now."

"Nobody's going anywhere," said a voice near the back.

The conversation petered out as the patrons turned to see who was doing the talking. Sully and Chief Dodge stood at the door. The warden stood with his hands in his pockets. Sully was holding a twelve-gauge shotgun in the crook of her arm.

"We just got hold of the county sheriff," said the warden. "Sheriff Delaney. You all know him. He's coming down here to conduct this investigation. They're also sending a team of deputies out to Axman's Ridge."

He looked at Andy and ran his gaze over everyone in the bar.

"Nobody is going out there," said the warden. "It's a crime scene. There will be an investigation, and when they find out who the perpetrator is, he'll be brought in."

"What do you mean, when they find him?" spat Andy. "I told you who did it. It was Will LeBarron. Will shot my brother. I saw him do it. So what the fuck are you going to do about it?"

Sully turned so that the barrel of the shotgun was pointing in the general direction of the bar.

"Careful, Andy," she said, her voice low and measured. "Don't do anything stupid."

"Hey, Andy," said Eddy, his voice causing people to turn. He hadn't meant to be that loud. "Here's that shot you ordered."

Andy turned, looked at him, and picked up the shot. He drank it, sat down, and glared at Sully. The door opened suddenly. Naomi walked in, glancing at the chief and Sully as she passed them.

"What's going on?" she asked.

No one said anything.

"Eddy?"

He looked at Naomi coming through the crowd toward him. She had on a new coat, some sort of a white fur. He felt himself frowning. She never wore white.

"What's going on?" she repeated.

"Will shot Bert Wilson," yelled someone in the back of the bar.

"What?" said Naomi, turning toward Eddy, eyes wide and mouth parted. She looked excited, eager, almost hungry.

Jesus Christ, thought Eddy as he watched Naomi smile slightly, her thin lip curling over her front teeth.

"Yeah," said Eddy. "Andy was there. He said Will went berserk."

"Well, what are we going to do about it?" asked Naomi, turning to face the crowd behind her. Andy Wilson raised his head off the bar, stood up, and looked around the room.

"That's right," he yelled. "Let's go get him."

A few of the others yelled and stamped their feet. Eddy saw Derrick Friendly and Bill Cobb clapping their hands and nodding. Others were shouting. The Redds, John Benson, Dickie, Jake, almost everybody was getting themselves worked up. Naomi stood at the bar with her back to Eddy, reaching behind and grabbing the edge rail, arching her back, and slowly raising her face to the ceiling.

She's loving this, thought Eddy, a small thread of loathing coursing through him. *It's like she's in a trance, some sort of rapture.*

Naomi turned suddenly, as if she'd read his thoughts. Her eyes shined with a cold silver light, like the sun on lake ice.

"Come on, Eddy," she said, grasping his wrist and pulling surprisingly hard. "Come on. We need you." She pulled again.

Eddy jerked his hand back, but Naomi hung on tight, her nails digging into his skin until bright beads of blood peeked out. He grabbed her hand and pulled it off.

"Stop it," he said.

Naomi opened her mouth to reply when a roar filled the room. Almost everybody hit the deck. Eddy ducked. Naomi didn't even flinch. The thick odor of gunpowder permeated the bar.

Sully stood at the door, holding the shotgun steady on her hip, glaring at them through the cloud of smoke.

"That's enough," she said.

Chief Dodge stepped forward.

"Until the county sheriff gets here, we represent the law in this town. You can ask the mayor or Bill Swanson here," he said, nodding toward Bill, who was lying on the floor. "One of your town supervisors." Dodge took a breath and continued.

"There will be no vigilante type of activity in Moon Lake," he said. "Not while I'm chief. We're going to act like civilized people and wait for the sheriff. He and the investigation team should be here shortly. They will conduct the investigation, and we'll do whatever needs doing—but I will not a let a mob loose out there to destroy a crime scene or to do violence to anyone. Anyone caught doing that will be arrested and prosecuted to the full extent of the law."

"He shot my brother," yelled Andy, getting up off the floor.

"If he did," said Dodge, "then he'll be arrested and stand trial for it."

"You can't let him get away," said Andy. A few others in the crowd shouted agreement.

Dodge smiled and exchanged a glance with Sully.

"Don't worry," said Dodge. "Will's not going anywhere. And, truth be told, if any of you are still thinking about going out there to get him, don't. You'd be fools to try it. Will knows that forest better than anybody. And if you go into those deep woods alone to go after him, there's a very real possibility you won't be coming out."

People were slowly getting to their feet and scowling at the two wardens. Sully hadn't moved a muscle. She was watching the crowd intently. Like a hawk. She was serious now, no joking or playing around. Eddy smiled to himself. *Wonder Woman. He knew Sully always had it in her, but still. This was outstanding.*

"Andy Wilson," said Dodge. "We'd like to have you come with us now to give your sworn statement."

Andy scowled, finished his beer, and stood up.

"Fuck you, Chief," he said. "Come and get me."

Bill Cobb and Derrick Friendly moved closer to Andy. A few others turned to face Sully and the chief. Sully shifted her stance slightly.

"It's your choice, Andy," said Dodge. "We just want your version of what happened. And the truth of the matter is, you either talk to us or you'll be talking to the sheriff." He shrugged. "It's up to you. He and his crew might not be as courteous as we are."

"I'm not going anywhere," said Andy. The others closed ranks around him.

"Suit yourself," said the chief. He turned. "Once again," he said, addressing the room, "no one is to go out there and violate that crime scene. If you do, you'll be charged with obstruction of justice."

He nodded to Sully, who started backing out of the room, keeping her eyes on the crowd in front of her.

"Fuck you, Chief," somebody yelled. "Fuck you, too, Sully."

"Get out and take that bitch with you."

Eddy watched as the chief opened the door and Sully backed through it. The chief followed. Eddy glanced around the bar. Andy was backslapping and shaking hands with Cobb and Friendly. Jake was standing at the bar and smirking. Dickie looked scared. Bill Swanson was making a phone call, probably to Mayor Coogan. Mattie stood with her back pressed against the bar. A few of the other patrons were glaring at her. She didn't quite look frightened, but Eddy had the sense she'd rather be somewhere else. He glanced over to Naomi.

She was standing on the first rung of the barstool, staring out over the crowd, looking like a beacon in her white fur coat. Eddy glanced at the wounds in his hand where she'd gouged him. He leaned over and put it under the faucet in the bar sink, washing the blood off.

"You crossed me, Eddy," the voice whispered, almost in his ear. He didn't look up.

"Why didn't you go after him?" she continued. "It was perfect. We could have run right over those two rangers."

Eddy continued looking down, scrubbing his wounded hand

"You're a coward," she said. Eddy finally looked up. Naomi was leaning up on the bar, her face inches from his. "You're weak, Eddy. You fucked up."

"Fucked up what?" he whispered, glancing around. He wasn't comfortable talking about this stuff out in the open. "Sending this crazy mob after my brother? Is that what you're talking about?"

"I'm talking about what we discussed," said Naomi.

"What we talked about never came close to this," answered Eddy, still whispering.

"Why are you whispering?" asked Naomi, leaning forward and smiling. "You have nothing to be ashamed of, Eddy. That land out there is yours. Ours. It belongs to us."

Her voice had risen to the point where nearly everyone in the bar was listening. Eddy turned away from Naomi, grabbed a glass, and poured himself a beer. He watched as Andy Wilson stumbled toward the door, followed closely by Derrick Friendly and Bill Cobb. Eddy looked back at Naomi, downed his beer, and said, "We'll talk about this later. In private."

Naomi glared at him but shut up, watching him as she eased herself down on the barstool. Eddy glanced around the room. Most of the others had turned away. *That's right. Move along.* Andy and his crew had left. *Shit.* He hoped to God they hadn't gone out to Axman's Ridge to look for Will. Not that he was worried about Will. Far from it. It was the other guys he was worried about. He felt an urge to follow them but couldn't with this crew hanging out.

The door opened again. Lewis strolled in. A path cleared for him as he made his way up to the bar.

"Hey, boss," he said, looking around the bar and then back. "Naomi. What's going on?"

"Hello, Lewis," said Naomi. "Will shot Bert Wilson this afternoon. Up by Axman's Ridge."

"What?" asked Lewis. "How did it happen?"

A few people started gathering around them. Eddy saw Mattie being pressed against the bar by Jake and a few others.

"Hey, Mattie," said Eddy. "Would you mind coming back here and washing a few glasses for me?"

She nodded quickly, ducked behind the bar, and started washing the glasses. She shot Eddy a look of pure gratitude. *Well, Naomi won't be happy, but tough shit.*

"Oh, yeah?" said Lewis. "Is Bert okay?"

"He's up at the hospital in Eagleton," said Eddy. "Doc's with him. I guess he lost a lot of blood. We haven't heard anything since."

"How'd you get him out of there?" asked Lewis.

"Me and Andy carried him to the landing. Doc was there with the ambulance," Eddy continued, "and then they ran him out there."

"Tell him about Sully and Chief Dodge," said Dickie, his voice high-pitched and excited.

"Tell him yourself," said Eddy. "You were here." Eddy nodded toward the front of the bar. "Lying right over there."

Jake and a few others chuckled. Dickie flushed.

"I don't know why the rest of you are laughing," said Naomi. "Almost all of you hit the deck when that gun went off."

A wave of assent passed over the group. A few of the guys laughed. Eddy caught Lewis' eye and motioned toward the back room. Lewis nodded.

"Hey, Mattie," said Eddy. "Would you mind watching the bar a little while? Lewis and I have some business."

"Okay," she said. "Eddy?"

"What?"

"Would you mind giving me a ride home tonight?"

Eddy couldn't help smiling. Mattie only lived two hundred feet away. Still. Eddy glanced at the crowd. He couldn't blame her. If he were a girl, he wouldn't want to walk through this bunch in the dark either.

"Sure," he said.

"I can give you a lift, Mattie," said Naomi.

Mattie looked at her, trying to make her smile look genuine, and said, "That's okay, Naomi. I wouldn't want to trouble you."

"No trouble."

Mattie glanced from her to Eddy uncertainly.

"I'll be back in a minute," said Eddy. "Just keep an eye on the bar, okay, Mattie?"

She nodded. Eddy went around the bar and into the back office. Lewis followed him. Eddy glanced back at Naomi, who was sitting at the bar watching him and smiling—not her usual forced expression, but a creepy grin that showed just a hint of teeth.

Christ, thought Eddy, following Lewis back into the bar kitchen. *What the fuck is happening?* He glanced back at the bar. Naomi sat with her arms folded in front of her, now staring at Mattie and half-smiling. Like a cat staring at a mouse. *If Naomi had a tail, it would be twitching. If she had a tail, it would probably be forked.*

Chapter 30

MAUREEN GLANCED OUT THE WINDOW. The sun was just beginning to set. She lay down her book, got a beer, and picked up her jacket. It was still chilly out at dusk, but she loved to watch the sun set over the lake. Going back to her childhood, she'd seen this sunset here a million times, but she never got tired of it. It brought back a lot of good memories.

She stepped out onto the porch and started down the hill toward the beach, patting her jacket pocket to make sure she had her cigarettes. Maureen stepped carefully. The carpet of pine needles was slippery. The day had been sunny and still; even now, there was virtually no breeze. The water was like glass. She cocked her head. Dead quiet. She could have sworn she had heard gunshots earlier, which was unusual out here.

Maureen glanced up at the old white pine on the far edge of the beach. It had been there forever and was over one hundred feet tall. Will had pointed an eagle's nest out to her a couple weeks ago. It was sitting in a sprawling branch about fifteen feet from the top of the tree and held two or three eaglets. From this angle, she could barely see a gleam of white peeking out. Mom already had the kids tucked in. Maureen walked out to the end of the pier and lit up a cigarette.

The sun was sinking slowly, the golden sky sinking into the darker blue just above the tree line. Beautiful.

"Maureen."

The voice startled her. She jumped a little and turned. Will was standing on the edge of the beach with his hands in his pockets. He looked nervous, jumpier than usual.

"Jesus, Will," she said, raising her voice. "You scared me."

"Sorry," he said. "Are you alone?"

She nodded. Will started walking toward her, glancing repeatedly at the path up to the house. He reached the end of the pier and just stood there. She waited a second and then walked down the pier to him. His face, even in the failing light, seemed pale. *Something's wrong*, thought Maureen. *Something happened.*

"Will, what's going on?"

He opened his mouth and shut it and then did it again, then took his hands out of his pockets, clenched his fists, and then put them back.

"I'm in trouble, Maureen," he said. "I shot Bert Wilson."

"What?" she said. "Jesus, Will. What happened?"

"He and Andy were over by Axman's Point. They killed the fox skulk over there. Four adults and three kits. All dead. For no reason."

There was real grief in his voice. Maureen had never seen a reaction like this from Will. Never. Not even at his dad's service.

"I'm sorry, Will," she said, putting her hand on his shoulder. He took a deep breath that hitched into a sob near the end.

"Is that why you shot him?" she asked, hoping to God the answer would be no.

"No. I was going to arrest them when Bert pointed his gun at me"

"Did you think he was going to shoot you?"

Will shrugged slightly. "Yeah. No. I'm not sure," he said. "I must have—otherwise, why would I shoot him?"

"Is he alive?"

Will shook his head.

"I don't know," he said. "I grabbed his gun and left. I took Andy's video camera, too."

"A video camera?"

Will nodded.

"Yeah, it looked like he was taping the whole thing."

Maureen felt herself frowning. Something stunk. *Why would Andy have a camera way out here?*

"Will," she asked. "What did they say when you tried to arrest them?"

"They were talking about killing the foxes, even the kits. Then they started getting after me, saying stuff."

Baiting him, thought Maureen. *Trying to tape him doing what? Losing it? Going nuts on them?* She tried to remember what Mr. Bradley had said. Something about evidence proving that Will was mentally unstable.

"Maureen," Will said. She looked up at him.

"I need help," he said. "I need a few things."

"For what?" asked Maureen. "What sort of things?"

"Salt, matches, some ammunition, a tarp, some rope, and," Will paused a moment. "Maybe some dynamite." He nodded. "That should do it, I think. I have everything else."

"Dynamite?" asked Maureen. "What the hell, Will? Do you really think I have dynamite lying around? And what in God's name do you need it for?"

"I can't let this happen, Maureen," he said. "I can't." He turned and gestured toward the lake and the shoreline, now bathed in the amber sunset. "It's too beautiful, too precious. What they did to those foxes will happen to every living thing out here. Everyone. The otters, the loons, the eagles, the trees, the fish. They'll kill it all if I don't stop them."

Will's hands started shaking as he spoke. He balled them into fists and stuck them back into his pockets. Maureen knew this was an old trick to keep himself under control. She also knew it almost never worked.

"What are you going to do?" she asked.

"I'm going to fight them," he said, staring at the shoreline disappearing into the blackness behind the setting sun. "I'm going to protect this place. I'm going to protect what my mother left me." He turned to Maureen. "And what my father left me, too."

"Will, we have a lawyer. We can fight them in court."

"That reminds me," he said, pulling the video camera from his backpack. "I took this off of Andy Wilson. The entire incident is on there. He taped the whole thing."

He handed the camera to Maureen.

"I want you to keep it safe, maybe give it to Mr. Bradley," he said. "I think maybe that shooting him was justifiable. Don't let Eddy get hold of it."

Or anyone else, she thought, looking up at Will and nodding. He looked at her a moment and finally said, "I can go and look in the shed and see if I can find that rope and maybe another tarp."

He started walking up the hill. Maureen followed him, her mind racing. What the hell was he planning? Some sort of war against Moon Lake? It sure sounded like it. She still couldn't believe he asked her for dynamite. If the situation wasn't so serious, it would be absurd—but Will was dead serious. She watched his silhouette framed by the tall trees. It seemed futile, one man against a whole town.

They had almost reached the top of the hill. Will kept close to the side of the trail, near the cover of the trees. When he got in sight of the house, he squatted down and watched. Maureen had left the kitchen light on. There were no other cars in the driveway and nobody moving around. Still, Will waited and watched. Maureen knelt on the pine needles next to him. She almost reached for his hand but stopped herself.

Finally, he stood and whispered, "It's clear. I'm going to the shed."

He padded away toward the back of the house. Maureen followed.

"Keep an eye out," said Will, as he entered the shed and flipped on the light. Maureen poked her head in. Mounds of dingy orange life preservers, nets, water toys, fishing tackle, and old air mattresses were heaped all over the shed. Rows of cross-country skis and poles lined the rafters. Will sidestepped past them to a locker sitting in the corner.

That was his locker, Maureen remembered, where he had kept all his junk when he was a kid—his science stuff, his telescope and his field books and his dissecting kit. He'd also kept a lot of camping stuff in there. She stepped inside the door to get a closer look at what he was up to.

"What do you have there, Will?" she asked.

He turned and looked at her, almost saying something, but then deciding not to. Will took a musty backpack out of the locker and started putting stuff in—a coil of rope, a tackle box, an old tarp, and a knife.

"Will," asked Maureen. "Where will you be?"

He looked at her and smiled, a full tooth-baring smile. She was surprised. Will rarely showed all his teeth. She realized he was—somehow—enjoying this.

"I'll be around," he said. "Maureen, do you have any of those big plastic storage containers? The real big ones?"

"I think so," said Maureen. She thought there were a few empty ones in the attic. "You want one of those?"

"Yeah," said Will. "I need to put something away."

"What?" asked Maureen. Will shrugged and turned back to the locker. Maureen put her hands on her hips. She'd had enough of this mystery man routine.

"Listen, Will, if you want my help, you talk to me right now. I want to know where you're going and what you're going to be doing. Until then, you can forget about me giving you any help."

Will turned and looked at her, frowning. She knew she'd disrupted his concentration, broken his train of thought. He usually hated that. *Well, tough shit.*

"Okay, Maureen," he said, leaning back on the workbench. "All right. I need the storage container to store my map."

"What map? What are you talking about?"

Will stood up straight and put his hands together, palm to palm, as if he were praying. He looked at Maureen a moment and then was instantly and completely focused on some point in the distance. Will began telling her about the giant map with every single geographic detail and every piece of data he'd ever gathered in his lifetime of working the land. He described migration patterns, population shifts, disease prevalence, and carrying capacity. Maureen crossed her arms and waited for him to finish.

"So," he was saying, "I need to take down the map and put it somewhere safe. There's too much information on it. They might be able to figure out where to find me, not just anybody, not Eddy or Jake or Bob, but Sully or the chief might. Sully definitely."

"Okay," said Maureen. Will stopped suddenly, taken aback at the interruption. "So, Will," she continued, "where are you going to put it?"

Will got that look on his face, that stubborn closed-off look. That defensive look. He wasn't going to say.

"Where are you going, Will?" asked Maureen again, walking nearer to him. He crossed his arms and just looked at her, his mouth set in a straight line.

"Where will you live?" she asked, although she was pretty sure she knew. "You should tell me, Will," continued Maureen. "Otherwise, I'll worry about you. I'm worried about you already."

She moved to put a hand on his arm. Will recoiled, stepping back toward the locker. Maureen stopped and put her hands in her pockets.

"I thought you trusted me," she said.

"I do," he stammered, suddenly his old self-conscious self. "I like you, Maureen. I like that we're closer now, but this is important—more important than anything." He blinked rapidly.

"Are you okay, Will?" asked Maureen, without moving closer. "Are you hearing the crows?"

He shook his head rapidly, almost like a dog shaking off water.

"No," he said. "Nothing like that. It's just that I have to say goodbye now." He sort of smiled sheepishly and looked away.

"What do you mean goodbye?"

"I have to fight, Maureen," he said. "And if I stay here, they'll get me. I'm going out there. If I go back, they'll arrest me and throw me in jail and everything out here will be torn up and destroyed. Everything. I just can't let that happen, Maureen. I can't."

"You know they'll send every cop they can find out there to get you. They'll probably be told to shoot first and ask questions later. You'll be a criminal, Will, an outlaw. And they'll go right ahead and start plowing everything under, anyway."

"No," he said vehemently. "That is one thing that will not happen. This I can do. This I can prevent."

"How?" asked Maureen. "How can you fight off all those cops by yourself? You know Sully and the chief will be out there, too. It's their job."

Will shrugged.

"They can try," he said, smiling his know-it-all smile.

Maureen thought a moment. If anybody could hide out back there, it would be Will. He knew where the food was, where the water was, and where to hide. *And, except for me, he doesn't have anything to lose. And he doesn't even seem that worried about losing me.*

"I wish you wouldn't do this," said Maureen, "but if you have to do it, do it right. I'll talk to Bradley and see if we can use the videotape."

"Thanks," said Will. "I appreciate it."

"Will you come back and see me every now and then?" she asked.

Will smiled a little, shrugged, and asked shyly, almost like a little boy, "Would you like me to?"

"Maybe," said Maureen. "If you promise not to be too much of a pain in the ass."

Will smiled and looked at the ground. *He's determined to do this. There's no way I'm going to be able to talk him into staying. And truth be told, it's probably what he should be doing. In a way, it's his fate. His destiny. He loves the land, and, well, now he was probably going to die defending it.*

"All right," she said. "You better get going, Will. I'm sure those cops will be here anytime. I'll go up and get your container."

Maureen went up to the house and brought the plastic bin back down to the shed. She put it down by the entrance, and Will nodded his thanks. He picked up his backpack and scooted past Maureen to the door. He turned off the light, glanced around outside, picked up the bin, and then glided away silently.

Maureen came to the doorway and looked out at the woods, now blanketed in night.

Will was already gone. Mr. and Mrs. LeBarron, Eddy, and now Will was as good as gone for her, too. What was left? *Well, she thought, trudging up to the hill, I have this place, the house where I grew up. There it is—brick, wood, cement, and glass. A house, just a place. Not a home. I have no family, no kids, no man, nothing.*

Well, she thought, opening the door to her house, *I have myself. And that's really all I've ever really needed.*

Chapter 31

Eddy came up the driveway to his father's old place—Maureen's house now—and turned off the engine. Danny Long and his crew had started clearing the land just to the west of the house and were about a quarter of a mile down the new access road they were building to Anderson Bay. A quarter-mile. Three months, and that was all they had been able to do so far. They should already be laying foundations for the new houses. Fucking Will.

Eddy got out of the old pick-up and wiped his face with his bandanna. It was hot, just past the Fourth of July—prime selling season, and they weren't even able to get anybody up here yet. They could have shown off the land with nothing on it, but word had gotten around about the attacks and people were spooked.

Eddy started down the dirt track, glancing up at the house as he went by. If Maureen was there—and where else would she be—she was still ignoring him. She was pissed at all of them ever since the sheriff had dragged her down to Eagleton. He was convinced—they all were—that she was protecting Will. "Harboring a fugitive," the sheriff had said. Maureen told him to piss up a rope and that she wanted a lawyer. She didn't give away one damned thing.

In spite of himself, Eddy smiled at the memory. He glanced back at the house over his shoulder. Empty windows, empty porch. Empty. She didn't want to see him anymore. She was done with him. She thought he was an asshole, a bastard. Well, he supposed he'd earned that. Still, he missed her. Eddy trudged along the road, little more than a dirt track, not even a logging road.

They'd managed to haul out a few trees, but that was it. Between the sabotaged equipment, the potshots taken at the crew, the booby traps, and the weird little twig and stone sculptures they'd found, Danny Long couldn't keep anybody worth anything on the payroll. The guys were spooked. They knew Will was out here somewhere and that he was on the warpath. They still thought he was crazy, but Eddy knew better. Will was cagey, he knew these woods, and he was determined; he could keep this shit up for a long time.

The sheriff and his men had combed the woods for weeks and never even gotten a whiff of Will. He was holed up, God knows where. There were only about ten thousand acres out here, and nobody really knew much about the land beyond Turtle Ridge. Eddy had only been up in the deep woods a few times himself. It was so quiet up there it was almost spooky. The sheriff had tried to enlist Sully to help them ferret out Will, but the chief kiboshed it, telling the sheriff it was out of their jurisdiction.

Eddy heard voices ahead. He mopped his forehead and his neck with the bandanna. It was humid in the woods, and there was no breeze. Eddy stopped and squatted down. Knowing Will and the way he planned things out, Eddy figured he'd be close by. He knew his brother liked to keep an eye on things. *The question is*, thought Eddy, *where would he be?* He scanned the trees above him carefully, looking for any odd movements or anything else out of place. Maybe a flash of the LeBarron blues. Nope. Nothing he could see. Could Will be on the ground, hunkered into a burrow? *Had he finally*, thought Eddy, smiling to himself, *crawled under a rock?*

Eddy considered calling out, trying to talk with his brother. No, that would be a non-starter. They were at an impasse. He stood, brushed himself off, and headed toward the voices.

Danny Long stood next to the front-loader, a map spread over its fender. He was leaning on his elbows and peering at it intently, as if it were hiding something from him. Two other guys were standing next to Danny. The shorter one kept looking nervously into the trees while the tall one was gazing at the map, too. Eddy didn't recognize either of them.

"Hey, Danny," said Eddy.

Danny turned.

"Hey, Eddy," he said. "I was hoping it was your brother."

"Fat chance of that," said the taller man. "He wouldn't dare show himself out here. He knows what would happen to him."

Eddy glanced at Danny, who raised his eyebrows slightly.

"Max," he said. The tall guy turned.

"This," continued Danny, "is Eddy LeBarron, the owner of this land."

"Oh," said Max, extending his hand. Eddy took it. Max was tall, well over six feet, and skinny. His angular face was covered with a dark stubble.

"And this is Terry," Eddy continued, nodding toward the smaller man.

"Pleased to meet you," said Terry.

He was a little guy, barely topping five foot four. *Naomi is bigger than he is.* He looked pudgy, too—out of shape. *What the hell is a guy like this doing out on a construction job? Danny must be really hard up for workers.*

"How's it going?" asked Eddy. Danny looked at him and shook his head. He reached onto the seat of the front-loader and grabbed a plastic black box with a tangle of wires attached to it.

"We found this next to the ash tree up ahead there," he said. "You know what this is, Eddy? It's a little bomb designed to punch through the tires on one of these loaders."

Eddy raised his eyebrows. That was quite a bit of firepower. Those tires were thick.

"It's a landmine," said Danny. "An IED."

"Holy shit."

"Yeah, there's plastic explosive in the box. Will means business," said Danny.

Jesus. Maybe he really has gone off the deep end.

"But the thing is," continued Danny, "this mine is set up so it only detonates when a vehicle goes over it. If you or me stepped on it, nothing would happen."

Eddy nodded, staring at the ugly little mass of red and black wires.

"Eddy?"

He looked up. Danny was staring at him.

"What?"

"How did Will build this? How does he know how to make stuff like this?"

Eddy looked at Danny and shook his head.

"I don't know. He's smart. It could be he found plans for this thing on the Internet. I don't know."

Danny looked at him.

"Eddy, this is going to mean another delay. We have to go on ahead and scout to see if Will laid any more of these up there."

"Can't you just keep going?" asked Eddy.

Danny snorted. "You know how much one of these tires cost?"

Eddy shook his head.

"At least five hundred bucks. We can't afford to blow one, let alone two or three. And then who knows what else could happen to these loaders."

Danny walked around the loader and motioned for Eddy to follow him.

"Eddy," he said, when they were out of earshot of the other men, "you have to find Will and work this out. This is not working."

"The cops are still looking for him, Danny. You know they've got that infrared thing out here and they're still using those drones to try and find him."

"He's shot down three of those drones already," said Danny. "C'mon, Eddy. We both know they're not going to find Will unless he wants to be found. He can live out here in the woods fucking up our operations for as long as he wants."

"It's just a matter of time, Danny—"

"It is a matter of time," Danny interrupted. "For me. I can give it two more weeks. If we don't have any movement on the project, I'm pulling everything out. We can't afford this, Eddy. I'm losing money every day."

Eddy nodded.

"Okay," he said. "That's fair. We'll figure it out, Danny." He turned to leave.

"What are you going to do, Eddy?"

"He's my brother," he said. "We'll have a beer and work things out."

Danny snorted and then started to laugh. Eddy smiled, shrugged, and turned around, raising his hand in farewell as he walked away.

* * *

Eddy stood on the porch of his father's house, waiting before knocking again. He knew Maureen was in there; her car was in the driveway. She had to be in there. He banged on the door again.

"Maureen, answer the door. I need to talk to you."

He paused and listened. Nothing. God damn her.

"Maureen, we have to talk," he shouted. "I have to get hold of Will. Listen, they're talking about bringing in the FBI now. Things could get really bad. I don't want to see Will get hurt. I know you don't want that, either."

Maureen knew where Will was or at least how to get hold of him. Eddy was sure they were in communication somehow. He'd told Sheriff Delaney that, and he had put the house under surveillance for over a month, but they hadn't seen a thing. Of course, the sheriff and his men were hardly Pinkertons—more like the Keystone cops. Will had probably been going back and forth right under their noses.

"What do you want?" said a voice behind him.

Eddy turned. Maureen stood there on the porch glaring at him. She was wearing a green bikini top and a pair of cut-offs. *She looks good. Sexy. She always looked hot when she was pissed. Her anger lit her up.*

"I need to talk to Will," said Eddy.

"What does that have to do with me?" she asked, crossing her arms.

"Listen, Maureen, I know you've been on his side ever since this thing started. All the way from that first meeting we had in the house here."

Maureen shrugged. "So what?"

"So I know you've been helping him out."

Maureen laughed.

"Even if Will needed help," she said, "and I don't think he does, why would he come to me? He has everything he needs."

"Really?" asked Eddy, taking a step closer to her. "What about ammo? What about electronics? What about this?" He held out the landmine.

"What is that?" asked Maureen.

"You know exactly what it is," said Eddy. "You got him the parts for it."

"You're full of shit," she said, turning away from him.

Eddy grabbed her by the shoulder and spun her around to face him. He felt anger—heat—rushing up inside, flooding him.

"You've got to tell me," he said.

"Don't touch me," she said, pushing him away.

Eddy pulled her close enough so that their faces were almost touching. He had control now—for once. A red mist rose behind his eyes. Everything else faded into the background.

"You used to like this, Maureen," he said. "Remember?"

"Fuck you," she said, shoving him hard enough so that he had to take a step back. He leaned forward, then stopped as a thought struck him—a revelation so true, so obvious, that he was surprised it hadn't occurred to him before.

"You know, Maureen," he said. "I was wondering why you suddenly got so tight with Will."

Maureen glared at him but said nothing.

"I thought," continued Eddy, "that maybe it was the whole idea of saving the land, of—what did you call it—preserving my mother's vision of the land? Maybe even siding with the under-dog, but that's not it, is it?"

Maureen opened her mouth as if to say something, but thought better of it. *I have her. For once I have her.*

"I know what it is now," said Eddy, stepping closer and whispering to her. "You're sleeping with him, aren't you?"

"Fuck you," she said.

I've got her. He could always tell when she was lying. *So I was right.* On some level, he had suspected all along that they were together, but he hadn't known fully, not consciously, until now. And, not too surprisingly, the fact pissed him off. She belonged to him, not to his brother. It made him want her back— it made him want to take her for himself, to steal her away from Will.

Maureen stood her ground, fists cocked. Eddy took a step to the side, keeping his eye on her.

"You're not going to deny it?" asked Eddy. He laughed. "My God. Sleeping with Will. Man, Maureen, you must have been some kind of horny."

"Go to hell," she said. "That's none of your business, Eddy. Not anymore."

"C'mon, baby," he sneered. "Don't you miss me?"

"No, I don't, Eddy," she said, suddenly deliberate. "I don't. You've changed. Naomi changed you. She turned you against your own family. Don't you see she's using you?" Maureen took a step closer to him. "She's using you to do her dirty work, isn't she? Like sending the Wilson boys after Will."

"That never happened," he said. "They came out here on their own. Nobody told them to do anything."

Shit. She'd gotten him on the defensive again.

"They told Will you sent them out there."

"Bullshit," he said. He realized he had been raising his voice and struggled to maintain control.

"Fine," she said. "Deny it, asshole."

"I need to know where Will is, Maureen. Right now. I need to speak to him."

Maureen shook her head. "No," she said. "If I did know, I wouldn't tell you. Besides, you know where he is. He's out there on his land. His land, Eddy. Where he belongs."

"Listen, Maureen, nobody wants to see Will get hurt. I want to see him come in and get help. He is my brother."

"Right," said Maureen. "Your brother. You're trying to steal his land and then you send those fucking knuckle-draggers out there to set him up. They could've killed him, Eddy. Your father would be ashamed of you. He never wanted anything like this to happen."

"Yeah?" retorted Eddy. "Look at this." He held up the improvised landmine. "Will made this and planted it. It's a fucking landmine, Maureen. It's designed to kill people. Do you think my dad would want to see that?"

"I think he would want to see the land that your mother loved be preserved. He told you that himself. His deal was fair, Eddy. It was fair to everybody, but then you and Naomi had to get greedy."

"Will is a killer," said Eddy. "He's sick. He tried to kill Bert Wilson."

"He was defending himself," retorted Maureen.

"That's a lie," retorted Eddy, who suddenly realized he was yelling. He took a deep breath.

"Bullshit," said Maureen between her teeth. "That's fucking bullshit. I know," she said, tapping her chest with her fist, "because I saw the tape."

"What do you mean?" asked Eddy, a kernel of fear forming in his stomach. "What are you talking about?"

"You know exactly what I'm talking about. You sent the Wilsons out here to provoke Will and get it all on videotape. You wanted to prove he was legally incompetent. You set him up. Your own brother."

Eddy stared at her. Andy had told him that he'd lost the camera, but he must have been lying. How else would Maureen even have known about the tape?

"Oh, yeah?" he said. "I don't believe it. Where is this so-called videotape?"

"In legal custody," said Maureen. "Where you can't get at it."

"Bullshit," retorted Eddy. "That's a load of crap."

"C'mon, Eddy," said Maureen. "You know it's true. The only thing," she continued, "is that you don't know what's on it and now you won't be able to find out. Not until they play it in court."

Eddy took a deep breath. *Shit.* He needed time to sort this out. If Maureen—more likely her lawyer—had that tape, he and Naomi had no case against Will. They needed the videotape. Maureen had to get it for him.

"You're cornered," said Maureen. "You're done."

She'd won again. Eddy looked at her. Standing there in that skimpy top, sneering at him. That slut. Then something snapped; his anger rose suddenly, uncontrollably. *No, I don't care if she hates me or not. She's mine.* He took a quick step across the porch and grabbed her by the wrist.

Maureen gasped in pain and surprise and then struck at his face with her free hand. Eddy felt her nails scratch him. He twisted her arm, spinning her around, bent her wrist up behind her back, and then put her in a half-nelson with his free arm.

"Listen, you bitch," he said. "We're going to get that land whether you like it or not. And if either you or Will get in our way, you're going to get hurt."

Maureen arched her back and kicked blindly, hitting him in the shin. It didn't matter; he couldn't feel it anyway. All he wanted was to take Maureen, to take her back from Will, to take her for himself. Eddy released her wrist, reached around and grabbed her breast. He squeezed hard and heard her whimper in pain through the roaring in his ears. She struggled against him; he tightened his chokehold until she stopped.

"If you keep protecting him, sheltering him, then you'll be in our way, too," he whispered in her ear. "And," he continued, "something bad might happen to you, Maureen. An accident. You might bump your head and fall in the lake. You could get into a car wreck. Or," he said, lifting her off the ground with the half-nelson, his other hand still clamped on her breast, "you could get attacked out here all by yourself."

She stopped struggling. Eddy lowered her to the ground where she lay gasping. She looked back at Eddy with a look he had never seen before. Fear. He felt himself smiling, a surge of power filling his chest. Eddy knelt behind her, forcing her flat to the ground. He grabbed her hair, pulling her head back, and reached forward to undo her pants. He stopped as he heard a creaking and then a sound of something rolling. Something big.

He looked across the yard and saw his red pickup starting to roll down the hill toward the lake. Eddy swore, got off Maureen, and jumped off the porch, chasing it. It was picking up speed as it careened down the path toward the pier, bouncing off the trunks of pine trees as it sped toward the water.

Shit. He'd never make it. He slowed and then stopped, watching as the truck rolled into the water, narrowly missing the pier. It went all the way in, floated out a little, and then slowly started to sink.

Eddy watched it a moment. How the fuck did that happen? He knew he'd put it in park. Will. It had to be Will. Eddy looked back toward the house and started trotting up the hill. When he reached the yard, he dropped to one knee and started scanning the tree line. Will would be in there by now, behind the trees, but he'd stay close enough to see. There was no trace of Maureen on the porch.

"Will!" he yelled.

Nothing. Eddy climbed to his feet and looked back toward the lake. The Ford was already completely underwater. *Fuck.* It would cost a fortune to get it pulled out of there. Eddy started taking out his cellphone when he felt a crack and a white flash exploded across his vision, jolting his head forward. It felt as if his brain had come loose and was clattering around inside his skull. Eddy staggered sideways, trying to keep his footing, when it hit him again. He instinctively reached back, trying to grab his attacker, but lost his footing. He fell heavily, oblivion close behind him.

Eddy opened his eyes. The light hurt. He was lying in the yard of his father's house. His head was throbbing and he couldn't focus. What happened? He remembered pieces—the white flash, the contact, and falling. Somebody had whacked him from behind. Eddy blinked, raised his head, and looked around. He seemed to be alone. He slowly raised himself up off the ground. Maureen was gone. Whoever had hit him was gone. Where was his truck? It slowly started to come back. Eddy limped over toward the lake. He could barely see the red of the truck glimmering through the water.

Fucking Will, he thought, touching the back of his head gingerly. It was him. It had to have been him. Will had rolled the truck down the hill to distract him and then snuck up and whacked him from behind. Eddy glanced back up at the house. He brought his hand around and looked at it. No blood. He supposed that was good, although he was still pretty woozy. Was Maureen still there?

"Maureen," he called out, wincing.

He started up the porch. He called out again and then tried the door. Locked. Maureen never usually locked her doors. He glanced around the yard again. She wasn't there—she'd gone. Will must have taken her with him. He thought he was protecting her.

Maybe he thought I was really going to hurt her, thought Eddy, remembering the chokehold and forcing her down. *No,* he thought. He was pissed at her, but he wouldn't have hurt her. He'd wanted her. Bad. That was all. Eddy suddenly remembered the look she'd given him, the only time he'd seen Maureen that scared, and felt a pang of guilt. What had he done? This was Maureen. His Maureen.

Eddy rubbed the back of his head and started down the road. He needed Danny to give him a ride back into town. He was going to have to get Vic Sereno out here with his rig to winch his truck out of the lake. It was probably fucking ruined and would cost a fortune to fix, never mind the fine the DNR would give him for immersing a vehicle in the lake. God damn that Will. God damn him. He'd make that little fucker pay. Eddy blinked again and started down the road.

CHAPTER 32

MAUREEN GLANCED BEHIND HER; EDDY lay face down in the yard and still wasn't moving. She hoped Will hadn't killed him. She looked ahead. Will was already some distance in front of her. He'd insisted she go with him, that she wasn't safe around Eddy anymore. And she had. She hadn't put up an argument or asked any questions. She'd gone into the house and grabbed a few things while Will stood guard over his brother with that two-by-four perched on his shoulder.

She left with Will because she was frightened. For the first time in her life, she was scared enough to run. Eddy really wanted to hurt her. He would've raped her if Will hadn't stopped him. Maureen was positive about that. She'd seen it, something ugly in his eyes that had never been there before.

Will was going into the deep part of the woods along a little-used path. Maureen tried to step up her pace but faltered. She couldn't seem to catch her breath.

"Will," she called out. He stopped and started back towards her.

She hadn't really had a chance to look at him before, but now she could see that he had grown a scraggly reddish beard and that his hair looked long and matted, as if he hadn't bathed for weeks. He was barely recognizable.

"Are you all right?" he asked.

Maureen shook her head and sat down.

"I don't know what's wrong," she said. "I feel sort of dizzy and I'm having a hard time breathing."

"You're probably in shock," he said, matter-of-factly.

Maureen nodded and grabbed her side. It hurt. She wasn't sure what Eddy had done to her down there.

"Can you take a deep breath?" asked Will, kneeling in front of her. She breathed and exhaled.

"No pain?" he asked. She shook her head.

"Okay," he said. "Your ribs are probably fine. Does your throat hurt?"

Without thinking, Maureen brought her hand to her neck. She nodded.

"It's sore, but I can breathe and swallow," she said. "I think it's just bruised." She took another breath. "I'm okay, Will. I'm okay. Just give me a minute. I just need a second."

"Okay."

He stood and stared down the path behind them, standing guard. She saw that he was wearing what used to be blue jeans, but that they were as brown as the earth now. He wore a long-sleeved work shirt; it was the same color as his pants. God. He looked off the grid, like a homeless guy. But he'd saved her. If it weren't for Will, who knows what could have happened.

"Thanks, Will," she said. "Thank you. I was really scared. I've never seen Eddy like that before. I thought he was going to kill me."

"He was assaulting you," said Will, still staring down the path. She could see his fists clench. He turned and looked at her. "He was trying to use you to get to me."

"Did you see it?" she asked. "Were you there?"

Will nodded. He squatted down beside her, a ripe smell clinging to him like a whiny child. It wasn't only a body odor smell; it was worse—musk, stagnant water, and some sort of fetid smell, like decaying wood. Maureen held her breath. *I'll get used to it in a little while*, she thought. *I will.*

"I was in the trees right behind the pickup today," said Will. "But I've been listening to all of them the entire time. I know exactly what they're up to, and I know exactly how to stop them. Look at them. Three months and they've barely gone a quarter mile. They won't be able to hold out much longer."

"Will," said Maureen, "are you all right? You look pretty ragged."

"I'm fine," he said. "Healthy as a horse."

"Will, when was the last time you changed your clothes or took a bath?"

"A long time," said Will. "But I can't wash off, Maureen. I've been living in the forest, lying on the ground, sleeping in the trees. I'm covered in the dirt and the water, the plants, all of it. The smell isn't just me. The smell is the forest."

"Will, I'm sorry, but whatever it is, it's pretty bad."

He stood and took a step backward from her, trying, she realized, to spare her.

"You don't understand," said Will. "This is my camouflage. I'm so much part of the forest now that they can't see or smell me. And, if they bring dogs, they won't be able to find me, either. I'd be invisible to them."

"Okay," said Maureen, nodding.

"It works, Maureen. Most of the time I'm right there, no more than ten feet away from them and they have no idea I'm there. Sometimes I'm up in the trees, sometimes I'm right on the ground, and sometimes I'm in one of my little burrows."

Maureen nodded. In a weird sort of way, his theory made sense.

"You think the dogs won't be able to smell you, Will? Really?"

"It's not me they'd be smelling," he said, smiling. "It's the forest, and they don't like the forest."

All right. Whatever you say. She rubbed her throat and hitched up her bikini top. It didn't feel right. She looked down. The strap was stretched and almost torn off. Eddy had wrecked it. And her boob ached deep down where he'd grabbed her. The cup was still covering her, but barely. She stood up and grabbed a t-shirt from the bag she'd brought and put it on.

"That's going to bruise," said Will. "Your throat, I mean. You need to get some ice on it."

"Sure," said Maureen. "Where's the fridge?"

"C'mon," he said. "We need to get moving anyway."

Will set off toward the east, toward Mirror Lake. He set a fast pace but kept looking back to make sure Maureen was keeping up. The trail they were on wasn't much more than a deer path, a narrow rut weaving between clumps of trees and boulders. The trees were thick here, and tall. Where the trail opened into a clearing, Will would stop and crouch, scanning the tree line to make sure everything was clear.

The day was warm, and while the interior woods were humid and still, Maureen felt comfortable. Safe. Will moved along steadily. He stopped by a large boulder, reached down underneath it and pulled out a metal canteen. He took a sip and passed it back to Maureen, who drank deeply, wincing as she tried to swallow.

"How is it?" asked Will.

"It hurts," she said.

"Hang on. It won't be long now."

"Where are we going?"

He took the canteen from her and put it back in its hiding place. *He probably has dozens of these stashed all over the forest.*

"I'm taking you to Sully's place," said Will. "She's got a fridge and ice and a real bathroom. You can freshen up, and then there's a radio there you can use to call the police if you want to press charges."

The cops. Shit. What was she going to do? Should she press charges? But what good would that do? It was her word against Eddy's. And what if he sent somebody after her for the video? She would need protection. Maybe Sully would help. *Maybe I could stay out here with Will until things settle down.*

"Okay," said Maureen. "That sounds like a plan. Will?" she asked.

"What?"

"Do you think I should press charges?"

Will stood up straight, his pale blue eyes boring into her, the rusty beard barely covering the anger etched on his face.

"He hurt you, Maureen." Will's voice was curiously flat. "He was trying to assault you."

"I know," she said, "but I don't know what to do. He got carried away, Will."

"That's no excuse," said Will, his eyes as sharp as crystals. "He shouldn't have done it. He shouldn't do that to anybody, but to you especially. You're family, Maureen. You can't do that to family."

Will looked down then and took a deep breath and then another. *He's trying to keep it together. He's that upset.* Eddy was lucky. Will didn't lose it often, but when he did, he could get pretty violent.

"I didn't want to hurt him," said Will suddenly. "I only wanted to knock him out."

"He'll be fine," said Maureen. "Eddy's got a pretty thick skull."

Will smiled a little, then turned and started walking. *Well, I guess that's that,* thought Maureen, hurrying after. As they plodded along, Maureen started going over her alternatives. She could have Eddy arrested for assault, but that probably wasn't a good idea. First of all, it was her word against his. Secondly, he had half the town in his pocket. And finally, everyone knew about her and Eddy. They would assume it had been consensual, maybe an argument gone bad. No, calling the cops was not a good idea.

The best alternative was probably to lie low until things settled down. She glanced up at Will, who was moving quickly along the path. Mirror Lake shimmered ahead through the trees. It wouldn't be long now.

What about Will? What could she do? He was fighting for everything he'd ever believed in; he wouldn't stop now. *And*, she thought, smiling at the thought, *he was winning.* Nothing short of an all-out assault or napalm would pry Will out of these woods. No, she'd be surprised if he ever came out now. Like he said, he was part of the woods now, and they were part of him. Down to the marrow.

Will slowed as Sully's cabin came into view. It was the first time Maureen had ever been out there. It was a small, pre-fab structure, not much more than a hunting shack. But Will said she had a shower and a fridge. He knelt down and motioned for Maureen to do the same. He waited, crouched in the bushes. Maureen lay on the cool grass, feeling it soothe her sore flesh. She closed her eyes and breathed deeply. It was nice here. So nice.

"Well, well, well." The voice came booming out of nowhere.

Maureen raised her head and blinked. Sully stood over her; Will was a little bit behind her.

"Hello, Sully," said Maureen, clambering clumsily to her feet.

"What the hell happened to you?" asked Sully, peering at her neck. "Was somebody after you?"

Maureen nodded and crossed her arms. For some reason, she felt shy suddenly.

"Eddy beat her up," said Will.

"You're kidding me," said Sully, glancing at him. "Eddy?"

Maureen stood there, her arms across her chest. She couldn't think of anything to say.

"Yeah," said Will. "I saw the whole thing. I had to knock him out."

"Good for you," said Sully, peering closely at Maureen's neck. "Those are some nasty bruises," she said. "Anything else damaged?"

Maureen paused a moment. *Nothing you can see.* She shook her head.

"Okay," said Sully, smiling. "Let's get you inside to put some ice on those bruises. I think we also need to take some pictures of these injuries."

She put her arm around Maureen and led her down the path to the cabin. Will stayed behind. Maureen turned and watched as he turned and trotted back into the trees, into the green, into the wild. Maureen leaned her head on Sully's broad shoulder and before she knew it, she was bawling like a baby.

CHAPTER 33

THE PURPLE ONION WAS NEARLY EMPTY. Lewis was tending bar as Eddy sat in the corner booth with Danny Long and Sheriff Delaney.

"So you think Will rolled your pick-up into the lake and then hit you?" asked the sheriff, his pen poised over his notebook.

Eddy nodded. His head hurt a lot worse now. He'd taken some Advil, but it wasn't doing much good.

"But you didn't see him," continued Delaney.

"No," said Eddy. "No, I didn't see who did it. I was up on the porch talking to Maureen when the truck began to roll. I went to chase it and somebody whacked me from behind on the way back up."

Even to him, Eddy's voice sounded stilted and lifeless, as if he were reading letters off an eye chart.

"Are you all right, Eddy?" asked Danny. "You don't sound like yourself. Should we take you to see Doc?"

Eddy shook his head. No. His head was fine. He'd been conked before; this was nothing new. Something else was bothering him, something he couldn't quite put his finger on. Not yet, but he had a feeling that it wasn't anything Doc could take care of.

"Maybe we should go out and talk to Maureen," said the sheriff.

"We went and looked for her after Eddy came and got us," said Danny, "but she wasn't around. The house was locked, and she didn't answer the door. A few chairs were knocked over on the porch." Danny glanced at Eddy. "There might have been a scuffle."

Sheriff Delaney looked at Eddy, too.

"What about it, Eddy? Was there any kind of scuffle?"

Eddy shook his head. He really didn't want to bring Maureen into this—he knew what it would lead to—but he didn't see a way to avoid it.

He finally looked up from his beer and said, "I don't think so. Not that I know of."

"All right," said the sheriff. "I'm going to take a couple squads out there to take a look around before it gets too dark. Eddy?"

He looked up.

"Do Will and Maureen get along? Are they friendly?"

Eddy blinked.

"Yeah," he said. "They're friendly." He hesitated and then swallowed; he had to do it.

"I think Will has a thing for Maureen," he said. "You know, he's attracted to her, but he never really could do anything about it." Eddy shrugged. "He's, you know, shy. That's part of his condition. It makes him kind of frustrated and angry."

The sheriff rubbed his chin. Eddy looked at him, wondering how long it might take him to finally get the idea.

"All right," said Sheriff Delaney, standing up and putting his notebook in his back pocket. "Stay in town, Eddy. We'll let you know if we need anything else." He nodded to Danny, who got up.

"Thank you both," he said and strode out.

Danny sat down opposite Eddy and took a sip from his beer. Neither one spoke for some time. Eddy lit up a cigarette.

"Funny," said Danny finally. "I never knew Will had a thing for Maureen."

Eddy shrugged. "Well, you know," he said. "It was kind of one of his little fantasies." He looked at Danny. "Will never really grew up that way. I don't think he's ever been with a woman. He'd never hurt Maureen, though."

"Yeah," said Danny, "but the sheriff doesn't know that, does he?"

"I guess not," said Eddy.

"I guess not," said Danny. He emptied his beer, took a long look at Eddy, then got up and left without saying another word. Eddy took a drag off his cigarette and continued to stare at the empty space where Danny had been.

CHAPTER 34

SULLY PULLED INTO THE DRIVEWAY JUST after dark. Maureen watched from the front door as she bustled out of the car and up the path to the cabin. Something was wrong. Sully seemed upset. Her eyes had a worried look underneath her thick black glasses.

"Hey, Sully," asked Maureen. "What is it?"

"They're coming after Will," she said, brushing past Maureen into the kitchen. She started putting items into a backpack. "Delaney has mobilized the county sheriff's office and the state patrol to do a manhunt. It's huge. They're setting everything up right now. There's got to be at least fifty or sixty officers."

"What?" asked Maureen. "Why? Why now?"

"Because," said Sully, stopping a moment and catching her breath. "Because they think Will kidnapped you."

"What? That's crazy," said Maureen.

"You know that and I know that, but those crazy cop bastards don't know that. And Eddy is saying nothing to contradict it. I think we need to get you back into town so they call off this circus. Are you okay with that?"

"Sure," said Maureen. "Of course." As good as Will was on his own turf, she didn't think even he would be able to withstand that amount of manpower.

"It's fucking nuts," said Sully. "They're bringing in helicopters, dogs, demolition experts, anybody you can think of."

"What are you going to do?" asked Maureen.

"I'm going to hike out and make sure Will gets himself tucked in nice and tight before the shit hits the fan. Can you get into town all right?"

"Yeah, of course," said Maureen. "I know my way out of here. Don't you want to come with me?"

"No, not right—"

Sully stopped, her eyes locked on the doorway.

Maureen turned. His huge frame filling the doorway, and cradling a shotgun in his arm, stood Lewis.

"Hello, ladies," he said, walking into the room. "It's good to see you."

Maureen instinctively took a step back, her mind moving toward flight. But there was no back door.

"What are you doing out here, Lewis?" demanded Sully.

"Just thought I'd stop in for a visit, Sully." He glanced around the tiny cabin. "You've got a nice little place here. Cozy."

"Thank you. Courtesy of your tax dollar," said Sully, crossing her arms. "You usually take a shotgun with you when you go visiting, Lewis?"

He smiled and shrugged. "It's dangerous out here in the big black woods," said Lewis. "You never know what, or who, you might run across." He glanced over at Maureen and gave her a slight wave.

"Why are you here?" asked Sully.

"Let's just say I'm doing a favor for a friend," said Lewis, sitting in one of the kitchen chairs. He glanced up toward Maureen. "Eddy's been worried about you, Maureen. He wanted to make sure you're all right."

"I'm fine," she said. "And actually," she said, sitting in the chair opposite Lewis, "I'm going back into town tonight, Lewis, so you don't have to worry about me anymore."

"I'm not the one who's worried about you," said Lewis, laying the shotgun on the table. "Eddy is."

"Is he worried about me or what I might say?" asked Maureen.

"Why'd you come here?" asked Sully.

"I figured you and Will might have Maureen squirreled away somewhere out here," he said. "Hiding out."

"Why would I be hiding?"

Lewis shook his head. He took a pack of cigarettes out of his shirt pocket and shook one out.

"Don't smoke in here," said Sully. Lewis lit up, looked up at her, and smiled.

"Fuck you, Sully," he said easily.

"I'm here because Eddy assaulted me," said Maureen. She felt her anger rising all over again as she said it. Lewis sat staring at her, not moving a muscle.

"Eddy asked me," said Lewis, looking at the both of them, "to keep you out of harm's way. You know there's going to be a big manhunt. The cops are in town, mobilizing right now. They'll be coming after Will—and they're going to get him, Maureen. And these are guys who won't stop and negotiate. They won't listen. They don't care. They'll shoot first and ask questions later."

Sully glared at Lewis, her blue eyes gleaming.

"And they won't care," continued Lewis, "who gets in the line of fire."

"I've got to talk to Chief Dodge," said Sully, moving toward the door. "I'm going to town."

Lewis moved sideways in the chair, graceful as a dancer, and tripped Sully, sending her sprawling to the floor. He took the shotgun from the table and placed it in his lap.

"Nobody's going anywhere," he said. "We're going to sit tight for a few days, girls. Now, Sully," he said, standing up, holding the shotgun in the crook of his arm, "where do you keep the duct tape?"

CHAPTER 35

WILL LAY ON HIS STOMACH JUST BEHIND the tree line on the southern rise, overlooking the town of Moon Lake, gazing down at the hubbub. The setting sun cast a thick orange blanket of light onto the array of people, cops, and vehicles, giving them an odd, otherworldly look, as if they were trapped in amber. Will took the binoculars out of his vest and trained them onto the intersection of Highway X and Ridge Road. He counted twenty-four squad cars parked along the road—from the Eagleton Police Department, the county, and even the state.

Will also noted a couple of unmarked black cars—maybe the Feds. There was also a canine unit. And he had seen a helicopter overhead earlier. *Well,* thought Will, *it looks as if they're not fooling around. But it was strange they'd mobilize a force that large unless someone was in danger.*

It couldn't be for him; why would they suddenly mobilize now? Could a kid have gotten lost in the woods? He wished he knew; he could have helped find a lost child. Or maybe there'd been a bank robbery and fugitives were loose. The worst of it was there were probably going to be seventy or eighty cops tramping around in his woods, scaring the wildlife, wrecking habitat, and leaving everything from cigarette butts to plastic water bottles behind. He felt a twinge of anxiety—the faint sound of crows—echoing in his consciousness. *Yeah, the sooner I stop this, the better.*

Will crawled backward until he was out of sight of the town and rose up. He tightened his backpack, shouldered his rifle, and started trotting toward Sully's cabin. It was nearly dark, and the moon didn't rise until after midnight, so he could afford to move fast; besides, it didn't look as if anybody was in the woods yet.

Sully's cabin was about six miles out. He could make that in about seventy-five minutes. Will pressed ahead, listening and watching. Some of the nocturnal feeders were coming out. He startled a small group of white-tails as he burst into a meadow barely lit by the purplish-gray dusk. They startled and ran into cover.

"Sorry," whispered Will, as he continued on. "This is an emergency."

Raccoons would be emerging from their dens, and the owls would be starting their long and lonely vigils. Will always tried to be as quiet as possible in the woods, but he made a special effort tonight. He glided along the narrow deer path, navigating between brush and boulders, using instinct and experience.

The air was growing colder; it was going to be a typical summer night. Chilly. Jacket weather. *But not,* Will thought, smiling to himself, *if you're on the move.* He felt warm and perfectly adapted to the environment. He loved moving through the forest like this, trusting to it and his own skill, becoming joined to its secrets and rhythms, its life, its heartbeat.

Will continued on, not seeing or hearing a soul. Sully's place was not as far south along Mirror Lake as his and was perched on a hillside right on the lake. He cut over to stay away from the shoreline where he could be spotted. He could still see glimpses of the water through the trees, black patches barely illuminated by the stars.

Will slowed as he got closer to Sully's. Something wasn't right. He stopped, kneeling down, and took a slow look around as he caught his breath. The cabin was still not in sight, maybe three-quarters a mile up the road, but something wasn't right.

Will waited. He could hear something faint in the distance; he concentrated. Sound was funny out here. It traveled a long way over the water. Sometimes you could hear a conversation taking place across a lake as clearly as if the person was standing next to you. This was not coming across the lake, though. It was up the road, coming from Sully's.

Could it be her and Maureen? Will cocked his head. Maybe. One of the voices was deeper. Maureen had a low voice. It might be her, but he didn't think so. Will stood up, crouching, and veered off the trail. He'd decided to come up on Sully's place from the western slope. That way he'd have a view of the place from above. Will started up the slope, taking care to make as little noise as possible. He reached the crest of the ridge and looked down on where the road snaked toward the cabin. There was an old van there. Not Sully's. Her little Jeep was further up the driveway. So she did have company, and it wasn't the chief. He drove a state car, one of those Fords. Will felt himself frowning. Who was it? Nobody else ever came out here.

Will took the rifle from his shoulder and held it in front of him. He scanned the ridge ahead of him and kept moving—slowly and carefully. Whoever drove that truck might be looking for him. Will crossed the point where the trail snaked between three boulders; he could see the front of Sully's cabin from here. Only one light was burning. The inside door was open, but the screen door was shut.

Will could hear someone talking—Maureen. She sounded angry. Someone answered her—a man. Will didn't recognize the voice, although it seemed familiar. Will couldn't place it. It wasn't the chief or Eddy or either of the Wilson boys, but he knew that voice. He strained to hear.

"So what are you going to do, keep us locked in here forever?"

That was Maureen. Somebody—the man—laughed and answered, but Will couldn't make out the words. He resisted the temptation to move closer. Another voice answered. Sully.

"You can't hold us here," she was saying. "That's kidnapping."

"Funny you should mention that," said the man, the stranger. "That's exactly what people think Will did with Maureen. But this isn't kidnapping. I'm keeping you here for your own safety."

"What?" said Sully. "What are you talking about, Lewis?"

Lewis. That's where he knew that voice. Eddy must have sent him up here.

"Well, think about it," he answered. "Somebody rolls Eddy's truck into the lake and then knocks him out. Then Eddy wakes up and Maureen is missing and nobody's heard from her since. What do you think they're thinking?"

Will took a breath. So that was the reason for all the cops. And the Feds. They thought this was a kidnapping. Eddy had sent Lewis up here to keep Maureen and Sully from going back, from talking, from telling the truth. They'd call off the manhunt if she showed up.

"That's not what happened," Maureen was saying. "Eddy assaulted me. That's why Will knocked him out."

"Nice story, Maureen," said Lewis.

"Why would she lie?" asked Sully. From her voice, Will could imagine the look on her face, that stubborn expression she got when she knew she was right.

Lewis laughed, a harsh grating sound like metal scraping metal.

"Rumor is that Will is sweet on you, Maureen," said Lewis. "People think he pulled a Tarzan and Jane thing on you, kidnapped you, and took you deep into the jungle."

"Will wouldn't do that," she said. Even from where he was perched, Will could tell that her voice had become less strident, less assertive.

"Maybe he would," answered Lewis, "and maybe he wouldn't. It's hard to tell with a crazy man. Anyway, I want both of you to go into the bathroom now. To be safe."

Will could hear Sully and Maureen protesting, a scraping sound and then footsteps, and then a door closing. Lewis appeared in the open doorway, his bulk nearly blocking out all the light, and whistled softly.

Will heard a rustling about fifteen yards directly below him. Someone was coming out of that little depression in the hillside beneath the rotted-out oak tree. Will caught a movement on the other side of the cabin. Someone else was moving toward Lewis. *There are three of them—and I didn't even have a clue.*

Will felt himself gritting his teeth. *Idiot. I didn't even realize somebody else was here. I didn't concentrate. I got distracted by the conversation, by Maureen.* He watched as the man trudged down the hill in front of him, loosely holding his rifle, making as much noise as five bears looking for food.

"Any luck?" asked Lewis.

"Nothing. Not one fucking thing."

Will recognized that voice. Andy Wilson. He heard someone come trudging up on the other side of Lewis. Will could barely make out the man's outline, but he was big. Probably Bert.

"We didn't hear anything, and you can't see a goddamned thing in this dark," said the second man.

It was definitely Bert Wilson. Will felt a thrill of anger at the sound of the man's voice. *Bastard. Shooting him hadn't been enough.*

"Okay," said Lewis. He stepped outside the screen door and stood next to the other two men.

"He's out there, though," said Lewis. "I know it. He's right under our noses. He's probably listening to us right now."

"Fucking loon," whispered Andy.

"Yeah," said Lewis, "but he's a dangerous loon. Did Eddy tell you about that bomb they found?"

"Danny told us all about it," said Bert.

The three of them fell silent, standing in front of the cabin, watching the dark and listening. *It's stupid to stand in front of the light like that. If I wanted to, I could take two of them right away and then take my own sweet time hunting the other one down. It would be child's play.* But he didn't move. Not yet.

"I heard Mattie Doolittle left town," said one the Wilson boys. Probably Andy.

"Yes," said Lewis, in a tone that didn't invite further discussion. "Eddy and I persuaded her to take a vacation."

"Bitch," said Andy.

Will felt himself bristling; Mattie was a good person. What rights did these bastards have to do these things? Who in the hell did they think they were?

Don't be stupid. Don't get mad. Breathe. Last time this happened, you shot somebody. Not that he didn't deserve it, but you can't keep doing that.

The men stood in front of the lit door, rifles dangling from the crooks of their arms. Bert swore as he swatted at the mosquitos. Lewis lit up a cigarette. Will watched them like a hawk, or more specifically, an owl; he didn't want to miss any detail that might come in handy.

"So," asked Andy after a few minutes, "what's the plan?"

Lewis glanced at his watch.

"Eddy wants me back in town by eleven," he said. "I'll have to leave in a few minutes. You guys have to stay and keep an eye on those two."

Andy stepped closer to Lewis.

"We can't keep them here forever."

Lewis took a drag off his cigarette and shrugged.

"That's not my call," he said. "Eddy and Naomi have it all figured out. They'll let us know what's up. You two just do as you're told." He glanced at his watch. "I've gotta go."

"How're we supposed to get back?" asked Bert, a belligerent tone in his voice.

"I'll be here to relieve you first thing in the morning," said Lewis. He started toward his van. "Remember," he called. "Keep your eyes open."

Lewis got into the van and drove off. Bert and Andy sat on the ground near the front door. Will wondered why they didn't go inside. The sound of the engine slowly faded, replaced by the silence and darkness of the forest. Will could hear Sully and Maureen speaking in low voices through the bathroom door.

"Hey," said Bert, "shut up in there."

The voices stopped. Will wondered what they were up to. Sully was resourceful, and she had guts. What would she do to get out of a situation like this? He knew what he was going to do. He could sneak up and take the Wilsons pretty easily right now, but waiting would be the better choice. They'd get tired, sleepy, and then he'd be able to come up and disarm them one at a time; that way nobody would get hurt—although he wouldn't mind it if they did.

* * *

THE MOON WAS HIGH. IT WAS probably after two. The boys were sitting with their backs against the cabin, and they hadn't stirred in over an hour. Will even thought he could hear one of them snoring. The light in the cabin was still burning, but Will couldn't tell if anything was going on in there or not.

Will stood slowly, wincing as the feeling slowly came back into his legs. He'd been examining and reexamining the terrain for hours, even though he already knew it like the back of his hand. The best way to approach Bert would be from behind the cabin on the side closest to the hillside. That way he'd be able to grab his gun from around the corner behind him.

After he got Bert's gun, Will would get the drop on them, tie them up, and get Sully and Maureen out of there. Sully could run down to her boat and take that to the north shore, get to County X, and walk into town from there. Will started moving slowly, stealthily, down the path. *Slow and silent now. Like one of the big cats.*

Something thumped. Sort of a slide into a thump. Like a window opening. Will knelt down again. He knew that sound. It was the access panel in the bathroom being opened. He knew it because he'd helped Sully replace the pipes that burst there last spring. It was a small opening, tight, but big enough for an adult to get through. *Good old Sully. She was going to sneak them out that little hole.*

Will started hearing small sounds, muted—grunts, creaks, something sliding over the ground. In the moonlight, he could see one shape moving around the corner behind the cabin, then another. Maureen and Sully were out and were making for the lake. Sully would probably take the canoe; they would have enough time to get across the lake before sunrise. The boys would never be able to find them in this dark anyway. Hell, thought Will. They probably wouldn't realize they were gone until Lewis got back tomorrow morning. He thought about going down to help Maureen and Sully, but that wasn't really necessary. They didn't need him, and he wanted to keep an eye on the Wilsons, anyway, just in case something happened. He'd wait until he was sure they'd gotten away.

Will backtracked a little until he was on the apex of the ridge; from here he could still see the cabin and the lake. He waited. Sure enough, about twenty minutes later, he saw a long, dark shape sliding over the black silver-streaked water, silently cutting through the slight fog that lay just over the lake's surface. Will waited until they rounded the nearest point and glided out of sight. He glanced over at the cabin. He could just make out the shapes of the Wilson brothers leaning against the cabin. They were both snoring now.

Will stared at them a long moment, his grasp tightening on his rifle. Part of him—the part that now belonged to the forest—told him to go ahead and do it—to rub out this threat against himself and his home. It would be easy enough now. No witnesses. They were asleep. Two quick shots and it would be over. The hard part would be sliding the bodies down to the water and onto the pontoon boat. After that, it would be easy. Just simply sinking them into the deepest part of the lake. No one would ever find them.

The other part of him, the part that still belonged to his father, his family—Maureen—made him stand up, turn, and start walking. Killing was necessary sometimes. To survive. The forest had taught him that. And this was not a matter of survival. Not yet. *But,* he thought, looking back at the still forms of the Wilson brothers, *when it gets to that point, I will do what I have to do, and I will do it to whoever I have to.*

But, then... The image of the slaughtered skulk of foxes popped into his mind, as clearly as if it were right in front of him.

His skulk, his family, his world. *No,* he thought, turning around. *This is a matter of survival.*

* * *

IT WAS NEARLY SUNRISE WHEN HE finished. The gray light of the eastern sky was becoming tinged with lavender. He knew he had a half-hour before light. Will started out; he was going to walk deep into the forest, as deep into it as he possibly could, into his caves. He could make new plans there. Plan while he waited for them to come. *Let them come,* he thought. *I'll be ready.*

CHAPTER 36

EDDY STEERED NAOMI'S LITTLE TOYOTA as carefully as he could. The old logging road was rutted and mostly overgrown in the middle. It wouldn't take much to tear out the oil pan of the little car. Naomi sat in the passenger seat, staring straight ahead. After Lewis had come into the Onion late last night, reporting that Maureen had been handled, Naomi insisted they go out there first thing in the morning.

Eddy wanted Lewis to handle it; he didn't want any part of this deal with Maureen anymore. It was spiraling out of control. They were only going to be able to keep her quiet for so long. Once she started blabbing about what had happened at the lake, his story would be shot to hell, and he'd be finding himself in deep shit. Lying to an officer, false imprisonment, maybe even assault—if Maureen wanted to press charges. Sully was involved now, too, which meant even more trouble. Technically, Lewis was the one who had locked her up, but that would come back and stick to him, too. And she wouldn't be like Mattie; there'd be no way to scare off Sully.

Eddy glanced over at Naomi in the passenger side. She sat staring straight ahead with that faraway look of hers, that look that had occupied her eyes more and more often. It was as if she weren't even in the car. She held up her hand to the window, fingers spread, and turned it, examining it from every angle.

And the buying—she'd been going crazy on the Internet, buying clothes, appliances, furniture. He had told her to slow it down, to wait until they were in the black with the land, but she'd ignored him; she hadn't even looked at him. It was like he barely existed for her anymore. She only spoke to him when she wanted him to do something.

Eddie was sick of the whole thing. Most of this shit was her idea, anyway. Making up the story about Will kidnapping Maureen, getting Lewis to track her down, and then hiring the Wilsons to keep her quiet; that was all Naomi. *And now*, thought Eddy, navigating around a boulder in the middle of the track, *now she wants to come out here herself. To do what?*

"We're almost there," said Naomi, suddenly, her voice cutting through his thoughts like a knife.

"No," said Eddy. "It's still a mile or so."

"No," she said, turning to him. "You idiot. I meant we're almost at the end of this whole ordeal."

"What do you mean?" he said.

He didn't see where she was going. Will was still on the loose. Nothing would be resolved until they brought him in, and even then he doubted things would go their way. If Maureen was telling the truth about the videotape, then they wouldn't have any kind of case for incompetency. If anything, he and Naomi could be liable for extortion or some other shit. *This whole thing is turning into a clusterfuck. Jesus, what was I thinking letting Naomi talk me into any of this?*

"I mean there's only one or two more loose ends we have to tie up," she said, turning and—for once—looking him in the face.

"Really?" he asked, glancing over at her. "What about Will? Nothing happens until we bring him in. And do you really think the cops are going to find him out there? Good fucking luck."

"They won't have to," she said.

Eddy looked over at her. He didn't say anything; he knew he wouldn't have to.

"He'll come after her, Eddy, when he hears she's in trouble. All we have to do is wait. And then we'll take care of him."

"Maureen? Why would he come after Maureen?"

"For the same reason you kept coming after her, Eddy." She turned and looked out the windshield. "Except that Will actually cares about her. You just wanted to fuck her."

Eddy didn't bother denying it. It wasn't like either of them cared anymore.

"What makes you think she and Will are together?" he asked, wondering how she'd figured it out.

"You saw them at the town hall. She was watching him like a hawk." Naomi reached into her purse and pulled out her pack of cigarettes. "She used to look at you that way," she said.

Naomi pulled out a cigarette and lit one up. "So did Mattie," she added.

"That's all over, Naomi," he said, almost out of reflex. She said nothing. He took a deep breath and let it out.

"That's right," she said, taking a puff. "Mattie's gone."

Eddy felt her turn in her seat and glanced at her. She was staring at him, those cold silver eyes boring a hole through him. He tried to hold her gaze but felt himself wilting underneath it.

"Don't back out on me now, Eddy. I don't have to remind you why we're doing this. We're doing it for Donny and Bella. For their future."

He snorted.

"Really, Naomi? For them? Is that why you've been buying clothes and makeup and God knows what else for yourself?"

Eddy felt her lean in toward him and then whisper, her breath hot in his ear. He kept his eyes fixed on the road ahead.

"I've earned this, Eddy," she hissed. "For all your fucking around and infidelities and inattention and selfishness. Pussy. That's what you got. This is what I get."

He felt her lean back and take a pull from her cigarette.

"When all this is done and the dust has settled," she said, "we'll see where things stand." Eddy glanced over at Naomi. She was staring out the window. "Maybe I'll keep you," she continued, "or maybe I won't."

They were rolling up to the cabin. *Thank God*. He stopped and got out of the car. There was no sign of the Wilson boys—no sign of life at all. Eddy started up toward the shack.

"Where are they?" asked Naomi.

Eddy held up his hand. He heard something, a clanging coming from the cabin. He went in. Pieces of crumpled duct tape littered the floor. A rifle lay on the kitchen table. Nothing else seemed disturbed. The clanging was coming from the only other door in the tiny shack. Eddy opened it. Bert and Andy were sitting on the bathroom floor, their hands bound to some plumbing behind the toilet. Their mouths had been taped shut.

Eddy leaned over and removed the tape from Andy's mouth.

"Eddy," he gasped, "it was Will."

"Really?" asked Eddy, leaning over to untie him.

"Where is Maureen?" asked Naomi. Andy looked over at Bert and then back at Eddy.

"Will must have let her out," said Andy, looking from her to Eddy and back again.

"You idiots," said Naomi. She turned away from them and took out her cellphone. Eddy finished untying Andy and started in on Bert.

"He snuck up behind us and knocked us out," said Andy.

Whatever. It doesn't really matter now. Once Maureen gets into town, it won't matter. We'll be done. The kidnapping story will be debunked, and once that tape gets out, Will is going to be exonerated. In a way, Eddy was glad. He was sick of it. He didn't care anymore. He just wanted it to be over.

"Shit," said Bert who stood up and started fidgeting. He unzipped, muscled past Andy to the toilet and started peeing.

"God," he said, "I've been holding that all night."

Naomi appeared in the doorway.

"All right," she said, addressing Eddy, Andy, and Bert's back in the tiny bathroom. "Lewis is on his way to pick you two up. Now listen," she said to the Wilson boys, in a tone as tight as a guitar string, "I want you two to do just one thing right. Just one thing. If you do this, everything else is forgiven. If you screw up, you pay. You understand?"

Andy nodded. Bert zipped up, turned around, and said, "Yes, ma'am."

"All you have to do," she said, slowly and deliberately, "is to keep your mouths shut. You weren't up here. You never saw us. Is that clear?"

They nodded.

"Leave the rifle, Bert," said Naomi. "And get out of my sight. Go out to the driveway and wait for Lewis."

Eddy watched them walk out sheepishly like two boys caught playing hooky. They started walking down the driveway. Eddy turned to Naomi, who was holding the rifle. She stared at Eddy, handed him the gun, and said, "Take them."

Eddy looked down the driveway where the brothers stood with their backs to them, waiting patiently.

"No," said Eddy. "No. Are you nuts?"

"Do it," hissed Naomi. "Do it and we'll blame it on Will. We'll tell them he murdered them. He hates them. Everybody knows it. They'll believe it, Eddy, they'll believe it."

Eddy turned toward the door, glanced back at his wife, her teeth shining under a smile as bright as a knife blade and threw the rifle on the table.

"No," he said. "We're not killing anybody."

"Well," she said, trying to pick up the rifle before he snatched it away from her. "I guess I have to do everything myself."

CHAPTER 37

WILL HEARD THE CAR COMING UP THE road. They were a good distance away, north, in the vicinity of Sully's cabin. He smiled to himself. Somebody was coming to get the Wilson boys. Bert would be pissed. He'd sure been surprised last night when he woke up with a flashlight shining in his face and a rifle muzzle two inches from his nose. Will had already gagged and bound Andy; marching them into the bathroom and tying them to the pipe was easy.

Will paused a moment, then continued moving. If he could keep up this pace, he'd be at the big cave by noon. He frowned as he heard an outboard fire up out on the lake. Nobody except the DNR had boats on Mirror Lake. Who was taking their pontoon? Sully? Was she back? Will walked along the top of the ridge, keeping his eyes toward the shore. He knelt down and watched. After about fifteen minutes, Sully's pontoon came chugging around the point. Will leaned his rifle against a tree, took the binoculars out of his vest pocket, and trained them on the boat. He focused in. Eddy was piloting the boat. Naomi stood next to him, her hand on his shoulder. She was talking. Eddy answered. It looked like they were arguing.

Will glanced all along the lakeshore—no troopers or helicopters or drones. Maureen and Sully must have made it into town and let them know what was happening. They must have, otherwise the cops would be all over the place. But what could Eddy and Naomi want? Were they after him? Good luck with that.

Will thought about the law. Eddy didn't have enough leverage to grab the land anymore. Maureen's lawyer had the videotape, and when she showed up, the kidnapping business would be dismissed. *The only thing I have to worry about*, thought Will, *is vandalism and criminal damage to property. That's not much. And, besides, it doesn't matter. I can live out here forever; I'm happy with the status quo. I don't need to go back.*

The pontoon boat came closer. They were almost into the near bay. Naomi was driving now, piloting the boat close to the shore. Eddy had the binoculars and was scanning the beach and the tree line. They were close, close enough for Will to see the rifle lying on the deck, close enough to see that Eddy wasn't looking good. He seemed tired, pinched.

Maybe they're out here to negotiate. Maybe they know they're beat. Will felt the urge to stand and hail them but waited. If Eddy had been by himself, he might have done it, but Will still didn't trust Naomi.

"Will!"

The shout rolled across the still water of the lake and was eventually soaked up by the trees. Will stood up. He knew it was nearly impossible to see him from the water.

"Will, I want to talk. I want to settle this thing," yelled Eddy.

Will watched them. Naomi was steering the boat as close to the shore as possible. Eddy was still scanning the shoreline. It was possible that Eddy was fed up, that he'd had enough of this crap. Naomi was responsible for it all. She'd been behind getting the town riled up, sending the Wilsons after him, all of it. Eddy had just gone along with her the way he always did.

"Will, this has got to stop. Too many people have gotten hurt," said Eddy.

He continued scanning the shoreline, passing right over where Will had positioned himself. He smiled to himself. Eddy would never find him, not in a hundred years.

"There he is."

Will started and looked down at the boat. Naomi stood at the wheel, pointing up, looking straight at him. How the hell had she spotted him? She shouldn't have been able to see him; no one should have. Her perception was spooky, almost animal-like. Will felt a shiver despite the heat. He grabbed his rifle and started trotting back into the forest, back to Turtle Ridge, his stronghold, his Alamo.

Will could hear Eddy calling after him and Naomi yelling something as they landed and secured the boat, but he wasn't going to wait. Something primal in him urged him to flight and he didn't resist, didn't think. Will accelerated into a loping run. As he got deeper into the forest, running along the narrow trail between the trunks of the great pines, the silence started to sink in on him. It was darker here, too. Sun only penetrated the deeper cover at certain times of day.

Will paused to catch his breath and listen. Nothing yet. There was no need to rush. It would be a while, if ever. Eddy wasn't very good at tracking. *Not that I leave much track.* It would take them some time to catch up. Will glanced around at the darkened forest, his forest. *It's still full of secrets. Secrets that only I know. There's no place like this anymore. Not anywhere. I've kept them out so far, but how long can one man last? Could I realistically live the rest of my life out here? And what about after I'm gone? Who'll protect it then?*

I don't know. Maybe Eddy's right. Maybe we could talk it out and go back to Dad's original plan. I could live with that. I was always ready to live with that. Most of the land would be safe then. And what rights would Eddy have after everything he'd done? He could go to jail. Yes, it's time to end this. But something told him not to expose himself. Not yet. Will trotted up the ridge a few hundred yards more to an outcropping of boulders that jutted out of the hillside, a place almost no one else knew, a place he had named Tabletop Rock.

Will clambered up to the flattened top and lay down. He would watch and if everything went well, he would talk. If he had to, he could run. The cave was nearby. Will lay on the soft moss on the rock, luxuriating in the cool air. It was beautiful here, as beautiful as the day he and his mother had sat here, watching the birds and the animals. It was taking them longer to find him than Will had thought. He was just about ready to go and look for his brother when he heard something crunching through the underbrush.

"Will," Eddy called. "God damn it, Will, where the hell are you?"

Will lay down flat. He didn't want to get overconfident and have Naomi spot him again. The crashing grew louder. Will poked his head up. Eddy burst onto the hillside below. He was covered in sweat and breathing hard. Naomi stepped in behind him. Her eyes scanned the hillside, over the outcropping, but she didn't spot him this time. Will took a closer look. Eddy was unarmed. Naomi carried Bert's rifle. Will reached over and touched his own rifle.

"Will, I know you're up here. I know it. Listen," said Eddy, pausing to catch his breath. "We talked. Everybody talked. Bert's not going to press charges. I'm going to talk to Maureen and make everything right with her. We want you to come in, Will. We want things to be the way they were."

Will said nothing. He could almost feel Naomi listening, watching, her antennae probing the forest.

"We're willing to go back to Dad's original deal," said Eddy. "We'll drop everything else."

Will waited. The old forest was still, so still it seemed to be holding its breath, to be on the verge. *That's why people didn't like it in here. It makes them nervous. They think it's watching.* Will listened; he could hear the slightest rustle or snap in the brush. He'd know when they were moving. And where.

"Maybe he's further up the ridge," said Eddy. He sounded tired.

"No," whispered Naomi. "No. He's here. He's right here. I can feel him."

Will heard someone moving on the hillside to his left.

"Will," called Naomi. She sounded as if she were talking to a child. Not one of her children, though.

"Will," she continued. "We want this to be over. We want it to end. Too many people have been hurt. We're lucky no one's been killed."

Yet. No one's been killed yet. Then a thought struck him suddenly. *Maybe that's their plan. Get rid of me, and everything else falls into place. Eddy would get the land, and Moon Lake would get their jobs. They would be happy, Naomi would be happy, everybody would be happy. But, Eddy couldn't do that. He's my brother. He wouldn't.* But he lay still. Something wasn't right.

Will listened; he wasn't sure exactly where Naomi was, but he could tell she was getting closer to the outcropping. She was trying to flank him. Will started crawling backward toward the woods behind him. He needed to fade back into the heavy brush and leave. There was a mouth to the cave complex not far from here—one of his hidden doors. No one knew about that one.

Will slowly raised himself to a squatting position, holding the rifle across his knees. He scanned the trees on both sides of the rock and started slowly making his way backwards toward the cover of the slope. He could hear Naomi—small steps, lighter weight—coming up on the west end. Will stopped. Where was Eddy? He'd forgotten all about Eddy.

"Hey, bro."

Will spun around. Eddy stood on the edge of the outcropping. He'd climbed up the front when Naomi had been coming up the side, distracting him. Will automatically brought the rifle up, but then lowered it immediately.

"Take it easy, Will," said Eddy.

Eddy was sweating and out of breath. *Climbing up those rocks must have taken a lot out of him.* He came forward with his hands raised.

"We do want to talk." He took a step toward Will. "We're serious. This whole thing has gotten out of hand. We need to settle it, Will."

Will heard a step and turned his head to see Naomi coming around the side of the outcropping, holding the rifle in front of her. He swung around. Naomi stopped, knelt down behind the rock, and gazed up at him, smiling her tight thin smile.

"Hello, Will," she said. "You're a hard man to find."

"Hey, hey," said Eddy. "Why don't we all put our rifles down? We don't want anything to happen. We're all family here."

Will actually laughed. He realized that it was the first sound he'd made. He looked at Eddy, then lowered his rifle.

"Family?" asked Will. "You tried to steal my land and sent those Wilsons after me. They tried to kill me, Eddy. Then you tried to prove I was insane. And you tried to rape Maureen. What kind of family is that?"

"Bert's the one who got shot," said Naomi. She hadn't moved an inch. Nor had the rifle. "And would we have to work that hard to prove you're crazy, Will? Look at you. You're like a wild man, a homeless person. You shot Bert. You tried to blow up the front-end loader and were planting bombs just like a terrorist."

"It was self-defense," said Will. His head started pounding and he could feel the crows beginning to stir. The old red mist started to rise in his eyes. *No*, he thought. *No. Stay calm. Breathe.*

"Self-defense, my ass."

"Shut up, Naomi," said Eddy.

"You're crazy, Will," said Naomi, her voice low. "You're schizo, just like everybody says. What would they say if they could see you now? What would the chief say? Sully? What would they think? What would your father think?" Naomi paused. "Or what would your precious mother think, Will? Would she be proud of you?"

"I said shut up, Naomi," yelled Eddy. "Leave him alone."

Will saw him take a step toward her and then move sideways toward him, trying to get between them.

"C'mon, Will, answer me," she said. "Would your mother be proud? Or would she be disgusted?"

Will could barely hear her over the crows. Naomi was still crouched down low, on the edge of the rock. He could barely see the rifle in her hands; he could barely see anything through the red mist. His hands were shaking. He was clutching his rifle so tightly he could barely feel his hands anymore.

"You don't deserve this land, Will," she said. "You don't deserve the LeBarron name. Eddy's the one. Your Dad wanted him to have it. He's the one who's going to take this land, to use it, to make something out of it. It's his."

Will blinked and saw Eddy looking at him. He then turned toward Naomi. The mist was dissipating. The sound of the crows was fading. Will could see Naomi hunkered down behind the rocks in front of him, her rifle pointed at his chest. He could just see Eddy out of the corner of his eye, but he didn't dare look away from Naomi. She reminded him of a raccoon he'd once found caught in a leg trap. It had snarled and snapped and lunged at Will, but had never taken its eyes off him. He'd finally had to sedate it before removing it from the jaws. Naomi was looking at him the same way now, her eyes full of rage and fear and hate.

Eddy moved into Will's field of vision; he was walking slowly toward Naomi, angling between Will and her. *He's trying to protect me,* Will realized. *Just like when we were kids.*

"C'mon, Naomi," he said. "Maybe we all need to take a step back and calm down a little bit."

"No," she shouted. "No. Not anymore, Eddy, not anymore. This ends now. No more."

She stood up and raised the gun to her shoulder, aiming it at Will. Eddy lunged toward her, reaching for the rifle. He got it by the barrel. Will instinctively hunkered down, raising his gun without aiming. Naomi's rifle went off. Will heard her cry out and saw Eddy crumple onto the rock where he lay without moving. Blood started pooling around his head. Naomi stared at Eddy a moment, her mouth working. Then she looked up at Will, raised the rifle, aimed deliberately—Will thought of his father's instructions to squeeze the trigger—and fired again.

The bullet caught Will in the chest and knocked him backward off the rock and into the brush beyond. The rifle was knocked out of his hand. He immediately struggled to all fours and clambered off into the alder thicket. That would give him enough cover to get to safety. He scraped past the dogwood and started crawling toward Turtle Creek. Will could feel a liquid rasping in his breath but the wound hadn't started to hurt yet. He had no idea how seriously he'd been hurt.

Will heard something behind him, crashing through the brush. Naomi. She sounded as if she were charging blindly into the thicket. The noise escalated and then veered off to the left, to the west.

Will waited a moment, until the sound was gone, then rolled over, unbuttoned his shirt, and quickly surveyed the damage. The bullet looked as if it had entered between the fourth and the fifth ribs. He reached around behind to see if it had gone through. There; it felt like a small exit wound. Thank God she hadn't been using hollow points; otherwise, he'd be dead for sure. As it was, she'd probably hit his lung.

Will tore strips from his shirt, stuffed them into the holes as best he could, and started crawling. It should be close. A few yards further and he could hear the slow-moving creek murmuring beyond the brush. Turtle Creek. This was good. Will looked up. The sun told him it was still morning. He was at the bottom of Turtle Ridge; once he got into the creek, he could float close to the cave entrance. He had bandages and antibiotics there. He'd hole up, get better, and figure things out. But he needed to rest awhile first. He shut his eyes, and the image of Eddy lying in a pool of his own blood rose up to him. Eddy was dead. Will had no doubt of that; he'd seen enough carcasses to know. His brother was dead.

Will hadn't seen whether it had been an accident or if Naomi had intended it, but he knew his brother had been trying to protect him. Eddy had looked after him one last time. A dull ache started within Will's chest; the pain was beginning. Will closed his eyes.

Naomi was dangerous—a predator—and now she was after him. She wouldn't stop until he was dead. But she didn't know the terrain, she didn't know these woods. Once he got into the caves, or to the beaver pond, she'd never find him.

Will raised his head as he heard something moving behind him. He started crawling again, then listened as the sound faded, stopped, came closer, and then became more deliberate, moving more quickly towards him. Naomi must have doubled back, spotted the blood, and started tracking him. She was close. Will scrambled off to the side of the trail and rolled into the under-brush in the thicket. He lay still. He heard nothing at first, then footsteps crunching on leaves. Coming closer. He saw a boot out of the corner of his eye. Naomi. She stopped at the point he'd gone off the trail, probably wondering why the blood trail had disappeared.

Will closed his eyes; he was part of the forest. He was blended into the earth, the roots, and the brush. He was invisible. He heard Naomi slowly moving to the other side of the trail and then coming back toward him. Will held his breath and closed his eyes. Invisible. He could hear Naomi's raspy breathing and smell the cigarette smoke coming off her. An eternity passed. Will thought of his mother, his father, and Eddy, now all dead. Now it was only him. Him and the land.

Naomi moved away.

"Goddamn it," she said. Will felt relief wash through him. She'd lost him. He heard her heading back the way she came, trying to pick up the trail.

Will took a deep breath and crawled silently through the brush until he caught sight of the slowly moving waters between the spindly trunks of the saplings. He paused, listening, on the outside chance that Naomi may have followed. Then he heard something moving on the trail not far behind him. She'd come back.

He crawled out into the stream and let it half-float and half-push him down toward the beaver pond, and—just beyond—his cave, his refuge, his home. The sun was higher in the sky; it was almost noon. It was quiet. Several deer watering near the mouth of the pond barely seemed to notice him. He couldn't hear Naomi anymore. Maybe she'd gotten sidetracked again.

When he reached the pond, he swam to the bank next to the abandoned beaver lodge, and pulled himself up to shore. The pain was constant now, the dull ache growing into an all-consuming throb. It hurt when he breathed, but—as far as he could tell—the bleeding had slowed.

He heard the shot and felt the bullet thud into the mud next to him simultaneously.

"Will!" she screamed.

Naomi. He forced himself to get up and half-ran and half-stumbled up the slope. Another shot rang out. He uncovered the tiny mouth to the cave, and burrowed inside. Will moved quickly along the cave passage; it was narrow here, but the corridor would soon open into the main chamber where he had his first aid equipment stashed. Then he could fix himself up. He paused as he heard a faint scraping and echoing coming from the cave entrance; she'd followed him. Will craned his head around. He could see the distant glow—her cellphone. Naomi was using the light as a guide. *Shit.* He hurried ahead, clutching his chest. The throb was becoming more intense; it was getting hard to breathe.

Will reached the main chamber, flipped on his flashlight briefly, and grabbed his medical kit. He could still hear Naomi, scrambling along behind him. Closer now. He flipped off his light and moved on ahead past the second entrance near the beaver pond. There was another passage further ahead that opened up on the other side of Turtle Ridge, into the deep woods. If he could lure Naomi into that corridor, she'd exit into deep forest. She'd be disoriented, maybe lost. And he'd buy enough time to be able to get out of the cave. He needed to get out of there, to hide somewhere else. She'd be back. She'd never give up. He'd have to go back to the pond.

Will moved on through the narrowing passage, past the large alcove in the cave wall where he usually stashed spare clothes. He stopped, smeared blood on the passageway wall, and then crawled back into the alcove, hunkering down. He waited.

It didn't take her long. Naomi came into the passageway, her sharp face outlined in the pale glow of the cellphone, and exhaled when she saw the bloodstains. She continued on. Will waited a moment as the noise of her progress faded. She'd come to the entrance and think he'd gone out and follow him. That would give him enough time to get away. Will listened a moment as Naomi's footsteps faded before he went back into the large chamber. He felt tired now, weak, but he couldn't give up. All he had to was dress the wound and go to ground. He stumbled ahead, feeling his way in the dark, until he saw a glimmer of light, the cave entrance—life.

Chapter 38

Where had Will gone? Naomi was lost. She wanted to go back to the cave, but after she crawled out of the mouth, she saw something moving in the trees. She had sprinted after it, the desire to kill Will—to end this thing once and for all—driving her forward, but after chasing the shadow down the ravine and up another hill, she saw it was only a deer. Naomi turned back but realized she didn't know where the entrance to the cave was anymore; she'd lost it. She felt a dull ache starting behind her eyes.

Naomi squatted down, breathing hard, surveying the land. She didn't know this place. There wasn't a lot of brush. These were old trees, big pines that blocked the sun and the wind. It was all the same, dark, still, and silent. Trees and more fucking trees. No other landmarks. Nothing. All she could hear was her own breathing.

The image of Eddy lying in his blood on Tabletop Rock rose in her mind's eye; she blinked it away and stood up. She remembered the gun going off and Eddy falling, but it wasn't anything serious; it couldn't be. He was fine; he was okay. He had to be fine. She thought a moment; she had to go up. If she got up to the top of the ridge, she'd be able to see where to go. She needed to get to the lake now, to the boat, to get back to town for help to go after Will. He was the key.

Once Will was gone, everything else would fall into place. Everything would be fine. If she couldn't take care of him, Lewis would. Naomi stood and moved up the trail, toward the top, the pounding in her head growing with every step, every movement, but she kept on and on and on until she realized she was looking downhill. She'd made it. Naomi took a deep breath and pressed the palms of her hands against her eyes.

She opened her eyes and looked for the shimmer of water through the trees. Nothing. She turned. Nothing but trees. More trees. She couldn't even see where the sun was. Old, overgrown, dark, silent, wise trees. That was it. A movement caught her eye. A black squirrel was perched on a pine branch above her, watching her. A snarl of rage catching in her throat, Naomi raised the rifle and fired. The squirrel, unscathed and unafraid, sat and continued to watch. Naomi sank to the ground, surrounded, engulfed, and consumed by the forest. Lost.

CHAPTER 39

SHERIFF DELANEY DIDN'T WASTE ANY TIME. Once Maureen had showed up in town and told her side of the story, it became obvious what was going on and who was behind it. Delaney had Lewis and the Wilsons arrested and taken to the Eagleton jail. His next step was to find Eddy and Naomi, who had gone up to Sully's that morning.

Sully and Maureen took the sheriff and the chief to Sully's cabin, where they found a faint trail and followed it into the woods to a big outcropping of rocks. One of the deputies found Eddy's body on top of the rock. He'd been shot in the head at pretty close range. Maureen could only look at the blood and the glassy eyes a moment before turning away, a cauldron of emotions bubbling inside of her. Even after everything he'd done to her, and to Will, he was still her Eddy, her friend and her brother. And her lover. A LeBarron. And now he was dead.

The sheriff said it had probably been pretty quick. There was no trace of anyone else, but they found a blood trail leading off the rock and into the thicket. Sully and the sheriff started to follow it when one of the deputies phoned in—they'd found Sully's boat nearby, moored to a tree branch overhanging the shoreline.

He looked at Maureen. "Was Will up here last night?"

"He might have been," she said, glancing at Sully. "We didn't see him."

Delaney grunted. He fell in behind the chief as he followed the blood trail from the rock into the thicket and finally to the banks of Turtle Creek, where it disappeared. The deputies found another trail that veered off after the first one before it, too, came to the creek.

"This trail ends here," said the chief, looking at the blood on the creek bank.

"What do you think happened?" asked Maureen.

The sheriff shrugged. "Hard to say. We knew Naomi was up here for sure and probably Will, too. Maybe all three were up on that rock. After Eddy got shot, the shooter, either Will or Naomi, shot the other one who got away and crawled here. The shooter followed. "We'll try to pick up their trails on the other side. It looks like whoever got shot is headed toward Turtle Ridge. It's awfully easy to get lost up there." He turned to Sully and Maureen.

"Will wouldn't get lost up here," said the chief.

The sheriff nodded. "I'll send a search party up there just in case," he said.

Naomi, thought Maureen. *Naomi had shot Will. Had she shot Eddy, too?*

"How bad was he hit?" asked Maureen. "Can you tell?"

The sheriff knelt down, examined the ground, and looked up at the chief before answering her.

"It's not good, Maureen," he said. "Whoever it was looks he lost a lot of blood." He stood up.

"But Will knows first aid," said Sully, "and not just broken arm first aid, but gunshot first aid. Wherever he holes up, he'll be able to fix himself."

If he doesn't bleed to death first, thought Maureen.

"Where would he go?" she asked, glancing around. A dense thicket ran along the creek, and she knew caves honeycombed the ridge. He could be anywhere.

"I think I know where we could start looking," said Sully. "Come on."

* * *

THEY MOVED THE KITCHEN TABLE IN the cabin and unfurled Will's huge map on Sully's kitchen floor. She explained that Will had brought it over from his own cabin for safekeeping just before he'd gone underground. *So*, thought Maureen, *this is it, Will's pride and joy.* And it was big. It covered the entire kitchen floor and still didn't extend fully.

"Okay," said Sully, pointing to a spot. "Here's my place, and here's that big rock where we found Eddy. Tabletop Rock." She pointed to some writing on the map.

Maureen found Turtle Creek and traced its winding course with her finger. Where would Will have left the water?

"What are these swirly marks?" she asked Sully. "Here. On the hillside."

"Those are cave openings," said Sully. "I know that's one for sure. Will uses it for shelter sometimes. I've never seen these others." She pointed. "This is closer to the creek. That might be where he's holed up."

"All right," said the chief. "Let's head out there right away. The sooner we find him, the better."

The sheriff nodded.

"What's this?" asked Maureen, pointing at another symbol on the map. Chief Dodge and Sully leaned in close.

"It looks like a nest," said Maureen.

"That's where that abandoned beaver lodge is," said the chief. "The one the wolves got at. They killed the entire colony a couple years ago."

Chief Dodge and Sully looked at each other.

"What?" asked Maureen.

"No," said Sully. "There's no way."

The chief rubbed his chin and leaned back on his haunches. "Knowing Will, he might have prepared it beforehand. Widened the entrance, brought in supplies."

"Maybe," said Sully. "Still. That's a stretch. Even for Will."

"What?" demanded Maureen.

The chief looked up at her.

"It's possible," he said, "that Will might be holed up inside that old beaver lodge here." He pointed at the nest symbol on the map.

"No way," said Maureen. "It's not big enough."

"You'd think that," said the chief, "but they can be surprisingly roomy on the inside. I've had to dismantle one or two in my time. Some of them would be big enough for a man to hide in. This one would be."

"All right," said Sheriff Delaney. "Let's split up. Sully, why don't you and me go up to the cave. He knows you. If he's in there and wounded, he might get squirrelly. It'd be better if you were there to talk to him."

Sully looked at the chief, who nodded.

"Okay," she said grudgingly. *She really thinks he's in the lodge,* thought Maureen. *That's where she wants to go.*

"Chief, why don't you go and check out the lodge. I'll send a couple of officers with you."

"No," said the chief. "That's not a good idea. The fewer people, the better. I think maybe just you and Sully should go to the cave, and I will take Maureen with me. If I can't get through to him, she might. And I'll take a chainsaw if you have one handy."

Sully motioned toward the cabin, where her ax leaned up against the woodpile.

"That's all I got, Chief," she said.

"All right," he said. "Let's go get him."

Maureen caught Sully's eye.

"You take care, Maureen," she said. Sully came over and gave her a hug.

"You too," Maureen whispered into her ear.

They turned at the sound of a car—no, cars—coming up the driveway. Sully walked out the front door. At least a dozen vehicles were coming up the long drive. Maureen recognized Jake LaRoche's black pick-up, Dickie Terwilliger's mini-van, Bob Singh's compact. Bill Swanson, Danny Long, even John Benson had come out. There were at least a dozen of them coming up behind the three prowlers parked behind Naomi's little car. They started to get out of the cars.

Jake strode up to the chief. Doc was right behind him. Maureen saw Jake had a pistol in his waistband and that Doc was carrying his doctor's bag.

"Chief, me and a few of the boys came up here because we're worried about what's going on."

Sheriff Delaney stepped forward.

"We appreciate your concern, Jake," he said, "but this is an ongoing investigation. You can't enter the crime scene."

"Is it true that somebody got shot?" asked Dickie, his tinny voice cutting through the still air.

"This is an ongoing investigation," repeated the sheriff, "so I can't comment on that. We'll fill you in as soon as we think it's the right time."

"This is our home, Sheriff," said Friendly, "and there might be a dangerous killer on the loose. We demand to know what's happening."

Maureen felt someone nudging her arm. She turned. The chief motioned for her to follow him.

"Let's go," he said. "We can't afford to waste time. The sheriff has a handle on the situation."

Maureen nodded and turned to follow the chief. A few of the deputies had come up and stood next to the sheriff, hands on their belts. Sully stepped backward and turned to follow Maureen and the chief.

"Where are they going, Sheriff?" demanded Jake, motioning toward Maureen and Chief Dodge. Maureen glanced back.

An angry murmur swept the gathering. Even Danny Long looked pissed. Sheriff Delaney nodded to one of the deputies, who took out his radio and started talking into it. The chief nodded and walked around the corner of the building. *Reinforcements*, thought Maureen, as they hurried down the trail toward Hourglass Road. It only took them a few minutes to get to the Thin Lake landing.

Chief Dodge went ahead, clearing brush aside until they finally reached the outskirts of the beaver pond. The lodge stood at the other side; the chief started working his way around, trying to stay on the high ground until they finally reached the lodge. It stood almost six feet out of the water and was nearly as big as a small car.

The chief climbed partway up and began pulling branches off the top layer; Maureen clambered up and started to help. It was easy to pull off the first pieces, but soon every branch seemed intertwined with the next or buried in mud. The chief motioned Maureen away and started chopping at the side layer. Most of the branches weren't very thick, and the chief started making progress. Still. Not fast enough.

"Will," shouted Maureen. "Will, it's us. Me and Chief Dodge. If you can hear us, come out. We know you're hurt. You need a doctor."

Nothing. The chief kept chopping away. Not fast enough. They had to get in. And now.

"Chief," she said. "Where would the entrance be?"

The chief stopped a moment, sweat staining his uniform.

"It's hard to say," he said. "Go around the perimeter, and you should find it. It should be pretty close to the waterline. But be careful."

"Are the beavers here?" she asked, stepping into the pond.

"No. The wolves picked them off one by one a couple winters ago."

Good. She didn't have to worry about running into any angry beavers underwater. She slid into the water. It was cold. The pond wasn't much more than waist deep here, and the water was a little murky. Maureen knelt down onto the pond bed, ducked her head underwater, and started looking. At first, all she could see were logs and sticks. She had to be careful not to get caught. It would be easy enough to drown down here. The sound of the ax striking the lodge reverberated through the water.

Maureen started to make her way around the structure, moving carefully over the logs buried in the mucky bottom. *Nothing*, she thought. *Just branches and weeds.* She couldn't make out anything. Wait. There. A darker spot near the edge. She reached her arm up into it all the way to the shoulder; there was nothing in the way. It seemed wide enough to get through. Maureen went up for air.

"I think I might have found it," she gasped and then went back under. She got underneath the gap and started to stand. It was tight, and she felt a moment of panic as twigs and smaller branches seemed to pull at her. Maureen straightened her knees, pushed, and was through. She was inside.

It was dark. Only a few pinpoints of light shone through where the lodge had started to disintegrate from disrepair. Maureen paused. All she could hear was her own breathing and the thud of the ax from above. Streams of dust and dirt loosened by the impact fell on her.

"Will," she whispered. "Will. Are you in here?"

She felt, rather than heard, something moving. Maureen was starting to get an idea of the size of the lodge's interior, even in the dark. It was bigger than she had imagined. The ceiling looked a little farther away than she could reach.

"Maureen?" whispered a voice.

"Will," she said. "I'm here. It's me."

"Chief," she shouted. "Chief. He's in here. He's alive. Will," she continued. "We need to get you out of here. Doc's here. He can patch you up."

Maureen heard steps above, then a splash, and then started when someone grabbed her leg. Chief. She felt a sort of shelf next to the opening and pulled herself onto it. A light shined under the water in the entrance, and then the chief's head popped through, his gray hair plastered to his head.

He played the flashlight around the inside of the lodge. Mud, branches, medical dressings, a water bottle, some food—and there, up against the wall, lay Will. The chief waded over next to him and started looking for the wound. Maureen tried to get closer, but there wasn't much room.

"Hello, Chief," said Will.

"Hey, Will," he said, examining him. "It looks like you stopped the bleeding."

"It was close," said Will, his voice thick. "The bullet hit my ribcage, probably between the fourth and fifth rib, and went through the lateral back there. It hit the lung. Pneumothorax. I could feel it." He lifted up his bloodstained shirt. A plastic tube was sticking out of his side. The chief played the flashlight on the wound.

"You did this?" asked the chief. Will nodded.

"I went to the cave," said Will, speaking slowly, "and got my stuff. When I got here, I inserted the needle between the ribs. "I got the air out and then put the tube in. It's good. I can breathe."

Barely, thought Maureen. *He sounds terrible.*

"You did all that without anesthesia?" asked the chief.

Will shook his head. "I had a local in my medical kit. I injected myself."

Enough shop talk, thought Maureen.

"Let's get you out of here," she said. "Can you move?"

"Yeah," said Will, starting to sit up. "But I'm not going into town."

"Will," said the chief softly. "You need a doctor. You probably need to go to a hospital."

"Everybody in town wants me gone," whispered Will. "Or dead. No. I'm staying out here."

There was a finality, the old stubbornness, in his voice. Maureen glanced at the chief in the dim backwash of the flashlight. This wasn't going to be easy. They couldn't haul him out, not without knocking him out first. They could cut him out, Maureen supposed, but how long would that take?

"Okay," said the chief. "Okay. I'll tell you what, Will. Let's get you somewhere dry first. Maybe back into your cave. Doc can look at you there. Once you're healthy, what you do is up to you. But you shouldn't stay here. Your chest will get infected in a heartbeat."

He paused. All they could hear was Will's deliberate breathing. Maureen detected a small whistle at the end of each breath, probably from the tube.

"I don't want anyone to know where I am," said Will.

"All right," said Chief Dodge. "That's easy. Is that good by you, Maureen?"

"Sure," said Maureen. "Of course. Let's get you out of here, Will."

"Okay," said Will. "Show me the light, Chief."

The chief did. Will took a small cork out of his pocket and placed it into the chest tube. "We don't want any pond water getting in there," he said.

"Okay," said Maureen. Together, she and the chief got Will through the entrance and back out into the sunlight.

"Will," asked Maureen, as they were wading to shore. "What happened?"

"It was Naomi," he said, keeping his eyes shut against the bright sunlight. "She shot Eddy and then she shot me. I was able to get away. I was lucky. She tried to follow me but couldn't." He smiled wanly. They reached the shore.

"Can you walk?" asked the chief. Will nodded.

"I think so," he said.

"Maureen," said the chief. "I want you to go back to the cabin and get Doc. The cave is about half a mile east up that little trail. He pointed to a little path about halfway up the hill.

"East?" asked Maureen.

"That way," said the Chief. She nodded.

"Bring Doc up there. Be quiet about it."

He stood Will up, supporting him, and started down the path. Maureen hurried back to Sully's cabin.

The deputies had dispersed the crowd, making everyone move their cars, but a few people were still standing around, waiting. Jake LaRoche and Dickie were still there, along with Bill Cobb and Derrick Friendly. Almost everyone else had left. She didn't see Doc. Jake saw her before she could duck.

"What's up, Maureen?" asked Jake. "You been swimming?"

"No," she said. "I fell in the pond back there."

"What's going on?" His tone was curt, sharp.

"Nothing," she answered. "They just wanted me to show them how we got out last night. Where we went."

"They believed your story about Eddy?" asked Dickie, peering at her like a bird looking at a bug.

"You think I'm lying, Dickie? Fuck you. Fuck the both of you. And if you two will excuse me," she said, stepping around them. "I need to get cleaned up."

Maureen walked into the cabin. Doc was sitting at the table with a deputy. Maureen smiled.

"Hey, Doc," she said. He looked up at her and smiled. She motioned with her head slightly.

"Hello, Maureen," he said. He narrowed his eyes.

"I was wondering if you could take a look at my shoulder. I think I sprained it."

"All right," said Doc. "Will you excuse us?" he said to the deputy, who got up and left.

"Will's hurt," she whispered. "He needs help."

"Badly?" said Doc.

"Yeah, but he stopped the bleeding. Doc, we can't let anybody follow us. He doesn't want anybody else up there."

"All right," said Doc. "All right. Let's not worry, my dear. I'll handle it."

He stood, straightening up slowly. It struck Maureen suddenly that Doc was old, really old. She knew that, but it hadn't really registered until he now as he stood before her, gray, wizened, a little stooped. His eyes, though, were vibrant, bright green, and as clear as a mountain lake.

"Don't worry, young lady," he said, as if reading her mind. "I walk two miles through the woods every day. I'll be fine."

They stopped outside the door. Doc motioned the deputy over and spoke to him a moment. The deputy nodded, walked over to the remaining bystanders and started ushering them to their cars. They waited a moment until everyone had cleared out and then started toward the cave.

True to his word, Doc kept a good pace, even through the uneven terrain. Will and the chief were sitting in the sun outside the cave mouth when they arrived. Doc knelt down next to Will and examined the wound.

"Did you do this triage?" he asked. Will nodded.

"Impressive work. I might have to take you on as a partner." Doc sat down on a rock. "The wound looks good. The bullet went through and through. The tube is stable. If it stays inflated, the lung will eventually heal itself," he said. "On both sides. For now, all we have to worry about is infection." He reached into his bag and pulled out a vial. "This is an antibiotic. Take two a day for two weeks. Don't quit early. I'd like to see you about that time or if any other symptoms occur. I'm going to give you an injection, too."

Will nodded. Doc tilted his face back in the full sun. He exhaled and opened his eyes.

"Beautiful day," he said. "I've never been up in this part of the woods," he added. "I can see why you like to stay here, Will."

Will said nothing. He started touching the dressing around his wound. Maureen checked the urge to stop him.

"I have to," said Will. "Now, especially. There's nothing left for me but this, my mother's land."

Maureen felt a pang as if she'd had the wind knocked out of her.

"My family's gone," continued Will. "Dad. Eddy. I have nobody. Except Maureen," he added. She was the afterthought.

"I won't sell the land, and I won't build, and everybody in Moon Lake is going to hate me. You're right, Doc. It's beautiful here. I've been here my whole life, up here in the woods. Nothing else compares. When I'm somewhere else, I'm thinking of here." He shrugged and looked at Doc. "These are my mother's woods. She's in here somewhere."

No one said anything.

"Yeah," he said, looking at Maureen. "I'm not going back."

"You might have to," said the chief. "At least until they finish the investigation."

"Naomi shot Eddy," said Will, his voice curiously flat. "And she wanted to. It was deliberate, not an accident. I saw it; I saw her face."

"Well, we'll know when they find her," said Maureen. "She's still out there somewhere."

Will said nothing, only staring at the dirt in front of him.

"We'll have to bury Eddy, too," said Maureen, reaching for his hand.

"Yeah," said Will. "Yeah."

"We'll bury him with your mom and dad," said Maureen. "He'd like that."

"Yep," said Will. "That way we'll all of us be together." He smiled then and giggled, as if at a private, coded joke.

Chapter 40

W<small>ILL CAME INTO TOWN TO BE INTERVIEWED</small> for the investigation. After the state forensics people had examined the murder scene, the trajectory of the bullets, ballistics, splatter patterns and whatnot, they determined that Will's story was credible, that someone crouching behind the rocks had shot both Eddy and Will. Burr, Eddy's lawyer, tried to grab some of the land for Eddy's kids, but the judge said no, that they'd get their share when they came of age. Burr disappeared as quickly as he'd shown up.

Will and Maureen scattered Eddy's ashes in Mirror Lake. Sully was there, too. Nobody said much. They didn't find Naomi until late in the fall. A couple of deer hunters ran across her body; she'd fallen into a pit deep in the back of Turtle Ridge. She'd broken her neck in the fall. The medical examiner's report stated that the break had probably caused complete paralysis but was not the primary cause of death. Naomi had probably died of thirst and starvation. He also pointed out that several parts of her body, including her face, evidenced bite and gnawing wounds, probably caused by small animals. Naomi's sister took in her kids. They were living over in Eagleton now.

No one ever saw Mattie Doolittle again. There was speculation she'd moved down to Chicago, but Maureen suspected that Naomi had hired Lewis to kill her. She hoped Eddy wouldn't have had anything to do with it. Lewis stood trial and was now serving time, along with the Wilson brothers, for extortion, conspiracy, and false imprisonment.

Will went back to his woods. Ostensibly, he still worked for the state, but he never showed up at the office in town anymore.

Sully and the chief were sometimes in touch with him, but they saw him less and less.

Occasionally, at night, Will would come and visit Maureen at his father's old house. Sometimes they made love, sometimes they'd talk, and sometime they'd just sit, but Will's silences were more frequent and lasted more often as the months went by. Maureen saw he was growing more distant by the day.

Maureen didn't tell Will she was pregnant until it became obvious. She knew what would happen—and she was right. Will smiled. He told her if it was a boy to name him Titus, and if it was a girl to name her Ariel. Then he disappeared back into the land, the deep tangle of life and earth, of sky and water, of death. She never saw him again. No one did. He would become a legend around Moon Lake as the years went by, the old hermit living up in the woods, protecting the lands.

The land was Will, and he had become the land—not LeBarron land, and not the vast empire that Naomi had envisioned, Instead, the spirit—the essence of the land—was nested deep in Will's heart, his soul, and in the tortured recesses of his mind. To know the land was to know himself; to know the land was to know his family and his place in the universe.

Maureen knew he was happy, as happy as Will could be, and that the land was safe. *And,* she thought, touching her swollen belly, *it will be safe for a long, long time to come.*

ACKNOWLEDGMENTS

I WOULD LIKE TO THANK KIRA HENSCHEL, my publisher, for her unwavering support. I'd also like to thank Dennis Curley and Lesley DeMartini for their outstanding editing skills, Michael DiMilo for his phenomenal artwork, Sue Ann Marciniak for advice on the Northwoods realty business, and Robert Carter for his photographic skills. A big thank you also goes out to Dave Thome and the Veggie Chips Writers' Group for their invaluable support and feedback. I would also like to thank Maryann Carter, Justine Hutchins, Paul Carter, Bob Carter, and Mark Mamerow for their input as my beta readers. I would also like to thank the rest of my family, particularly Sue Kletzke Carter, Rae Williams DiMilo, Suzanne Carter, Barbara Gillespie, my wife Kris, and my daughter Frankie for their unwavering support.

ABOUT THE AUTHOR

GEOFF CARTER GREW UP ATTEND-
ING public schools in the
Milwaukee area, eventually
graduating from the University
of Wisconsin at Madison with a
degree in Communication Arts.
He has been teaching English in
Milwaukee Public Schools for
twenty-eight years in both
traditional and non-traditional
settings, working almost
exclusively with at-risk students. Mr. Carter is a proud and
active member of the MTEA, the local teachers' union.

He holds a PhD in English and has also taught at the
University of Wisconsin-Milwaukee.

Mr. Carter lives in Milwaukee. He is married and is the
proud father of a remarkable daughter. In his spare time, he
enjoys fine wine, sailing, fly-fishing, organic gardening, and
reading.

Please visit his website for more information and blog:
https://geoffreymalcolmcarter.com/

ABOUT THE AUTHOR